CHRIS POURTEAU

INVASION

WAR FOR EMPIRE

3

aethonbooks.com

Invasion

Aethon Books
www.aethonbooks.com

Print and eBook formatting by Josh Hayes.

Published by Aethon Books LLC.

ALSO BY CHRIS POURTEAU FROM AETHON BOOKS

WAR FOR EMPIRE

Legacy

Warpath

Invasion

STAND ALONE NOVELS

Optional Retirement Plan

PROLOGUE

PERSONAL CORRESPONDENCE

TO: Bathsheba Toma, Lieutenant Colonel / CO; 214th Marine Battalion, First Drop Division, Alliance Ground Forces

FROM: Benjamin Stone, Captain / CO; Dog Company, 214th Marine Battalion, First Drop Division, Alliance Ground Forces

SUBJECT: Threat Assessment: New Alien Species ("the Skane")

CLASSIFICATION: Personal Correspondence, Encrypted

FORMAT: Video Deposition, with Retinal Verification and Voice Pattern Recognition Enabled

Colonel Toma:

I am recording this message within the scope of my sworn duty as a Marine to protect the Sol Alliance from any and all threats. I'm addressing it specifically to you as my commanding officer in the 214th Marine Battalion of the First Drop Division of the Alliance Ground Forces. I make this recording of my own free will and knowing that I am of sound mind and body. I am under no physical, mental, or emotional coercion or any known influence of a pharmaceutical, psychological, or telepathic nature. The information I relate here represents to the best of my ability the truth as I believe it to be.

Okay, Sheba, now that the formalities are over, let's get to it. This will sound like crazy talk. You'll probably think it's one of my patented, fast-talking desperate attempts to divert from consequences: the fact that I'm AWOL, destined for court-martial, and probably the Alliance's Most Wanted fugitive behind a certain teenager. Or maybe you'll think it mere Archie propaganda meant to weaken our defenses. But I'd ask that you hear me out. If you want to dismiss what I have to say after that, well ... that's on you.

I have a good-faith belief that the Arcœnum fleet recently picked up on the subspace sensor network might not, in fact, be an invasion fleet. Yes, I know that's a bold (and some might say *insane*) assertion following the loss of Canis III. But an individual, whom the citizens of New Nassau trust implicitly—full disclosure, he's a trade representative from the Arcœnum—has identified a cloaked fleet pursuing the Archies. Let me give you a minute to absorb that. Rail against the logic of trusting an Archie later. But right now, *listen.*

According to Light Without Shadow—the pirates call him Louie—the pursuing fleet represents an ancient enemy of the Arcœnum called the Skane. The Skane are apparently the same "shadow-spiders" Alice Keller encountered on Drake's World. Yes, I know—that's a little too coincidental for me, too. But set that aside for the moment. According to Louie, the Skane are hive-like, sharing a common cognitive neural connection through subspace. This provides them a natural resistance to Archie mind-control. And we've now reached the end of my knowledge on that particular topic.

This message is already too long—or maybe too short for the number of "are you kidding me?" moments in it. I'll wrap it up shortly so you can have the intelligence geeks begin dissecting it for subterfuge. I'm reaching out to alert you, the Admiralty, and the AGF that a threat even more deadly than the Arcœnum might be lurking in the shadows. I mean that quite literally—according to Louie, the Skane can manipulate subspace in ways our sensors can't register. If he's right—and I know that's a big "if"—these shadow-spiders can pop up in our backyard, and we won't even know they're there till our ships are burning in space.

Science has a concept called the survival imperative. For humans that means killing, eating, fucking, and protecting the offspring that result from the fucking at all costs. We drive our DNA into the future that way. The Skane's survival imperative is to conquer other species, take the resources those species squat on to gear up, and then move on to the next target. They're like locusts. Expansion. Extermination. Avoiding extinction. This, in a nutshell, is what the Skane do. Mercy is weakness to them. And now they're in our space.

Believe me or don't, Sheba. I'm not sure I believe it myself, actually. But I've recently come to realize that following the rules isn't always the right thing to do. I know that will come as a great shock to you, my saying that. But protecting Alice Keller was the right thing to do, and I did it, whether anyone but me ever recognizes that. Passing along this intel to you—whether it's right or wrong, mere Archie propaganda or the ravings of a madman who only thinks he's sane—well, you'll have to decide that. But I've told you what I think I know based on others' testimony whose honor I trust. My conscience is clear.

Good luck. Keep your powder dry. You're going to need it.

Ben Stone (aka Shitbox), Capt., 214th Marine Battalion, First Drop Division, Alliance Ground Forces

---

BEN REACHED to the chest plate of his battlesuit and turned off the cam. The light faded, and a quick chirp let him know the recording had saved.

"Shitbox?" Torque asked.

"Long story," Ben sighed. "But it should help convince Sheba I'm telling the truth. If anything will."

"Think she'll believe you?" Alice asked.

"Not a chance in hell," Ben answered.

The others in the hold of the *Junkyard Dog* stood in a kind of reverent silence. Light Without Shadow made a gesture with his four arms.

"He says your sincerity will count for much in how the message is received," Torque informed them.

Cinnamon Gauss scoffed. "You were right about one thing, Stone—you sounded like a crazy man telling boogeyman stories."

"Maybe," Ben said. "Probably. But like I said, my conscience is clear."

"I thought you did great, Ben," Alice said. She offered him a supportive smile, which he didn't return. "And I know I've said it before, but ... thank you for standing by me."

"Sure, kid," he said. "Wasn't even a question."

"Hey guys," Gal Galatz, ship's navigator, said over intraship comms. *"Coming up on the rendezvous. Ionia awaits."*

"Copy that," Torque said. To those around her she said, "Once we're off the *Dog*, Gal will launch the buoy with the message. Should reach New Nassau in a few days."

Ben grunted a *for-what-that's-worth* sound.

"Remember, Stone," Gauss said. "On Ionia, we do things my way. You and your famous face lay low. When it's safe, we'll make the run for Sylvan Novus and get Alice home. Feel me?"

Ben met her gaze and held it. "Aye-aye, Captain, *ma'am*."

"You too, little sister," Gauss said to Alice. "No one can know you're there."

"Sure. I understand."

Gauss nodded and headed to the cockpit.

Ben turned to Torque. "I'm putting myself on the line here." Nodding at Louie, he said, "You'd better be right about him."

"I am," Torque answered simply before following her captain forward.

Alice slipped her hand into Ben's and squeezed. "I have faith in the future, Ben. It's gonna be okay."

She's young, he thought, feeling unexpectedly, uneasily old.

"Sure, kid," he said. "Sure, it is."

1

WHERE DREAMS COME TRUE

IT WAS HOT, and no breeze moved the heavy air.

Ben Stone assumed the atmospheric recycler was offline again. The environment in their small two-room apartment felt physical. Beyond discomfort—like a cloak of fat wet molecules overlaying everything. As if Ionia's surface world were sweating into the nooks and crannies of its underground—what the locals called the Underside, where the laborers and maintenance crews lived.

The so-called pleasure planet maintained the best of both worlds from the customer's perspective. Ionia's surface—bright buildings promising anything the customer could want, for a price—was like the smooth, nutrient-fed skin of a fashion model that made other, lesser planets complain with envy about the unrealistic standard it set.

The Underside was where the cogs lived—those who helped maintain the fantasy sold on the surface. The place where maintenance and cleaning crews crawled up from to do their work, three shifts a day. Where more daring patrons came to purchase substances and satisfy cravings unavailable on the extensive but legal menus aboveground. The desperate ones could even purchase devices for hacking slot machines at "regular but random intervals to avoid detection." Which was a joke, of course, with the joke on those who purchased the devices. The casinos were in on the scam, and so cheaters were arrested by the local constabulary—part of the racket—who extorted the poor shmucks with outrageous bribe-or-bail demands, depending on your definition of what constituted a bribe or bail. The offender was then escorted off-planet with a wagging trigger finger. For those with more sordid tastes, the widespread extreme sexual violence in the Underside was often celebrated in private-knock snuffsex clubs, and rarely if ever prosecuted—unlike the hacking scams. Probably, Ben thought acidly, because human life was held less dear on Ionia than casino profits.

As he sat considering the moral pliability of Ionia's business model, sweat trickled down the back of Ben's neck. His body was anxious with the need to cool itself. Even the *Junkyard Dog*, with its creaking, claustrophobic bulkheads, would be preferable. But Gauss's ship was standing off, hiding in the Malvian Triangle, where ionized haze and random asteroids obscured ships from sensors. Too recognizable, that pinnace, too infamous to dock anywhere, what with Sayyida al-Hurra's hunters on overwatch, a Fleet bounty on his head, rewards for Alice Keller promised by President Bragg in amounts so exorbitant they'd make a snuffsex pimp blush, and oh yeah, a war on. They'd had to go to ground somewhere after escaping Tower's Fall, and Ionia, with its well-known contempt for Alliance oversight, seemed the natural choice.

But even here, they'd had to be discrete, and they'd needed a place to be discrete in. Which rumination brought Ben back to their shabby little apartment in the Underside, the sewer where Ionia's runoff ended up, literally and otherwise. Ben gave that image for their current billet its due consideration, dismembered its component parts from the body whole to ensure each fit properly the sewer motif. The oppressive closeness, check. The rusty hinges on the pressure door, which he was sure wouldn't stand up to an actual vacuum emergency, check. The black grime left caked in the corners by a hasty landlord's underpaid cleaning crew, check. All of it fit well enough. But what sealed the deal was the constant, thinly masked odor of human waste. Ben had once had a conversation with Gal Galatz about Tower's Fall, the pirate retreat nestled inside a massive asteroid—a shithole by any other name. Looking back now, sitting in the dank, shit-perfumed, dimly lit sweatbox of his surroundings, Ben felt almost apologetic toward the Fall. Closing his eyes with nostalgia, he began picturing the cove in his head. The busy docks. The Swashbuckler's Leap with its Archie bartender. Compared to the Underside of Ionia, the Fall was a penthouse. A cultural mecca. A shining trophy of human achievement meant to inspire—

"What'cha thinkin'?"

He felt slightly annoyed as Alice slipped cautiously beside him on the wall bench. He'd been enjoying his revelry in self-pity. It distracted him from the constant itch at the back of his neck.

"Nothing, really," he answered without opening his eyes.

"The air recycler stopped working again."

"I noticed."

"Torque can look at it when they get back," Alice said hopefully. She seemed to feel the need to make him feel better.

"Yeah."

"Too bad Moze isn't here. She'd have it fixed right up."

Ben wanted to bark in response to her brightness. That had become so easy to do lately. For all of them. He controlled the impulse, despite his longing for a taste of liquid oblivion. Just one burning swallow of it coursing down his throat. But Alice was trying, and that alone deserved respect, not a biting comeback. The last thing she needed to deal with was his drunk ass.

"Torque's a good mechanic," he allowed.

"They should be back soon."

Ben finally cracked an eye. Across the room, manufactured sunshine died in dark corners. The light was a ghost of the vibrant sun that hung over Ionia, its amber light gleaming off the silver buildings on the planet below. Its luminescence was fairly constant, an approving god smiling down on its creation. There was hardly ever bad weather on the surface.

"You know, I researched this place when I was on the *Archimedes*," Alice said.

I know, Ben thought. *You've told me. A hundred times.*

Still, conversation was better than listening to the eighty-proof imp with the shitty attitude squatting in his head and urging him to go out and drink. "Yeah?" he prompted.

"I guess I told you already, didn't I?"

"It's okay." Ben smiled, doing his best to make it genuine. "I like talking to you."

Alice smiled too, and it was clearly no effort. Was it the shadows from the poor lighting playing across her face, or had her cheeks just flushed? "I like talking to you too, Ben."

He was tempted. Bored, tempted. Letch from a bygone era, tempted. Alice was seventeen, but it was hard for him to see her as anything other than the frightened fourteen-year-old he'd first met. The imp's middle finger poked the back of his neck, urging him on. He reached up to bat it away. The planet must have infected him with its dark fantasies best left to bad dreams.

"Think of anything new?" Ben asked quickly.

"From the research? No. But, Ionia? It's not like I imagined."

Ben nearly laughed out loud. "I wouldn't think it would be."

Alice did laugh then. "You must think I'm a child," she said. It had that lilting quality of a hesitant statement hoping for contradiction. "A Marine like you—you've probably been here on leave. Seen things." Her voice dropped a level or three. "Done things."

Ben caught her drift. Alice was about as subtle as Ionia itself. But she was venturing into dangerous territory, especially in his current frame of mind, and it wasn't the first time since they'd arrived. Alice Keller was bored too. And, it seemed, hopeful of chasing that boredom away with Ben.

"Not so much," he said carefully, and adding in his mind, *not here anyway*. "You've grown up a lot since I first met you, Alice."

"Really?"

Oh, geez. He'd meant it as a compliment. Not a leer with a hook on the end of it.

She looked up at him from beneath raised eyebrows. Alice Keller could easily find employment on Ionia. All she'd have to do is stare like that, and they'd frame her face in snap-ads. *Come and get to know the girl next door...*

Stop.

Alice dropped her eyes into her lap. "Monitor: on," she said sharply.

The lone wall display in the flat's common room came to life. The first image, as always, was a smiling, blonde woman with her chin dipped, gaze furtive with secret knowledge, lips wet with promise. She wore a more mature, more experienced form of Alice's coquettish expression. *Maybe that's where Alice learned it*, Ben thought. Maybe she was emulating it for his benefit? Behind the woman, pastel-colored walls and a doorway through which another woman, quite possibly her twin, escorted a male customer. The twin was laughing, and so was he. The woman in the foreground looked over her shoulder, watching them like a voyeur, then returned her gaze to the viewer with a wink.

"Ionia: where dreams come true," a sultry narratrix purred. *"And so can you."*

Alice's cheeks were burning red now.

"I just wanted to see something positive," she said, as if apologizing.

Ben decided to save her further embarrassment and himself further temptation. "Monitor: local news."

The commercial faded, replaced by chyrons scrolling right-to-left and a talking-head announcer discussing Ionia's current economic woes. The war had disrupted the standard rotation of Fleet personnel taking leave on-planet. Casino revenues were down. Whore downtime was up. No one was happy, least of all Damianos Blackmore, now being interviewed for the story. Their savior. Their jailor. The man who controlled the underworld of Ionia and was, at the moment, the only thing standing between them and an un-boring, much more dangerous life on the run.

There was no mention of the Skane, no images of the huge, arachnoid ships Louie had revealed aboard the *Dog*. It'd taken Alice half an hour to stop shaking after Louie had shown them all the combined Archie fleet burning hard for Alliance space, chased by the giant spider-like starships. An old enemy of the Arcœnum, Louie had informed them afterward. As far as subspace news was concerned, however, the Skane didn't exist at all.

The pressure door to the corridor slid aside. Alice hopped away from Ben as though afraid her parents might catch her at something untoward.

"You're home early," Alice said as Cinnamon Gauss charged through the doorway. Torque followed close behind.

The pirate captain's eyes sought out Alice. Her expression

was one of relief, and she nodded in passing as she headed for their shared sleeping quarters.

"Hey, blaggard," Ben called after her, using the common slang name for Blackmore's Blackguard, the private army of enforcers he used to control Ionia. "Roll anyone for cash today?"

Gauss hesitated only a little, then pushed forward toward the bedroom.

"Ben..." Alice said, and it was almost pleading. The apartment door swished shut behind Torque with a sharp whine and hiss.

Ben sat up on the bed-bench and raised his voice to reach his target, now out of sight. "Maybe evict a mother and child when the deadbeat husband missed his payment?"

He thought he'd never get used to Gauss's new look. Her pirate ensemble was gone, replaced by a ninja's all-black leather obsession and a black sash—the mark of a member of the Blackguard—hanging opposite the single handgun on her left thigh. The orange spikey hair was gone too, hacked off her head, the remaining stubbiness dyed black to match the horizontal mask painting the upper half of her face.

Ben felt eyes on him and turned to see Torque standing in the middle of the common room, staring. She too was dressed in black but hunched over to disguise her naturally impressive height. She rolled her shoulders back and stood up straight as she growled, "Today's not the day for it, Stone."

He stared back innocently, tempted to wink, and thought it'd be too much.

"Torque's right," said Gauss, who'd returned to stand in the doorway between the rooms. "Today's not the day. Leave it. For once."

It threw Ben at first, her reasonable request. Tempted him to a kind of conciliatory geniality. But he was so damned bored. And tweaking Gauss, who could take it and dish it back like an athlete in a playoff game, was infinitely preferable to his mind wandering into Aliceland. It was she who put a hand on his shoulder now, as if tempting him to reconsider that option.

"Well, I mean," he said, "with the president's declaration of martial law, Blackmore must be having a field day. Collecting on old debts. Maybe collecting on debts he's not even owed. Perfect opportunity to squeeze the locals." Then, inspired by the cackling imp in his head, Ben added, "That's something I'd think you were good at, Gauss—squeezing."

"Ben!" Alice said.

A hand jerked him around, and he had half a thought that Alice must have been working out before realizing it was Torque who'd adjusted his posture for him.

"Whoa, big hoss!" he said when she pulled him up off the bench by his smartfatigues. Two or three inches separated his toes from the gritty floor.

"This is my intervention face, *little* hoss," Torque said. "I know I look angry, but it's been a long day and not a good one either. Think I mentioned that already. This is just my concerned-for-your-safety look. So, today's episode of 'punching Cinnamon till she punches back' needs to end *now*."

"It's okay," Gauss said from the doorway. With effort, Ben turned his head and found her leaning there in a kind of apathetic version of her hip-cocked swagger-stance. "I understand you're suffering, Stone. I should have been more considerate."

He had no idea what she meant, but he felt the trap being laid. Her eyes tracked slowly down the length of him, tarried on the air beneath his dangling feet, then scanned back up again.

"Next shift," Gauss said, "I'll bring you a bottle. Bourbon, maybe. Or rubbing alcohol. You can't be too choosy at this point."

Ben flashed a look to Alice, who saw the fury in his eyes and turned away. She'd told Gauss? He'd confided in her as a friend, as someone he thought he could talk to about his constant temptation to drink—and she'd *told* her?

Alice mustered the resolve to look at Ben again. There was contrition in her gaze, swimming in sorrow. He didn't care. He was pissed.

"Put me down, Bertha." Ben turned away deliberately from Alice to face Torque. He knew he was smiling but it felt like the skinless smile of a bleached skull. He could see the disappointment in Torque's face. It was on, now. And the match was going to be epic. "I said, put me down." Ben reached up and grabbed her wrists.

"Stop it!" Alice shouted.

He glared at Torque. The big woman didn't rile easily, but when she did, it was like waking a mama bear from her den in winter. Slow to rouse, but deadly once disturbed.

"I said—" he began.

"And I said, stop it!"

Alice was on her feet and standing next to them, eyes flashing between them. "Put him down, Torque." When Torque didn't move, Alice added, "Please."

Ben's feet touched ground again. With exaggerated, slow-motion intent, Torque brushed off the wrinkled material of his tunic where she'd gripped it.

Alice rounded on Cinnamon. "Too far," she said.

Gauss's face was disbelieving. "*I* went too far? Little sister—"

"And *you*," Alice said to Ben, "you do this *every* time they come back. It has to stop!"

"Look, kid—" he began, anger at her betrayal still fresh.

"Stop calling me that!" She laughed but it was cruel, not joyful. "In this room? I'm the only adult!"

That shut them all up for a moment. Alice stood fuming,

staring at each one of them in turn. "We're all we've got, guys," she said, her voice calming. "I know it's hard. I'm bored as anybody. But I'm alive! We're all alive! Can't we be happy about that? Just once?" Alice turned to Ben and said simply, "I'm sorry."

"Hey, Alice..." Torque reached out one large hand, but Alice shrugged it off and stomped across the room, pushing her way past a surprised Cinnamon Gauss. She might have been crying or she might have been cursing as she disappeared into the bedroom.

"You know," Ben said to Gauss, whose gaze jerked up in warning, "if you'd let me pull some credits from my account, we could at least get better accommodations."

"You're right for once, Stone," Gauss answered. "We need to find new quarters."

Ben eyed her, thrown by her surprising agreement. "What's wrong?"

"You and I need to talk," Torque said to him. "Cinnamon, go get some rest."

Gauss followed Alice into the bedroom without another word. Looking at Torque, he realized the worry he saw on her face had been its dominating feature since she'd entered the apartment. It seemed to be inspired by something well beyond their current, pressure-cooker living situation.

"Yeah," he said. "I guess we do."

2
ANOTHER PERSPECTIVE

ALICE YANKED THE THIN, black drape closed behind her. Torque had hung it to separate their shared bedroom from the common room. As an attempt at privacy, it was poor. As a sound barrier, it was useless. But at the moment, it was all she had to claim her space as her own. To achieve a necessary distance.

Need first.

She threw herself onto her bed, one of four lining each wall of the fifteen-by-fifteen room. Even the beds, Alice thought, felt far apart in spite of the room's size. Shoved flat against each wall, leaving a luxury of shared, empty space in the center. Cinnamon's bed seemed the most isolated of all, its frame shoved firmly into one corner. If she'd been able to knock down the wall and move her bed into the adjoining apartment, Alice figured Cinnamon would have done it.

The pirate captain bolted through the curtain but didn't spare a look for Alice. Instead, she collapsed into her own bed, then turned away toward the wall.

They were at each other's throats constantly, now. Two weeks of close-quarters co-existence had seen to that. Two weeks of routine and boredom and nerves fraying like the strands of a rope barely tethering them all to sanity. How people who cared so much for each other—or at least for her and, through her as a kind of conduit, valued the welfare of one another—could be so cruel, could stick a thumb into an emotional wound just to watch the other person squirm ... Alice couldn't understand it. But now, even as an impulse to cry from frustration coalesced in her gut, she held it in check—swallowed it back down before it was born.

Anger made it easy. She was mad. *Furious.* Ben seemed to delight in nothing else these days but egging Cinnamon on. Poking at her for taking the job that was the only thing allowing them to stay here in this soggy, stinking hole of an apartment. Now, wasn't that a joke? And yet...

Be grateful, Ben! If it weren't for Cinn and Torque, we'd be out there and running from—everyone!

Pirates loyal to Sayyida al-Hurra. President Bragg and the Alliance military. Shadow-spiders.

Alice shuddered.

Be grateful, Ben, she thought again, her anger ladled over with memories of her rushing, stumbling, terrifying flight in the underground of Drake's World.

The Terror Planet.

Alice shook her head, trying to banish the image. But the memories persisted, flashing with a *tap-tap-tap* cadence, dominating her mind. So, she tried another tactic. Instead of running from the tapping as her mind-self ran from its multi-legged makers, Alice made herself present with the sound. Embraced it. Counted the taps as she had her steps in the tunnels then, with the shadow-spiders pursuing close behind. Counting made her feel centered and in control. She metered the taps in triplets and doublets. Her mind-self stumbled and fell and caught herself on the rocky floor, a ghost of that impact echoing in her palms. Then there was her father's voice in her head.

And that moment when she'd become determined to live after all.

In her mind, Alice stood up in the tunnel. In reality, in the room with four beds, she opened her eyes. The counting had worked again. And now she was back and facing problems that, however difficult they were, didn't include being chased by shadow-spiders. And that was something, anyway.

Cinn hated the work and Ben knew it, and he poked at that bruise nearly every time she and Torque returned from a shift. Cinnamon Gauss was a good person, an honorable person, whatever Ben's general opinion of pirates might be. But Cinn did the work anyway because she had to—for Alice.

All of this is for me.

The hitching emotion returned, but she bit her lip and fought it off again. She had half a thought to reach out to Cinnamon, to see if she was okay, but the pirate's stiff back warned her off. Despite the wet heat, Alice pulled up the thin blanket and curled up into a ball on the bed. The programming of the smart mattress worked most of the time, and now it sculpted itself beneath her, accommodating the fetal shape her body made. Alice stared at her left palm, and even in the low light, she could see the crevice of an old wound. But it wasn't from her stumbling fall beneath Drake's World. Though broken, the palm sensors of her environmental suit from the SS *Seeker* had largely protected her then. No, this wound she'd given herself in a fit of desperation on Tarsus Research Station, when fear and aggravation had ruled her life. Alice had carved her pain out of her own flesh, given herself something physical to feel to distract her from the emotional pain invading her from the inside. In the past, she'd reveled in seeing the bright red blood welling, in feeling the sharp, acrid ache of self-inflicted penance.

Though her insides roiled—and the relentless, festering dread of losing her new family as she'd lost everyone else simmered inside her—Alice didn't feel compelled to bring the bloody scar back to life. Even now, after the latest confrontation between Ben and Cinnamon. She found it strange, and strangely heartening, that she didn't need to. She tried to analyze that feeling, a dim recollection of her father's challenging, measured voice directing her.

"What is it you want to understand?" Marcus Keller asked, his tone professorial but kind.

"Why I don't want to cut," Alice answered.

"What does your gut tell you?"

"My gut?" Alice said, skeptical. "What does my gut have to do with the scientific method?"

"Everything, when the broth of the science is boiled down."

Alice didn't understand. She'd never heard her father speak that way. He sounded more like her mother. Or what he'd said sounded more like her mother's words, anyway.

"What does your gut tell you?" Now it *was* her mother, Annabelle, asking the questions.

"That I don't want to cut," Alice said without thinking first.

"Why?"

"Because I don't need to."

"Why?"

"I don't know!"

God! Now her mother sounded like Andre Korsakov.

Why? Why?

Try! Try!

"Look at it from a different perspective." Her father again. *"Pick it up, turn it around, and look at it again."*

"Like Sudoku?"

"Like Sudoku."

When he'd first taught Alice the game, Marcus Keller had let his daughter struggle with the impenetrable wall of empty squares demanding numbers, one through nine, seemingly randomly scattered across a grid of nine squares, with nine more squares nested inside the larger grid. The game appeared impossible at first, overwhelming in its complexity of 670,903,752,021,072,936,960 permutations, until her father had shown her the fairly simple way in which the numbers related to one another. No two instances of a single number could occupy the same row or column, and once you began to see the pattern of each one's placement in relation to the others, determining what went where was relatively easy. The first time she'd conquered the game with ten-to-the-twenty-first-power quintillion possible solutions—with no hints or errors—had been one of the proudest moments of Alice's life. Viewing how each numeral fit together by examining first where each could coexist without conflicting with its same mates was key to solving the whole puzzle.

"Sudoku's like life, you know," her mother had once said, looking over Alice's shoulder as she'd struggled with a particularly troublesome placement of numbers. "Seems complex. Simpler, though, when you stare at it long enough from another perspective."

Alice did that now, setting aside the more opaque question of why she didn't want to cut in favor of the more distant, less thorny one—why had she wanted to cut before? She'd been alone in her quarters after nearly killing Korsakov. Wondering if maybe she'd gone even further and murdered her own family, was horrified by that possibility, half-convinced it was the reason they'd simply disappeared. She hadn't felt that alone since waking up by herself on the *Seeker*, clueless as to who she was, *what* she was. And in that moment in her quarters, in the wake of injuring Korsakov and suffering Ian's accusing stares, of feeling Zoey's cold distance and her own isolation inside herself, of feeling like a freak, she'd needed to feel something else—something solid, something real and external and distracting.

Two families, lost. The second at Tarsus, her doing for sure, the result of her ability and her inability to control it. The first ... well, what had happened to that family was still an open question, wasn't it?

Alice reached beneath her shirt and took out the locket. Her one piece of evidence she still possessed of a former life with her birth family. She unsnapped the clasp and angled the image inside to gather the most light possible from the lone lamp in the corner of the room. Her father, Marcus, looking stalwart and curious as always, as if counting the milliseconds needed by the cam to capture their image. Annabelle, her mother, smiling and proud and knowing whoever saw the image in the future would know what a loving family looked like. Ollie, her little brother, lover of action vids and scrawler of no-nonsense, personal warnings, like the *KEEP OUT* sign he'd carved outside his cabin door on the *Seeker*. He was smiling but reluctantly, the way little boys do. *He looks so young*, Alice thought. As she did herself. She was, of course, only fourteen in the photo, but more than that, she appeared world-foolish, a girl with dreams of wedding dresses and following her father into science and looking forward to the next time they climbed Mount Maraschino on Sylvan Novus. Looking so much like her mother and father, as if their DNA had been dropped into a bowl and swirled together with a spoon. She had her father's penetrating stare, constantly on the lookout for new knowledge, but also her mother's calmness, her unwavering faith she'd carried into every situation: that everything happened for a reason and therefore, whatever the outcome, it would be all right.

A strange mixture that, Alice thought, staring at their faces. From her father she'd inherited the rigorous certainty that knowledge sprang from data and, interpreted within the realm of the known, could be spun out to create what could be. How he ever managed to woo her mother was a mystery. His approach to life was so at odds with what Alice remembered of her mother's personality. "People should be less uptight." How many times had Alice heard Annabelle Keller say that about her academic friends and their quest for success among their equally anxious peers?

"Easy to say, Mom," Alice whispered to the tiny, serene face staring out from the locket. "I don't know how you did it. Kept faith in the future, I mean." The reality of everything happening right now flooded her mind. Their constant hiding from those meaning them harm. The war.

The shadow-spiders.

Alice released a long, slow breath. "Sometimes it's not so easy."

But, at least, she and the others were doing it together. She, Ben, Cinnamon, and Torque. And the others, Gal and Moze and even Louie, back on the *Junkyard Dog*. They might be running and hiding, avoiding detention and death and constantly looking over their shoulders for both, but they were doing it together. And that's when the answer clicked for Alice in the finest tradition of great discoveries. The answer to why she didn't need to cut came with the certainty of her father's reasoning wrapped in the warm glow of her mother's smile.

Alice wasn't alone. She was with friends who'd become her family. Those she loved and who loved her in return. Neither expecting anything of the other, but only too glad to give of themselves. It wasn't the first time she'd realized what they meant to each other, but it was the first time it seemed a magical talisman, a sprig of hope hanging over the front door, shielding against bad omens.

"How you doing, little sister?"

Alice glanced over the lip of her blanket to find Cinnamon sitting up and facing her. She didn't get up or approach Alice's bed. Maybe trying to respect boundaries, Alice thought, noting the distance. Or maybe defining her own.

"I'm okay," she said. "But I hate it when you fight with Ben. I *hate* it."

"I know," Cinnamon said. "I'm sorry."

"It's not just you."

"No."

"And I get it. This sucks. This planet, this place. I hate that you have to do what you do, just to protect us." It spilled out of her all at once, pent up before and now released. "But you went too far, Cinn."

"I know." Cinnamon sighed and stood. Walking to Alice's bed, she said, "Mind if I sit?"

"Sure," Alice said. "I mean, yeah, go ahead." Truth was, she'd been a little surprised by the question. Six days out of seven, Cinnamon Gauss, number one, didn't sit next to anyone she didn't have to and, number two, didn't ask permission to do anything. It somehow made Alice feel special that Cinn was doing both for her.

"You're right," Cinnamon said, "I went too far with Stone. I—"

"His name is *Ben*. Maybe if you two would go by first names, things would be a little easier."

Cinnamon pursed her lips but nodded, almost like it was a thing she'd consider doing, if pressed. "You're probably right about that, too. But Stone ... Ben ... and I have a tough relationship."

"Because you both make it that way."

It was weird. She could tell Cinnamon was making a real effort here—*trying*, Korsakov said in her head. But the more Cinnamon talked, the harder she tried, the angrier Alice got. She didn't want to be mad, but she was. Alice said, "I told you about Ben's problem with drinking because we're *family*. So you could maybe better understand where he's coming from. What he's dealing with."

Cinnamon drew back a few inches. Her brow furrowed beneath its stubbly skullcap, her eyes flashing light emerald inside their painted-on, ebony frame.

"What *he's* dealing with? He has no idea what real pressure is, Alice."

"That's not fair. He—"

"He sits here, day after day, and plans ambushes and doesn't let me get in the goddamned door before he..." Cinnamon broke off. She'd stood as she'd spoken, and now seemed frozen in self-righteous indignation. She backed away from Alice a step. "I'm sorry. I didn't come over here to say that."

Alice stared up at the woman who'd dedicated her life to protecting her. "No, I'm the one who's sorry. We're all so tired. So stressed out. I'll talk to Ben, I'll smooth it—"

A loud banging came from the other room, startling Alice. It took her a moment to realize it'd come from the corridor outside their apartment.

"Stay here," Cinnamon said.

The pounding came again, along with a muffled demand to open up.

The black curtains breezed aside, and Ben Stone hopped into the room.

"Stay with her," Cinnamon ordered as she passed him. "And don't make a sound."

For once, Ben didn't argue.

3
NIGHTMARES AND OPPORTUNITIES

EVA PARK HAD GOTTEN USED to waiting. That didn't mean she'd learned to like it, not one damned bit, but she was used to it. Just part of her new normal under a military regime.

One aspect of that reality she was fairly sure she'd never get used to? Alliance Marines in New Nassau's Command and Control Center. Eva stared across the round table in Hadrian al-Hurra's office at the quiet efficiency humming along in the C&C next door. After a brief transition period wherein Lieutenant Colonel Bathsheba Toma's handpicked substitutes had debriefed al-Hurra's command staff, the pirate officers had been unceremoniously rotated out to house arrest. Replaced by their occupiers, the 214th Marine Battalion, First Drop Division, of the Ground Forces of the Sol Alliance. The former staff now stood down, along with the other thirty-eight thousand or so of New Nassau's population, confined to quarters unless explicitly permitted to be outside them.

When the Marines had first landed two weeks ago, most everyone had sighed their relief at bloodshed avoided—a majority sentiment, if not a unanimous one, the first few days of occupation. But that collective sigh had turned tense with anticipation over an ill-defined, yet-seemingly-inevitable conflict to come. New Nassau's calm acceptance of the new normal, much like Eva's patience with waiting, had begun to erode. Slowly, at first, but it wasn't long before personal grousing behind closed doors morphed into the public griping of like-minded individuals gathered in small groups. The rate of erosion was quickening. The tension between occupiers and formerly free pirates, increasing. The citizens of the Malvian Triangle, suckled on a diet of libertarian idealism from an early age, naturally resented the confines imposed by martial law and its lockstep enforcement by Toma and her troops. Oppressors, some called them. Others, jackbooted thugs. Armed rebellion had yet to break into the open, but it festered in the darker corners of the colony like a bad smell that was impossible to find but ubiquitous. Graffiti had even begun appearing in public spaces after curfew.

Eva had initiated more than one conversation with al-Hurra about her concerns over the simmering tension, and she'd even—once—persuaded Sayyida, his daughter and current political rival, to join them to talk strategies for defusing it. But Sayyida's cozy association with Colonel Toma had been tantamount to treason in her father's eyes, a usurpation of his authority as leader of the colony, and much as he wanted nothing more than to keep his people safe, their one summit with Sayyida had descended quickly into political attacks and personal recriminations. Barely five minutes after the meeting began, the daughter stalked away from the father, who'd sat stubbornly fuming at the very table where Eva now waited impatiently. And so, the bad mojo in New Nassau continued to grow, catalyzed anew by the increasingly personal animosity within the al-Hurra family. The need to discuss that problem—again—and perhaps this time to find a solution that didn't involve mass casualties had brought

Eva back to the table, where she tapped her toe and admired the quiet competence now occupying New Nassau's nerve center.

The pressure door securing that room from the outer corridor rolled open, its hydraulic moan drawing Eva's attention. Hadrian al-Hurra, colony commander—now a merely ceremonial rank with a lower-cased "c"—had finally arrived in his former command only to be stopped short by a Marine corporal. They exchanged perfunctory pleasantries, and Eva could imagine the dialogue going something like this:

"Please hold for a security scan."

"You know who I am, Corporal. I come in here every day."

"And yet, I need to verify your identity."

"My face isn't enough?"

"Sure, sir. Once I scan it."

"I nicked myself with a razor this morning. You might need to recalibrate your scanner from yesterday."

"Sir, do we have to do this dance? Every time?"

But whatever the actual exchange had been, the corporal on duty conducted the required ID scan and passed al-Hurra through the checkpoint. The corporal stood aside, and al-Hurra made his way through the C&C with his gaze fixed forward. The door to the office passed into the wall, briefly allowing the white-noise operations in the adjoining room to pass through. Then it shut again behind al-Hurra's entry. Eva stood to receive him, grateful for the excuse to stretch her lower back.

"Eva," Hadrian said by way of greeting. He threw himself into a chair opposite her, turning his back on the bustling room behind. "I don't think I'll ever get used to that, checking into my own C&C."

"I know what you mean," Eva replied. She didn't point out the obvious fact that it was no longer al-Hurra's C&C.

"Sorry I was late," he said. "Trouble sleeping last night."

"No problem. Gave me time to get my thoughts together."

"I've been having this recurring dream lately," al-Hurra continued, as if she hadn't spoken. "I don't remember many details."

Eva decided the purpose for the meeting could wait a little longer. "A dream? What do you remember about it?"

He brought his eyes up from the smooth surface of the conference table. "New Nassau, full of corpses."

She watched him closely. Tried to keep any reaction off her face. Practiced more of those well-honed political skills she planned to highlight on a resume one day. One day soon, maybe.

"That is," he went on, "the ones not blown out into space by the destruction of the dome."

Eva nodded, agreeing on their shared vulnerability behind the sealed engineering wonder of polysteel, plastinium, and hexacrete that allowed them all to breathe inside an iron-nickel asteroid that would have otherwise been uninhabitable vacuum.

"You know how the Specter War began?" he asked, focusing on the wall behind her. Before she could speak, he continued, "Of course you do, being the president's communications director."

Former communications director, Eva corrected in her head.

She watched al-Hurra. Gave him some space and silence to void himself of whatever negativity the dream had left him with. She needed him thinking, not distracted. They'd spent too long distracted already. Disaster loomed.

"Miscommunication," he said. "No one knew what the Arcœnum were. No human had ever seen an alien before. All we saw was what we feared they were."

Eva nodded, more acknowledgment than encouragement. He'd only related what most agreed was the tragic truth of the worst event in recent history. And it had begun principally because two different otherwise advanced, arguably intelligent species—each with its own perspective on the universe and why they existed in it—were unable to find any common ground upon which to base a peaceful coexistence. Not even the common ground of mutually desired survival.

"It didn't help that the Archies had no spoken language. So miscommunication, I suppose, was inevitable."

"War didn't have to occur," Eva noted.

His eyes found hers again. "No, I suppose not." Al-Hurra exhaled heavily. "And yet war happened anyway."

"Wars don't just happen. People make decisions."

"Politicians, you mean?"

She offered him a small, world-weary smile. It was macabre, not mirthful. "Most of the time, yeah."

"Looking back on the war," al-Hurra said bleakly, "it seems like God tossed a pebble from on high. It landed on a mountain-side and started an avalanche—which buried tens of thousands on both sides."

Eva noticed her toe was again tapping softly against the floor. She quieted it with effort. "Dreams are supposed to be the subconscious subtly working out our daily trials via metaphor."

Al-Hurra grunted. "Nothing subtle about *my* dream."

Time to press the point. "So, you see New Nassau going the way of Sirius?"

"No, I see it being more of a tragedy than that."

More of a tragedy? More than two species attempting to expunge one another from existence? All because—

"The difference is, *we* know how to communicate with each other," al-Hurra said wearily. "Whichever faction, we all speak the same goddamned language."

Eva bobbed her head in sympathy with his point. Symbolically transparent dreams aside, at least he'd returned, however roundabout, to the reason for their meeting.

"I think we should approach Sayyida again," she said, fully prepared for his bristling response. The elder al-Hurra appeared to swell up in his chair. Like a puffer fish, getting defensive.

But just as quickly he deflated again, seeming even smaller now than he had pressed beneath the weight of his nightmare. "It's the right course of action," he said, and Eva was struck again by how the man could surprise her with his lack of ego and persistent propensity for doing what needed to be done, however distasteful he might find it. But then he said, "But there's too much history there."

She blinked, trying to reconcile his refusal in light of his agreement on the best way forward. "Time might be running out," Eva pressed.

"I know," he said. "I just don't see how Sayyida and I—"

"I'm not just talking about your family squabble." She could hear it in her voice. The impatience for bullshit in the face of life-ending events. Eva's entire foot began rhythm-keeping below the table, no longer satisfied by a single, tapping toe.

Al-Hurra stared at her a moment, his brain slowly slipping past his personal issues with his daughter. "The Skane, you mean?"

"And the Arcœnum." She hesitated to put too fine a point on it, but the time for friendly debate felt about three days out of date. The graffiti was getting nasty. "There are larger conflicts we need to worry about. But we have to be united in how we approach those. We can't have humans killing humans if we hope to—"

Al-Hurra raised a hand to stay the lecture she was gearing up to give. "I know," he said. "I know."

He didn't bother challenging the controversial assumption

that the so-called Skane even existed. Word of the new threat had come in as so-called intelligence based on Arcœnum claims relayed through a back-channel, encrypted communiqué from Ben Stone to Toma—the one contact they'd received from Gauss and her crew since they'd fled New Nassau. But there'd been no actual sighting of any "spider fleet," no evidence confirming that it even existed beyond the word of Louie the Shadow, or whatever his name was, currently on the run with Gauss. That the intel had come from fugitives openly defying a presidential *habeas corpus* order to turn over Alice Keller only deepened suspicions of its veracity. As far as military intelligence was concerned, the Skane were mythical, likely created as propaganda by the Archies to distract the Alliance military—something even Stone himself had suggested as a possibility in the communiqué. Eva would be in that camp too, if she'd been asked outright. But the Archie fleet had also disappeared from the subspace network, and Alliance forces waited in Sol, Alpha-C, and The Frontier for them to reappear. Waited for the chance to strike. Louie the Shadow's assertion that it was a refugee fleet running from the Skane... Well, neither Eva nor the military leaders of the Bragg Administration believed that one, either.

She sat in silence with al-Hurra, whose eyes fixed on the table between them as he debated internally with himself. It looked painful. Maybe he was trying to figure out a way to reach Sayyida after all, despite his reservations at the likelihood of success. But, Eva had to admit, he might be right. Sayyida had her own agenda, and it hinged on successfully ingratiating herself with the Bragg Administration to facilitate reunion for her outlaw brethren with the larger Sol Alliance. To do that, she'd subjugated herself to Toma, acting as a calming liaison with angrier voices in the colony, which as far as that went was a good thing. But flaccid assurances weren't enough, even when offered by someone as well liked as Sayyida. She was spending all her political capital with her followers while rubberstamping Toma's rule and biding her time for an opportunity to exploit. What Eva could see, and Sayyida apparently could not, was that their current state of occupation would be the status quo for the foreseeable future. And the residents of New Nassau and the rest of the pirates across the Triangle, too used to charting their own course, were growing too restless to endure it much longer. The dissension, growing bolder every day, was evidence of that fact. Eventually, Sayyida's bedding down with Toma would be her own downfall. Eva was sure of it. Then, as it often does, inspiration rode into her mind on the back of a horse named Irony.

"There might be another way," she said before her own thoughts had fully formed. Certainly before any strategy for success had suggested itself. "A side entrance to the solution."

Al-Hurra woke from whatever daydream he'd been indulging. "What do you mean?"

Before she could answer, the door chime sounded. Al-Hurra turned, annoyed at the interruption. The door swept aside, revealing the corporal who'd stopped the commander on the way into the C&C. He didn't wait for permission to step forward.

"Yes?" al-Hurra said.

"Colonel Toma needs to see you, Commander al-Hurra."

"Now?"

The corporal eyed him coldly but respectfully. That they still referred to al-Hurra by his defunct title was an attempt at the same, Eva knew.

"Well, sir," the corporal said impatiently, "she wasn't making a reservation." He stood in the doorway, making it clear he wasn't going anywhere except as an escort.

Al-Hurra turned to regard Eva. "I wonder what *this* is now..."

"An opportunity, maybe," she said.

"What do you mean?"

Instead of answering, she stood up and said to the corporal, "Mind if I tag along?"

4
SINISTER BUSINESS

"YOUR CHIME DOESN'T WORK."

Oromo Bello's first words were straight to the point after Cinnamon opened the door. Explanation without excuse for pounding so loudly. Civilized in a utilitarian kind of way but shorn of all social pretense. Like the pounding itself had been.

"Mister Bello..." Cinnamon knew they'd be coming—or that someone would. But she thought she'd have more time. She hadn't guessed that Blackmore would send his second-in-command.

The tall, bony man with the close-cropped hair and bleak face stretched his lips into a toothy smile. Gratified, or satisfied, that she'd recognized him. He adjusted his old-fashioned, round-rimmed glasses to squint at her, as if to verify who *she* was. As though choreographed, each of the three henchmen behind Bello crossed their hands in front of them. They wore red sashes, the mark of Damianos Blackmore's elite enforcers who ranked several tiers above Cinnamon. They stood with fingers unlaced should the need arise to draw their weapons.

Like his manner, Bello's clothing was crisp, clean, and

precise. He needed no sash. Anyone who needed to know who he was knew it already.

Cinnamon said, "This is unexpected, Mister Bello."

His thin lips stretched wider. "I doubt that." Bello arched his neck left and right to peer into the apartment behind her. Cinnamon didn't try to prevent it. His eyes lit on Torque. "Frida," he acknowledged.

Torque nodded. "Mister Bello." Without looking, Cinnamon knew Torque would be doing her best lazy dog impression, lounging on the bed-bench, maybe one hand hanging loosely off a knee. Presenting a picture of fatigue and relief after a long day. And no threat to any surprise visitors.

Bello's eyes reacquired Cinnamon, pinning her in place. From the impressive arrowhead of his nose, he stared down at her like a predator bird preparing to dive into a hatchling's nest.

"May I ask the reason for your visit?" Cinnamon said. She was kicking herself for not having gathered up Alice and the others and vacating the apartment immediately upon returning from her shift. And then Stone, the selfish, self-indulgent sonofabitch, had derailed her. And now it was too late.

"Oh, I think you know, Asta," Bello said with no patience for foreplay. He held out one hand. "Your weapon, please."

Please sounded a lot like *now*.

Cinnamon inched her hand toward the pistol hanging low on her left thigh. The smaller henchman behind Bello separated his hands and turned his right palm up to reveal a small sidearm of his own.

"Use the other hand," Bello said to Cinnamon.

Her left hand almost on her weapon, Cinnamon ceased all movement. The henchman targeted his pistol at her solar plexus. She considered leaping forward while she drew her own gun and pushing Bello into him. Maybe the man's gun would go off and he'd shoot Bello in the back. As her mind calculated the possibilities, time dilated. The old, familiar buzz of adrenaline caught like fire under her skin. Her center of gravity dropped from her sternum into her stomach.

"Don't be an idiot," Bello said. "I'm a practical man, Miss Merck. If I wanted you dead, you'd be dead."

Her eyes tracked from the henchman's pistol mouth to Bello. "I didn't do anything wrong."

Bello shrugged. It was almost sympathetic. "Not for me to say." His expression hardened. "Weapon. *Now.*"

Behind her there was the rustle of cloth and leather across the 4D-printed stone of Torque's bed-bench. And a resigned exhalation from Torque that translated to *here we go again.*

"Keep your seat, Frida," Cinnamon called over her shoulder. "This won't take long."

Bello's anorexic grin returned. "Again, we agree."

"Asta—" Torque began but Cinnamon raised her hand. She understood Torque's impulse to draw, shoot, and hope for the best. It'd served them well enough in the past. But the stakes were higher now, and circumstances arrayed against them. The space was too tight. There were four adversaries, including Bello. Sure, Cinnamon might get Bello and one of his henchmen, but one of the remaining Red Sashes would clip Cinnamon and maybe Torque before she could join the fray. That'd leave only Stone to protect Alice. And while he'd proven his resourcefulness on the rooftop of the Swashbuckler's Leap, she didn't think Stone could get Alice out of here and off Ionia before being caught by Blackmore—not alone. So, for one of a handful of times in her life, Cinnamon Gauss ignored the ballsier angels of her nature.

"Keep your seat, Frida," Cinnamon said again. "That's an order."

Cinnamon dropped her left hand and, in slow motion, reached around with her right. The small man's pistol didn't waver. She extracted the sidearm with her fingertips and handed it to Bello, who wedged it into his belt.

"Be careful with that," she said. "It's unique. One of only two of a kind."

"Oh, I will," Bello said. "You know, Merck, it's not every day a new hire like you, a Black Sash no less, gets an audience with the boss. Search it." Bello stepped aside, and two of the Red Sashes entered the apartment, pushing their bulk past Cinnamon with little effort.

One frisked Torque, who was clean, then made her get up so he could search the cushion she'd been reclining on. With a sneer, he pulled out the pistol hidden beneath it. He moved on to the closet in the common room, rifling its meager contents. The second man breezed through the black curtains and into the shared bedroom. There came distant noises of searching, more grunting. Cinnamon glanced at Torque, knowing it would look perfectly natural to Bello. Who wouldn't commiserate with a comrade while their apartment was tossed? Torque arched her eyebrows, but only slightly. Cinnamon shook her head, but only slightly. The henchmen returned, one brandishing the pistol he'd taken from Torque.

"Nothing else, boss."

"You scanned?"

"Sure," the Red Sash said, producing his bio-scanner for proof.

Cinnamon looked back to Bello.

"Shall we?" He gestured to the corridor.

The two enforcers who'd searched the apartment took up positions outside the door. Bello was leaving them behind. Insurance against an attempt by "Frida" to, perhaps, attempt an ill-advised rescue. Cinnamon took a step forward, then stopped in the doorway, turning to look at her oldest friend. "Hold the fort, Frida," she said. "I'll be back."

Bello bent down, leaned in close. Cinnamon felt his breath in her ear. And the nearness of his hawklike nose, air whistling in his nostrils as he inhaled her scent.

"I wouldn't count on it," he said.

The Red Sash led the way with Cinnamon behind him. Bello brought up the rear. Residents of the Underside went about their business, some noticing them and more pretending not to. Cinnamon had a flashback memory of a similar public parade, when she'd led Ben Stone and Eva Park across the docks of New Nassau, welcomed by the accolades of her fellow pirates. Victorious again—Cinnamon Gauss, pirate captain and queen of rogues, with two prizes so valuable this time that...

Why hadn't she simply killed Carletha Lutz and been done with it? What was one less self-proclaimed prophet come to cure Ionia's visitors of their addictions? There was always another would-be savior to take her place, ready to become another huckster on a planet of hucksters, selling absolution instead of luck. Instead, Cinnamon had knuckled under to an acute attack of morality, and look where that had landed her. With Alice put at greater risk than she had been since Tower's Fall.

They took the lift to the tube central exchange, where the regular lines crisscrossed the Underside to a dozen destinations, every one of them strategic to ensure the cogs had consistent access to work. The henchman led them past the public lines and into a private alcove where, thanks to Oromo Bello's familiar face, they weren't even stopped for ID scans. They boarded Blackmore's private tube train that would make only one stop.

Bello hadn't said a word since leaving the apartment. Cinnamon almost wished he would. The voice inside her head kept assailing her with doubt. She felt keenly the empty holster on her left thigh and half-regretted her earlier instinct not to fight. But she'd known better then, and she still did, if she were being honest with herself. Fantasy and wishful thinking, that's all that particular regret was.

The train slowed, and she side-eyed Bello. He stared straight ahead, his face emotionless. His posture erect but also relaxed, an odd combination. He struck her as a walking, talking moral void with good fashion sense. No, Cinnamon thought, she shouldn't have risked delivering Alice into his hands. Every minute she remained alive, there was hope to prevent that from ever happening.

Still underground, they transferred to a lift, and it was a long ride to the ninety-ninth floor of Blackmore's penthouse-fortress. When the doors opened, the light of Ionia shining through the windows blinded Cinnamon. By the time she could see again, Bello and the guard had melted away into the cavernous room somewhere. At its far end, seated at a table long enough to accommodate twenty, sat the king—make that kingpin—who'd summoned her.

"Ah, Asta Merck." Damianos Blackmore rose. "Please, come in."

Cinnamon walked cautiously forward, her eyes still adjusting. Blackmore's appearance met all her expectations. He was tall with fiery red hair, short on top, thick sideburns on his cheeks and a jutting ginger goatee on his chin. He was dressed like the local tycoon he was: business suit with an amber pendant representing Ionia's sun on the lapel.

Her tactical sense assessed the room. Spare, except for the

long table and a cart hovering nearby, liquor on display. Various representations of Ionian art adorned the walls, mostly demurring nudes. Aphrodisiacs for art lovers, but nothing anyone but a fundamentalist preacher would consider pornographic. Ionia's sun bathed the room in a reassuring, honey-colored warmth through the bank of windows to the west.

"You're wondering why you're here," Blackmore said.

"Not really," Cinnamon said respectfully. She was within a few feet of him now. The purr of the liquor cart's anti-grav servos filled the space between them. "I get it. I refused to carry out my assignment."

"Ah, well, yes, there is that," Blackmore said. "Will you sit?"

Cinnamon said, "I'd rather stand"—then, realizing the attitude that had accompanied the declaration, added—"if you don't mind." If her earlier prudence had destined her to die without a gun in her hand, she'd at least go out on her feet.

Blackmore smiled, and there was something reassured in it. As if, had she taken him up on the offer to sit, he would have been disappointed.

"Practical, like Mister Bello over there," Blackmore acknowledged. "I like that. Time is money, after all. No need to waste either."

Cinnamon found Bello to her right pretending to admire a fleshy piece of art.

"You're familiar with the current state of affairs on Ionia?" Blackmore asked.

"I assume you don't mean all the cheating spouses."

The pleasure planet's de facto ruler offered a hollow chuckle in response. "Only indirectly. I refer to the larger issue of the decreased business these days."

Shrugging, Cinnamon said, "War is usually bad for business."

"That's exactly right. Unless, of course, your business *is* war." Blackmore began to move around. Not toward her, exactly. But not away from her either. "Mine, alas, is not. Did you know I brought Carletha Lutz to Ionia?"

That surprised Cinnamon. "You did?"

"We had a deal." Blackmore about-faced on his heel, and Cinnamon wasn't sure whom "we" included. He walked toward her. "She could come here and moralize to the masses, and I'd pay her expenses on-planet."

That made zero sense. No business sense, certainly, since Lutz and religiosos like her had the specific goal of interfering with the profitable vices Ionia's visitors typically sought out.

"I see the obvious question on your face," he said, diverting his path in Bello's direction. "Think of it this way, Asta—human motivation is rarely straightforward. And symbols are important. And the more *conflicted* visitors to Ionia need to feel a little guilty about what they do here. It's the way they balance the impulse—compulsion, in many cases—to, shall we say, indulge themselves. Feeling like shit afterward about sinning is how they give themselves permission to do it in the first place."

He was being obtuse, but Cinnamon thought she understood. "Sinning is fine, as long as you're sorry on Sunday?"

Blackmore stopped mid-step and turned to face her directly. "Exactly, Asta!"

"So, you had Lutz here as psychological counter-programming to your customers' immoral impulses."

"'Psychological catalyst' would be a better way to put it."

Before Cinnamon could avoid the landmine, she stepped squarely on top of it. "Then, why kill her?"

"Ah," Blackmore said, "now we get to why you're here." His tone had changed from genial host to dissatisfied boss. "The good sister of virtue has been doing her job a little too well. When business was good, not a problem. In bad times—a liability. In war, people begin to take stock of themselves. Worry about meeting God sooner rather than later."

"Why not just ship her off again, then?"

He observed her a moment. "Because others, whose loyalty should be beyond doubt, are beginning to respond to her. An example needs to be made. Remind those whose faith is wavering, if you'll pardon the self-indulgence of the pun, who runs the show around here." Blackmore became reflective. "But I think I know where things went wrong with the assignment."

Cinnamon couldn't resist asking. "Where?"

"Direct involvement in daily business isn't something I do much anymore, you see." Blackmore began to pace again. "I rely on others for that, like Mister Bello there. I solve bigger-picture problems. But sometimes those who work for me fail me."

A screeching sound of heavy dragging called Cinnamon's eyes toward the lift behind her. Two Red Sashes hauled a beaten man roughly across the floor. He was still wearing his Blackguard outfit, complete with blue sash, the symbol of a supervisor. His face was so bruised, she hardly recognized him. The Red Sashes dropped him to his knees, and he collapsed onto his face.

"Rader?" she whispered.

Bello had ceased his artistic appraisal and was casually making his way over.

"Job screening is—and I know some disagree—the most important part of hiring someone," Blackmore pronounced. "Do your homework right, and you minimize potential for problems down the line."

Bello pulled Cinnamon's pistol from his belt and leveled it at Rader's head.

"Ours is sometimes a sinister business. And termination of an employee can be so distasteful." Blackmore's tone—fatherly, patient, even amiable before—had frozen solid. He sighed.

"Harder on the terminated than the terminator, I suppose. Alas, Mister Rader here failed to vet you properly."

"Please—" Rader said. "I didn't know!"

Bello cocked the pistol.

"But that's the point, Mister Rader," Blackmore said. "Had you done your homework—"

"Wait..." Cinnamon said, taking an involuntary step toward a man she'd hardly known and had little regard for.

The shot echoed in the airy, empty space of the oversized conference room. Rader's head jerked sideways. His blood spattered a coarse maroon across the golden floor. His corpse slumped over, a muffled squeak marring the perfectly maintained tile with gore.

Shock morphed into hatred inside Cinnamon. Became a supernova, a sudden need to end a murderous CEO and his psychopathic second-in-command.

My own gun...

"Now, you have a choice," Blackmore said. "Save your life or lose it."

That checked Cinnamon's impulse to charge him, scratch his eyes out, stick her fingers into the sockets and dig Blackmore's brains out as poetic justice for the way Rader had died.

"It's simple, Miss Gauss," Blackmore said. "Tell me where Alice Keller is."

Cinnamon barely registered his knowledge of her real name. But she'd heard Alice's plainly enough. Then she felt the cold barrel of her own pistol pressed against the back of her head.

Blackmore's eyebrows lifted expectantly. The self-satisfied expression of a man who'd known exactly how a meeting would go and stood only to gain from its outcome.

Bello cocked her pistol a second time.

Fuck it, Cinnamon Gauss spat at the universe. She'd drop,

whirl, take Bello's legs out, take the gun from him, and shoot Blackmore before they gunned her down.

Take care of her, Stone.

A sharp pain erupted from one side of her skull.

Then, oblivion.

5
A DESPERATE PLAN

HE WAS SO CLOSE. But the smell of Ben's sweat wasn't altogether unpleasant, Alice decided. Even pressed tightly against him inside their hiding place in the wall. She couldn't help being embarrassed by what she must smell like to him, or cringe at the thought of his being offended by it. Or if, like her—

"Could you move to the left?" Ben whispered.

"Sorry," she said, shuffling quietly.

When Cinnamon opened the apartment door, they'd dashed into the narrow wall compartment to avoid discovery. They'd held their breath, and each other, while their meager belongings were picked up, examined, and cast aside by the man searching the bedroom. They'd listened to the muffled exchange from the common room, heard Cinnamon and Torque trade words, then the closing of the apartment door.

Alice breathed, "Ben, maybe—"

"Shhh."

"But—"

"*Shhh.*"

He maneuvered against her—again, not a totally horrible sensation, despite her annoyance at him—and pressed his ear to the panel. From the main room they could hear what sounded like Torque talking to herself, and salting it with expletives.

"Help me with this," Ben said. "Don't make a sound."

Together they disengaged the polysteel panel with a light, metallic click and shifted it aside along the wall. It was heavier than it should be, and Alice remembered why Cinnamon chose this shabby little underground apartment. Criminals who'd feared nuclear annihilation during the Specter War—or, worse, the loss of their contraband—had reinforced the polysteel and hexacrete construction of Underside's subterranean apartments with a lead polymer shield. Great for protecting against radiation, but the lining made the dense panels even heavier.

"Just set it aside for now," Ben said. They leaned the panel against the wall. Once Alice was out and inhaling the less stuffy air of the bedroom, he reached back inside the wall and removed Torque's scattergun from its back scabbard. "Stay here."

He froze when they heard Torque opening the front door again. There was more conversation, and the sound of a man's deep snark.

Ben stepped to the curtain separating the two rooms. He squinted, reconnoitering the common room. Alice moved up behind him.

"I told you—"

"*Shhh*," she said, squatting to see.

At the apartment door, Torque made obeisant apologies.

"You're lucky you're still standing, Frida," a man said.

"I understand," she replied and tried to swipe the door shut.

The man wedged his foot in, put one flat hand against the door to keep it open. He was dressed like Torque but wore a red sash instead of a black one. He had a pistol in his hand.

"Best make no trouble," the man said. "You might even get out of this alive, boss willing."

"Good advice," Torque said. "I'll take it."

The man nodded and stepped back. Torque touched the control pad again, and the door closed.

"What the fuck was that?" Ben asked, breezing through the curtain. Alice followed closely on his heels.

Torque keyed the lock on the door, then hop-skipped toward them on tiptoes. Like a tank pretending to be a ballerina.

"Where's Gauss?" Ben demanded.

"Keep your voice down!" Torque said, doing her best to follow her own advice. "Not every wall in this place is reinforced."

When Ben approached her directly, Torque centered herself. But he only handed her the back scabbard followed by the shotgun. Warily, she took them.

"I knew this was a bad idea," Ben growled. "This whole planet is infested with grifters and killers." Then, staring straight at Torque: "No wonder you two fit in so well."

Alice was about to say something, to tell him to stop his grumbling, but the quiet regret in Torque's voice stopped her.

"Not well enough," the big woman said. "Stone, calm down. I need to think." She headed for the bedroom.

Ben walked after her, asking, "What happened? And cut to it this time. No vague details like earlier."

Torque went straight for the open wall panel and began pulling the rest of their gear out. A small, boxy device with a large, complex antenna strapped piecemeal to one side. Another sidearm in its holster, the mate to the one Cinnamon always wore. A pack of food. Water bulbs.

"We were assigned a clip job," Torque said simply. "Cinnamon refused to do it."

"Clip job?" Alice wondered.

Ben clarified, "Murder."

Alice's eyes widened. "Oh, no..."

"It was inevitable, wasn't it?" Ben said. "Live among rats,

you get diseased. First it was, what, making collections from shop owners? Then last week, you guys practically separated a father from his family—and his life."

"We worked that out," Torque said, replacing the panel on the wall. "No one was hurt, you know that." She began sorting the items she'd removed from their hiding place.

Ben wouldn't let it go. "And yet, here we are."

Torque stopped what she was doing to stare at him. Hard, but also wearily. "Give it a rest, would you, Stone? I told you I need to think!"

"Shhh," Alice warned. "We'll figure it out. Now please, just stop."

"We have to get Cinnamon back," Torque said. "But first things first."

Torque set the square component on the floor next to the antenna parts, which she'd meticulously arranged on the floor. She was murmuring as she began putting the pieces together.

Alice moved to stand next to her friend. "I can help."

"You don't know anything about transmitters," Torque said brusquely. She added, "But thanks, little sister."

The anger welled up quickly inside Alice. Born of weeks of anticipation, of waiting to be discovered. And now fear for Cinnamon, for all of them. She felt weighed down with worry and powerless—that old, hated feeling of lack of control over events spinning off their axis.

"I didn't mean with the transmitter! And don't call me that!"

Torque looked up at her sharply, caution etched across her face.

"Ben calls me 'kid.' You call me 'little sister.' Korsakov called me 'child.'" Alice restrained her volume but not the fury churning behind it. Ben and Torque weren't her parents. She didn't have parents anymore. Didn't they know that? "I'm not helpless! I'm not!"

Torque reached out one large hand and lightly grasped Alice's arm. "I know you're not. But now's not the time..."

"Look, I know you're scared, Alice," Ben said, stepping forward. "We all are." Alice looked over at him. "But Torque's right. We have to keep our heads. Now, more than ever."

He didn't reach out as Torque had, and Alice was grateful for that. It would only confuse her more.

"I'm sorry," she said. "I'm sorry, Torque."

"It's all right—" But she caught herself and offered a light smile. "It's all right, Alice. And you *can* help."

"Yes!"

Alice kneeled beside Torque and the transmitter, still in pieces.

"So, how do we get Cinnamon back?" Alice asked, excited. "Maybe I could—"

"First things first," Torque said again. "Help me put this together. You too, Stone. You have training in subspace comms, right?"

He grunted acknowledgment. All three of them were soon cross-legged on the floor, Torque directing them as they connected individual components.

"This thing won't penetrate all the shielding," Ben declared, gesturing at the surrounding walls.

"That's why we're taking it outside," Torque said.

"You *do* remember the two thugs preventing our—"

"Stone, one thing at a time," Torque said, focused on the task at hand.

The three of them resumed their work in silence, which didn't last long.

"So, what's your plan?" Ben asked Torque. But without malice or sarcasm, Alice noted.

Torque grumbled, "Desperate."

More silence, more tinkling of metal-on-metal. Torque took

their individual efforts and completed the array's transmitter disc.

"Well," Ben said, looking from Alice to Torque, "sometimes desperation is the difference between defeat and victory."

"That is absolutely true," Torque responded.

Alice smiled, grateful to see them agreeing for once.

"Understand, Alice?"

She nodded at Torque.

"I hate this plan," Ben said. "She's too exposed—"

"Ben, I'll be fine," Alice assured him. She reached up to stroke his chin. "Let me help."

He seemed surprised by her touch. "Okay."

"Curtain time," Torque said. "Up against the wall, Marine."

Each of her companions took up their stage positions: Ben with his back against the wall beside the door to the corridor, and Alice moved into the bedroom. When the curtains were still again, Torque opened the door.

Both men were startled, but only briefly. "You again? What now?"

"I want to know where my friend is," Torque said.

"*You* want?" the Red Sash said. He drew his weapon but kept it pointed at the floor. "Back up. Go on, now."

Hands raised, Torque did as she was told. That was Alice's cue.

Alice thrust her face into the common room. "Hey, what's going on out here?"

The enforcer jerked his gaze to the sound of her voice. He did a double-take at Alice's innocent, smiling face framed tightly in the black curtains.

"Hey! It's you!"

He advanced two more steps, his gun rising. Torque had backed away far enough to allow him into the apartment, then ceased retreating. They were like two dancers pirouetting, one armed and astonished at his good fortune, the other's face calculating with hands raised in evident surrender. The Red Sash was so focused on Alice, he missed Ben lurking in his blind spot.

"Get out here!" the man ordered Alice. "Right now!"

The second Red Sash drew his weapon and advanced through the doorway behind his partner.

Ben brought Torque's scattergun crashing down on the second man's arm. The Red Sash cried out and dropped his pistol. Ben reversed course with the shotgun and shattered the enforcer's jaw on the upswing. The man went down, out cold.

The first enforcer swung toward the scuffle, leveling his pistol at Ben. "Who the hell are—" But Torque took advantage of his surprise and barreled into him, both her large hands grappling his gun arm. She forced it down and away, the momentum of her charge forcing him backward and off-balance. Ben slammed the panel on the wall with the flat of his hand, and the apartment door swished shut.

Torque kicked the enforcer's feet from under him and he went down, the impact of his hand with the floor sending his gun skittering into the grime. The struggle between them was brief and bloody. Torque stomped him once, twice in the face, and his nose burst like a ripe tomato smashed with a hammer. One groaning attempt to breathe, and then he lay still.

"Lock the door," Torque said, her breath heaving. Less from exertion, Alice guessed, and more from the surprising and welcome knowledge they'd all just survived.

"Already done," Ben replied. "I can't believe that worked. Too bad we couldn't just shoot them."

"Too much noise," Torque said. "Who knows who'd hear."

Grinning, Alice said, "Glad I could help!" as she stepped from the bedroom.

"And a good job of it, too," Torque said, smiling with relief. "Now, we stow these two."

Ben cleared his throat. "We could kill them *without* noise..."

Instantly, the room filled with tension again. Alice's face fell to a horrified expression. "Ben!"

He turned to her. "I'm sorry, Alice, I don't want to do it anymore than you do .But it's the smart move here to make sure—"

"We're not killing them," Torque declared sharply. "We can keep them unconscious long enough to rescue Cinnamon and get the hell off this damned planet."

Looking back and forth between them, Ben raised his hands. Truth was, he loathed the idea of cold-blooded murder. But he loathed the idea of risking Alice and, hell, even Cinnamon Gauss a lot more. "Fine. But we're using whatever that knockout drug is you and Gauss take to sleep at night, Torque. I want them out a *long* time."

"Fine," Torque agreed. "And once that's done, it's on to phase two."

Ignoring Alice's stare of judgment burning holes in the side of his head, Ben said, "Which is?"

Torque released a breath. "Let's just say that was the easy part."

"This poncho is itchy," Alice murmured, fiddling with the hood.

"And yet, oh, so fashionable," Ben said, attempting humor. "Try not to draw attention to yourself."

She smirked, though he didn't see. Ben was overwatching the bar. Torque sat in her own slate-gray poncho, hood down around her neck, chatting up the bartender. Most of the patrons wore the light ponchos, a staple piece of clothing among the working class of the Underside. Every minute they spent here was another minute the men from the apartment might fend off the sedative they'd dosed them with and wake up. Or Cinnamon might die. But Torque had emphasized—and Ben agreed, amazingly enough—that patience was vital if Torque's plan were to succeed.

"Are you sure you're okay to be in here?" Alice asked. "The bar, I mean."

"I'm fine," he replied less than convincingly.

The tension between them from earlier was gone, displaced by the need to focus on the mission to free Cinnamon. They'd dosed the enforcers with a drug called Kick, which the locals used to crash hard on restless nights, then stored them in the wall compartment of the bedroom. They'd be unconscious for hours yet.

In theory, Alice thought.

Torque had led them to Underside's entertainment district, where she'd made some inquiries, chosen a venue, and planted herself on a barstool serviced by a particularly chatty bartender. Ben and Alice, disguised as locals, sat watching at a table in one of the darker corners.

"What, exactly, is she doing?" Alice asked, her neck itching again. She was starting to think it wasn't the poncho, after all, but her own skin, which tingled with a nauseating combination of stress, hope, and crawling dread.

"Well," Ben ventured, "she's throwing hooks in the water."

"What does that mean?"

"It means she's probably offering you up."

"What?"

Ben flashed her a look. "First, keep your voice down.

Second, not really. She's pretending to get drunk and letting things slip out. Bits of information."

"Are you sure she's pretending?" Alice asked sarcastically.

"Well," Ben replied, "she *does* appear committed to the part. Hey, see the bartender? There must be half a dozen customers to take care of. Over the last half hour, he's hovered longer and longer over Torque. He's getting interested."

"Okay, and then what?"

"He'll make a call, if he hasn't already," Ben said. "Ah."

He flicked a finger and Alice followed its direction. A lithe man, powerfully built but not huge, approached Torque from behind. He nodded once and furtively to the bartender, who moved off.

The man mounted the stool next to Torque. The bartender returned quickly with a drink, then departed again. The newcomer struck up a conversation with Torque, who now seemed less inclined to talk.

"See how she's clamming up now?" Ben said. It sounded almost admiring. "She's making him work for it."

And working for it he was. Persistent with his overtures, and it soon paid off. Torque laughed and crowded into his space, almost too far, and the man helped right her on her stool. His coat lifted, and Alice noticed the belt holster and sidearm. Cautious in his movements, he reminded her of Cinnamon. Torque, on the other hand, seemed about to fall on the floor. The two talked for another couple of minutes.

"That guy looks familiar," Ben said. "But I don't know where from."

The man rose from his stool and helped Torque from hers. She was taller than him, but then she was taller than most men, and more muscled. He struggled for a moment to keep her on her feet. The man passed payment to the tender, who nodded in acceptance. The weaving couple began to make their way toward the bar's batwing doors.

Ben reached under the table and picked up the pack they'd brought with them from the apartment. "This is us. Follow my lead and do exactly what I say. Because now is when it gets dangerous."

6
THE LITTLE THINGS

EVEN A KNIFE WOULD HAVE *trouble cutting the tension in here*, Eva thought.

She stared directly at Bathsheba Toma. "Hadrian al-Hurra is a proud man. You didn't need to send him away like that."

Toma had her back to Eva, hands clasped behind her, body rigid, legs spread. In some kind of bastard compromise between erect attention and relaxed at-ease, she stared up at a small monitor. It showed a tactical display of the magenta-tinted cloud called the Malvian Triangle with blue and red triangles scattered across it representing Fleet and pirate assets. The red significantly outnumbered the blue, since most of Rear Admiral Malcolm Thorne's Third Sector Fleet had been redeployed from patrol duty in the Triangle to guard strategic assets within the sector. Notably Gibraltar Station, which still served after nearly one-hundred years as the hard-point bulwark between the Sol System and the rest of the Alliance like some fort along the Roman frontier intended to deter barbarian incursion.

"That's part of his problem," Toma said, watching the screen. "He hasn't yet accepted that he no longer commands this colony. I should never have taken your advice. I should have thrown him in the brig when we first arrived." She shook her head once and hard. "Half the problems we have now might never have manifested had I done so."

"You're making another mistake," Eva said.

It seemed impossible given her statue-like posture, but Toma appeared to stiffen further. After a moment her clasped hands released, and she turned to face Eva, a curious eyebrow raised.

Eva didn't retreat. "And a classic military mistake, at that."

Toma took her time approaching the small table. "Please, Miss Park, enlighten me." The colonel sat down, back erect, as though a teacher were standing over her with a ruler.

"These people have been here for decades. They carved out a life from the dead rock of the Triangle because they were given little choice by the Alliance fifty years ago. At least, that's how they see it. That chip on their shoulder? It's made of nickel and iron. It's as cold as the hollows in this asteroid. Just as empty of sympathy, too."

"Forgive me if my own capacity to sympathize with thieves and kidnappers is a bit lacking, Miss Park. 'These people' are traitors and the progeny of traitors. They abandoned their duty at a critical time, when humanity could least endure such irresponsibility. They deserve to be tried by military tribunal and incarcerated, if not *spaced*, for treason! Starting with their leader, as an example."

Eva held Toma's eyes. In them, she found an absolute belief in the correctness of a cause. Right and wrong, black and white, good and evil. Eva could see it in every movement Toma made, in every order she gave. Binary thinking was like a religion with her. And yet, Eva knew there was something more to Bathsheba Toma. What made Eva so good at politics was her uncanny ability to suss out human motivation. It was almost a sixth sense, what Leo Byrne—her comrade-in-arms and worst-kept-secret lover in the administration—called her superpower. Toma cloaked herself in regulations and chain-of-command to grapple with life, day after day. Eva understood the appeal for her. Toma had chosen the military to escape the slums of Mars, Ben Stone had told her. But she'd been Bathsheba Toma long before she'd become a Marine. Eva thought she could work with that.

"Colonel, these people are used to representative government through their elected captains. Arguably, they've formed a more direct democracy than the Alliance: a republic of pirates used to determining their own fate. You've taken that control away from them. You've shown them the value of taking personal liberty for granted. Good for you. Now they want it back."

"I'm still waiting for you to enlighten me," Toma said ungenerously. She paused, took a breath, and put her arms on the table. Like she was acting out steps from a manual on how to appear more relaxed. "These people are criminals, Miss Park, as I've said. You don't negotiate with criminals. You put them in jail." She inhaled and, slowly, exhaled. "But to your point of defusing tensions—if not incarcerate al-Hurra, perhaps replace him as the figurehead he's become. Sayyida al-Hurra would be a logical—"

"If you want a civil war, change leadership now."

Toma lifted her chin, regarding her. "You seem very sure of yourself, Miss Park."

"Call me Eva. I've asked you to a dozen times, now."

"Fourteen, actually. I started keeping count at three."

Of course, you did.

"Technically," Toma went on, "I should call you Presidential Liaison to the Colony of New Nassau."

"Miss Park is fine," Eva sighed. *Jesus!* "But whatever you think of them, you need to try to meet these people where they are, Toma. Not where you think they deserve to be."

"Call me Colonel."

Eva closed her mouth once she realized it was hanging open. *Lockstep* was too loose a word to encompass the padlocked sphincter that was Bathsheba Toma. Time for a different tack.

"The Skane and Arcœnum fleets have gone completely off-grid," Eva said, meeting the colonel on military ground. "You're essentially alone here, with no Fleet assets to back you up. Maintaining the peace is a first imperative, not to mention a strategy for survival for your Marines and the people they're ordered to guard."

Toma said, "I don't disagree with that. No one wants unnecessary casualties. But this 'Skane fleet'—all we have for evidence of its existence is one extremely suspect transmission from Ben Stone, a fugitive, that cites unconfirmable intelligence from an Archie refugee." This last Toma said with what sounded like disappointment.

"And yet, Thorne and Third Fleet have been redeployed."

"That was in response to the appearance of the Arcœnum invasion fleet. Not some invisible spider ships supposedly chasing them. One enemy at a time, Miss Park."

"Fine," Eva said, "maybe you're right about the Skane. But the Arcœnum fleet is missing too. My point is, whatever you have to do here is what you *need* to do. Compromise is not capitulation, Colonel."

That suggestion seemed to make an impression. There was a crack, the slightest glimmer of light in the armor of Toma's body language. The colonel's expression became thoughtful. Her eyes, less hard.

She doubts herself, Eva thought, seeing opportunity in that possibility. *She's scared.*

But then the wall sealed itself closed again, and Toma declared, "My job is to occupy peacefully the—"

"Yes, that's exactly right," Eva interrupted, pressing her advantage before the mortar re-set into place. "This place is a powder keg, and all it needs is a single spark. You've literally seen the writing on the wall lately. That graffiti's gotten dangerous. And you've heard the rumors."

"Marines don't move on rumor, Miss Park. We react to specifics we know to be—"

"*I'm* speaking now, Colonel," Eva declared, standing. She propped her weight onto the conference table. "With the full weight of the Office of the President of the Sol Alliance. Who's your boss, if you'll remember."

Toma closed her mouth but not with acquiescence. In fact, her jaw clenched as she braced in her chair. She almost appeared to be standing at attention while sitting down.

"Let's talk specifics," Eva said. "These passes the colonists are required to carry to leave their homes? Onerous and unnecessary—as if the people who know this colony better than anyone couldn't sneak out if they wanted to. They see armed jailors in Marine armor everywhere they turn. Regular maintenance of colony systems has deteriorated, impeded by the stringency of your articles of occupation. Hell, even the damned toilets in the Havens are backing up!"

Toma absorbed what she said. "We can certainly review the maintenance schedule to—"

"Read the tea leaves, Colonel!" Eva's back was up, the time for tiptoeing long past. "Do you know what starts revolutions?"

"Usually, it's when someone fires a weapon."

"Wrong. They begin far earlier than that. Colonel, it's the little things that make revolutions. When mothers can't buy bread to feed their children. When living conditions become so intolerable, the people have nothing to lose. *Listen* to the whispering populace, Colonel. *Read* the graffiti—have you noticed its evolution? From nostalgia for yesterday to a desire for a better tomorrow. A call for action to make that tomorrow a reality is next. The people in New Nassau are trying to communicate with you, to warn you. You have to start *listening* instead of issuing harsher orders. If you truly want to avoid unnecessary bloodshed, then you have to *talk* to these people."

Eva had bent so far over the table, she was up on her tiptoes. She expected Toma to jump up, to explode with a recitation of policy and procedure. To retake the moral high ground, loudly and with flag waving, obliterating whatever doubt Eva had glimpsed behind the colonel's well-maintained façade of button-down control. But that didn't happen.

"How do you suggest we begin, Miss Park?" Toma said, folding her hands on the table between them. Her expression was open. So, it seemed, was her willingness to finally entertain ideas not already existent in the Marine manual.

"I'll arrange a meeting," Eva said quickly. Now, she decided, was as good a time as any to press her luck. "In the commander's office. I'll let you know when to be there."

Without awaiting a reply or even an acknowledgment, Eva turned on her heel and exited the room, feeling more like herself than she had since leaving Earth.

The high of her victory carried Eva along as she walked back to her small apartment in the Havens. Her Marine escort, a private with freckles and an earnest need to please, marched dutifully in her wake. She was so used to his shadow, she hadn't even noticed him falling in behind her when she'd left the C&C.

As was Eva Park's wont, the clean, uncomplicated elation of her triumph didn't last long. Questions niggled in the back of her mind. Why hadn't she confronted Toma sooner? Tried to force the colonel to see the wisdom of compromise, say, a week earlier?

Ahead, two dour-faced residents, a man and a woman, squabbled with a Marine corporal, who was demanding to scan them for entrance to a shop. She and her armored shadow passed by them like everyone else. Such verbal fencing matches were common and becoming more so—symptoms of the very disease she'd been haranguing Toma about.

But Eva doubted she'd have been successful if she'd pressed Toma sooner. Having this second week of increasingly inflammatory rhetoric, both spoken in secret and scrawled in the wee hours, had helped Toma come to that decision on her own—with a little nudge from Eva, maybe.

She stepped out of the close corridor and into the colony's commons. The sensation was almost as nauseating as walking on a planet's surface after relying for months on artificial gravity. Eva grasped the reassuring hardness of the pressure door to orient herself.

"Are you all right, Miss Park?" asked the Marine private.

"Fine, Rusty," she said. "I just need a minute."

"Ma'am, yes ma'am."

Across a cavern sprinkled with New Nassauers and their Marine minders stood the Havens, and Eva focused on it to settle her stomach. The stacks of condominiums were starship quarters salvaged and welded together, then affixed to the iron-nickel rockface of the pirates' home asteroid. Whenever she saw it, especially from a distance like this, Eva was awed by what it had taken to build it. Her gaze wandered upward to the curved pressure dome of reinforced plastinium braced by a polysteel superstructure. The reliable but fragile cocoon holding in New Nassau's atmosphere, shining with an infinity of stars beyond it.

Emblematic, she thought, of the scope of the problem Toma faced. Any people who could build such a wonder out of what others would consider scrap and dead rock ... as an ally, they'd be invaluable. As an adversary? Damned hard to defeat.

"Miss Park?"

Eva focused herself and stood up straight. "Yes?"

"Ma'am," the private said, raising one armored arm between Eva and the woman who'd spoken, "please step back."

The colonist, about Eva's age, turned her shoulder to him and placed one hand protectively over the face of the baby she held in her arms.

"It's all right, Rusty," Eva said. The woman offered her a grateful smile. "Do I know you?"

"No ma'am. My name's Althea. Althea Murray."

"Eva Park."

"Yes ma'am, I know."

Sneaking a peek past the rough blanket swaddling the infant, Eva asked, "How old is your baby?"

Murray repositioned her arms, tugging the blanket down to give Eva a better view. A round, rosy-cheeked, cherub face framed moist lips with a tongue just visible between them.

"She's barely a week old," Murray said.

"Ma'am." Rusty the Marine came forward again. "Maybe you shouldn't—"

"Afraid the baby will go off, Private?" Eva chided.

The young man's freckles faded to dark spots against a crimson background.

"You can't be too careful, Private," Murray said, with a wink toward Eva. "It's happened before."

The Marine looked at both women, confused.

"Don't worry," the proud mother reassured them, "I just changed her diaper."

Eva laughed and motioned for Private Rusty to back off.

"Thank you for that," she said to Murray. "It's been a *day*. Now, you were introducing me to..."

"Her name's Eva."

"Oh! What a coincidence." Eva peered closer at the baby girl, who made a gurgling sound and opened her eyes. They didn't quite fasten on Eva's face, but they might just as well have. Somewhere deep in Eva's core, nervous strings were plucked.

"It's not a coincidence, ma'am."

"What?" Eva pulled her eyes from the child to Murray. "What do you mean?"

"My husband and I named her after you, ma'am." She'd said the words with a broad if tentative smile.

Eva stared at the young mother, unsure she'd heard right. "You named ... but why?"

"We know what you're doing, ma'am."

"What I'm doing?"

"You're fighting for us. Every day. Some of us ... we don't hate the Marines. My great-grandfather was a Marine officer. We know they're here because they have to be." She glanced at the private. "But we feel like, without you here, things could be so much worse."

"It's really Commander al-Hurra who—"

"Yes, we know that too," Murray said, and it was as if the whole of New Nassau had elected her to speak for them. "And Miss al-Hurra, too. But ... well, you're from the outside. No one from the outside has ever fought for us before. *Ever*. That's why we're here in the first place, isn't it? Anyway, I don't want to take up your time, Miss Park. I just saw you standing here and thought you'd like to meet, well, Eva."

Take up my time? How about make my day? Year? Career?

"I certainly have enjoyed meeting her," Eva said. She reached a hand out to touch her namesake. Murray raised the child in her arms again as if seeking a blessing for her baby's future.

One piece of advice, kiddo. Eva stroked Little Eva's forehead. *Go big or go home.*

"And I've enjoyed meeting you too, Althea."

"Thank you for your time, Miss Park," Murray said, stepping back. "And for all you're doing here to keep the peace."

"No, Althea," Eva said, "thank *you*. For talking to me today. Thank you very much."

7

DEALS AND DECEIT

CONSCIOUSNESS RETURNED, but it was a nebulous thing that required effort. For Cinnamon, waking was like pulling a heavy rock up a steep slope.

The pain came next, radiating from the back of her head. Cinnamon ignored it, all her energy tasked with steadying her sight. All was dark, at first, but tinged with light at the edges. She moved, but the pain in her head flared brighter. She moved anyway, pushing herself slowly into a sitting position.

She was sitting on a sofa. A very nice sofa. Her salvager instincts kicked in automatically, cataloging its composition for sale later on the black market simulated leather or the real thing? Hard to tell sometimes for someone who'd only ever used a synthesizer. Onyx factory stitching that approximated human hands, individual cushions times three. This was no prison bunk.

Turning slowly, supporting herself on the posh sofa arm, Cinnamon scouted the rest of the office. The custom, cherry wood shelves that took up one entire wall were full of 4D motion images depicting pivotal moments in history. Battles and speeches. The ornate, contemporary smartdesk with curves that more resembled a star yacht's sleek hull than office furniture. It matched the sofa in color and design, as did the receiving chairs positioned like props in front of it. This was no prison cell.

The view outshone it all. When she looked straight at the wall of windows, Cinnamon had to shade her eyes against Ionia's radiant sun.

"About time you woke up."

She jerked her head around and instantly regretted it when the wave of nausea came. Across the room, a Red Sash stood guard inside the closed office door. The third enforcer who'd escorted her and Bello from the apartment. His eyes roamed over her for a moment, perhaps assessing her threat potential, perhaps for other reasons.

"Where am I?" she croaked.

He exited the room without responding, securing the door behind him. Cinnamon stared after him a moment longer, then tracked her eyes along the wall like a blind man feeling his way. There was respectable art, the kind of subdued nudes she'd seen in Blackmore's conference room. This must be his office. Confirming it were the 4D motion images arranged in the window behind the smartdesk, no doubt as background atmosphere for business calls requiring a more intimate setting. A woman and two children—one boy, one girl—moved merrily in the images. A man with short, red hair and without the wrinkles of a dozen years of running a criminal underworld stood by, looking proud and happy. Cinnamon wondered if the images were real or manufactured to humanize Blackmore. But something about them seemed genuine. Maybe it was the smile on his face.

How long have I been out? she wondered.

Gingerly, she reached up, touched the soft lump on the side of her head just above her left ear. Whoever had knocked her out had aimed for the thickest part of her skull. Well, she thought with sarcasm, it was good to know they'd tried to avoid hurting her seriously.

When she stood up slowly, her brain felt like it was sloshing around on a sea of vertigo. Cinnamon steadied herself against the sofa and stared hard at a single, wavering spot on the carpet until her head stopped churning and the spot stopped moving.

One step at a time, Cinnamon made her way to the window-wall, despite Stone's voice snarking in her head that walking was a bad idea. The guard would return soon enough and likely not alone. She needed a drop in the cold, deep end of the consciousness pool if she were to gather her wits back.

Bad idea.

Dizziness tried to drown her again. Cinnamon choked down the impulse to vomit. She braced herself on the window frame, focused on a tower half a kilometer away. Silver and reaching, an optimistic finger pointing at the golden sky overhead. After a few moments and multiple swallows, she managed to steady herself. The giddy sensation of falling to her death surrendered to a swift, fierce appreciation of the city's beauty.

Aponia, often called the Silver City in the snap-ads aimed with confidence at gamblers and fetishists. Its self-indulgent scope awed Cinnamon, especially after weeks spent in the close darkness of the Underside, distracting her even from the pounding that threatened to crack her skull wide open. Every line of the city was cheerful, its brightness a complement to the abundant sunshine. The promise of riches in every spire, the city was a fool's goldmine of opportunity. Aponia had been first founded as a paid vacation spot for the agricultural workers of Covenant, the miners of Monolith, and the ship crews that hauled it all back to Sol. A way for corporations to generously give back to employees with an almost worthless assurance that they too could be rich, with a little luck. Now Aponia served as a playground for the captains of industry and the military personnel who protected them.

On the one hand, it disgusted Cinnamon, who was used, like all the Separated, to scrambling and scratching for a regular meal. On the other, Ionia's existence felt almost justified to her. As if God allowed the city to thrive as a counterbalance to all the shit humans had to deal with, from disease to a universe determined to suck the air from their lungs in the cold vacuum of space. Maybe seen in that light, Ionia was a necessary thing. Maybe even a *good* thing in a thumb-in-the-eye-of-the-universe sort of way.

"I see you're awake."

Cinnamon didn't startle. She didn't turn around quickly, and her unsteady brain was grateful. But she couldn't help but notice the scant weight of the empty holster hanging on her left thigh. She turned around in a measured fashion, trying her best to make it seem relaxed instead of necessary to keep her feet.

Damianos Blackmore was there, of course. The enforcer who'd been her babysitter entered behind him, and the door slipped into the wall, sealing the three of them in.

"Nice office," Cinnamon said. "Nice view."

Blackmore made an open, appreciative gesture. "I like it. Somewhat necessary for getting business done. Maintaining an image, so to speak." He stepped farther into the room, returning the enforcer to door duty.

"You almost sound apologetic."

"Oh, I don't apologize for anything I do," Blackmore said, pausing near the sofa. "Everything I do is absolutely, precisely necessary for survival. Join me?"

Cinnamon carefully, casually walked past the desk as Blackmore sat down at one end of the sofa. She sat at the other, apart. They stared at one another, the distance between them the width of a comfortable cushion but, more fundamentally, quite a bit more than that.

"Survival?" Cinnamon said. The throbbing in her head from crossing the room reduced to a dull thud. "I'd say you're thriving here."

Another gesture, less open this time. "I make do."

Cinnamon grinned, and it was mostly sincere. She waved a hand at the images going through their perpetual motions behind the desk. "That family real? Or just a prop for the people you bring here to impress?"

"Oh, they're quite real. Estranged, but real."

She absorbed that. First, that Blackmore was so open with her—assuming his claims on the family and their estrangement were true—and second, the knowledge that people had managed to escape the web of Damianos Blackmore before, and two of them children.

Hope springs eternal.

"Mister Blackmore, why have you brought me here?"

She didn't ask the other question—why it'd been necessary to kill Rader—because she already knew the answer. To impress her. To show her that Blackmore wielded the absolute power of life and death, of a god, in his own domain. The only real power that all other forms of power obeyed.

"Call me Damian."

"Not 'Damianos'?" she asked.

Blackmore made a face that reminded her of a young boy told to eat his vegetables. "A name imposed upon me by my traditionalist mother. I prefer 'Damian.'"

Joseph Gauss, Cinnamon's grandfather and the marshal of New Nassau, had taught her long ago to look for tripwires. Not just on the ground but also in conversations. The point at which an adversary offered you their first name was a transition point from formality to assumed intimacy. Dangerous, like all things pleasant. Conversations, like combat zones, were always full of traps, he'd said. *Don't let the camouflage of courtesy keep you from seeing what's really there.*

"Damian," she said, as though tasting the word. "Another prop?"

He shrugged. "The long form is more impressive, I admit, so it has its uses. As I said, whatever it takes. Speaking of which, my apologies for that lump on the side of your skull, but you looked ready to tear me apart earlier."

How observant of you to notice, she thought. Cinnamon adopted a grimace from the toolkit of useful expressions her grandfather had bequeathed her. "Rader's death shocked me—"

"Oh, come now, Cinnamon," Blackmore said, and she noted the presumption of familiarity in using her first name. "That wasn't it at all. Don't insult my intelligence. We've reached a juncture in our relationship where honesty saves time, if nothing else."

His patronizing tone threw her off-balance, so Cinnamon decided to return the favor. "Where's your bug-eyed better half?" she asked.

Blackmore seemed to take no offense at her slight toward Oromo Bello. "He's managing some personal business for me," he answered, revealing nothing.

It was like they were two cats, prowling around each other. Looking for one another's weaknesses.

"I understand you're feeling out of sorts," Blackmore continued. "But I don't want you to worry."

"No?"

He made a dismissive gesture. "Nah."

"You didn't answer my question. Why have you brought me here?"

"Ah, that," he said, as if hiding a racy secret. "I wanted to show you your future, Cinnamon."

She took a moment to digest the implications. "You thinking of retiring? Giving up the big office?"

"Not anytime soon, no."

"Then, what?"

"When Asta Merck refused to kill Carletha Lutz and that fact was brought to my attention, at first, I was merely furious." Blackmore said the last two words as if they wouldn't translate into a death sentence for anyone else on Ionia. Rader, for instance. "But then I began to wonder why. I had Bello pull your cases—every one of them peacefully resolved. Not good for the reputation. Mine, that is. So, I had you checked out more thoroughly. Rader should have DNA'd you before bringing you on. But he was sloppy. Lazy. Fooled by that sooty skullcap and black eyeshadow."

"I did *my* research, though," Cinnamon said. "On him. He had a reputation for being ... less than thorough."

"Of course, you did," Blackmore nodded. "As for his reputation, well, that's why he's no longer with the organization."

"You said something earlier about honesty saving time?" She knew she was testing his resolve. Not to mention his patience.

But Blackmore only smiled. "I told you earlier: I want Alice Keller."

"Who? You mean *The Castaway Girl* girl?"

"You know whom I mean."

"Never met her. She probably has an agent, though. They can maybe hook you—"

"Now who's wasting time?"

Cinnamon made a helpless movement with her hands. She sure did miss her guns.

"I know all about what happened on New Nassau," Blackmore said. "Sayyida al-Hurra and I—well, let's just say, we have a relationship of convenience. You give me Keller, and I'll make you my number two here. You can bring your own crew on, too."

"All this and more?" Cinnamon said, sweeping a hand around the office. She flicked her middle finger at the window view as if it were a fly.

"Not to mention the greatest prize of all," Blackmore said.

"Yeah? I'm pretty sure you're gonna mention it."

"Your life."

The door chime sounded.

"Wouldn't Bello have something to say about you offering me his job?"

"My bug-eyed better half?" Blackmore seemed to enjoy lobbing Cinnamon's insult back at her. "In the interests of saving even more time, let's just say he's a liability."

"Like Lutz?"

Blackmore nodded. "Like her, there was a time when he was useful. Constructing a business in the dark doesn't require the same skillset as maintaining it in the light. Bello is too—"

"Crazy?"

"I was going to say 'unpredictable.'"

Cinnamon shrugged. "Tomato, tomahto."

The chime came again, insistent. Face clouding, Blackmore called to the enforcer at the door, "Tell them to come back!"

The door slid open, and low murmurings burbled into the room.

"We found our two operatives in your apartment," Blackmore said to Cinnamon. "We ran DNA scans on the room, of course, and in that secret compartment of yours. Very clever, using the old shelter-rated walls. But we know the girl was there."

Cinnamon didn't flinch, but her insides felt suddenly much lighter. But Blackmore didn't have Alice, that much was clear. And if he'd "found our two operatives," that meant Torque and

Ben must have escaped with her. Whether from the percolating nausea of the blow to her head or the mixture of relief and fear roiling inside her, it was all Cinnamon could do to avoid projectile vomiting all over Blackmore. But the knowledge that he didn't yet have them settled her. Maybe they were even on the *Junkyard Dog* and halfway out of the system by now. That possibility would console her in the moments before Blackmore executed her.

"Boss," said the enforcer at the door, "Mister Bello says it's urgent."

Blackmore's cheek twitched. Cinnamon thought the tick might be the most honest thing she'd seen on his face since she'd met him.

"Think about it, Cinnamon," he said. "No more struggling to survive. No more patching holes in the hull with whatever's at hand. I need talented people who aren't afraid to take the initiative but understand that subtlety can be an asset. Who are not only tough, but smart too. You qualify on both counts. You and yours can have a life here. Your father, too," he said, as though it were an afterthought and not the sweetener meant to seal the deal. He rose from the sofa. "Now, if you'll excuse me a moment."

Cinnamon nodded her unnecessary permission. When Blackmore reached the others, whispered deliberation followed. She took the time to scan the room for weapons. There was an amber model of Ionia on the desk. It sat atop a base of black quartz. Assuming she could stand again, she could amble that way and snag the model while engaging Blackmore in conversation. If he walked with her, followed her closely enough, she had a chance to bash out his brains before the Red Sash killed her. Petty, maybe, but when death is knocking, you take what pleasure you can.

She stood when he returned, as if from courtesy. Her head

complied without complaining, and that helped fuel Cinnamon's resolve. If she could reach the model, with a little luck, she could kill Damianos Blackmore with his own planet.

"Circumstances have changed," Blackmore said. "We have your woman."

What? Alice?

Cinnamon kept her face neutral, but her head began to throb again.

Bello stepped aside in the doorway, and the last person in the world Cinnamon expected to see stumbled through. She looked terrible. Haggard. Drunk.

"Sorry, boss," Torque said. Her whole body seemed slumped in shame. "They offered me too good a deal."

"That's the thing about pirates," Bello observed with a serpent's smile. "At the end of the day, they're loyal only to themselves."

Cinnamon stared at her oldest friend and the abject defeat on Torque's face. Betrayal weighed heavily on her.

"I understand you can lead us to Alice Keller," Blackmore said.

"I can!" Torque exclaimed, straightening up and flourishing one arm like a magician completing a trick. Bello steadied her to prevent her toppling over. "For the right price, bossman."

Slyly, Blackmore regarded Cinnamon. "Looks like your friend gets a deal instead."

She let herself sink to the sofa. She knew she had to appear lost, to seem to realize her life was forfeit now, the bounty for a best friend's betrayal. She was desperate to make herself believe it, to play her part in this impromptu charade so Blackmore wouldn't see through it.

Cinnamon worked to muster crocodile tears to sell the con. All the while thinking, *What are you up to, big sister?*

8
ONE SMALL VICE

"JUST KEEP AN EYE OUT," Ben told Alice as he pulled the mobile comms array from the pack. "But don't *look* like you're keeping an eye out."

He was clearing a space inside a small copse of bushes to hide the transmitter. She smirked down at the back of his head, then surveyed the park. Visitors wandered the green space, enjoying the open air. Birds cooed and twittered in the golden-boughed trees, reminding Alice of storybook covers. Violet leaves made her think of Drake's World.

"Won't they track the signal?" she asked.

"It's tight, scrambled, and programmed to piggyback on local navigation frequencies," Ben said. "By the time Blackmore's people notice something strange, we'll be long gone. In theory."

A hundred meters or so away, a man threw himself down to rest beneath one of the golden trees. Alice couldn't tell if he was merely exhausted or contemplating suicide. Maybe both, she thought.

Ben flipped a switch on the side of the unit, and a small red light began to blink. He touched the skin just below his right ear. He was plugged into the frequency through his personal comms device, the one the Marines had implanted.

"Well?" she said.

"Seems to be working. The *Dog* should be here soon enough."

"In theory?"

"Yep." Ben stood and raised the hood of his poncho over his head. "Come on, let's get away from this thing."

He led her a little deeper into the grove where they sat on a bench canopied by two trees. A different genus from the others, with burnt ivory bark and finer, piney orange leaves.

"Now what?" Alice asked, feeling the need to fill the silence.

"Now we wait for Torque's signal."

Past the park's grass perimeter was an immaculately maintained square where the flags of Ionia and the Sol Alliance fluttered over a fountain. Beyond that, the tall spire of Blackmore's headquarters reached skyward.

Alice sighed, preferring the natural wonders around her to the impressive architecture. "This place reminds me of the Terror Planet," she said.

That got Ben's attention. "Drake's World? Why?"

"There, the surface is beautiful too. The silver desert. The sky with all those shades of purple. The three moons and so many stars at night. But as pretty as it is, the surface is mostly dead. It's the underworld that's alive. I saw a lake there ... so many amazing species!"

"I think I know that lake," Ben grunted. "But even the air here is fake, y'know."

"The air?"

"Sure," he said, peering hard at Blackmore's building. "They regulate it inside. Artificially suppress the oxygen level. Makes humans overproduce dopamine, which stimulates the pleasure center in the brain." His tone slid from instructive to sarcastic. "Makes desire for—well, *whatever*—addictive. Drives shlubs back to their credit vendors for one more draw."

"That's horrible," Alice said, disgusted by the manipulation. Was everyone everywhere just someone else's lab experiment?

"That's Ionia." Ben rose to his feet. "There's that guy again. Damn—I know his face, I just can't place him."

"What guy?" Alice scanned the square, saw a man walking with a determined stride in their direction. When she stood up too, Ben said, "Stay here. And keep that hood up."

"But—"

"I won't be long." Her anxious expression prompted him to add: "I won't leave you alone in this place. I promise."

The touch of Ben's hand caused Alice to shiver, though not with fear. "Okay."

He'd hardly taken three steps when Ben stopped short. He began talking in a way she'd come to recognize as his half of a two-way conversation occurring through his embedded comms.

"Who is this?" he demanded.

There was a pause.

"Well?" Alice said. "Who is it?"

Ben motioned her to silence with a wave of his hand.

"That's not good enough, Mister No-Name," Ben said. "I want to know who you are. And where's Torque?"

It wasn't until Ben mentioned Torque that Alice realized the man coming toward them across the park was the same one who'd escorted Torque from the bar. It must be that man Ben was talking to.

"You have ten seconds," Ben was saying. "Then I cut the connection before you can track it."

The man began walking away from Blackmore's headquarters and toward the fountain. In their direction, in fact, still talking.

"Ben..."

Another wave at her, more insistent.

"Five..." Ben said, beginning a countdown.

The man's stride quickened.

"Three..."

Ben's finger poised beneath his ear to cut off contact.

There was a rustling of leaves, of foliage brushed aside. One step on the soft green grass, then two. Then two more.

"Ben!"

He turned at the urgency in her voice, saw two Red Sashes taking up position, one on either side of Alice. Ben reached for his sidearm, but the bulky poncho made it clumsy.

"I wouldn't," said one of them, a woman, once Ben managed to pull the pistol. She waved her own weapon in Alice's direction.

The second Red Sash spoke into his wrist. "We have them."

Alice flashed a look to Ben. She could handle this. A single thought, directed with purpose and pushed forward to knock these two off their feet, and then she and Ben could run, have a fighting chance at escape. She could even control it, she was sure she could. No one would have to get hurt. And Gal would be here soon in the *Dog*. If they could just find Cinnamon and Torque—

But Ben shook his head slowly, adjusting his grip on the pistol in his hand. She could tell that he, too, was struggling against his own instinct to fight. But he didn't raise the weapon.

"Calm down, everyone," said a new voice, raised to be heard over a distance. The man from the bar was now halfway across the skirt of green between the bench and the park's perimeter. "No need for anyone to get hurt here."

Alice moved forward, closer to Ben. The Red Sashes tensed but didn't try to stop her. Ben felt her behind him and positioned himself between her and the approaching man.

"Where do I know you from?" Ben asked warily.

The man opened his hands. It might have been a gesture of *who knows?* or it might have been reassurance that he, at least, had not drawn his own weapon. "I travel widely, or I used to anyway. Miguel Casca, at your service." He offered his right hand, which Ben ignored, still holding a pistol in his own.

"Casca! That's it!"

Drawing nearer, her arms pressing his poncho around his waist, Alice asked, "Who is he?"

"The 214th had a set of 'personality ID snap cards' when we were assigned to the Triangle a few years ago. High-priority targets for capture. This guy was the jack of clubs," Ben said. "Bounty hunter."

"I prefer the term 'mercenary with focus,'" countered Casca, sounding professionally slighted.

"Bounty hunter?" Alice blew out a breath. "What the hell is going on?"

"Drop the weapon, Captain Stone, and I'd be happy to explain," Casca said.

Ben nodded to the Red Sashes flanking Alice. "Them first."

Casca nodded at the enforcers, and they holstered their sidearms. Ben followed suit with his pistol, pulling it back beneath his poncho. But he didn't drop it. Casca appeared satisfied.

"Our formidable friend said you'd be reluctant to trust me, Captain," Casca exhaled. "She said to tell you that, since Desi's unavailable, you'll have to do. Whatever the hell that means. In any event, I need you both to come with me."

Alice recognized the reference to Desi but, like Casca, not its meaning. What did Ben's battlesuit secured aboard the *Junkyard Dog*, and more specifically its AI controller, have to do with anything?

"We're not going anywhere with you," Ben told Casca.

"One cryptic reference you might have beaten out of 'our formidable friend' doesn't buy you jack shit for trust."

"Your friends are running out of time, Stone," Casca warned.

"More cryptic crap," Ben answered. "Why would I trust a bounty hunter with a known preference for hauling in dead bodies over live ones?"

"Because you're both still alive, for one thing," Casca said. "But the answer to your question is that nowadays I prefer a more predictable salary."

Alice stepped around Ben, tired of being a bystander. "What does *that* mean? Who are you really? Where's Torque? Where's Cinnamon Gauss?"

Casca turned to face her for the first time, scanning beneath the hood of her cloak. "Talk about your bounties of a lifetime," he muttered. He raised a placating hand when Ben's gun hand got restless beneath his poncho. "As I said—I prefer less-exhausting ways to make a living now. And a regular paycheck. I'm too old to dash around the galaxy trolling for people who don't want to be found."

"Who would employ *you* full-time?" Ben said.

"Oromo Bello." Casca said the man's name like a watchword, a spoken ward against evil. Or, in Bello's case, perhaps against good.

"Blackmore's second-in-command is your boss?"

Casca smiled with an abrupt calmness. "So, here's the deal..."

When she walked into Damianos Blackmore's office, Alice was awed by its grandeur. This was nothing like Korsakov's subdued, traditional rooms back on Strigoth. The lines of the office, the large glass wall overlooking the city. She was so captivated it took a moment to find her friends who were already in the room, or notice the large, redheaded man staring out at the city.

"Cinnamon!" Alice ran to her, and the pirate captain stood to embrace her. "I'm so glad you're all right!"

"I'm okay, little sister," she said, "but carefully, please."

"How touching." Approaching them, Blackmore resumed, "And quite the pleasant surprise. Nice work by your man there, Bello. And more quickly than I expected." He regarded Cinnamon with a paternal expression. "You see? Good management really is about hiring well."

"So, you're him, huh?" Ben said, unimpressed. He advanced a step toward Blackmore before Casca stopped him.

"Captain Stone!" Blackmore exclaimed, seeming to notice him for the first time. "The Hero of Canis III himself! Though, I suppose, you'll need to find another title, now that Sirius has fallen." He let the barb hang between them a moment. "Still, there's always The Rescuer of Alice Keller to fall back on." He reached out to stroke the side of Alice's face. She pulled away, repulsed.

"You can't sell her back to Bragg," Cinnamon said, wrapping a protective arm around Alice.

Weighing his options, Blackmore moved closer to both of them. "A *habeas corpus* order is no small thing. He clearly wants her badly. I suspect I can strike a deal that keeps the Alliance out of my business for at least as long as Bragg's in power. Maybe longer."

"But you can't—" Cinnamon's plea was cut off by the sharp slap of Blackmore's backhand across the side of her face. She went sprawling across the black sofa.

"Cinnamon!" Alice dropped to her side. Cinnamon rolled against the arm, moaning, then went still, breathing hard but only semi-conscious. Alice glared up at Blackmore. "You didn't have to do that."

Blackmore addressed Bello. "Get Gauss out of here. Take her to the Underside. It should be easy enough to make it look like she was the loser in a fight among the cockroaches."

Cinnamon was moving again and struggling to rise.

"Cinn, stop. You're in no shape to—"

But the pirate captain shrugged off Alice's attempts to restrain her. Bello strode toward them, and Cinnamon lurched away toward the desk. She grabbed up a small, round statue, turned around, nearly fell over again, and raised her hand with its heavy prize. Her intent was clear enough that Blackmore retreated a step.

Bello pulled Cinnamon's pistol from his belt and easily knocked the statue aside. It fell to the carpeted floor. Cinnamon stood swaying, squinting, trying to focus. Bello placed the pistol barrel against the side of her head.

"My own gun..." Cinnamon murmured.

"No!" Alice screamed.

Torque yelled, "Alice, don't!"

Alice rounded on the big woman. Torque stood confident but imploring, and Alice was confused. She turned back to Bello to find him no longer holding the pistol to Cinnamon's head. He now aimed it at Blackmore.

"What are you doing?" his boss demanded.

"Making a change in personnel," Bello said. "It's time you retired."

Blackmore blinked. "Don't be a fool. We can talk about this. You don't have what it takes to run this place—"

"I have a gun," Bello stated flatly.

"You there!" Blackmore said, addressing Bello's enforcers. "Casca! Stop him, and his job is yours."

But no one moved, only regarded him at a distance. Some with pity. Others, anticipation.

"He says that to everyone, Casca," Cinnamon said, leaning against the desk.

"Oromo," Blackmore said, taking a step toward him, "you know how much I—"

Bello cocked the pistol. Blackmore halted. "Working in the casinos, you learn people's tells. You know what your tell is, Mister Blackmore? You become friendly. In your case, it's how you signal you're about to lie."

"What do you—"

The report from the pistol boomed like a cannon shot. One neat, round hole marked Blackmore's forehead and his head jerked back. A less perfect exit wound exploded from the back of his skull. Brains and blood streaked the smooth surface of the onyx couch.

Alice cried out. Blackmore's eyes rolled up and he collapsed to the ornate office floor. Blood began to flow from the hole in his forehead, staining the dark carpet.

Torque rushed to Cinnamon's side, where she took her friend's weight onto her shoulder.

"What the fuck—what the fuck just happened?" Cinnamon said.

Ben pushed Casca aside, ignoring the man's drawn weapon, and went to Alice. She turned into him, shaking, but refused to hide her head. Bello lowered the pistol.

"To answer your question, Captain Gauss," he said, "Your friend made a deal to save your life." He waved casually at the room. "All your lives."

"Big sister?" Cinnamon said, still hazy. Her eyes held Torque's. Alice thought she could see that old iron bond, the indestructible connection the two women shared that no danger, no opportunity, no promise of heaven or threat of hell could break. Despite her pounding heart, Alice felt it there, strong as ever.

"Our ship will arrive soon," Ben said, all business. "They'll need free passage to land. And we need any record of our ever having been here scrubbed."

Oromo Bello turned to regard him. To Casca he said, "Miguel, see to it."

"You're just going to let us go?" Alice asked. She couldn't help herself. The very idea seemed ridiculous. "What about Bragg? What about—?"

"Alice!" Torque said in warning.

But Oromo Bello offered Alice a satiated smile. "Learn when to take the win, Miss Keller. I told you before, Captain Gauss—I'm a practical man. A man with but one small vice: *ambition*. I have achieved my immediate goal for advancement. I can, in other words, afford to be generous."

"You're a psychopath," Cinnamon said.

"You people really need to learn when to shut up and take the win," Bello said, exasperated. He walked forward and once again aimed the pistol at Cinnamon's forehead. The pirate, seething, did not flinch.

Ben uttered something foul.

Alice prepared herself to unleash whatever power she had against him, and damn the consequences. There was no Bell Jar here, no shroud to neuter her power.

But Bello abruptly turned the weapon around and handed it butt-first to Cinnamon. "The kingpin of Ionia has just been murdered by this pistol," he said. "A unique weapon, its owner once told me. Once the bullet is analyzed, I suspect that owner will become *persona non grata* on Ionia. And a warrant issued for her arrest—for murder."

Cinnamon's eyes narrowed.

"Y'know," Torque said facetiously, "one more warrant for the collection."

The look Cinnamon gave her was anything but amused. "*This* is the deal you made? Blackmore's assassination?"

Torque's face became grave. "Whatever it takes to survive, right? To protect the ones we love."

"Boss, the outer defense grid has registered their ship inbound," Casca reported. "Orders?"

"Find a quiet space for them to set down, somewhere outside the city. And Casca?"

"Boss?"

"Get a cleaning crew in here," Bello said, turning up his prominent nose at the bloody mess. He turned a hard stare on Cinnamon. "As for you and your people?" His gaze passed over each of them in turn: first Torque, then Alice, then Ben. "Get the fuck off my planet."

9
A BRUTAL FINALITY

THE SEAGULLS WERE LOUD. How was she supposed to enjoy sitting here with Leo, holding hands and watching the waves roll in, when those damned birds wouldn't stop screeching?

Eva snapped open her eyes. The pitch dark was strange because her mind's eye held such a vivid after-image of Florida sunlight shining down on Yellow Bluff. The lingering flavors of the picnic they'd been sharing—fruit and lean turkey on crackers, washed down with half-glasses of red wine.

"Lights," she said softly.

The room brightened to reveal her quarters. Its lean lines and low ceiling a reminder of the crew cabin repurposed from a long-dismantled starship. The open air and bright sunshine of her dream had already begun to fade.

The comm unit chirped. Not nearly as annoying as her unconscious mind had made it sound a minute ago. Not merely a dream of Leo now, but the real thing. He was calling.

Eva dragged her fingers through her hair and wiped away any embarrassing sleep drool. The chirp came again, and she accepted the call.

"Hi, Leo."

"About time!" Leo's face was carefully sculpted in fake outrage for her amusement. But he couldn't quite maintain the façade or prevent a genuine smile of joy when he saw her. "I was beginning to think you didn't want to talk to me."

"Sorry. It's the middle of the night here."

"Ah. Right."

But not on Earth, Eva noted. There, it was late morning. The Japanese sun angled in behind Leo through the window of his Citadel office. He'd loosened his tie a bit, hardly noticeable except to someone who knew him as well as she did. An unusual conceit on a workday, especially before noon. And maybe a commentary on the old stress. His face had more lines than she remembered.

"You look tired."

"Yeah, well, 'tired' is the new normal here. Double-checking before we go on—did Colonel Toma set you up with that encryption unit?"

"Yeah," she said. "We're secured."

Leo nodded. "Good. Now we can actually talk about something other than hiking."

So, he'd missed her, too. Eva smiled. More than her face, more than her body, more than her ability to drink him under the table after a long day. Maybe he'd missed their shoptalk too, just as she had. It had been their way of refining strategy as a team when they'd first begun working together on Bragg's campaign. And later, as their romance bloomed, that meeting of the minds had become like an aphrodisiac hors d'oeuvre.

"The president is gearing up for a big address," Leo said, explaining the cloud of fatigue hanging over him. "How's the situation on the ground there?"

"About the same. No, check that—it's getting worse. I can feel it coming, Leo, like you can smell a storm on the air and know there's nothing you can do but stand around and wait to get wet." She sighed, wanting to change the subject. "How's the new building coming along?"

"Making good progress. The upper floors are about done. They're actually being proactive for a change and reinforcing the foundation."

Eva took a moment to parse the code. The new *Monolith*-class dreadnought, as yet unnamed, was almost completed, and it sounded like the Admiralty wasn't rushing it, despite the war. Taking their time, doing it right. At least her mission to the Triangle, as sideways as it'd gone, had delivered on its principal objective. The lonsdaleite had safely reached Mars and was now being forged into hull plating, its molecular structure uniquely resistant to Arcœnum psychic attacks.

"Any word on the in-laws?" Eva asked. "I know how anxious the president is to host them."

Leo shook his head, and there was more than a little worry in his expression. "None. And we've kept a light on in the window."

"I suppose you have to be ready for whenever they drop in."

"Exactly."

So, the Arcœnum fleet spotted weeks ago on subspace was still off-grid. Where they'd pop up eventually was unknown. And of the supposed Skane fleet, not even an initial sighting had yet occurred. More and more the consensus was that Ben Stone had either been coerced, delusional, or worse, collaborating with the enemy, when he'd sent his briefing to Bathsheba Toma.

"So, what's the president going to say?" Eva asked.

"How should I know?" Leo snarked. "I haven't written it yet. How's your relationship with the crabby aunt going?"

"Better, actually. Sometimes you just have to set boundaries."

Leo's expression showed firsthand empathy with that sentiment. Though his leeway in defining boundaries with Piers Bragg was considerably narrower than hers with the colonel.

"I'm convinced she's the key to solving our family crisis," Eva said. "We regularly pull everyone together to check the thermostat. Some days are hotter than others."

"I understand." Leo paused, searching for the right words. Then, quite deliberately, he said, "I miss you."

It took her a few moments to realize there was nothing to reinterpret there, nothing to sift through her internal decoder to determine Leo's meaning. No, he'd said exactly what he meant in the way he'd meant to say it. Her insides fluttered.

"I miss you too." Maybe it was the hundreds of lightyears separating them, but she quickly determined those few words weren't sufficient to express what she was feeling. "I miss hiking up Oku-Hotaka with you and talking damage control."

His expression of fake outrage returned. "Hiking? *That's* the first thing that comes to mind when you miss me? And here I thought more secure comms would broaden our conversational palette."

"Well," she smiled mischievously, "maybe not the *first* thing. Especially lately." Her voice was breathy and soft. When she bent closer to the cam lens, her blouse fell open a little. "It's been very tense around here lately..."

"Stop that." Leo loosened his tie a little more. "I will *not* have subspace sex with you in code. From my office in the Citadel. In a time of war."

She laughed at all the barriers he'd just erected. So to speak. "You know military intelligence monitors these calls, right?"

"Well, I bet they're awake *now*."

Eva laughed again. God, she really did miss him. His lion's growl when they discussed politics, ready to pounce on the issues he believed in. His standing in the middle of her Tokyo apartment, holding a drink in the air as enticement after a long day, one eyebrow raised like the serpent with the apple. How he whispered her name, tickling her ear with his warm breath, when they made love.

A klaxon blasted, quashing the moment.

"What's happening?" Leo asked.

"No idea," Eva sighed. "I gotta go—"

"Hey! One more second."

"Leo..."

She was already getting to her feet. *Could it be a year instead?* she thought in answer to his delaying her. *How about a lifetime?*

"I love you, Eva. Take care of yourself out there. I want to climb that mountain again with you. I fucking mean that —literally."

She smiled. "Me too. And—me too. Have fun writing the president's address."

Leo rolled his eyes. "Oh, yeah."

She reached forward and turned off the feed. There'd come a day again, Eva assured herself, when she'd be able to walk across the room and touch Leo's shoulder for no better reason than he was there and she wanted to. *Whenever* she wanted to.

But the klaxon persisted, and Eva saluted its unwelcome intrusion with a raised middle finger. *Now*, she thought, gearing up her gut to deal with it, *what fresh hell is this?*

Toma's lockdown alert had achieved the opposite of its intended effect. Haven residents milled about in the hallways murmuring speculation as to the cause of the alarm. Women and children stood in apartment doorways, mothers clutching infants in their arms or resting firm fingers on gawping children's shoulders, keeping them near.

"What's going on?" Eva asked Private Rusty, who stood his post outside her apartment. He looked every bit his freckle-faced age amid the excitement, younger maybe, with an anxious expression at odds with the hard readiness of his battlesuit.

"Trouble at the docks, ma'am. I know the lockdown order doesn't apply to you, but maybe you'd best go back inside before—"

"Fuck that." Eva locked her quarters and pushed past him. Over her shoulder she called, "You coming?"

The private followed Eva like a shadow as she marched through the corridor. She nodded at citizens as she passed, trying to demonstrate that, while as curious as they were about the alert, she wasn't worried. Groups of them stood staring through the plastinium windows overlooking the docks below. It was hard at this distance to see exactly what was going on, but colonists, with growing anger by their body language, were confronting armed Marines. Eva quickened her pace.

On the ground floor, a large crowd was attempting to exit the main entrance to the Havens all at once. They were barely held in check by a single squad of Marines. Voices demanded to know what was going on. The Marines had to shout to be heard over them. Anxious colonists at the back of the group pushed forward, forcing those up front to resist to avoid being pushed into the armed Marines.

"Let me through!" Eva yelled. "Please! Let me through!"

No one gave ground. Private Rusty moved up next to her, enduring without comment the pirates who, on principle, cursed his presence. "Ma'am, let me, I can—"

"No, wait," Eva said, placing a hand on his chest plate. It was cold. "The last thing we need is you shoving these people aside..." She decided to try a different tactic. "Just follow me. And I mean, *follow* me."

She edged around the left side of the burgeoning crowd,

away from the pressure point of the entrance. Slipping through the stiff shoulders of two feuding colonists, Eva identified a lieutenant among the Marines, likely the squad's commander.

"Call that officer over there," she told Rusty. "But tell him to be nice!"

"We don't really do nice, ma'am."

"Make do, Marine!"

Rusty engaged his comms, and the lieutenant quickly located them. He and another member of his squad used their rifles, butts extended, to begin to clear a path to Eva. She pushed her way forward to meet them, with apologies and gratitude toward the people around her, and Rusty filed in behind.

"Eva Park, Presidential Liaison to the—"

"We know who you are, ma'am," the officer said. "Lieutenant Lawson. Come this way."

Lawson passed Eva and Rusty through the entrance and onto the docks. What Eva found there filled her with alarm. The throng of locals had grown considerably. More Marines had also arrived, including Colonel Toma, who now stood at the eye of the storm. The al-Hurras were there too, and Eva wondered if their rough relationship would hinder or help the situation. Two distinct groups of colonists became evident as she drew nearer, their allegiances obvious—older, grimmer pirates behind al-Hurra and younger, more fiery agitators around Sayyida. At last, she spotted what seemed to be the cause for all the hubbub. A child of New Nassau, a teenage girl, was on her knees on the deck in a posture of submission. She looked frightened.

"Nevertheless," Toma was saying, "I'm taking her into custody. Get up, girl."

"What's going on here?" Eva said.

"Miss Park," Toma acknowledged. Was that a hint of relief in her voice? "This young woman was caught defacing the hull of a dropship. My Marines were in the process of arresting her when they were confronted by these—" She seemed to have trouble getting the word out. "—citizens. Things escalated from there, so I instituted the lockdown."

"Joe Gauss is on his way," Hadrian al-Hurra said. "He can detain the young woman until we get this sorted, Colonel."

Toma shook her head. "That won't be possible, Commander. I'm glad to discuss the reasons why in a more suitable location. For now, you need to convince these people to disperse."

"Colonel," Sayyida said, "I understand the need to take Marya here into custody. But I agree with my father. To keep events from escalating further, let us handle this as a colony matter. She'll face suitable consequences."

"Marya!" A teenage boy pushed through the pirates on Sayyida's side. His face was flushed, his brow sweating from the effort. He locked eyes with the girl on her knees for a moment, then turned a furious look on Toma. "You let her go!"

"Step back, son," al-Hurra said. "We'll make sure your friend is—"

"No!" The boy reached behind his back and produced a small pistol.

"Gun!" yelled a Marine.

A collective gasp rose up from the crowd. Those nearest the boy stepped away. Toma's Marines shouldered and aimed their combat rifles.

For a heartbeat, no one moved.

"Hold your fire," Toma ordered, her voice calm.

"You let her go!" yelled the boy, pointing his pistol at Toma.

The colonel said, "Listen to me now. We're in dangerous territory here. I need you to lower that weapon before someone gets hurt. Then, we can talk."

"No!" the boy insisted. "You let her go!"

"What's your name, son?" al-Hurra asked and took a half-step forward. He was waving a hand behind his thigh at Toma, telling her to back off. "Mine's Hadrian."

"I know who you are," the boy said in a tone implying that al-Hurra had said something stupid. "Everyone does."

Eva was close enough to see the boy's hands shaking, and the pistol with them. She couldn't take her eyes off the small barrel, and the hole at the end of it no wider than a fingertip.

Pleading with the boy, Marya said, "Richard, don't. I'll go with Marshal Gauss when he gets here."

The boy, Richard, shook his head. "I'm taking you home. It's just graffiti!"

"That won't be possible," Toma said. "We'll treat her fairly, Richard. Just put the gun down. *Now*."

"Richard!" Marya urged him. "Do what she says. *Please*."

But Richard shook his head. The rest of him seemed paralyzed, frozen with the gun pointing at Toma. "I'm taking you home."

"No one move," Toma said. "No one fire. That's an order." She stepped toward the boy.

Richard's pistol shook harder. What happened next seemed to move at the speed of light. And, Eva would think later, in slow-motion at the same time.

She saw the blaze from the barrel, then heard the sharp crack of the shot. Al-Hurra was already moving, jumping in front of Toma. Something massive and irresistible hit Eva from behind and slammed her to the ground. Marya screamed, the whole of the docks erupted with a moan of anguish, and pirates on both sides shoved one another hard to escape the hot zone of inevitable return fire.

But Toma's Marines held their discipline.

Eva opened her eyes, saw the chaos unfolding from her sideways perspective on the deck. She could feel Rusty, propping his armored weight off her body to keep from crushing her while also protecting her. Her hearing was deadened from the nearness of the shot, save for distant screaming and the pulsing blood between her ears. A second body hit the deck beside Eva, and she expected to see Colonel Toma diving for cover. But it wasn't Toma.

His eyes were open but unseeing. His gaze, teetering on the edge of awareness but finding Eva, fastened to her. His face held a shocked expression, as though he'd denied the possibility of dying all his life only to have Death itself dispel that hope with a brutal finality. She could see it—physically see it—when the light left his eyes.

Is that what it looks like, Eva wondered, *when the soul leaves the body?*

Hadrian al-Hurra was dead.

10
THE CALM

"THAT BULLET WOULDN'T HAVE PENETRATED my armor." Toma said it as though describing someone else's dream. "He died for nothing."

Inexplicably, despite knowing what had happened wasn't Toma's fault, Eva wanted to unload on her. Shout at her for everyone to hear, drive home that this was exactly the kind of tragedy Eva had wanted to avoid. But she checked herself, opting for a half-hearted statement of hope instead.

"No one dies for nothing, Colonel."

They stood inside the infirmary observing Sayyida al-Hurra through a window. She stood next to her father's corpse, head bowed, fingertips stroking the thin sheet that covered him from the chest down. Beside her stood Joseph Gauss, the marshal of New Nassau and Hadrian al-Hurra's former quartermaster from their pirating days. He put his arm around her and pulled her close. Sayyida placed her head on his shoulder as he spoke softly to her.

"I don't know what that means," Toma said. It wasn't harsh or angry. Sounded a bit apologetic, in fact.

"It's okay. Neither do I. Not yet, anyway. But his death, however tragic, has to count for something."

Inside the room, Sayyida broke down. She folded against Joe Gauss's chest and clutched him to her as though he were a life preserver and she were alone in the middle of the ocean. For all their recent disagreements, Eva had read between the lines how much love and respect Sayyida and her father had shared. Else, their disagreement could never have been so fiercely personal. Or so deeply painful.

"Any word on the boy?" Eva asked.

The shooter, the boy Richard, had been yanked backward into the crowd while others jumped to their commander's aid. Someone had secreted him away. Extensive questioning by Toma's Marines had, as yet, turned up nothing on the boy's whereabouts. Toma met with calm assurance the loud calls for swift justice from Hadrian's faction, while deftly handling similar pleas for mercy from Sayyida's followers, who claimed the boy as one of their own. Toma had issued standing orders to, for now, pursue a vigorous but controlled search. Since flights out of New Nassau were forbidden, as they had been since the occupation began, the boy wasn't going anywhere.

They'd come here together to offer Sayyida their shared condolences but were waiting for the appropriate time. *If there ever is such a time*, Eva thought.

"What do you think will happen to him?"

"Who?" Toma asked.

"Who do you think?"

Toma seemed vexed by the question. "He'll be found, tried, and, if found guilty, sentenced under the articles of occupation."

"You mean executed?" Eva stared at the side of Toma's head, her barely contained anger returning. "You soldiers and your binary thinking."

"More likely life in prison." Toma's cheek flexed. "What

would you have me do? Suspend the law because the murderer is young?"

"I..." Eva had to admit, she was at a loss to answer that question in any way that wouldn't sound naïve.

"Come on, Miss Park," Toma pressed, her own frustration bubbling up. "You've done nothing but criticize the rules of engagement under which we operate here. The ones agreed to by both sides, by the way. Tell me which rules I can bend, and which are acceptable to break."

A knock on the window startled them. Both women turned to find Joe Gauss's disapproving glower, unsoftened by the tears on his cheeks. He mouthed two words, staccato and tart. The most amateur of lip readers could interpret the crude suggestion with little effort.

"Maybe we should leave the family alone to mourn," Toma said.

"Yeah," agreed Eva, offering Gauss an apologetic nod. "Maybe we should."

Eva and Toma walked to the C&C via strangely quiet, nearly deserted corridors. The emptiness felt unnatural. The colony was enduring a collective shock following al-Hurra's killing a few hours earlier, and most of New Nassau's residents had retreated to their homes to mourn. In one of those, Eva knew, was a terrified boy named Richard who would have to answer for ending his commander's life.

The C&C was similarly subdued. Toma's people were less vocal than usual, as if their efficient competence had switched to autopilot. Eva couldn't shake the feeling that the colony's atmosphere was less about respect for a dead leader and more the calm before the coming storm she'd mentioned to Leo.

They entered the conference room to find Toma's battalion captains already there. The officers stood when the colonel entered the room, and she put them at ease. Everyone took seats at the round table.

"Sit rep?" Toma said.

"House to house searches continue," Victor Taikori reported. Toma had appointed her senior company commander to be her right hand and coordinate the others. Eva liked him. He reminded her of Rusty—earnest, true-blue, a little embarrassed at but appreciative of others' deference to him. He'd either get his entire command killed one day, she thought, or become one of the most thoughtful generals the Alliance Ground Forces had ever produced. "The shooter is still at large."

"Sector reports, starting with Alpha," Toma said.

The captains went around the table. Eva focused on internalizing details rather than trying to remember the names of the captains reporting them. Their reports confirmed that New Nassau was indeed in communal shock, though not all dissent had been quelled, particularly from Hadrian al-Hurra's followers. They were understandably angry and directing most of that ire at the object of easy blame for his murder, Sayyida, whose supporters harbored his murderer. But it was still easier to hate the Marines, and conspiracy theories had risen up, expressed in new physical graffiti and untraceable messaging permeating the colony. The rumor gaining the most traction posited that Toma's Marines were actually the ones behind the killing, having recruited an impressionably young, sympathetic member of Sayyida's faction to do their dirty work for them.

"This place is a ticking time bomb," Eva said. "It's been that way since you got here, but the ticking is getting louder."

Toma eyed her, but her silence was tacit agreement with Eva's assessment.

"We shut down the nodes as soon as one of these messages pops up," Taikori explained, "but it's like cutting a head off the Hydra. Two more pop up."

"They're channeling their grief," Eva said. "They've resented the occupation since day one, and Hadrian al-Hurra's death is catalyzing that potential energy into action." She was a little surprised to see Toma nodding as she spoke. "It's easy for them, particularly al-Hurra's followers—older, more jaded, less trusting of Alliance authority—to translate the need to hold the boy accountable into blaming your people for what happened."

No one spoke for a long while.

"We're on our own here," Toma said quietly. Taikori sat up a little straighter. "To date, we've followed the letter of the insurgency doctrine. As we should have. And we won't abandon that, but now we're in a new situation. And what do Marines do when they're cut off from command in dangerous territory?"

Improvise? Eva answered reflexively in her head.

"Whatever we have to," Taikori said solemnly, "to complete the mission."

Head nods and gruff acknowledgment around the table.

Taikori's statement scared the shit out of Eva with its lack of specificity. She remembered standing in the galley of the *L'Esprit de la Terre* with Ben Stone after the Alliance's formal declaration of war against the Arcœnum, and the *oo-rah* enthusiasm of his Marines. The bristling electricity in the room had felt suddenly in need of a target for violent expression. That kind of response in New Nassau would spell disaster. Eva opened her mouth to speak.

"Ladies and gentlemen," Toma said, "now is the time for restraint."

Eva closed her mouth.

"We must be vigilant. Diligent. Methodical in our search for the shooter. But disciplined with this populace." Toma stood but restrained her officers from following suit. She clasped her hands behind her armored back and began to pace thoughtfully. "Our core mission here is to pacify the populace while Fleet prosecutes the war against the Archies. We've done that to date by locking them down. Recent events require that we adapt our methods. While New Nassau will never welcome us—especially now—we must do everything we can to coexist peacefully with its citizenry without, as Captain Taikori points out, compromising the integrity of our mission." Toma stopped and effected a precise about-face. Her gaze, like a targeting reticle, found Eva. "Your help will be key, Miss Park."

Eva blinked. "Of course. Whatever I can do." So grateful Toma hadn't proposed the kind of dynamic response she'd pictured in her head, Eva was tempted to promise her firstborn to whatever the colonel said next.

Toma turned her attention back to her captains. "Ladies and gentlemen, your watchwords going forward are these: patience; restraint; understanding. Brand these backward on your boots' foreheads so they can read them in the mirror before morning chow. Do whatever you have to so they internalize these concepts, especially by example of your leadership. We were walking a knife's edge before here, captains. The knife just got sharper."

Taikori cleared his throat. "Ma'am, point of clarification. Are you changing the rules of engagement? Should one of the pirates produce a weapon or otherwise threaten—"

Definitively, Toma said, "I am *not*." She scanned the officers around the table. "Our mission here hasn't changed. Nor has the greater strategic situation inside or outside the colony. Operationally, however, we're in a new ballgame."

"What's our new operational objective, ma'am?"

"Glad you asked, Victor," Toma said. She pulled her chair out, retook it, and leaned forward. "Our new operational objective is to install a new leader for this colony." Eva was startled by that. "One who will reduce tensions and return homeostasis. And, thereby, help reduce the likelihood of a clusterfuck of historic proportions."

Regime change? Eva thought. Was that really the right...? Then again, there *was* no regime, now. Someone had to fill the power vacuum left by al-Hurra's death, and better it was someone of their choosing, she supposed. Eva felt slightly oily at how conniving that notion sounded.

"Who would that be?" she muttered.

"There's only one choice," Toma said solemnly. "Sayyida al-Hurra."

"That is all, ladies and gentlemen."

Taikori and the other captains stood, saluted, and filed out of the conference room. Toma had given them their orders. Work with Joe Gauss's marshals to find the shooter—Toma would approach Gauss personally to lay that groundwork. Restrain any Marine response not dictated by the rules of engagement. Keep the peace with the populace. Stay on mission. And until further notice, no rec time outside Marine barracks; no alcohol or other recreational substance; and all fraternization with any locals that might be happening off-book was to end immediately. Any interactions with the colonists would occur only in service to the mission and their current tactical objective of locating al-Hurra's killer. That was key to reestablishing stability and preventing further bloodshed. Meanwhile, Toma herself, and with Eva Park's assistance, would work to convince Sayyida al-Hurra to step into her father's shoes as leader of the colony.

"You certainly know how to clear a room," Eva said for

something, anything, to lighten the heavy cloud still hanging over them.

"My people know their jobs," Toma stated.

Eva had no doubt. "What, specifically, do you need me to do?"

"This is unusual terrain, Miss Park, for Marines to traverse. There's no hill to take here. Our mission, more than ever, requires subtlety. Listening more than talking. And a willingness to compromise."

"I agree."

"Those characteristics are not top of mind for AGF Marines."

Eva almost offered her agreement again, then thought it might sound too much like *I told you so.*

"Ben Stone told me something similar once," she said.

"Oh?" Toma's tone betrayed a perverse curiosity. "And how did Captain Stone put it?"

"When we first came to the Triangle to negotiate for the freighters, I think it bugged the shit out of him that I was here. Negotiation, he said, is not something Marines are trained for. He thought treating with pirates was a mistake. That it presented weakness."

"And he wasn't wrong." Toma grunted, and there was a surprised quality in the sound. "Maybe he learned something in OCS after all. But this situation is different, as I just explained to my officers. Now, diplomacy is our most important weapon in securing peace."

Eva laughed. "You *do* realize what you just said?"

But Toma was already thinking of something else. "Where's President Bragg?"

Stumbling over the non sequitur, Eva said, "I'm sorry?"

"Leadership. This colony needs it, right? The whole Alliance needs it, too. People need to hear from their leaders when they're in crisis. They need to know someone's in charge. Knows what to do, even when they don't. Especially then."

"Was that what this was?" Eva teased, motioning at the non-existent officers around the table. "Faking it till you're making it?"

"Of course not," Toma said. But there was a good-natured pause. "I always know what I'm doing."

"Of course you do."

They sat eyeing one another for a moment until it became awkward. "He'll be giving a speech soon, the president," Eva said. "Be careful what you wish for."

"Speaking of wishes," Toma said, rising, "I need to talk to Marshal Gauss. And you to Sayyida." The colonel waited for Eva to stand.

"What?"

"You asked how you can help," Toma said. "That's how. Convince Sayyida to pick up her father's crown."

"Now?" Eva was reluctant. "She hasn't even buried him yet—"

"And every moment we delay risks more deaths," Toma said. "You heard my officers' reports. The colony will wake up from its shock soon, and if there's no one to lead them, to focus them on the future, then we'll be in trouble. More casualties, including some of my Marines, no doubt. I can't have that if I can prevent it. With your help, I believe I can."

"But why me? Sayyida doesn't even like me. I sided with her father against—"

"It has to be you. I'm the occupier, you said it yourself. The enemy. The only reason Sayyida approached me was as a wedge against her father. I was a means to an end to curry favor for reconciliation. Now I'm just the head cop. You, however—you're still useful to her. Leverage that and convince her to step up for the good of New Nassau."

That slick feeling from earlier returned. Eva felt like she needed a shower. But try as she might, she couldn't fault Toma's reasoning.

"How do we know the colony will accept her? Half believe she's at least partially to blame for her father's murder. They might even see her taking his position as the final step in a coup."

"You'll figure that out." To Eva's questioning gaze, Toma said, "You're in charge of messaging from now on, colony-wide. As for Sayyida al-Hurra, she's her father's daughter. With the right packaging, she'll be the natural inheritor of his mantle, not the usurper of his office. So, on your feet, soldier." But she'd said it in a friendly way, Toma's face softening to match her tone. "I need your help, Eva. Help me prevent more casualties."

Eva felt a quickening in the middle of her chest. Her life in public service had focused on shaping policy. On selling abstract doctrines to the public that were intended, somewhere far down the line, to have real impacts on real people. Now, she had the chance to make a difference, to save lives as Toma had said, and see that happen in real time.

Standing up formally, Eva was almost tempted to salute. "I'll do my best, Colonel."

"Your best is a good place to start," Toma quipped. "And when it's just us? Call me Sheba."

The colonel spun on her heel and led them from the room. Her about-face had been so quick, she'd probably missed Eva's face breaking into a smile.

11
THE STALKING HORSE

"YOU KNOW WHAT I HEAR?" Mango "Gal" Galatz said with a leer in her voice. "I hear they employ Arcœnum consultants to train the whores."

Ah, that gets the game going, Alice thought. Hoping to learn the basics of celestial navigation, she'd been spending more time with the randy pilot in the two days she'd been back aboard the *Junkyard Dog*. Her familiarity with human sexuality—if not from firsthand experience—had expanded considerably while on Ionia. Now that she was back home, Alice knew she only had to wait long enough before Gal's mind would wander around to the pilot's favorite obsession. Inevitably, one of those wandering thoughts would pop out of Gal's mouth, and that's when the fun began.

Alice cocked her head to one side. "What do you mean?"

"Well," Gal said, the corrupted leather of her seat squeaking as she adjusted, "not for mind-control, of course. The consultants help train the, um, human staff in certain techniques."

Alice bent forward, wide-eyed. "Techniques?"

No topic was taboo. If anything, Gal delighted in embarrassing others with her brazen, nothing's-off-the-table attitude toward sex. It was one of her most endearing qualities, in Alice's opinion. She enjoyed watching the other person squirm—except when it came to Alice. Like the rest of the *Dog*'s crew, each of whom had adopted "the castaway girl" in their own way, Gal felt the need to protect her. So, when the pilot's mind ran down the rabbit hole of sexual speculation and Alice happened to be around, Gal would grow beet red with embarrassment when she remembered whom she was talking to. But once the box had been opened, it became a principle of personal pride that Gal had to finish what she'd started.

Alice found it downright delicious catching Gal in a self-conscious trap of her own making. There really wasn't much else to do while hiding from everyone in the known universe until an opportunity presented itself to make a run for Alpha Centauri.

"Um," Gal clarified, "visualization techniques."

Alice affected a curious expression. "Like what?"

A red light flashed on the navigation console. Gal touched a switch, and the light stopped blinking.

"Fantasies ... I guess."

"Fantasies?" Alice's eyebrows rose, her stare as vacant as the space between planets.

The pilot's eyes flitted right and left. Quite like a rabbit's, Alice judged, that smelled a predator nearby.

"Yeah, you know," she said, "sexual fantasies."

"Ohhh," Alice replied innocently. "I wonder, how would that work?"

Behind them at tactical, Torque made an impatient noise. Alice had forgotten she was there, she'd been so quiet during her duty shift, quiet even for Torque. The time they'd been back aboard the *Dog* had been oddly tense between Torque and

Cinnamon. The two, usually sympatico enough to finish one another's sentences, had hardly spoken a word.

"Well," Gal said, "the Arcœnum help the ... staff ... by projecting ... scenarios ... into their minds and having them describe out loud what they see."

"I see," said Alice.

"It supposedly makes them able to better appreciate another's perspective. Be, uh, more creative with their partner."

"Partner?"

"Um, yeah. Y'know, sex partner."

"Ohhh."

Gal tinkered with the controls on her console.

From the few lessons Alice had had in the principles of navigation, Gal was merely keeping her hands busy. With a tone both curious and conclusive, Alice said, "I bet it makes the ... *whores* ... great at sex talk."

Gal cleared her throat. "Have we gone over how to use the targeting scanner to guide navigation in the Triangle? It's short ranged, sure, but that's the point. When you're navigating around large objects—"

"I used to love romance vids," Alice said.

"You did?"

"Oh, yeah. *Loved* them."

"Huh."

There were distant footfalls approaching the cockpit from the crew compartment amidships.

"Practically lived in them," said Alice.

"Guys," Torque warned from tactical. "Cap's on her way up."

"Huh," repeated Gal. "'Used to,' you said?"

"Yeah."

"You wouldn't still happen to have any of those—"

The comm chirped.

"Yeah, Moze?" Gal prompted.

"Any more hops planned for the next hour?" the engineer, Serena "Moze" Mozart, asked. *"I need to take the TLD offline and clean the injectors. All this starting and stopping is caking up my throughput."*

"Sounds painful," Gal said, clearly glad to be talking ship's business. The playfulness in her voice dried up when Cinnamon Gauss appeared in the door. Alice smiled a greeting at her, but Cinnamon merely frowned back. Her forehead was mottled with angry red welts, a prolonged reaction to the black paint she'd used to disguise herself on Ionia. The effect made her forehead appear perpetually flushed with measle-like sores.

"Captain," Torque said formally, acknowledging her arrival.

Without responding, Cinnamon said, "I need my seat, Alice."

"Oh, sure." Alice worked to pop her safety harness free.

"Nah, not at all," Moze was saying to Gal, oblivious of the cloud now hanging over the cockpit. *"The explosion will happen too fast for our brains to register pain."*

"Status?" Cinnamon demanded, sidling roughly past Alice's wrinkled nose. Cinn smelled like she hadn't showered since they'd come back aboard.

What's going on with you?

"I asked for a status report." Directing her annoyance at Gal, Cinnamon situated herself in the co-pilot's seat. Then, before the navigator could reply, the captain cut her off. "Moze, something wrong with the engines?"

There was a pause wherein Moze, given the tone of her reply, seemed to clue in to her captain's dark mood.

"Nothing, boss." The engineer's tentative tone reminded Alice of when Andre Korsakov would launch into one of his Russian-laced tirades. You felt like every step you took was like walking on eggshells. Moze took her time, saying, *"I just need*

about half an hour to scrub the injectors. Routine maintenance is all."

"Tactical," Cinnamon said without so much as a glance at the duty station, "threat assessment?"

Alice stood frozen in the doorway of the cockpit and watched as Torque stared daggers at the back of Cinnamon's scalped skull.

"Clear," Torque reported tartly. "Next hop in fifty-eight minutes."

"Acknowledged," Cinnamon said. "Moze, do your maintenance. Be ready to lock everything back up on short notice and cold start if we get any visitors."

"Uhhh," Moze said, *"cold starting wouldn't be advisable, boss. I mean, if there's any chance—"*

"I said be ready." Cinnamon finished buckling herself in. "Now, get on with it. You're burning starlight."

"Hey, Moze," Torque said, "need a hand?"

There was a moment of quiet contemplation from engineering. *"Sure. Might make it a little fast—"*

"Great! Be right there." The big woman's fingers worked her console. "Feeding my tactical readouts to your screen, Gal. You don't mind double duty for a few, do you?"

"No problem," Gal answered, trading a knowing look with Alice. Whatever was going on between Torque and Cinnamon was getting worse, not better. "Long as the cap doesn't mind."

There was no answer from the co-pilot's seat. Cinnamon was somewhere else in her head. *Unplugged* was the word that came to mind for Alice as Cinnamon stared out the window at something only she could see. Pretty soon, Alice knew, she'd snap back to their shared reality and bark something at someone. That pattern had begun to emerge in the past couple of days.

Gal said, "Cap?"

"What?" Alice saw Cinnamon plug back in. "Sure. Whatever."

But Torque hadn't waited for permission anyway. She was already walking past Alice in the narrow doorway.

Gal nodded her head at Alice, then after Torque. Alice got the hint.

"I think I'll see what's up with Ben," she said.

"See ya," Gal answered, attempting to sound casual. "Tell Captain Stud Muffin I said, 'Hi.'"

Anxious to be where Cinnamon Gauss wasn't, Alice hurried after Torque. She found a comforting normalcy in the crew compartment, where Ben fiddled with his battlesuit and Light Without Shadow hibernated on his haunches like a piece of ethereal furniture.

"Hey, Torque, got a second?"

"Not really. The longer those injectors are offline, the more vulnerable—"

Alice reached out and snagged Torque by the crook of the elbow. The big woman's momentum pulled her along for a couple of steps until Torque finally stopped.

"I said—"

"What's going on with you two?" Alice demanded.

"I don't know what you—"

"You know *exactly* what I mean!"

"Yeah," said Ben, "you and Gauss have been stomping around each other like a married couple with lawyers."

Sighing, Torque said, "You'd have to ask the captain. She's treated me like shit since we got back." Torque seemed ready either to punch a bulkhead or collapse to the deck. With a soft glance, she said, "I need to be somewhere else, okay Alice?"

Alice let her go, and Torque nodded gratefully, then continued on to engineering. The woman's sadness trailed behind her like a ship's wake. It made Alice want to grab

Cinnamon by the front of her leathers and shake an answer from her. On Ionia, the constant bickering between Ben and Cinnamon had been bad, but at least it had been understandable. They didn't like each other much, and hiding there had kept them all under high pressure. But this thing with Torque—this felt personal. Vindictive. With intent to wound.

"Never thought I'd see her back down from a fight," Ben said.

Alice ripped her gaze from the empty hatchway, ready to pounce, but found Ben staring up at her with genuine concern.

"What's Cinnamon got to fight about?" she demanded to know. "Torque saved her life!"

"I wasn't talking about Gauss." He motioned for her to come and sit beside him on the bulkhead, made a final adjustment to Desi, and shut her access panel.

"That's the funny thing about Torque," Alice said. "She never *wants* to fight."

Ben slipped her a sideways glance. "She's just really good at it."

Knowing Ben was trying to make her feel better, Alice managed a weak half-smile.

"It was bad enough on that fucking planet," she said. "With you and Cinn at each other all the time."

"I know. I'm sorry about that."

"So was Cinn."

"She said that?"

"Yeah."

"Huh."

The ship fell unexpectedly quiet. The perpetual hum of the engines was gone, the result of Moze's maintenance. A low murmuring filtered back from the cockpit. Gal was trying to engage her captain in polite conversation. From astern, where you'd expect to hear Moze and her temporary mechanic's mate working together, there was only silence.

"She seems haunted," Ben said.

Alice turned toward him. "Torque?"

"Gauss."

Haunted—that seemed an old-fashioned word to use. An odd word with specific meaning. Alice regarded Ben a moment, since he seemed to have more to say on the subject. When he didn't go on, she asked, "What do you mean?"

He hesitated. "Did I ever tell you..." But then he shook his head, as though the nays inside had vetoed the motion to say more after all.

"What, Ben?"

He looked her in the eye then. "The last time I told you something about myself—something I didn't want anyone else to know—you spread it all over the ship."

Alice pulled back. "That's not fair!"

"You know what I'm talking about—"

"I told Cinnamon, and *only* Cinnamon, about your drinking," she said. "I told her to get her to lay off you. I was so tired of all the squabbling. I just wanted a little peace and quiet!" She looked away and found only Louie, unmoved by her outburst, serene as ever. Alice lowered her voice. "I've said it before, but I'll say it again. I'm sorry about that, but I had good intentions."

Exhaling a long breath, Ben said, "Yeah, you did. I just ... this is very personal. Maybe more personal than the alcohol thing. But it might be relevant to what's happening with Gauss ... I dunno."

"Cinnamon," Alice said, calmer now. "Her name is Cinnamon."

He looked at her then, a pale smile teasing at the corners of his mouth. "Always the peacemaker, eh?"

"I hate conflict," Alice whispered, revealing a hidden secret of her own. "People take family for granted. I don't. Not anymore."

The compartment grew quiet again. Light Without Shadow appeared not even to need to breathe. It was kind of eerie. One more uncomfortable detail aboard the *Dog* these days. Alice would never wish to return to Ionia, but sometimes, compared to this...

"I didn't choose that word at random, you know," Ben said.

"What word?"

"Haunted."

Alice wanted to leap forward to satisfy her curiosity but gave him time and space instead.

Ben said, "I see ghosts sometimes."

Alice absorbed that revelation. "Like, real ghosts?"

Ben grunted. "That's the question, isn't it?" He looked at her, a kind of earnest nakedness in his eyes. *Haunted*, she thought. Yes, that was the right word for it. "I have no idea."

Alice asked, "Is that why you drink?"

Ben thought about that, as though he'd never contemplated the question before. "Maybe."

"What do you see?"

"Not what, *who*." He shrugged, like now that he was telling her he wasn't even sure himself. "Old comrades. Casualties of a war we didn't even know we were fighting yet. On Drake's World."

A sudden dread drained through a hole in the bottom of Alice's heart. It filled her gut with a kind of heavy, stony coldness. Obviously, Drake's World still held them both. She wanted to reach out and hug Ben close to her. Let him know he wasn't alone, he and his ghosts, the way she'd been alone with the shadow-spiders in the dungeon.

Just as she was about to reach out, Ben went on. "I haven't seen them in a while." Then, as if realizing that for the first time: "And only a couple of times on Ionia, actually. Huh. Maybe that's why I'm less tempted to drink than I used to be. I mean, it's still there, but—"

"Isn't that a good thing?"

Ben thought about it. "Hell, I'm not even sure of that. But Gauss—Cinnamon—she has that look. Like she's somewhere else; maybe some*when* else. Stuck there."

"Unplugged from here," Alice said.

His eyes homed in on hers. "Yeah, exactly."

"But why take it out on Torque?" Alice wondered. "She saved Cinn's life!"

Ben shrugged again. "That's something you'd have to ask Cinnamon. I can tell you this, though: experiencing death can change a person. Their feelings about it become like a stalking horse, following them everywhere. Always just out of sight. But always there."

"I don't know what that is," Alice said, frustration creeping back into her voice. "A stalking horse?"

"It's a blind that hunters hide behind when stalking prey. Long time ago, they'd make it look like a horse to keep from spooking the target."

"So, people who are haunted by death are like the prey." Alice wrinkled her forehead. "But Cinnamon didn't die, that's my point. No one died."

"No one?"

"Well, only Blackmore, but—"

"Only?"

Alice flushed scarlet at Ben's one-word reprimand. Who was she to judge the value of one life over another? And after losing everyone she'd lost, too. Even Damianos Blackmore had deserved better than cold-blooded murder.

"Sorry," she said, "you're right. But I still don't understand why Cinn's so mad at Torque. I mean, what choice did Torque have if she was going to save her?"

"Like I said, that's a question only Cinnamon can answer."

"I'll talk to her again," Alice said.

Smiling his support, Ben said, "Good luck."

12
AN EXCESS OF ENEMIES

"THE ARCHIES ARE ONLY RESPONDING DEFENSIVELY, *Admiral,"* Commodore Marcus Isakov sent over subspace. *"I don't understand it."*

Neither did Natasha Ferris. But why the Arcœnum fleet wasn't taking offensive action against Alliance forces didn't matter, as long as they kept doing it. Or not doing it, as the case may be. After weeks avoiding the subspace sensor network, the Arcœnum had popped back up in Alpha Centauri. The system's outer defense platforms peppered them with missiles to limited effect, since the Archies' point defenses were largely successful at countering the incoming fire. Now the Archies' hodgepodge fleet of elegant, Arcœnum vessels and Alliance ships captured half a century earlier was advancing on Sylvan Novus itself.

Ferris, commander of the Alpha-C sector, had scrambled every Fleet asset in the system to meet them. Isakov and Battle Group Bravo were already halfway to the point of incursion. Ferris's Alpha Group had spent the last half-hour recovering personnel from scheduled shore leave. But they'd just about hooked them all back aboard their respective vessels, and Alpha was mobilizing to join Isakov's defense.

"They certainly showed no such restraint at Canis III," Isakov grumbled. *"Maybe they're keeping their powder dry for planetary bombardment."*

"Let's keep speculation to a minimum," Ferris said. "And prepare for every contingency."

"Aye, ma'am." Isakov turned to deal with a request by one of his bridge officers.

Her response had been tight as a bedsheet prepped for inspection, but internally, Tasha Ferris was smiling at Mark Isakov's archaic reference to the ball-and-musket weaponry of eight centuries earlier. Isakov was the kind of officer her old mentor, Nick Stone, would have said had the military in his bones after generations of service. That quality, as much as his military acumen, was why she'd recruited Isakov into her orbit decades earlier, guided his postings. In much the same way Stone had guided her, now that she put two and two together.

Tasha enjoyed paying that privilege forward. And now Stone was happy at home, enjoying his storybook ending to a slow-burn, if distant, decades-long friendship with Maria Hallett. Why he hadn't pursued her prior to retirement, Tasha had no idea. Or maybe she did, thinking of the scene in her office when she'd shanghaied Stone for the Alice Keller mission at the behest of Piers Bragg. She thought she'd been doing Stone a favor, giving him a final opportunity to make a difference—not that he'd needed it after saving the human species. But Tasha had wanted to send the man who'd made such a difference in her own life into retirement with one last victory, and the easy grab-and-go mission to rescue a marooned teenager had seemed just the thing. Then, when Nick had balked at the assignment, Bragg had had the nerve to threaten Nick's pension if he didn't play ball. So, he'd played ball, and Tasha had too, acknowledging the incoming president-elect's power, duly voted and certified, to marionette events to his liking. She'd felt bad enough about the part she'd played in that fiasco that, when Nick had requested a favor—to press Morgan Henry to accompany him for the mission aboard the refitted *Rubicon*—she'd been only too happy to oblige. Even if she'd had to call in a marker with the old coot to do it. Were Henry still among the living, he'd probably use the word "extort" to characterize their exchange.

But she'd owed it to Nick. Some people deserved happiness. Most, Tasha figured. She counted Nick Stone at the head of that group of folks.

"Fifteen minutes to weapons range, Admiral," Isakov reported on-screen.

"Excellent. I'll command from *Thermopylae*. Alpha should reach your position in five."

Isakov's expression went from confident to concerned. *"Ma'am, I really wish you'd reconsider leading the attack yourself. The Admiralty ought to be ashamed of saddling us with these old ships. The old girl included. She was long in the tooth during the Specter War, and between the barnacles on her hull plating and—"*

"Barnacles? Commodore Isakov, your anachronisms are showing."

Her old protégé made a sour face, though it was subtle. Couldn't show that kind of insubordination to the subordinates now, could he?

"You know what I mean, ma'am."

But Tasha wasn't done tweaking him. "And I assume by 'the old girl' you're referring to *Thermopylae*?"

Isakov shifted in his seat. *"Admiral, I merely meant—"*

"I know what you meant, Mark, and I realize we're on an encrypted channel, but let's confine any grousing about our well-aged assets to the bar after the battle. You go to war with the navy you've got."

His lips stretched into a tight, decidedly unsatisfied smile. *"Aye, ma'am."*

"I'll call you back when we're in position. Ferris, out."

Isakov's face disappeared, replaced by the tactical situation in Alpha-C. On the other screen at her desk was a running commentary from an older human. Dressed in a uniform that hadn't been regulation in fifty years and a mere dusting of gray at his temples that clearly indicated he wasn't quite old enough to be an officer from that era. Ferris had muted the transmission when Isakov called, so closed captioning ran along the bottom of the screen.

...pursued by a fleet of hostile ships determined to end us, read the text tracking across the bottom of the screen. *The Arcœnum call them the Skane...*

The man named himself Patrick Hirtz and a descendant of an officer captured during the Specter War. He claimed that the Arcœnum had dropped from translight to open talks with Alliance representatives in Alpha Centauri. Ludicrous on its face, Tasha knew. Especially after their attack on Canis III, where Archie aggression had cost the lives of hundreds of Fleet personnel and destroyed a dozen ships. Using their human captives to subvert Alliance morale—as she was sure they were using Hirtz now—wasn't a new strategy for the Archies. Hirtz's claim that the Skane were a mutual enemy sounded like classic Arcœnum misdirection straight out of a wartime documentary. Nick Stone had taught Tasha too well for her to believe such a transparent tactic.

Archies couldn't be trusted.

Ever.

For any reason.

As Hirtz's lips moved, as the transcription scrolled at the

bottom of the screen, Tasha Ferris had the grim realization that soon, very soon, she would likely have to issue a fleetwide directive: Containment Protocol, the zero tolerance policy dictating the isolation, imprisonment, and summary execution of Fleet personnel even suspected of being compromised by Archie mind-control. But these kids serving today? She wondered if they could step up and make, at so young an age, the hardest decision they'd likely ever have to make in their entire careers. To put to the sword—or to the pistol—their own comrades to secure victory over the Arcœnum. It only partially reassured Tasha that, two generations earlier, Fleet commanders during the Specter War had likely wondered the same thing. Their concern had been, in the vast majority of cases, unwarranted. Under fire and driven by training, necessity, and duty, most had done what they had to. And paid the psychological price afterward for doing it.

At least they were alive to wrestle with the fallout from that decision, Tasha thought.

The bosun's whistle filled her ready room. *"Admiral to the bridge. We'll be in weapons range of the Archie fleet in twelve minutes."*

"Acknowledged," Tasha said. "On my way."

Methodical. Merciless. Indiscriminate. The transcription crawled from right to left beneath Hirtz's expression. *That's what the Skane are. The only way to defeat them is together...*

Part of Tasha wished she could trust him. What she was about to do would no doubt be costly here, as resisting the Archies at Canis III had been costly. But paying that price now, in lives and ships and materiel ... well, that was a price *she* was willing to pay. Even up to and including her own life.

Tasha sought out the holo-image on her desk: her granddaughter Joanie back on Earth, playing with her new kitten. *Hi Grandma*, the little girl's lips said. Her hand waved vigorously beside her smile, and the kitten, seeing an invitation to play, swiped at Joanie's fingers with its tiny paws.

Tasha Ferris stood up, smoothed her uniform, and took a long last look at Patrick Hirtz's face. He appeared earnest enough, but how many times had mind-raped humans seemed just as sincere during the Specter War? And how many times had someone's desire to believe in their sincerity resulted in a horrendous loss of human life?

Not on my watch.

Joanie's smile filled up the corners of her heart like sunshine. Her stride determined, Admiral Natasha Ferris, sector commander and captain of the Alliance dreadnaught *Thermopylae,* left the silent sanctuary of her ready room for the bridge.

"What do you mean 'they just disappeared,' Lieutenant?"

Keric Bradley at tactical took a moment to double check his readings before responding. *Try not to embarrass yourself in front of the flag officer, son,* Tasha thought.

"Scope's clear, ma'am," Bradley said. "They just..." He couldn't quite bring himself to say the word again.

"...disappeared," she finished for him.

He looked up from his sensor readouts, his eyes apologetic. "Aye, ma'am."

Curioser and curioser, Tasha thought, *is this Archie "invasion."*

"Their hails have stopped too," reported the communications officer.

Tasha's eyebrows rose. "No more Hirtz?"

"No, ma'am. But Commodore Isakov is calling."

"I'll bet he is. Patch him through."

Isakov's face came up on the main screen. He was looking older. Tasha resisted speculating on how she must look to him.

"I guess you're seeing what I'm seeing."

"Or not seeing what you're not seeing?"

"Right."

Tasha caught her chin between her thumb and forefinger the way she always did when kicking her brain into translight. "They had a number of civilian ships. And a lot of old captured Alliance vessels. Maybe after the outer defenses plinked at them, they thought better of picking a bigger fight."

Isakov nodded at the logic. *"A sound military strategy, going back to translight before coming under the guns of two fleets."*

His latest archaic reference to Fleet's sailing-ship ancestors made Tasha smile.

"Admiral!" Bradley barked. "New readings. Bearing one-one-two, mark five-one."

"Well, that reprieve was short-lived," Isakov groused.

"The Archies?" Tasha asked her tactical officer.

Bradley's head came up slowly. "Negative. A second fleet."

The Arcœnum call them the Skane.

Hirtz's words came to mind like a ghost rising from a grave. Tasha's skin went cold.

"Analysis?" she requested of Bradley.

"Admiral, are you—"

"I see it, Mark," she said, though staring impatiently at her tactical officer. "Lieutenant, today, if you please..."

Bradley stared at his readouts a moment longer. "Sorry, ma'am. We're having a hard time getting a fix on them. Some kind of subspace inter..." He trailed off, staring intently at his sensor data.

"Lieutenant?"

"We just lost three satellites on the skirt," Bradley reported. "Make that four."

The perimeter satellite network, commonly called the skirt, comprised a series of booster satellites at the edge of the solar system. They served as an early warning system against unwanted incursion by enhancing the sensitivity of the wider subspace satellite network. It was the skirt that had alerted them to the arrival of the Archie fleet. Now, it was warning them again.

"A second fleet," Tasha repeated, as though trying to convince herself.

On-screen, Isakov muttered sardonically, *"Admiral, we seem to have an excess of enemies."*

"Eight satellites gone now, Admiral," Bradley said, his voice settling into a monotone.

"Admiral," Isakov said, *"I'd like to take the* Everest *forward with Battle Group Bravo before they hit the real defenses."*

"Hold on, Mark," Tasha said, her blood getting up. The satellites were part of an unmanned sensor web, but the new ships would be on top of their second line of defenses, manned weapons platforms, soon enough. The Arcœnum hadn't fired back when challenged by them earlier, so there'd been no casualties. But Ferris felt certain that particular statistic was about to become something more than zero. The hairs on the back of her neck prickled. "Tactical, any sign of the Archie fleet? The first fleet, I mean."

"No, ma'am," Bradley said.

To the screen, she said, "Go, Mark. I'm holding Alpha in reserve for now in case—"

"—the first fleet shows back up. Acknowledged." Isakov issued orders to his command crew, then nodded at the screen. *"Look forward to that talk at the bar afterward."*

"Godspeed, Mark," Tasha said.

The screen faded back to its default tactical display of Alpha Centauri. A cloud of green icons represented Isakov's

Battle Group Bravo, already speeding forward. A cluster of red icons, twice as many as Alpha and Bravo groups combined, made steady progress toward them from the outer system.

"First blood, ma'am," Bradley reported. "They've destroyed two defense platforms."

Tasha closed her eyes briefly out of respect for the loss of life, then snapped them open again.

Here we go.

She squinted, made sure she was seeing what she thought she was. "Why are they blipping?" she asked. On-screen, the red icons were blinking in and out in what seemed a random pattern. Gone one second from the tac display, back again the next.

"It's the subspace interference, Admiral," Bradley said. "Whatever they're doing, it's playing havoc with our ability to track them."

Another oddity. Or, maybe, a next-generation Arcœnum tech innovation the Alliance had never seen before. But if that were the case, why hadn't the first fleet employed it as well?

"A sensor cloak?" she asked.

Bradley hesitated. "Hard to say, ma'am. But *something* we're not familiar with."

On-screen, Bravo's green cloud began to spread out. Attack Maneuver Omicron. Specifically designed to minimize the devastation a chain reaction of starship explosions could cause. Mark was expecting to lose ships, and he wanted to make sure one of them detonating wouldn't take out another close by. Tasha told herself he was just being prudent. Like she'd taught him to be.

"Bravo's range to enemy?" she asked.

Bradley said, "Fifty thousand kilometers."

One of the green icons winked out. Then, another.

Tasha asked, "Has Bravo fallen inside whatever sensor cloud the enemy is generating?"

The Omicron formation loosened as Isakov put further distance between his starships. A third green marker disappeared.

Bradley looked at her, his face draining of color. "No, ma'am. That's not it."

"Lieutenant!" Ferris insisted. "Report with efficiency!"

"We've never seen these ship designs before, Admiral," Bradley said. "If they're Archies..."

On-screen, another ship icon from Battle Group Bravo vanished.

"Helm," Ferris ordered, "flank speed. Send to Alpha Group: Attack Maneuver Zeta."

"Who are they?" Bradley asked, and now it seemed he was the one desperate for information. "*What* are they?"

Methodical.

Merciless.

Indiscriminate.

Hirtz, back in Tasha's head again. As he spoke, a chill traced at translight speed along her skin from head to toe. But she didn't answer Bradley because she couldn't answer him. All her thought now focused on how to defeat an enemy she'd never before encountered.

"Admiral?" prompted Bradley.

Tasha Ferris exhaled. "The Skane."

13
SIEGE

"WHAT'S HAPPENING?" Eva asked Bathsheba Toma.

"A bar fight between the factions got out of hand. Didn't take much for the mob to form. The commander's people marched on the Havens, and now they're besieging it."

"A siege? Like in medieval times?"

Toma treated the question as rhetorical. The colonel and twenty of her Marines had established a defensive position behind crude fortifications. Across the flat expanse of the docks, hundreds of Hadrian al-Hurra's followers had formed a wall outside the Havens, blocking egress. There'd be more Marines inside, Eva guessed, preventing Sayyida loyalists from stepping out to meet them.

A standoff.

"What do Hadrian's people want?" Eva asked.

"Not what, *who*. It's been two days. That shock we were talking about? It's worn off."

"I can see that," Eva said, her anger forming. "Why didn't your Marines stop it before it—"

"They tried. But the situation spun up quickly." Toma's

implication was clear. Lowering the boom on the combatants had come close to causing the very casualties they'd hoped to avoid. "I finally ordered my Marines to stand down."

Eva knew that was a dangerous precedent to set. If the colonists suspected the Marines wouldn't, if pressed, enforce the articles of occupation, it was game over for Toma. They could overwhelm her with vastly superior numbers, though at the cost of a high body count. Toma would have to reestablish her position as the apex predator in New Nassau, and soon, or any hopes the pirates had of reconciliation with the greater Alliance would be lost.

"At least no one's been hurt so far," Eva said.

"I didn't say that."

"What?"

"Three dead, four wounded in the bar fight. The Sayyidists broke off, fought a running retreat, were reinforced, then fell back to the Havens."

"Were any of the dead—"

"Pirate on pirate only," Toma assured her. "Now do you see why I ordered my Marines to stand down?"

Eva did. So far, the bloodshed had occurred only between the factions. There was still hope for a peaceful resolution here.

"What about your people inside the Havens?" Eva asked. "Did they stand down too?"

"They're holding defensive positions inside the structure, same as we are. Orders are to fire only if fired upon. Any progress with Sayyida?"

Eva had been waiting for the question. "No." Despite her best efforts at subtle influence, Sayyida al-Hurra had resisted Eva's suggestion that she nominate herself to the Captains Council to lead the colony. Even Joe Gauss had enthusiastically endorsed the idea. But Sayyida, for all her frustration at her father for his reluctance to turn over Alice Keller, found the notion vulgar, disrespectful to Hadrian al-Hurra's memory. Eva suspected Sayyida blamed herself for her father's death like so many of his former sympathizers blamed her. She was in mourning and focused on past regrets and in no mood to care about, much less consider, the needs of the future.

Joe Gauss and two of his deputies emerged from the corridor behind them.

"What's the situation, Colonel?" asked the marshal.

Toma repeated the brief history of the conflict. She'd formed a guarded but respectful relationship with Gauss since al-Hurra's shooting. Tense at first, their combined investigation had settled into a kind of mutually respectful routine.

"I want to address the people outside," Gauss said. "They know me."

"Someone has to be held to account for what happened at the bar," Toma said. Her voice was cautious, like a foot probing at potentially unsafe ground. "The assaults, the killings."

"I know my job, Colonel," Gauss said, his hands dropping to his beltline where his marshal's star hung. Not a subtle gesture, but effective. "Now, you gonna let me talk to my people or what?"

Toma considered her options. "Miss Park goes with you."

"Fine by me. But I do the talking."

"Maybe I should go."

Everyone turned toward the sound of the voice. Sayyida walked toward them. Her appearance surprised but pleased Eva, though it also made her a little bit nervous.

"Not a good idea," the marshal said. "Those are your father's people out there. Folks are edgy enough as it is."

Sayyida gathered herself to argue, then acquiesced. "Okay, Joe."

Gauss turned to Eva. "Shall we?"

Private Rusty slung his rifle, preparing to escort Eva.

"Not this time, son," Gauss said. "The last thing we need is a Marine standing in the middle of everything. Too tempting a target for some, I think. I'll look after her. Although, from what I've seen, she can take pretty good care of herself."

"Stand down, Private," Toma said before turning to Eva. "Help me keep this from going any more sideways."

With a deep breath and not a little apprehension, Eva followed the marshal into the open space between the barricade and the pirates surrounding the Havens.

"This is Joe Gauss! I need to speak with someone empowered to treat for you folks!"

A man emerged from the ranks of al-Hurra's people. Tall, gray like Gauss, with a dour face. Eva couldn't tell if it was just the natural grouchiness of age she saw there or something aimed personally at the marshal.

"Poopdeck Pete Cooper," Gauss said. "Must say, I'm a little surprised."

"Nice to see you too, Joe."

"You parlay for these people?"

"'pears so," Cooper said, haughty.

"Well, then."

The two men stood, sizing one another up. Which was odd, Eva thought, considering they'd apparently known each other for years.

"What exactly you hoping to accomplish here, Pete?"

"Justice. For Hadrian al-Hurra."

Around him a chant began. Low at first, but then it took on a life of its own as it spread through the crowd.

"Justice for King Hadrian! Bring the boy to justice!"

Gauss let it go on like that for about ten seconds. Eva wasn't at all sure that was a good idea. And the "King Hadrian" talk worried her.

"Kinda hard to hear through all that," Gauss said.

Cooper raised his arms and flapped his hands slowly. He looked like an elderly buzzard too lazy to actually take flight. The chanting ebbed away.

"This how you expect to get that justice?" Gauss asked. "Fighting your own folks?"

"Wouldn't be the first time we settled a disagreement the old-fashioned way," Cooper said.

"True," Gauss allowed. His eyes fastened on Cooper when he said, "But there weren't hundreds of Marines with itchy trigger fingers around then."

Cooper spat, "Fuck the Marines."

The marshal let that stink dissipate into the air.

"What's she doing here?" Cooper asked, jerking his head at Eva.

"She's the negotiator who's going to bring all this to a peaceful resolution."

No pressure.

"An outsider?" Cooper scoffed. "We'll handle our own business, thanks all the same. And it's too late for parlay. We lost family today."

Gauss made a humming sound in the back of his throat. "Way I hear it, both sides lost folks. That's why firearms and bars don't mix. I'll hold those accountable who need to account."

Cooper's jaw jutted out. "Hadrian's dead, and your day's over, Gauss. New Nassau needs new blood—"

Gauss advanced on Cooper quickly until the two men stood nose-to-nose.

"Now, you listen to me, Pete," Gauss said, speaking in a whisper Eva could barely hear. "I know what this is *really* about. You never had no love for Captain al-Hurra. Not when we were taking merchant vessels together twenty years ago, and not when the captains elected him colony chief. You were always an opportunist, someone looking for circumstances to make yourself respectable cuz respect weren't a thing you could earn for yourself."

Cooper appeared immobilized, like a bug pinned to a collector's display. His bluster gone, a boy caught out by a knowing parent. Gauss moved in closer, stood on tiptoe to whisper into Cooper's ear. The longer Gauss spoke, the paler Cooper's face became.

"Hey, Pete!" someone in the group called out. "What's he saying? Don't let him buffalo you!"

Gauss returned to his natural height. He held out his right hand. "Do we have an accord, Pete, you and me?"

Cooper's eyes held the marshal's a moment longer before dropping to the deck. They flitted up once at Eva and his gaze narrowed in resentment. But whatever had passed between the two men had dampened the fire motivating Cooper. He reached out and gripped Gauss's forearm.

"Aye," growled the gangly man. "We have an accord."

Gauss turned to Eva. "Pete's going to accompany us forward to treat with the folks inside. Come along, Miss Park. This is where you earn your keep."

The mob parted down the middle to let them pass. A smattering of questions peppered Pete, who offered a few mollifying comments along the way. When they were within spitting distance of the entrance to the Havens, the doors opened. Eva spotted Lieutenant Lawson and his squad, observing from inside but following orders to stand down.

Three individuals emerged. Leading them, to Eva's amazement, was Althea Murray.

"Hello, Miss Park."

"Hello, Althea," Eva replied, recovering quickly. "How's little Eva?"

"She's fine. She's with her poppa. She's safe."

"That's good. That's very good to hear."

The group of six settled into an uneasy silence. If the negotiation had seemed abstract before this moment, it had suddenly grown very personal for Eva. Every daughter needed a mother. And Althea Murray was one poorly chosen word, one kneejerk reaction by a true believer away from her daughter losing hers.

Murray said, "We have wounded."

"We want the boy," Cooper said.

"You won't get him," one of Murray's companions snapped. "But you're welcome to try and take him."

"Gentlemen, please," Eva said. "Althea, how many wounded?"

"Three. We're caring for them, but Diallo needs a doctor."

"Okay. Marshal Gauss, can you guarantee safe passage to the infirmary for their wounded?"

"I can," Gauss said.

"I can't."

"Shut up, Pete," Gauss said. "End of the day, Al, I'll need to take the boy into custody. He'll stay in a Nassau cell and he'll be judged by a Nassau jury. Give you my word on that. You've known me long enough to know I'll keep it."

"I have. And I do." Althea Murray stared at him for a long moment. "You know why this happened, Joe?"

Gauss shrugged the way old people do when acknowledging the random nature of the universe. "I was there."

"Because Richard Brown is in love with Marya Jacobson," Murray said. "Or what a teenager thinks is love. You remember back that far, Joe?"

Gauss made a face. "Sometimes. Through a glass darkly, usually with whiskey in it."

"This isn't a laughing matter."

"No, Al, it isn't."

Murray said, "I'm talking about back when everything seemed consequential. Every love intended to last a lifetime. Each and every time you felt it filling up your heart."

"I remember," Eva said.

"He thought he was saving her," Murray said, gazing at her. "He wanted to be her hero."

Seeing the evident emotion in Murray's expression, Eva thought, *A new mother with tears in her eyes looks like art.*

Gauss nodded. "I understand. And yet, a man lies dead. And now more besides, as a consequence of Richard roaming free. This is bigger than one boy, Al. The whole colony's future is on the line."

Murray sighed. "What about Toma? She's got Marya in the brig for defacing that dropship."

"That can go away," Eva said with more confidence than she felt. Surely, with the stakes so high, Toma could give a little there. "But Richard has to give himself up to the marshal."

"Hadrian al-Hurra wouldn't have wanted more bloodshed," Joe Gauss said. "Whether you and yours supported his decisions lately or not, he was our chief, duly elected."

"We can fight," one of Murray's companions urged at her back. "We have people. Resources."

Eva heard a commotion behind them. She refused to turn, to be distracted. One wrong word here, one sudden move...

"I've known you all your life, Al," Gauss said. "And that newborn you got, she'd like that privilege too."

"The boy made a mistake," Murray said. "I know that's no excuse, but it's a simple fact."

"He'll have to account for that mistake." Gauss took no pleasure in his work here, that much was clear to Eva. It was simply what had to be done. The colony needed justice to heal.

Gasps from behind them. Murray's companions stared past Eva's group. Then, Murray's eyes widened too.

"Althea." Eva turned to find Sayyida al-Hurra walking across the open space between her father's besiegers and her own supporters holding the Havens. Angry murmuring erupted from the besiegers, but no one was moved to violence. "It's time this ended."

She drew up beside Eva. "If the Captains Council approves, I will take over leadership of New Nassau. We must unify among ourselves, and peacefully, if we're ever to rejoin the Alliance. That must start here."

Something in her voice struck Eva. Something new and grounded in wisdom. As though Sayyida had somehow unlocked a portion of her father's DNA or maybe her mother's. Something that had remade the scowling, demanding young woman into someone who was much more than that.

Sayyida turned to Cooper. "You speak for my father's people?"

"I do."

"And you for mine?"

Murray nodded.

"Then here's what's going to happen." As Sayyida spoke, she regarded each of them in turn. "Richard Brown will be taken into custody by Marshal Gauss, who will guard him around the clock until a trial date is set. Any extenuating circumstances will be considered, but the boy is old enough to be held to account for his actions. If the jury finds him guilty, he'll pay the consequences under colony law. Do we have an accord?"

There was angry dissent behind Murray, but it was muted. She said, reluctantly, "Agreed."

Sayyida proceeded. "As for those who were killed or injured in the bar fight, their families will meet in arbitration and a blood price set between those responsible and the survivor's kin. You, Pete Cooper, and you, Althea Murray, will serve as co-captains of the arbitration board. You may each pick one other person to serve, and I will act as the fifth member. The board's final decisions regarding responsibility and the blood price assessed will end the matter there. Any reprisals of any kind or further acts of vengeance will face the consequences of colony law. Agreed?"

Cooper began to grumble, but the marshal cleared his throat over him.

"Agreed," Cooper said finally, with a resentful look at Gauss.

Murray nodded.

"We also have Colonel Toma to account for. Marshal Gauss, going forward, do you agree to work hand-in-hand with her to secure the citizenry? To provide them a quality of life that accommodates greater freedom of movement, a greater degree of normalcy?"

"Sure," Gauss said, "but Toma won't go for that. She'll see it as—"

"I think I can convince her," Eva said. "If I can get you two in a room with me, I'm confident we can make it happen."

Gauss's grunt was doubtful. "I'm willing to give it a try."

"Miss Park, I'd like you to serve as special advisor to the arbitration board. You won't have a vote, but we need your skills if we're to successfully reconcile these two citizen groups."

Eva answered, "I'd be honored."

Sayyida turned to Cooper. "Have your people disperse. I don't want anyone tempted to rush justice when they bring the boy out. And emphasize what I said about facing Marshal Gauss's wrath. And Marshal, the bars are closed until after my father's funeral."

"Aye, ma'am," Cooper and Gauss said together.

"Now come on, all of you," Sayyida said. "This siege is over. Let's let everyone else know."

She whirled and marched back toward her father's faction. Sayyida seemed to fully expect the parlay's representatives would follow her. No one disappointed that expectation.

Well, Eva thought, *seems the colony has a new leader after all.*

14
WRECKED

HER DUTY SHIFT couldn't pass quickly enough.

By the time Cinnamon made her way back to the spare compartment that served as her cabin, it was all she could do to walk standing up. Head pounding, vision blurring in and out of focus. Hails from Alice went unanswered as Cinnamon passed her in the mid-section of the ship. She didn't want to chance whatever she might be tempted to say, to snarl at her, or worst of all, look like a weak captain to the little sister depending on her for strength. And besides, Cinnamon wasn't sure she could start moving again if she stopped.

The door to her quarters slid shut mercifully behind her. She fell backward against it. Propped up and precarious as a three-legged chair.

Safety. Isolation. A cocoon surrounding her.

Cinnamon shivered. Her skin pimpled with goose flesh, cold under the breeze from the overhead vent. Her whole body oozed sweat. The hammer slamming the inside of her skull dropped ten sizes smaller when she was still, and so she rested against the pressure door for a few more moments, recovering her strength. The air recycler wafted the stink of her own armpits into her nostrils. When was the last time she'd showered? She couldn't remember.

But none of that mattered. Or wouldn't matter soon.

She slid down the door to her knees, then slowly, carefully, shuffled to her bunk. Wrenched the bottom sheet loose from the mattress. Working her hand around, Cinnamon felt a flash of panic when she couldn't find the slit. Relief flooded through her once she located the hole in the mattress. Her fingers worked the gel packs aside, probing farther.

There. She touched the small medical case and yanked it out. Cinnamon stared at the case, its efficient, dull lines the perfect camouflage. How had it come to this? How had she fallen so low in so short a time? Her stomach rumbled at her. It didn't give a shit about Cinnamon's feeling sorry for herself, couldn't care less about anything but the respite waiting inside the case. The chill came again, mingled with nausea. The metal deck pressed into her knees, as though the *Dog* were passing judgment on her captain.

Fuck it.

Cinnamon unsnapped the case. On Ionia, there'd been a reason for the stuff. Even Torque had taken a hit or two to sleep after an especially offensive outing on Blackmore's behalf. *We did what we had to do to survive.* The rationale echoed in her throbbing head, a ghost flitting through an old window. Cinnamon had hit the stuff harder than Torque had on-planet, but not so hard she couldn't sleep without it. Not so now.

Cinnamon stared down at the tiny vials. Half the diameter of her little finger and less than half as long. The tiny needle at the tip so small. Too small, it seemed, to provide such deliverance. But she'd proven that theory wrong since returning to the ship, now hadn't she? How many times, she couldn't remember. Only four vials left, the last of their stash from the pleasure planet.

A new wave of chills made her shiver. Her knees ached. Her heart was heavy with disgust at her own need for the drug. Hiding in the Triangle and with no new source, she'd tried hard to extend the effect of each dose. Had even tried injecting a half-dose once as an experiment, to see if it'd be enough. But the injector was made to deliver the entire amount of each vial, and she'd ended up watching the last half-dose spew onto her cabin floor, wasted. And no, the half-dose hadn't been enough. So she wouldn't make that mistake again. And the supply issue was tomorrow's problem. Today, Cinnamon had what she needed.

She worked a vial from the case and held it firmly between thumb and forefinger. Her gut grumbled again, anticipating. She stared at the tiny injector, feeling the weight of the pistol on her left thigh. A whisper inside her head tempted her to its more final solution. But she wasn't there. Not yet.

Spreading the first and second fingers of her right hand, Cinnamon thrust the thin needle into the webbed skin between them. The slight stick, a welcome sting, followed by the slightly chilly injection of what she would soon feel as pure pleasure. Or the lack of any feeling at all, actually, which is where the pleasure came from. In ten or fifteen minutes, she wouldn't even know her body existed. Her mind would float free on a serene, weightless ocean, detached and distant from anything tactile. Hollow and happy inside. No more memories of Ionia or Rader's brains streaking Blackmore's floor. No more half-remembered nightmare of the darkness before she'd woken in Blackmore's office, wondering if she was dead. No more vague fury at Torque for some reason Cinnamon could neither fathom nor, very soon now, feel.

She snapped the case closed, shoved it back between the gel packs in the mattress, and fixed the sheet back over the hole. Pushing herself up from the deck, she collapsed—carefully, reverently—onto the more forgiving softness of her bunk. Rolled over onto her back, the motion sloshing around inside her head, and let her weight sink into the body-shaped warmth of the bedcovers. Cinnamon closed her eyes and waited for her soul to relax, determined not to count the seconds as they thudded by in her pounding skull. Time had already begun to slow down. Awareness, to drop away. The *Dog* seemed to withdraw around her, as though the walls and bulkheads of the cabin were dissolving. All Cinnamon could hear was the ragged sound of her own breathing. The rapid beating of her heart. The nausea in her stomach was at last subsiding. Her insides emptying out, gutting themselves as the hollowness filled up the space.

The cabin door chimed. Cinnamon ignored it. Had barely heard it. If she squeezed her eyes tight enough, maybe whoever it was would just go away. She was beginning to drift away, from the ship, from herself. The burden of being captain, and the fatigue that came with it, finally beginning to lift. The effect, she had the solid thought, seemed not unlike dying, or how she imagined dying to be. Deeper than sleep, a permanent laying down of—

The door chimed again, almost petulant in its persistence.

"Go away!" Cinnamon yelled. Or thought she did. Maybe she'd just imagined yelling. Maybe she'd even imagined the door chime itself.

The chime came twice more.

"Goddamnit!"

She could run, Cinnamon thought, and she could even hide. But she couldn't get away on her own ship. But she still had time—time enough to fake it, if she could just get rid of the asshole quickly. Time enough for the Kick to work its magic.

"Enter!"

The voice command unlocked the door, which slid aside. Turning her head, Cinnamon pried her eyes open. After a moment or two of seeing twin teens in twin doorways, her vision coalesced into one Alice standing there, concern etched in her face.

"What is it, Alice?" Cinnamon exercised a supreme force of will to avoid shouting at the girl. She thought it a remarkable effort, all things considered. "Really tired here."

Alice stepped inside her cabin.

No, no, no, no, no...

The door shut behind her.

Fuck.

"So, this is the cupboard, huh?" Alice said. She made a show of looking around, like a child seeing the wonders of a zoo for the first time. "Never actually been to your cabin before, Cinn. It's nice."

Neither Alice's use of the crew's joke name for her tiny quarters nor her lie about its aesthetic appeal did a thing to mollify Cinnamon's mood. The clock was counting down. She should be working with the Kick, not fighting it. Too much pushback by her, and the drug would simply shrug its shoulders and lose its potency, and then where would she be?

Left with only three more doses, that's where.

But she had to be cautious. Walk that fine line between appearing normal and getting Alice the fuck out of her quarters.

Attempting a genial tone, Cinnamon said, "Closest thing to a captain's cabin on this bucket of bolts. Quiet. Remote."

Usually.

Shit. Alice's expression suggested that Cinnamon had missed her target of appearing friendly. "Sorry. I'm just really tired—"

"What's going on, Cinn? Between you and Torque?"

Cinnamon stared at her. Heat rose up the back of her neck. Embarrassment or anger at the personal nature of the question? Cinnamon wasn't sure. One thing she *was* sure of was that any attempt to answer it, any attempt at all, would likely take more time than she had. She could already feel sensation returning to her skin. The Kick, chased away by the warmth of her angry blush.

"Look, Alice—"

"Would you sit up, please?"

Cinnamon blinked. "What?"

"Would you please sit up? It's hard to have a conversation with you when you're—"

"I'm tired!"

She'd roared it. The shock on Alice's face appeared at the same time as the expansive warning inside her own head. It was like Cinnamon's shout had dropped a pebble into her brain, and the waves of pain that followed thrummed against the inside of her skull.

"I lied before," Alice said.

Cinnamon's eyelids squeezed closed. Her eyes ached. Feeling was returning all over her body. She wanted to vomit.

"What?" she said, trying to catch up.

"Before, when I said the cupboard is nice. It's not. It's a wreck. Looks like the *Seeker* after the crash!"

"Alice," Cinnamon murmured, as much in anguish as angry now, "please, get out."

But Alice wasn't listening. She moved around the tight space like an officer on a tour of inspection. "It's a mess. *You're* a mess."

"Alice—" Cinnamon tried to raise herself in her bunk, managed to get to her elbows. She'd passed the point of no return now, and her heart felt sick at the utter waste of it.

Only two doses left after I hit again.

Oblivious, Alice marched on with her mission. "Why are you acting like such a bitch to Torque? What did she do that—"

"Alice, get the fuck out!"

Everything stopped. Alice's short-stepped pacing in the

small space of the cabin. Cinnamon's waning grip on the fantasy of disconnecting from, well, everything. It was like God had stuck a fingertip in the clockwork gears of the universe, just to be a shit.

Alice, who'd had her back to her, about-faced. Cinnamon managed to achieve a sitting position on her bunk. Her pistol, still strapped to her left thigh, pressed into the mattress, which adjusted to absorb it in a perfectly shaped cavity. Vomit felt ready to march up her gullet and explode from her mouth.

Go ahead, she thought. *Yell back*. Then, viciously, *Let's get this party started, bitch.*

But Alice didn't yell back. She only stared at Cinnamon with a judge's knowing look at the guilty in her eyes. Ready to pronounce the verdict, make it official.

Cinnamon sighed, and her fatigue felt like a physical weight bearing down on her. The last of the drug, petering out of her system. She could almost hear its fading footsteps echoing in the blood between her ears.

"What do you want, Alice?"

The girl's anger flared, sudden and hot. "Nothing." With a go-fuck-yourself look at Cinnamon, she stomped to the cabin door, which opened to allow her exit. Then Alice halted, spun around.

"No, that's another lie. I want my *friend* back. I want you to stop treating Torque like shit." Alice's cheeks were crimson with disappointment and fury. Her fists, clamped at her sides. Cinnamon wondered if she were about to experience the girl's power, dormant for weeks now. Maybe that would solve all their problems. "I want my family back!" Alice shouted before whirling and bolting from the cabin.

The door closed behind her.

Cinnamon sat staring at the cold polysteel, alone again in the quiet seclusion of her quarters. Part of her was sad, feeling guilty even. It's not like Alice didn't have a right to be angry. But most of her felt only the left-behind numbness of the Kick, and that vacuum was at the core of who she was now. As though someone had poured liquid metal down her throat and it had hardened to fill the cavity of her insides.

"Captain Gauss, your presence is needed in command."

The summons came like the voice of God. But it was only Stone, using a formality of language far more appropriate to a Fleet starship than the *Junkyard Dog*. When was the last time anyone had called her "Captain Gauss" on her own ship?

"Captain Gauss, acknowledge."

She punched the comm panel next to her bunk with the side of her fist. "Yeah! On my way."

Mistake. Cinnamon's skull pulsed like a drive reactor on overload. The nausea tickled her insides. Maybe if she just stopped eating. Maybe that could solve at least one of her problems.

All of them, eventually.

It took all Cinnamon's willpower to slide off her bunk and stand on her feet. No, not all of it. The last bit she used up in resisting the overpowering urge to drop to her knees and rip open the mattress again.

But she'd never done Kick on duty. And she wouldn't start now.

Adjusting her gun belt before it spilled her pistol to the deck, Cinnamon took one, then another jerky step from her refuge. The door opened.

Three more doses. Only three more.

15
A CLOSE-RUN THING

INTERNAL EXPLOSIONS ROCKED *THERMOPYLAE*.

"Keep those fingers nimble, Lieutenant," Admiral Natasha Ferris called out.

Over the clamor of blaring klaxons and shouting personnel, Bradley yelled, "Aye, Admiral!"

Thermopylae twisted along its horizontal axis like a whale in the water, her point-defense cannons surrounding the ship with a ring of protective slugs. The tracer rounds cut much of the enemy's incoming fire to pieces, but not all of it. Some of the tiny ninjas—what Bradley named the alien projectiles for their resemblance to ninja throwing stars—scythed through the aging dreadnaught's hull. Once the latest innovation in starship defense tech, the quadranium yielded like butter to a hot knife.

"Damage report," Tasha stated calmly.

"Hydroponics and main ward room venting to space," said a woman's voice. "Force fields in place. We lost a few—"

"Thank you, Ensign." The admiral cut her off. They didn't have time to count the dead—not yet. To the helm: "Lieutenant, get us in closer to that mothership." To Bradley: "Open all tubes. Prep a port broadside and target enemy engines and weapons. If you can find them."

Acknowledgments came from her bridge officers.

Tasha wasn't sure at all they *would* find those vital systems. The Skane ships were spherical, dark, with yardarm-like extensions that made them look like spacefaring arachnids. Not only did their uniform design make it difficult to identify where vital systems were located, it made them damned terrifying too. Called up some primal, hardwired fear from the deep recesses of the human psyche. At seemingly arbitrary locations around the globe-like main hull were lights—whether sensors or targeting scanners or some alien attempt at soliciting the favor of the gods, Tasha had no idea. But they completed the nightmare portrait, appearing as random, bulbous eyes scattered around the ship's central core.

Thermopylae shook again. "PDC rounds down fifty percent," Bradley reported.

They'd lost nearly half their complement of ships to ignorance of the new threat. Not just that the Skane existed or even the fact of their surprise attack, but also ignorance of how they fought, their weaponry. The aliens were adept at controlling subspace, that much was clear, and could use it to cloak their ships. Even use it as a weapon, carried by the ninja projectiles. If they weren't shot down first, those tiny flywheel-like delivery devices used subspace mechanics to pass through the molecular makeup of a starship's hull and cut into vital systems like trans-light engines, breaching containment and exploding vessels from within. It was only by the virtue of Bradley's tactical expertise that *Thermopylae* still existed.

"Ma'am!" exclaimed Bradley. "The Archies ... they're back!"

"Tactical!"

The main screen switched from the immediacy of the battle around them to the sector map. Beyond the hex representing

Sylvan Novus, red icons winked into existence, one by one. The Arcœnum fleet, returned to finish the job...

"Incoming hail from *Everest*," communications announced.

"On-screen," Tasha ordered. Then, when the commodore's face appeared: "Sit-rep, Mark?"

"Everest *is badly damaged, but we're still here.*" Mark Isakov appeared stretched thin. *"We lost six ships before we figured out the subspace thing."* He tilted his head, getting a report from off-screen. *"Shit."*

"Yeah," Tasha said. "They're back."

Isakov's expression, grim before, became gray as the grave. "Orders, Admiral?"

"Incoming!" Bradley warned.

Thermopylae hulled over against the latest barrage of ninjas. Her point-defense cannons spread a fresh shield of slugs around the length of her hull as she rolled. Artificial gravity took a moment to catch up, and Tasha Ferris fought back a level of nausea she hadn't felt since her first zero-g classes at the Academy. The ship's superstructure shuddered with internal trauma from the subspace bombs that had penetrated her shield of PDC counterfire.

The female ensign assigned to damage assessment, her voice shaky, began her report. "Admiral, we've taken hits in—"

"Later," Tasha said. If there was a later. The ship hadn't exploded. Knowing that would have to do for now. "Dispatch damage control teams."

"Admiral, caught between two fleets, we're between a rock and a hard place here," Isakov pressed on-screen. *"What are your orders?"*

"Something odd, ma'am," Bradley said. "The Archie ships that jumped in—they're all our old ships."

Tasha Ferris turned to him. "What?"

Bradley checked his scope again. "Confirmed. They're all

captured Alliance ships from the Specter War. No Arcœnum ship profiles so far."

Tasha looked back to the main screen. Isakov had heard him, too.

"Interesting," was all he said.

"Admiral, incoming hail from the lead Archie ship," communications reported. "It's Hirtz. He's asking to speak to the fleet commander."

"We've lost the *Mawrth Vallis*," Bradley reported.

Ferris turned her chair to face communications. "On-screen. Pass to *Everest*, too."

Patrick Hirtz's face came up. He was sitting in the captain's chair of his ship, one of a dozen that had reappeared from the void. Tasha opened her mouth, but he spoke first.

"If you won't believe our words, maybe you'll believe our actions."

Before she could reply, Hirtz killed the feed.

"Admiral," Isakov said immediately, *"I strongly suggest we redeploy to defend the planet—"*

"We don't have the ships for that," Tasha said, her voice mechanical. *The only way to defeat them is together*. Hirtz's words, haunting her conscience again. "What are the Archie ships doing?"

"Heading for our line, Admiral," Bradley said. "I could order the *Liberty* and *Ticonderoga* to redeploy to the rear to intercept—"

"We don't have the ships!" Tasha reiterated. Despite the heat of battle, despite the sudden appearance of an old enemy in their rear, despite the certainty of facing impossible odds, the bridge quieted in response. Admiral Tasha Ferris gathered herself, embarrassed by her outburst. The last thing they needed to see was the pressure getting to her. To the screen, she said, "I'm taking a gamble, Mark. Ignore Hirtz and his ships."

"But Admiral—"

"That's an order, Commodore," Tasha said.

His face sank from confusion into swift, solemn purpose. *"Lieutenant Bradley, prepare to relieve Admiral Ferris under Containment Protocol."*

Tasha blinked at the screen. *He thinks I'm turned. He thinks the Arcœnum have mind-raped me.*

"Mark, I'm not compromised."

"Lieutenant," Isakov said, half rising from his chair, as if he could step onto *Thermopylae*'s bridge and carry out the order himself. *"You are to relieve—"*

Tasha cut the transmission using the override button on her chair. She looked to Bradley. "I'm fine, Keric," she said. "Man your post. We can't be distracted now."

She saw it warring in Bradley, the decision—duty versus instinct; to follow Isakov's order or hold faith with Ferris, his commanding officer. Her earlier speculation about younger officers today having what it took to make the hard decisions came back to her. And which would be the harder choice here? Bradley had only her word she wasn't a pawn of the Arcœnum. And every reason in the book, literally, to follow Isakov's duly given order. She resisted the urge to glance down at the sidearm resting, for now, in her lieutenant's holster.

Holding her gaze, Bradley decided. "Aye, Admiral."

She nodded, hoping her relief wasn't as obvious on her face as it felt in her gut. "Status of the Archie vessels?"

Bradley returned to his scope. "Closing on the Skane. And —a portion of the Skane fleet has broken off. They're accelerating to meet them. And ma'am..."

"Spit it out, Lieutenant."

"The Skane are launching smaller versions of their ships."

"Fighters?"

"No idea, ma'am. But..." He looked directly at her, as

though reconsidering his decision to ignore Isakov. "They're on a direct course for Sylvan Novus."

On the planet, cities burned.

The Skane launch of smaller ships hadn't been ships at all, but autonomous subspace bombs. Larger than the ninjas and aimed directly at population centers on Sylvan Novus. Planetary defenses detonated much of the bombardment as far out as the exosphere, but some had hit their targets on the ground. Tens of thousands of civilians lay dead, many more trapped in the rubble of collapsed buildings. Some wandering aimlessly in the streets, shocked and dissociating but alive.

On the bridge of *Thermopylae*, Tasha Ferris absorbed the silence around her. All aboard had loved ones on Sylvan Novus. None knew whether they were dead or alive. They wouldn't likely learn any different anytime soon. The civilian communications network was so jammed with calls, no one could have gotten through to anyone back home had their duty allowed them to make the attempt.

"Ma'am..."

The sound of Bradley's voice was offensive. Heretical.

No one should be speaking now, Tasha thought. *No one.*

"What is it, Lieutenant?" she said softly.

"The Archie ships."

Tasha closed her eyes, indulging herself in her own isolation, just for a moment.

Let it be over. Just do it. I'm tired of feeling hopeless.

"Report," she said.

"They're ... they're ramming the Skane, ma'am!"

Tasha opened her eyes. "What?" She focused on the main screen and its tactical display, flooded with red icons. "What did you say?" She needed differentiation. Other than the few remaining Alliance ships painted in green, she couldn't tell unfriendlies from friendlies among their enemies. And what a ludicrous thought that was on its face.

As if reading her mind, ten of the symbols turned blue on-screen. Bradley, painting Hirtz's old Alliance vessels to distinguish them from the Skane.

A blue icon overlapped a red, then winked out. As did its target.

Then another.

And again.

Tasha turned to communications. "Hail Commodore Isakov."

On the main screen, two more Skane vessels disappeared, as did the compromised human ships targeting them. The irony somehow made itself known over the shock and awe of what was happening on-screen. Hirtz's ships, coopted by the Arcœnum, were employing the very tactic Nick Stone had used to defeat them at Gibraltar Station half a century earlier. A tactic inspired by sea battles of the Ancient World, when galley slaves laid into their oars, driven by overseers' whips and the rhythmic pounding of drums, to propel their ships into ramming enemy vessels to sink them. What, she wondered, would Mark Isakov make of that anachronism...

But there are so many more of them than of us.

Huh. And wasn't that a thing, now? Tasha had begun thinking of Hirtz and his crews as part of *us*.

Isakov's exhausted face appeared on half the split-screen. And yet, through the exhaustion, a kind of contrite expectation of comeuppance.

"Admiral, I—"

"Save it, Mark. Hirtz is showing us the way."

He acknowledged the point but his expression remained

grim. "We're still outnumbered," he said. In his voice, Tasha could hear it. They were on the same wavelength regarding the Archie fleet of human ships. Maybe it'd help if she stopped thinking of Hirtz's fleet in those terms.

"Ma'am!" Bradley called, surprised. Excited. Unsure.

But she knew what he was going to say before he said it. And Tasha Ferris smiled. Almost laughed out loud as their ludicrous situation devolved into the farcical.

"The Arcœnum fleet—the rest of it I mean. They've just jumped back into the system. Right on top of the Skane!"

On-screen, a grunt. *"Well,"* Commodore Mark Isakov said, *"looks like I was wrong."*

"Good hunting, Mark."

"And you, Admiral."

"Bring us in close," Tasha called through the acrid smoke of fused circuitry. She held her burned hand against her bloodstained tunic. Useless now, but by holding it up, she'd managed to reduce blood flow. Even the pain had subsided to a dull, throbbing ache.

Around her, small fires flickered from control consoles, the result of overloaded systems. A triage crew of Fleet med-techs performed yeoman's work around the bridge treating survivors. There were fewer of those, now. The corpses of heroes were left lying where they'd died, no time or personnel available to remove them.

Instead of carrying out Ferris's order to advance *Thermopylae*, the helmsman slipped from his chair to the deck. One of the med-techs stumbled toward him. The ship shook again under fire—more like shivered, it seemed to Tasha—and this time the old girl felt like she might shake the fastenings right out of her hull plating. The Skane weren't surrendering.

Methodical. Merciless. Indiscriminate.

You might add 'fucking relentless' to that list.

When her ship ceased quaking, Tasha Ferris rose from her center seat to collapse in the vacant chair at the helm. With her one good hand, she clumsily plotted a course to bring *Thermopylae* alongside the largest of the Skane vessels—the mothership, as Tasha thought of it. Analysis indicated the attacks were coordinated from there, so maybe if they could take that node out...

There were far fewer Skane ships now, but still more than the Alliance-Arcœnum fleet combined. Isakov and *Everest* were gone, so Ferris coordinated what ships Alpha-C Sector had left. Hirtz was gone, too. His vessel—the aptly named *Audacious*, she'd learned—was one of the first to ram the Skane. Together, the Alliance fleet and its unexpected allies had done considerable damage to the enemy.

But the good guys were still outnumbered.

And math doesn't lie.

Without hesitation, Tasha Ferris swung the bow of *Thermopylae* around. The Skane mothership's subspace drive, or whatever it used to travel faster than light, had either been knocked offline or, confident in final victory, she'd simply refused to retreat. The Skane had reason to be confident, Tasha allowed.

Well, motherfuckers, we can be relentless too.

She addressed Bradley, one of only two uninjured crewmembers remaining on the bridge. "What do we have left, Lieutenant?"

"PDCs exhausted," he reported. "We have a final brace of reserve nuclear missiles loaded in the fore-quarter portside tubes."

"Well," Tasha said, inexplicably feeling like an officer far younger than her age, "I'll aim that side at the Skane then."

"Aye, ma'am," Bradley said, sounding far older than his. "Good idea."

The stellar theater had opened up. What once had felt dense with starships—enemy and friendly and friendly-enemy—now seemed nearly deserted, save for scattered clouds of ionized gas that had once been engine fuel and ammunition, and floating debris that had once housed life, human and alien.

Much of that wreckage used to be starships shaped like spiders, Tasha thought with gritty satisfaction. In the name of the dead that had paid that butcher's bill, she intended to add a bit more to the Skane side of the tally sheet.

"Incoming," Bradley reported. "One-one-two, mark fifty-five."

Ferris saw it on her navigation board. A second Skane ship, a mid-size vessel, on an intercept course to prevent *Thermopylae*'s reaching the mothership.

"Don't think so," Tasha murmured to herself. Adjusting the course of *Thermopylae* to starboard with one hand took more effort than it should, but considering how many maneuvering thrusters her ship had lost, she wouldn't complain. The arc of *Thermopylae*'s course lazed away from the approaching Skane vessel. "Lining up the fore-quarter tubes on the new signal."

From tactical: "But ma'am, then we'll have nothing left."

Tasha regarded Bradley, who gazed back at her. "This is it, Keric. Make sure those launch doors are open, yeah? Wouldn't want to blow ourselves up ... prematurely, anyway."

He offered a pale grin of understanding. "Aye, Admiral. Launching in five ... four ... three..."

Tasha fancied she could feel *Thermopylae*'s effort when she released her final payload of missiles at the enemy. That was fantasy, of course. Between stellar physics and the ship's gravity compensators, there was no tangible recoil at the missile launch. But Tasha imagined it just the same, the old girl giving her last, full measure of devotion to her designed purpose. To throw one last handful of nuclear rocks at an existential enemy before falling away among a battlefield of stars, never to sail them again.

The smaller Skane vessel exploded in a corona of hellfire.

Thermopylae passed through the cloud of fiery radioactive dust, still aimed dead-on at the Skane mothership.

"She's changing course, Admiral," Bradley said. "Trying to—"

"I know what she's trying to do. But we're not going to let her get away, are we?"

"No, ma'am. We're not. Ninety seconds to impact."

Tasha checked her navigation board. Whatever engine capacity was left to the Skane vessel, *Thermopylae* had more. She was gaining. Now, it was just a matter of time.

Math doesn't lie.

Adjusting her injured arm, Tasha Ferris gazed down at her old-fashioned wrist communicator. She'd refused to get the new subdural implant all the younger officers now had. Still preferred seeing the face of the human she was talking to. The communicator hadn't been nearly as damaged as her arm had. Tasha pulled up a miniature of the motion image from her ready room. Her granddaughter, Joanie, waving. The kitten, trying to catch her hand.

Clearing his throat, Bradley said, "One minute."

She'd barely heard him over that goddamned klaxon.

"Silence that, would you, Lieutenant?"

Bradley pressed something on his panel, and the klaxon muted.

With her good hand, Ferris lifted her mangled arm and pressed Joanie's image to her lips.

"Open a channel," she said. "Prep the log buoy for launch."

On-screen the mothership grew in size. It now filled half the screen. A handful of ninjas launched from an aft eyeball at them. With nothing left to shoot them down, *Thermopylae* let them land.

Just let us last a little while longer.

"Channel open," Bradley reported. "Recording."

Ferris reached deep inside herself. Addressing future history was, after all, a daunting thing. "Log addendum. The actions of the enemy have left me with no alternative. But with Arcœnum assistance, I believe we've managed to stave off total annihilation, and that's something. Now, there's just one last thing to seal the deal. I hope it'll be enough. This is Natasha Ferris, sector commander of Alpha Centauri and captain of the Alliance dreadnaught *Thermopylae*. See you on the other side." She turned to Bradley. "Launch the log buoy."

He pressed a control on his console. "Launched. Twenty seconds, ma'am."

She missed Mark Isakov in this moment. Hadn't shed a tear when *Everest* exploded. Hadn't had the time. But in his memory, she wondered what he'd say. Something antiquated. Something historical. He was fond of the Duke of Wellington's diagnosis of his near-defeat by Napoleon at Waterloo: *It was a close-run thing*. For herself and Bradley, she settled for something a little more personal.

"Been an honor, Lieutenant."

"Back at you." He was ignoring rank protocol, trying to sound brave. "Old girl."

Natasha Ferris smiled. She ran her healthy fingertips along the helm console.

He was talking to you, y'know. Tasha projected the sentiment straight to the spirit of her starship. *Thank you for your service. Now, just one last duty to perform, old girl.*

16
ONE SMALL SHIP

ALICE COULDN'T BELIEVE what she was hearing. None of them could.

The crew of the *Junkyard Dog* sat or stood, huddled in the cockpit and frozen in rapt attention, listening to the scattered reports from Alpha Centauri. It sounded almost like a subspace drama, missing only the mood-shaping music. Only, the events unfolding on her homeworld were real, Alice realized with rising horror. *Had* actually happened. Were already in the past, and as real as the tears on her cheeks. As real as Torque's heavy gasps of disbelief.

The reports came in, schizophrenic and random, mere snippets of longer pleas from dozens of sources as Gal Galatz surfed subspace. Private citizens and planetary officials trying to reach family, even some military transmissions. Individual messages peppered them with a kind of methodical desperation.

"*...brought Danny down from the mountains just before the attack,*" a man was saying, his voice shaky. "*If anyone has seen them, we live in the Riverwalk District of New San Antonio. The aqueduct is destroyed, and homes are flooding, but I've taken refuge with neighbors. If you see them, please call me...*"

Gal rolled the receiver to another channel. Subspace was so clogged with calls for help, together they were like a coordinated chorus of voices, each hoping one of the others could render the aid no one seemed able to find.

Her knees shaking, her palms sweating, Alice felt as helpless as the people of Sylvan Novus. The terror in their voices gripped her. The anguish and tragedy at the sudden attack. The shock and sorrow and valiant efforts across the planet to save lives. And yet, there were messages of hope, too. Triumph at finding a loved one. Assurances to family back on Earth or in The Frontier that someone they cared about was safe. Still alive.

And what of her own family? Her Uncle Isaiah and his wife and kids? How silly the family squabble seemed now that had kept her father and his brother apart. She should have reached out to them, Alice admonished herself, instead of hiding on Strigoth. No matter the risk to herself. She should have ignored Morgan's warnings and reached out to them! And now, would she ever be able to talk to them again? Or were they just more casualties, more corpses on a planet with tens of thousands of dead now counted?

"*...Mama and I are in the cellar.*" The old man croaking the report wheezed with exhaustion. "*I managed to stop her bleeding, but the collapse ... we can't get out! I can't wake her, but she's breathing. Thank God for that miracle. Please, anyone listening to this, we are in the Giv'at Shapira settlement in Port Bukhara...*"

Gal scanned the network again, as if she could only take so much of one heartbreak before searching for the next.

Around Alice, the scale of the loss had stunned the rest of the *Dog*'s crew as much as it had her. Torque slumped unmoving in the co-pilot's seat, grim and grumbling. Next to her, Gal kept busy with her channel surfing, as though her hands were processing the emotions she did her best to restrain behind pursed lips. Ben sat at tactical, rigid and at attention like he was waiting for orders to attack something. His hands gripped the console with white knuckles.

All of them would remember where they were when they heard the news of Alpha Centauri. Alice was sure of it. They might live to be a hundred, but they'd remember. And something else—they'd remember hearing the news together.

Rapid steps came from the crew compartment. Still at her duty station when the subspace network lit up with the news, Moze had said something about joining them up front. But the shoulder that moved Alice aside wasn't the engineer's.

"Status report!" Cinnamon Gauss barked. "What's so damned—"

"Shhh!" Alice said again as a new story filled the cockpit.

"...was out with the scouts at Camp Artek," a mother said. She was weeping but trying to hold it together, to be coherent. *"I've tried the scoutmaster, but I can't get anyone to call me back! Does anyone know what's happening, goddamnit? Tell Rafael if you see him not to come home! The whole neighborhood is gone. We're at his Aunt Ellie's in Ebony Hills..."*

Alice closed her eyes. *It's just so horrible!*

Next to her, Cinnamon looked like she'd caught Gal's fidgeting disease. Her brows knitted together in concentration but her feet refused to keep still. "What are we listening to?"

"Civilian subspace chatter," Ben reported.

"Sylvan Novus," Alice said.

"What's happening?" Cinnamon demanded.

"Invasion," Torque answered. "It's the Skane."

"I've got a military channel," Gal said. "Hang on..." She piped it into the speakers.

"...left me with no alternative. But with Arcœnum assistance, I believe we've managed to stave off total annihilation, and that's something." It was a woman's voice. She sounded exhausted but

determined. *"Now, there's just one last thing to seal the deal. I hope it'll be enough. This is Natasha Ferris, sector commander of Alpha Centauri and captain of the Alliance dreadnaught* Thermopylae. *See you on the other side."*

"How are you getting that?" Ben wanted to know. "That's a classified channel!"

"Pirate magic," Torque murmured. But it had none of the pluck, none of the tongue-in-cheek razzing of Cinnamon's usual.

"Transmission ends," Gal said. "Came from a buoy, though."

Cinnamon grunted. "Well, I guess we're not taking you home after all, Alice."

Appalled, her skin bristling with shock at the thoughtless remark, Alice turned to face her. Cinnamon's expression was sleepy and sardonic in response, almost drunk in fact. Her eyelids closed and opened again, but slowly.

"Captain!" Torque scolded from her position forward. The look she shot Cinnamon was incredulous, hateful at the other's callous disregard for Alice's feelings.

"What a fucking asshole you are, Gauss," Ben spat.

Though limited by the tight doorway, Alice pressed herself away from Cinnamon in return. In all their time together—from that first moment the pirate poked her head into the *Archimedes*, to their long hours of conversation in New Nassau, and straight through to facing Cinnamon in her cabin earlier—Alice had never harbored ill will toward the woman. Not even when she and Ben were abusing one another in their Ionian apartment. But that was no longer true.

Gal silenced the constant stream of tragedy coming through on the speakers. In the aftermath of the cries for help from Alpha-C, in the shocked silence following Cinnamon Gauss's callous pronouncement, the crew in the cockpit seemed unable to speak. Only the low, constant hum of the returns from the sensor sweeps around the ship's position filled the quiet. A chill current of air whispered across the back of Alice's neck, and she remembered to breathe.

"Alice, I'm sorry," Cinnamon muttered lamely. Alice raked her with an unforgiving stare but only received more heavy-lidded blinking from Cinnamon. And, perhaps—were Alice feeling generous—a lazy-eyed kind of repentance. But she wasn't feeling generous. "I—I haven't been myself lately."

Ben snarled, "No fucking shit."

Once more, stillness descended over the close quarters of the cockpit. It was like no one knew what to say or do next. As though they'd been walking together in the wilderness and the path forward were suddenly cut off by an unbreachable tangle of forest.

"What now?" Moze whispered. Alice jumped at the hissing crackle her voice made through the intercom. *"Where to from here?"*

Simple as it was, Alice didn't understand the question. "What do you mean?"

Gal said, "Our plans have changed, haven't they?"

"No," Alice replied with a sideways glance at Cinnamon, daring her to disagree. "I need to go home—to Sylvan Novus—now more than ever."

No one responded. What was there to say?

"They need our help!" Alice exclaimed. Her voice was shattered, like a brittle vase of memories dropped on the floor. "You all heard!"

Ben released a breath, slow and severe.

"It's too dangerous, Alice," Cinnamon said, reaching out, sounding remarkably normal and not at all like the total asshole of mere moments earlier. "We're only one small ship."

Alice shrugged her off. "I don't care! We have to help!"

"The trip's too dangerous," Torque said softly. "The Skane are everywhere."

"I'm not afraid of them!" Alice shouted, knowing she was lying. Just as everyone else knew. They all knew how terrified she was of the shadow-spiders because they knew her story. But no one argued the point.

"Orders, Captain?" Moze said.

When Cinnamon didn't answer, the crew in the cockpit—even Ben with his fiery gaze—watched her, waiting. She was still the captain of the *Junkyard Dog,* whatever their personal animus toward her might be. However disrespectful, however cruel she'd been toward Alice. Each and every one of them looked to her now to set their course forward. She was still the captain.

Alice watched Cinnamon from beneath a creased brow, so angry at the woman for what seemed like too many reasons to count. She felt herself sinking into that familiar feeling of forlorn helplessness. *Again.*

"Captain?" Torque prompted.

Cinnamon opened her mouth to speak.

"There's something else coming through," Gal said. "Another message."

Ben asked, "From Alpha-C?"

"No, this is from New Nassau. It's an official communiqué from ... Oh, no."

Alice closed her eyes. What now? More death. More heartache. She heard it in the space between Gal's words.

I can't take it, she thought. *Not one more thing.*

"What is it?" Torque wanted the news, good or bad. Whatever it was, she needed to know.

Gal looked over her shoulder directly at Cinnamon. Her captain, swaying in the doorway, stared blankly back.

"What?" A shadow of the old Cinnamon rumbled in her

throat.

"Captain, I'm sorry," Gal said. "But Hadrian al-Hurra is dead."

For a moment, Cinnamon seemed not to hear. She put one hand to her temple and her head drooped left as though all the ballast in her brain had shifted portside.

"Any word," she whispered, closing her eyes. "Any word of my grandfather?"

"It was Marshal Gauss who issued the communiqué." Somewhere, Gal had found a kernel of hope to inject into that. "He's fine, Captain."

Cinnamon gave a lopsided nod of acknowledgment. It was quickly followed by the rest of her body leaning into a leftward loll. Instinctively, Alice moved to steady her. She was surprised so short a woman could be so heavy. Cinnamon reached up to anchor herself on Alice's shoulder. Her anger displaced by concern, Alice held her up with both arms. Cinn had been close to "King Hadrian." No wonder, then, that she was so disturbed by his death.

"I can't believe it," Torque said. "I can't—" But she cut herself off when she saw how her captain was leaning into Alice. "Captain?"

"Help me!" Alice shouted. Cinnamon's full weight was on Alice now, her chin drooped onto her chest, her hold on Alice gone limp.

Releasing her crash harness, Torque thrust herself so forcefully from the pilot's well, she knocked Gal Galatz, also rising to help, back into her chair with a squeak of surprise. Torque's large hands cradled Cinnamon's armpits, and Alice gasped with relief when she took the weight.

"God, she's heavy as a corpse," Torque murmured. She scooped Cinnamon into her arms like a mother with a limp child.

"What's going on up there?" Moze asked.

Gal said, "Cap's down."

"How many times have I said we need a proper sickbay on this fucking ship?" growled Torque. She held the unconscious Cinnamon tighter. "Cinn? Cinn!"

"Take her to the crew compartment amidships," Ben said. He stood, hunched over tactical, carefully holding himself out of Torque's path. "Desi has an advanced field triage system."

"Is she breathing?" Alice asked anxiously. "Is she alive?"

"Yeah," Torque reported as she moved past her through the doorway. "Hurry up, Stone!"

"Right behind you."

Alice exchanged a look with Gal, whose eyebrows had nearly joined with her deep auburn bangs. Alice had never seen the coolheaded pilot look so worried.

"Gal, what's going on?" Moze demanded again.

"Go on," Gal said to Alice. "I'll hold the fort here." Alice was already sprinting after Ben but heard Gal say, "Stay at your station, Moze. I'll keep you updated."

Ben detached the left vambrace from his battlesuit and passed it, head to toe, over Cinnamon. Readouts chirped and blinked. Desi seemed in no hurry to render a diagnosis.

Cinnamon lay on her back on the deck, her color pallid, her breathing shallow. They'd placed Ben's helmet over her head to enhance the field kit's scanning capability. The bulky helmet obscured Cinnamon's face, and her frame seemed even tinier than usual with her head inside. Did everyone look this way when they were unconscious and defenseless? Though Cinnamon was a decade older than Alice, she seemed as helpless as a small child. Alice reached out and took Cinnamon's hand, setting aside her anger from before.

"How is this thing in any way useful during combat?" Torque snarked.

"It's a field app version of an autodoc, not a med facility AI," Ben replied, examining a readout.

"Exactly!" Torque said. Her fear for her friend was evident in every word. "A Marine's bleeding out on some alien world, and this thing's cataloging Cinn's vitals like it's never seen a human body before!"

"We want it right, not fast," Ben said patiently, swiping settings. The chirping resumed.

"We want both!"

Moze appeared from aft. "How's she doing?"

Ben grunted. "We'll know in a second."

"I see you're as good as ever at following orders," Gal said as she joined them also.

"Right back at ya, Mango," Moze said. "Who's flying the ship?"

"The *Dog* can take care of herself for a while. I wanted to be here."

Moze flashed her an understanding smile. "Ditto."

"Maybe you two could get a room," Torque snapped, though there was little fire in it. Rather, she'd almost sounded relieved. Maybe even grateful. They were all gathered now, the full complement of the *Junkyard Dog*, all their shipboard family, holding anxious vigil around their matriarch and captain. Only Light Without Shadow, sitting stoically on his haunches behind Alice, appeared disinterested in Cinnamon's condition.

"Huh," said Ben.

"'Huh' what?" Torque took a step forward. "Out with it, Stone!"

Ben angled the arm so she could read its results. "Subdural

hematoma."

Looks of concern passed between them.

"What's that?" Alice asked.

"I've only had the basics," Ben said, "but it means she's bleeding inside her skull."

"Oh..." Alice gripped her friend's hand a little tighter.

"How the hell did that happen?" Torque demanded.

"Does that matter right now?" asked the ship's engineer. "How do we fix it?"

Ben said, "How should I know?"

"You're the Marine!" Torque's tone was more desperate than angry.

"I'm not a field medic!"

Moze said calmly, "What does the suit recommend?"

Ben turned the vambrace around, worked the display's menu.

"Two options—we can remove a piece of her skull and clean out the clot."

"What?" Torque said.

"Or," Ben continued, "we can bore a couple of holes in her skull to decrease the pressure."

"Jesus!" Moze said.

Gal said, "She needs surgery, then."

"We need a real sickbay on this fucking ship!" Torque yelled.

Gal shrugged. "We'd still need a proper doctor."

Torque's expression made Gal take a step back.

"Whatever we're going to do," Ben said, "we need to do it fast."

Alice cleared her throat. "I know where we can take her."

All eyes turned to her.

But it was Gal Galatz whom Alice looked to. "How fast can we get to Strigoth?"

17
A GOOD MAN GONE

ON THE THIRD day following his death, Hadrian al-Hurra's remains returned to the cosmos. That high-minded final act of appreciation for a life of service was preceded by compromises of politics, logistics, and the working out of security concerns. Eva was at the center of it all in her role as special advisor to the newly formed arbitration board, whose first contentious outcome was orchestrating their former commander's funeral.

Al-Hurra's body laid in state at the docks, preserved in a small cargo container that Joe Gauss insisted was perfect, for all its commonness, to serve as his coffin. Its utility, its simplicity, its lack of pretention—all fit its occupant to a T. In their youth, Gauss said, he and al-Hurra had shared many a meal and not a few slugs of hooch whiskey over just such a "table" while planning raids on merchant ships passing through the Malvian Triangle. Al-Hurra would have appreciated the nostalgia of it, Gauss said, had it been Joe lying in the coffin instead of him.

Bathsheba Toma provided an honor guard of Marines for the container, though they weren't really needed. No one would have dared to desecrate their beloved leader's remains. Though, Gauss said only half-jokingly, the bottle of twenty-year-old hooch whiskey he'd placed alongside al-Hurra might have disappeared if not guarded. He'd never gotten around to drinking the bottle with his old captain, had been saving it for a special occasion.

In the final day leading up to the ceremony, it seemed the entire colony had filed past the container for a final glimpse at the man who had, for the past decade, helped them navigate the treacherous currents of competing factions, Fleet admirals on the hunt, and even the Triangle itself. No one, whatever their al-Hurra affiliation, picked a fight with the taciturn Marines surrounding Hadrian al-Hurra's body—or one another, for that matter.

Reflecting on that encouraging fact, Eva watched the rites of the ceremony unfold. They were ritualistic, respectful, and deliberate. Handpicked by Sayyida, an old pirate dirge played. Her father had sung her to sleep with it at night when she was a little girl. She was holding up well, the demands of her new office a constant distraction from her loss. The docks, as full of people as Eva had ever seen them, were a sedate portrait of polite cooperation. There were no obvious divisions, no "Hadrian's people here, Sayyida's people there." Families, once divided by age as much as loyalty, now stood shoulder to shoulder.

Toma too had accommodated the spirit of the moment. In addition to the honor guard for al-Hurra's coffin, Toma provided a ceremonial guard of twenty-eight Marines during the funeral itself. The Marines formed a tight square around the dais, seven per side, where those who'd chosen to speak on Hadrian al-Hurra's behalf now sat. Toma sat with them in her formal dress uniform and nothing else, the only time Eva had seen her without her armor since the beginning of the occupation. Toma was taking a risk with that, making a gesture of trust. Eva resolved to pull her aside later and thank her for it.

Hadrian would have liked this, she thought. *Not out of any ego; not him.* But seeing everyone together, angry voices quieted; no threats, no conflict at all. Peace between factions within the community, a détente between pirates and Alliance Marines—everyone putting aside their differences in service of a common cause. And all it had taken was the death of the man who'd commanded their respect in greater or lesser measure. It wouldn't have surprised her to know that al-Hurra might have considered whether or not his own death could achieve the very result he'd worked so hard for when he was alive. But no, she decided, that required too egocentric a view of one's own self-importance. And that wasn't Hadrian al-Hurra.

The chaplain had finished a reading of scripture. The crowd murmured assent. The old man of God doddered back to his seat. Gauss stood. On his way to the podium, he wiped his nose with a handkerchief the way men do to hide their tears.

"I'll keep this short," he grumbled, his voice amplified by the public address system. Someone in the crowd showed appreciation for his promise of a brief address, and was answered by a spate of laughter.

"Cap and I served together aboard the *Nicomo's Luck* longer ago than I care to admit. He was an in-your-face, up-and-coming type with more mercy in him than anyone in the pirating business should have. In charge of ship's inventory as quartermaster, I was just a crusty asshole who said 'no' a lot."

"So, nothing's changed!" someone called out. More laughter. Including from a few Marines.

"Nope, not much," Gauss allowed. "But once he'd risen to second mate, we became tight through our duties. By the time he was named first mate, I thought maybe I'd discovered the only pirate who ever lived who thought fairness was the noblest of shipmaster qualities. When the crew voted him captain, hell, I thought maybe I'd found a son I'd fathered somewhere and forgotten about."

There was more laughter, but less easy than before. Eva noticed Sayyida cracking a sad smile. It gave her cheeks, glimmering with tears, a lovely radiance.

"Sometimes he had to tack across the wind, but Cap's course always arced upward." And here Gauss faltered. He wiped his nose and croaked, "Still does."

The marshal turned quickly from the podium and headed back to his chair, but Sayyida intercepted him and wrapped him in her arms. Gauss hugged her back hard, and close, then retook his seat. He sat down, it seemed to Eva, just before he might fall over.

At the podium, Sayyida took a moment to take in the vastness of the crowd who'd come to pay their respects. Eva had prepared talking points for her at Sayyida's request, remarks they both hoped could quicken the healing of any remaining rivalries between the factions. Sayyida had thanked her but, preferring to speak from the heart, set the prepared remarks aside before the ceremony.

"We've come here today to honor my father," Sayyida said. Her voice, like Gauss's before her, filled the hollowed-out cavern of the asteroid. "Not to grieve him, though his loss will certainly be felt keenly. By none more so than me. But to celebrate his life. And the legacy he leaves us all." She turned to Joe Gauss, who gazed up at her from his chair. As full of pride as any father would, were she his own daughter. "Joe, you said my father was like a son to you. In case he never told you, he considered you like a father the moment you two stepped off the *Luck* together for the last time. You were his family. You're still mine."

Gauss nodded his appreciation, then wiped his nose again.

Sayyida surveyed the crowd. "My father believed in you. Each and every one of you. He believed in New Nassau. In our right to exist as a community when the Alliance abandoned us. In the moral certitude of taking from those who have more than they need to keep our own children from starving. Call us pirates or patriots, call us what you like." Eva knew Sayyida was speaking to Toma or anyone else who might doubt her father's actions over his lifetime. "Of all the men I ever knew, I trusted Hadrian al-Hurra, my father, to know the difference between right and wrong. And there's nothing wrong, he often told me when I was a child, in feeding the hungry or housing the homeless. Any law that prohibits that is the thing that's wrong.

"We will not question his wisdom here," she continued. "I said when I began that we're here to honor him. But not with words. Words are flimsy things, easily manipulated to meaner motives. Actions, though—actions are what matter. Actions express true beliefs. They are measures of true character, not promises to be broken.

"My father's actions as your commander can be summed up simply: to ensure the safety of his colony, her people, and their future. While we disagreed on the speed at which reconciliation with the Alliance should happen, we agreed that it *should* happen. Now, we're at that crossroads, and the rightness of our choices is muddied by war. You've no doubt heard the reports of a near-total loss in Alpha-C. Humanity's relationship with the Arcœnum is tenuous at best, perhaps more so than ever since the Specter War. Uncertainty is all around us. This is not a time to stand separated by petty differences."

Sayyida took a long breath, in and out. "Life has a way of slapping you in the face. You grow complacent, then God or Fate or the laughing monkey that spins the universal wheel shows you how fragile your reality actually is. Alpha-C is that for the Alliance. My father's death was that for me. And for you, I hope."

Murmurings arose among the mourners. Ascent, mostly, for simple wisdom shared. Some questions were voiced, one person to another. Some apologies were made for past wrongs. Sayyida let it continue for a few long moments, then raised her hands.

"My father was a good man, and he's gone now. But his legacy is your future," she said. "We must press forward with reconciliation now. I'm calling on all of you to support that effort, in my father's name—whether you agreed with him or not, whether you liked him or not, whether you voted for him through the Captains Council or not. We can no longer afford to let philosophical disagreements separate us. We no longer have that luxury. We are all one colony, one community, one people. We have a moral obligation to lend our aid to the Alliance. And, perhaps in return, they will welcome us home when, together with them, we have defeated the Skane. In my father's name, I ask this of you. Each and every one of you."

Sayyida al-Hurra stepped back from the podium, put her hands together and lowered her head, a supplicant before the will of the people she served. The people she now led.

Yes, Eva thought, *here is a commander worthy of the title "leader."*

Her thoughts were drowned out by the sudden, spontaneous eruption of applause and shouts of "Huzzah for al-Hurra! Huzzah for al-Hurra!" Thousands of voices raised as one, not just for a notion or even an action, but for the person who could carry them all forward into a better future. Sayyida turned to her father's coffin, placed one hand on the lid.

Standing with everyone else to honor Sayyida al-Hurra's words, Toma commanded, "Present: Arms!" The Marines surrounding the dais obeyed, and there was the snap-crack of rifles on armor. It was a hopeful and surprising sound in Eva's ears. Sayyida made her way back to the row of chairs.

"Sayyida, that was fantastic," Eva said.

Gauss reached out a hand, touched Sayyida's shoulder.

There were tears on his cheeks. "Your father would have been very proud of you. *Is* proud of you."

"Please, Joe," Sayyida said, leaning into Gauss for support. "Please get me the hell out of here."

"I've pressed so hard and long for this," Sayyida al-Hurra said. "Now I'm not sure how to actually make it happen."

Eva couldn't help but notice her body language. Hunched over, tired, wrung out. After her father's coffin had been launched into space and the funeral party dismissed, the people of New Nassau had returned to a more relaxed reality than they'd enjoyed of late, the bubble of the tension having burst finally in the wake of Hadrian al-Hurra's death. Alliance Marines still guarded sensitive areas like the colony's power plant, and ships were still grounded. But the day-to-day life of the community was approaching a kind of normalcy that felt nearly like its former freedom. Internal commerce within the colony was spinning up, and the toilets were working reliably again. Eva had to credit Sheba Toma for following through on her new enforcement policy of patience, restraint, and understanding.

"You mean the next steps for reconciliation?" Eva said. "Now that the Captains Council has ratified your position as colony commander, I'll reach out to Sam Devos, the president's chief of staff. That their vote was unanimous—that will impress him, I think."

Sayyida nodded absently. "I used to give him shit, you know. When I was a little girl."

"Ma'am?" said Toma.

"He was never home. This was after captaining the *Luck*. He started ascending the ranks of colony leadership quickly."

Her tone was wistful, as if watching a memory and narrating it for the benefit of those who couldn't see. "Now, I get it."

"Leadership isn't a burden," Eva said. "Or it shouldn't be. It's a privilege. An opportunity to know, after you're gone, that you've made a difference for others as much as yourself."

"I still feel him here," Joe Gauss said. His gaze took in the conference room. "It's not a sad thing."

"No," Sayyida said, then again, "no. It's reassuring." She straightened in her chair and made an effort to look around the table at each of them. "I'm passing the word to all the coves. I'm calling off the hunt for Alice Keller."

"Ma'am?" Toma said again.

"No offense intended, Colonel, but finding her is your problem. My father was right. We can't begin this way with the Alliance. Trading one life for a colony's? Where does that bartering end?" Sayyida held Toma's gaze, level and firm. "I will not hinder your efforts to implement President Bragg's order. But I will no longer help them, either."

Toma said nothing. She appeared less displeased by Sayyida's sudden shift in policy than Eva would have expected her to be.

The commander of New Nassau turned to her chief law enforcement officer. "Joe, what's the status of the trial?"

"Jury selected," Gauss answered, glad to have something positive to report. "Six from your—from the folks who sympathized with you. Six from the group who sided with your father."

"I hope the trial itself is swift," Eva said. "Whatever the outcome, uncertainty can only encourage people to speculate. And that could mean more trouble."

"It'll be what it is," Gauss said. "Puppy love is not a defense to murder."

Those in the room allowed him his moment of bitterness.

He was entitled to be angry at the boy who'd shot his oldest friend in cold blood, so long as he carried out his duties related to the matter as the law prescribed. No one present doubted he would.

"The president is speaking soon," Eva said. "Once we've heard what he has to say, I'll reach out to Sam."

"Good," Sayyida said. "Thank you all for your support in these past days. I believe, with your help, we can achieve reconciliation."

Eva smiled. "Your father would be pleased to see you there, Sayyida. In his seat."

"Yes," she said, her tone melancholy but hopeful. "Yes, I think he would."

18
SOMETHING NEW, SOMETHING OLD

"MY FELLOW HUMANS—I come before you today not just as your president, but as a member of our shared humanity. I come before you today as an advocate. Not simply for our survival, but for our right, as a species, to exist."

Piers Bragg looked tired, Eva thought. He reminded her of a college student who'd goofed off all semester, then suddenly realized his entire academic career hinged on passing his final exams. His hair seemed as though he'd just hastily run a comb through it.

"Today is not a day for dissembling. Or politics as usual or rosy predictions of guaranteed success. Today is a day for truth-telling. For transparency. We are at a crossroads, my friends. We have a choice before us unlike any humanity has faced before. Together, I truly believe we can make our destiny for ourselves and our children's children whatever we wish that future to be. But if we stand apart, if we remain divided over trivial, political disagreements—trade bills, monetary policy, intersystem immigration limitations—we practically guarantee our own extinction."

Eva cast her eyes around the colony's leadership seated at

Sayyida al-Hurra's round table. Sayyida, newly elected commander by the Captains Council, and Joe Gauss, marshal of New Nassau and one of the few remaining colonists who remembered firsthand the Great Separation. Both generations now sharing one objective: to return to the larger fold of humanity. Sheba Toma, military governor of New Nassau, who'd agreed to share power with those whom she ostensibly ruled, a sign of admirable personal growth since dealing with Sayyida's father. And Eva herself, Presidential Liaison to the Colony of New Nassau, personal advisor to its new commander and confidant to its military governor. She wore three hats now, each with its own agenda, and each of those more often than not in competition with the other two.

"That includes the media," Bragg was saying. He held up a hand, a gesture Eva recognized as acknowledging the potential for debate but warding it off at the same time. "I'm merely asking the Fourth Estate to exercise discretion. To resist feeding the rumor mill. We can't afford panic. There's no time for it, or to rectify the misdirection it causes. We must pull together across all the traditional lines of division which separate us. We must stay united."

It was a familiar message, and shared more than a passing resemblance to what Sayyida al-Hurra had said to the citizens of New Nassau at her father's funeral. Eva quirked an eyebrow, knowing it'd been her own summary of that speech for Leo that had provided his inspiration for the theme of unity he'd woven into Bragg's speech.

"United behind *him,* I suppose," grumbled Gauss.

Eva sighed. "He's who we've got. But he's not alone."

He's got Devos, a first-class strategic mind. And Leo, who could sell water to a fish.

"I even have your first story for you," Bragg told his listeners with a hopeful smile. To Eva, who knew him so well, it almost looked authentic. "In the spirit of cooperation and to show my own commitment to this course of breaking down old barriers, I've authorized the release of Miranda Marcos."

That shocked Eva, given how recently the president had reincarcerated Miranda. Then, her cynical political sense figured she knew why he'd so suddenly reversed course. Releasing the reformer was likely a ploy to distract from the disaster at Sylvan Novus—which Bragg had failed to address right away, she noted—but at least Miranda was free. Again. His next words all but confirmed Eva's thinking.

"Miranda will be heading up the humanitarian mission to Alpha Centauri," Bragg stated. "She will be the administration's ambassador to that wounded system, which is also her home. I've vested in her the complete authority of my office to provide relief and effect recovery in the most expeditious way possible. You have our thoughts and prayers, Miranda. Whatever else you need, you have but to ask."

Bragg was not only distracting from the tragedy, he was doing so by putting it centerstage, with Miranda Marcos as the star. Eva had to admire the audacity of it.

Go big or go home, indeed.

The people of Sylvan Novus had a home-grown champion who'd haul them back on their feet herself, if she had to. Bragg's gamble there was bold. Perhaps, as he had to defuse the Psycker crisis, this was his way of co-opting a popular public figure in the name of his own cause. Eva thought about that, about its cleverness. And, flipping that coin over, its deviousness. Bragg was looking for a public relations win in the face of near-disaster in Alpha Centauri. She wrinkled her nose at her internal cynic. Maybe she was being too hard on Bragg. Maybe he really had turned over a new leaf and was acting in what he believed to be humanity's best interests. The species was facing an extinction event unlike any it had experienced before. He'd said it himself.

The president took his time lauding Miranda's qualifications for the office he'd drafted her into. Her passion, her strength of character, her formidableness as a political opponent.

"These core qualities," Bragg said, "will aid her in her work to help the people of Sylvan Novus, whom Earth considers her own children."

As he praised her, Bragg ran a hand through his hair. He was nervous. His confidence seemed to waver. But he delivered what were clearly Leo's words with a certainty honed in many a board meeting when quarterly earnings had been less than stellar. And on the campaign trail speaking to supporters, who told their children boogeyman stories of alien abductions at bedtime.

"And now, I will practice some of that transparency I spoke of earlier. I must share with you an uncomfortable truth. A truth that, under normal circumstances, a president would think twice before sharing with his people because of the potential for panic. But, as I said, there's no time for dissembling, for spoon-feeding you small doses of what you need to know.

"We face a new alien threat. A species from the distant past of our old adversary, the Arcœnum. The Archies call this new threat the *Skane*. And the Skane represent as great a threat as the Arcœnum to our continued existence."

Eva glanced at Toma, the petty need to say "I told you so" rising in her again. To remind the colonel of her doubt over Ben Stone and his Arcœnum-sourced intelligence, to reprimand her for it. Sheba met her eyes briefly, her lips drawn taut in a thin line. No need to, then. She was already doing that herself.

On-screen, Bragg shifted in his chair. Another tell that Eva recognized. He was taking time to think; transitioning, changing tracks in the speech.

"For her courageous defense of Sylvan Novus, I've posthumously promoted Fleet Admiral Natasha Ferris to Grand

Admiral of the Fleet. Her sacrifice will not have been in vain. It's courage like that demonstrated by Tasha Ferris, her brave crew, and all those who've given their lives in this war that will help us achieve ultimate victory over the Skane—and any alien that seeks to subjugate humanity, or deny our God-given right to exist among the stars."

He went on like that for a while. Lionizing the armed forces, emphasizing the economic resilience of the Alliance, citing half-baked historical precedents of how humanity had prevailed despite overwhelming odds predicting failure. Eva attempted to parse the strategy of the speech, which seemed a bit scattered at this point. The president had begun by assuring his viewers that he'd avoid the platitudes and empty assurances he was currently serving up. In the wake of Sayyida's eulogy-cum-homily of her father, it sounded a lot like the typically hollow, high-minded promises of a political candidate. And it didn't seem like the kind of thing Leo Byrne would write. The more the president talked, the more uneasy he appeared, the more irritated his demeanor became. With a kind of locomotive zeal, his voice grew angrier. And Eva found her own anxiety growing as she wondered where the train of his argument was headed.

"Humans first," Bragg said.

Eva snapped out of her rhetorical analysis.

Bragg's expression was grave. "You might remember that theme from my campaign three years ago. If you walk away from my address tonight with nothing else, I want you to embrace that idea. *Humans first*. Go to sleep and wake up in the morning with it firmly in your hearts. I said earlier we could only ensure our collective survival by working together. Well, when I was in the corporate world, what that required first was sharing a single *vision*. To ensure our survival, we must embrace the notion of *humans first*. Regardless of party or political persuasion. Here, we must be of one mind."

If it had pinged before, Eva's off-script radar now flashed a red alert. Bragg used to do this all the time on the campaign trail. Get bored with the redundancy messaging crafted by his speechwriters and start injecting his own slogans. And when the audience clapped and shouted their enthusiasm, he devoured it like a starving man would food. Leo would be beside himself. Bragg was, counterintuitively, employing the divisive language of his campaign from three years earlier to suggest people should come together—as long as it was on his terms. But he risked dividing them back into the very political tribes he claimed to want to transcend. His own speech seemed at war with itself.

The president's chest heaved dramatically. "My friends, my call for 'one mind' is not accidental—it is, in fact, one way we can fight fire with fire. Based on analysis of the Battle of Sylvan Novus, we believe the Skane coordinate their actions through a hive-like central intelligence." Eva watched his eyes track ever slightly left to right. He was reading his speech again. Back on script. "Our working theory is that it provides them some kind of immunity to Arcœnum mind control. Unlike humans, whose independent brains—unnetworked, if you will—makes them vulnerable to the mental enslavement of our old enemy. I share this belief—which is very much a working theory—to emphasize my call for unity. Put simply, we need everyone rowing in the same direction.

"My administration will make regular reports to you. Like this speech, they will be unvarnished. Obviously, my fellow humans, we don't want to cause panic. What we *do* want is for you—each of you and your loved ones—to understand the dire nature of our situation as a species. Every choice you make from this day forward is really leading to only one choice: to survive or to perish."

Bragg ran another hand through his hair. He was deciding,

again, what to say next. Something you didn't do when you had speechwriters. Especially ones as good as Leo.

"I warned us all of this moment," Bragg said. "During my campaign, you'll recall."

Eva closed her eyes. She knew what was coming.

"I said that aliens couldn't be trusted. And here we are, facing not one but two alien species bent on our destruction."

"What?" Sayyida said. "The Arcœnum helped at Alpha-C!"

Sheba's brows knit together as she put her elbows on the conference table.

"Some see the Arcœnum as allies now," Bragg said. He clasped his hands together on the desk in front of him and stared directly into the camera, as if addressing Sayyida al-Hurra personally. "I would say they are 'the enemy of my enemy' and nothing more. A convenience of circumstance, perhaps. We'll fight alongside them until the Skane are *eradicated*. But we can't afford to trust them."

The old campaign fire. The blatant, dog-whistling appeal to xenophobia regarding the Arcœnum. Was that really what they needed to do to survive? Eva wondered. And if it was, would survival be worth it?

"Back then, I had my detractors. Bleeding hearts who insisted my ideas were a form of speciesism. And yet, here we are. You might even say I saw the future." A look of earnest determination settled onto Bragg's face. "I was right then, and I'm right now. But, my fellow humans, *together*—together we can pave the way forward to greatness for our children. Thank you for your attention. Good night, and God bless the Sol Alliance. And God bless all humanity, everywhere."

The Seal of the President of the Sol Alliance now occupied the screen. In the C&C next door, oo-rahs erupted. The duty officer caught Sheba Toma's gaze and, seeing her reproval, calmed his command staff. Sayyida sighed.

"What the hell was that?" Joe Gauss wondered.

"A president," Eva said, "going off script."

"I thought it was a pretty effective speech," Toma said. "Especially if you voted for him."

"I don't disagree." Eva tapped her index finger on the conference table. "First, the loss of Canis III; then, we almost lose Sylvan Novus. President Bragg is in damage control mode. That speech, the parts I recognized by Leo Byrne? An administration's attempt at leveling with the people. That 'we don't have time for business as usual' stuff was pure Leo. The unscripted parts? Classic Piers Bragg: 'I was right all along. If only you'd listened to me. Best listen to me now...'"

"That's a pretty cynical interpretation in desperate times," Toma suggested.

Eva shrugged. "I know him. And I know Leo. I'm telling you, Sam Devos is already fielding angry calls on subspace from congressional leaders."

"At least he acknowledged the new threat," Gauss said. He rose from his chair. "I should call my people. Who knows what kind of reactions we'll get? Colonel, I'd suggest you do the same. Let's at least make an effort to endorse the president's larger message of all working together."

"Agreed," Toma said, pushing away from the table. "I'll start with the C&C."

"Eva," Sayyida said, "I'd be grateful if you'd stay for a few minutes. We should start drafting my official reaction to share with the colony. Provide some direction for how we'll do our part."

"Of course," Eva said. "That would certainly stand us in good stead with the administration when we approach them about reconciliation. We can even cite the president's call to action as having inspired the idea."

Sayyida raised an eyebrow as Gauss and Toma left the conference room. Once the door had slid shut behind them, she said slyly, "Take advantage of thc situation? I do believe you'd make a good pirate, Eva."

Eva returned her amused expression. It was good to see Sayyida loosen up a bit after the past week. "Well, Commander al-Hurra," she said, "I'm afraid that, being in politics, my moral compass is a bit too broken for me to be a good pirate."

"Lucky for me," Sayyida said. "Now, what should I say to my people?"

"First lesson," Eva said, "is stay the hell on script."

19
SOMETHING BETTER

THE CROWD SHUFFLED around the main dock of New Nassau, as though every person claimed Richard Brown as family. A sister or brother. An aunt or uncle, maybe. A mother or father.

After Hadrian al-Hurra's funeral, the political distinctions between his followers and his daughter's seemed to melt away again into the soup of shared community. The aftermath of the sentencing, Eva thought, was the next test of those tenuous new bonds. Beside her, Bathsheba Toma seemed more uneasy than she'd been since the siege of the Havens. It had fallen largely to her Marines to defuse any tensions during the trial. There had only been a few drunken dust-ups, the offenders handed over to Joe Gauss and his deputies, in most cases to merely sleep it off.

Would the people accept the boy's sentencing? Eva wondered. Would they grab the better future now within their reach and rejoin the human community at large?

"Nine years is a long time," she said aloud. In Eva's present frame of mind, that translated to: *Most people can't see past tomorrow.*

"Some will say not long enough," Toma observed.

On Eva's right, Sayyida al-Hurra sighed. "If I can accept it, others can. Others must."

"Emotions are rarely simple," Eva said.

"No," Sayyida agreed, "but acting on them is a choice."

Motion dockside caught Eva's eye. One person embracing another. A brother and sister? Or a father and mother, maybe. Halfway across the carved-out cavern, two women shared a hug of their own. One of them holding an infant might have been Althea Murray.

"Thank you," Sayyida said, turning to Eva with a soulful look. "Your work on the arbitration board... Without your calming influence, this colony would be in a very different place today. Maybe even embroiled in a civil war."

"I..." Eva wasn't sure what to say. As a practical matter, Sayyida was likely right. There were times—discussions that became shouting matches—when Eva thought the boy's trial would strike that match. But somehow the two sides had stepped away from the finger-pointing, other-side-is-evil brink that hallmarked a society on the precipice of self-immolation. She'd helped them to discover self-interest in empathizing with one another, to turn aside from the self-centered prejudice that thwarted cooperation. All that running from crisis to crisis to clean up Piers Bragg's messes had finally paid off. Sayyida's gratitude made Eva uncomfortable, but it required acknowledgment, nonetheless. "I was happy to serve, ma'am."

"We'll be back here again," Toma said. She was still in overwatch mode, observing the milling crowd below, awaiting a flashpoint.

"What do you mean?" Eva asked.

"The sentence," Toma said, as if that made her meaning self-evident. "Taking the death penalty off the table was understandable. I suppose." Her tone made it clear she was unconvinced of that decision's wisdom. "But when the boy turns twenty-five and the tribunal reassembles to decide whether to keep him incarcerated for life or...?"

Toma left it hanging. What if that future tribunal decided to release Richard Brown? What would be the public's response? Eva wondered if she had really helped New Nassau avoid a civil war, or merely delay one.

"Questions for tomorrow," Sayyida said. The docks were beginning to depopulate. "Today, we have peace. And a chance for something better."

"As a Marine, I'm not in favor of kicking the can down the road. Usually results in a waste of resources and, sometimes, lives. And as far as efficiency goes, it's about as—"

"Not everything is a balance of weights and measures," Sayyida said forcefully. She wasn't angry, Eva thought, but lacked the patience in this moment for Sheba's doomsaying. "Not everything is about solving an equation. Where people are concerned, sometimes the best you can do is the best you can do."

Respectfully, Toma acknowledged the point. "I understand, ma'am."

She'd been distracted by their conversation, so Eva hadn't noticed, at first, the opening up of space below. Here and there, citizens had begun to drift away, walking together, from the periphery to their homes or duties or wherever their joint paths took them. The body language of those who remained sent relief flooding through her. And with it, a kernel of hope formed. Maybe, just maybe, New Nassau was finally beginning to heal.

"There they are," came an ambling voice from behind. All three turned to face a gruff but amiable-looking Joe Gauss approaching. "The Triumvirate."

Toma snorted and returned to overwatch duty.

"What?" Sayyida said. "What's that one supposed to mean?"

Lately whenever he found the three of them together, Gauss had taken to naming them something that highlighted their unity of leadership. The Triad. The Three Fates. The Furies, when their shared mood proved fiery. The Threesome, which had especially irked Toma for some reason. Eva's personal favorite was Macbeth's Three Witches of Prophecy, which sounded darkly romantic to her, like the name of a cursed ship doomed to forever sail the stars. And now, the Triumvirate.

"Colonel Toma gets it," Gauss said, joining them. His eyes tracked downward to the crowd. *Like Sheba*, Eva thought, *always on duty*.

Sayyida looked to the colonel for the explanation.

"He's referring to the Roman trio of rulers," she said, her lips twisting. "There were two trios, actually."

"Rome?" Sayyida said. "We're Roman, now?"

"Well," Gauss said, mischief in his voice, "pirates *do* travel a lot."

A collective *ugh* issued from the women. Old men and their puns. There were some constancies in the universe one could do without, Eva thought. Cockroaches, hangovers, and old men's puns. *Get on that, God, would you?*

"And, on that note," she said, "I have a call to make."

Sayyida regarded her. "Do you really think there's a chance?" There was little of the decisive commander in her voice. More, the trepidatious little girl, unsure of what to do next.

"After Alpha Centauri?" Eva said. "I think there's more than a chance."

"If anyone can make reconciliation happen," Gauss said, gesturing at the docks, which were nearly empty now, "it's you, Eva."

She smiled her thanks. "Wish me luck anyway."

Ever the pragmatist, Toma grunted, "Good luck."

In a time of war, official communiqués are scheduled down to the micro-second. It's not just a matter of efficiency, which is always an issue when military protocols are involved, but also of security. Multiple levels of encryption and backup monitoring are required, which translates to using military assets to ensure secrecy and avoid inadvertently betraying intelligence to the enemy.

The net effect of all that precision was that Eva arrived in al-Hurra's conference room a few minutes before her scheduled call to Sam Devos at the Citadel. So she caught up on the news-feeds, a habit she'd neglected amid the drama of Richard Brown's trial and the seemingly constant meetings with Sheba and Sayyida surrounding it.

Despite administration news releases attempting to minimize their impact, the images flooding subspace showed the true devastation of Alpha Centauri. *The price for living in a free society*, Eva thought. Several major cities in smoking ruins. Tens of thousands of Centaurians dead or injured. The Alliance military presence, what was left of it, still engaged in supporting civilian efforts to deal with the devastation. Soon, those would transition from rescuing survivors to recovering corpses. It was a horrible reality that every image of faces streaked with tears, every wailing mother grieving a dead child who was shown, only seemed to put a fresh face on a deepening pain that transcended the vast, interstellar distance between its source and Eva Park. She thought again of Althea Murray and little Eva and was grateful they were here in New Nassau, even with all its problems, and not on Sylvan Novus.

One shining light in the darkness of that tragedy was Miranda Marcos. No sooner had she arrived on-planet than she seemed to be everywhere. Not digging out bodies, maybe, but doing what she did best: speaking to the cams, pleading for more resources, imploring the Bragg Administration to "lend all aid and assistance to the people of Sylvan Novus, your progeny, your pioneers—and the best hope for humanity's future." Miranda's empathy for those suffering citizens on Sylvan Novus was evident to anyone with the eyes to see it, and a clear contrast to the *me-me-me* chest-beating of Piers Bragg's disastrous speech. Bragg had tried to score points with the public by sending her to Sylvan Novus, but Eva wondered if he might come to regret that decision in the next election cycle. And then, that oily, slick feeling crept across her skin again, her conscience lecturing her for letting such mercenary thoughts intrude on a moment of human suffering.

The comm chimed. Eva glanced into the neighboring C&C to find one of Toma's officers waving. Eva nodded to the major, then turned her back on him. She wanted that official activity in her background. She wanted Sam Devos to see it.

"Eva," Devos said in greeting. "Good to see you again."

Eva felt conflicted at seeing his face. There was camaraderie, sure, forged in the shared stress of dealing with Piers Bragg on a daily basis. But it was tinged now with resentment. Had been for a long time. It had the oppressive, sweaty smell of the Boys Club about it.

"Hi Sam," she said.

"Seen the latest news?"

"About Marcos? I was just—"

"Not about Marcos."

The president's chief of staff sounded tired. Looked it, too. The dark circles under his eyes, the sagging skin of his jawline, which had once seemed cut with a straight-edged razor. More tired even than Leo had looked when last they'd spoken.

"I guess not, then," she said cautiously.

"The media has the freighter story."

Eva blinked. "Okay." It sounded like a non sequitur. There was a time, before her journey aboard *L'Esprit de la Terre*, when they'd feared the story breaking about the captured freighters and their lonsdaleite cargo. What had bothered Eva most then—because of its blatant illegality—was the use of military assets to escort the president's corporate freighters under the thin guise of carrying classified materiel, the lonsdaleite. But then, the freighters had been recovered from the pirates and delivered to Mars, where their precious cargo was even now being fashioned into the hull of the greatest warship the Alliance had ever launched from an orbital drydock.

She said, "I don't understand—"

"They're following the money."

"Sam, quit being cryptic. I've had a long month. What are you—"

"'TREASURE FLEET PROFITS PAID FOR WITH PUBLIC FUNDS.' Today's trolling teaser. Part of a series of exposés currently exploding over subspace. Its only real competition for public eyeballs is what happened in Alpha Centauri."

"Jesus, Sam. Is that, literally, what the teaser says?"

"It is."

The fact that the report referred to the freighters as a "Treasure Fleet" was a telltale sign. Very few people inside the administration had ever heard the flotilla called that. Eva Park was one of them.

"You've got a leak somewhere, Sam."

"Bullshit. We've got a fucking gaping hole in the side of the ship of state." He pushed a claw-like hand through his hair in very much the same manner Bragg would have. "You *did* see the speech?"

"Yeah."

"You won't believe the phone calls I've received from the Joint Congress. And the public polling? The two system parliaments are carving out funds to build the guillotine. Seems their biggest challenge is, How do you cut Piers Bragg's head off twice?" Sam closed his eyes a moment, calmed himself. "I'm speaking metaphorically, of course. But I didn't call to unload on you. I know you're dealing with a lot there." His patronizing tone made Eva want to reach across the hundreds of lightyears separating them and yank him forward by his skinny necktie.

Game face, girl. Let Daddy think he's in charge. We know better.

Eva said, "Actually, I'm glad you told me. I think I might know of something that'll help."

Devos's gaze of fatigue became keenly attentive. "Yeah? I'm all ears."

"It's something I haven't mentioned before, but I think the president can really benefit from giving it serious consideration."

"Now who's being cryptic? Spit it out, Eva. I'm busy as hell trying to manage—"

"The pirates of New Nassau want to come home."

"—little patience for..." Devos's brain caught up with his ears. "Say again?"

"Some forty thousand citizens of New Nassau and her satellite communities seek reconciliation with the greater Alliance. They want to come home, Sam."

"'Citizens?'" Devos's voice was far past dubious. "They're murdering bandits! These are the same people who ransom Alliance *citizens* for credits, Eva. There's a reason we deal with them militarily—"

"They're mothers and daughters, fathers and sons. And they want to come home, Sam."

"I don't give a good goddamn what they want. Are you serious? Do you have any idea what the interplanetary business sector would say if they knew we'd even discussed this? Our reelection coffers would dry up! Jesus, Eva, I thought you were smarter than—"

"If you'd shut up a minute, Sam, you might be able to save Bragg's ass."

Oh. Oops. She'd used her out-loud voice, there. The shocked expression on Sam Devos's face proved it. So much for leaning into Daddy's need to be dominant.

But Devos, made desperate by circumstance, placed his hands quite deliberately on the desk in front of him.

"I'm listening."

Now was the time to press for everything. Negotiation couldn't start from the middle ground if she hoped to secure for Sayyida and her people the future they wanted.

"In exchange for the administration's recognition of New Nassau and its satellites as an independent republic, in perpetuity, Sayyida al-Hurra will guarantee free passage through the Triangle for all Alliance-affiliated vessels, private or military, without fear of attack. In addition, she'll pledge New Nassau's military assets to helping stop the Skane. All they ask in return—after the war, of course—is for New Nassau citizens to have the freedom to settle wherever they wish in the Alliance, like anyone else. Blanket amnesty for past offenses, right up to the date the reconciliation treaty is signed."

Sam Devos stared blankly at her, as though there were a delay in the subspace feed. After a moment of his Adam's apple bobbing up and down, he said, "Is that all?"

"Let's start there," Eva said, trying hard not to make it sound smug. That wouldn't do, not at all. Sam Devos didn't react well to being overtly coerced. Covertly was bad enough.

"No," he said. "Not in a million years."

She let him have the victory because she was sure it was only momentary. In the final analysis, Bragg couldn't *afford* to say no. If the loss of Fort Leyte in Sirius and the humanitarian disaster in Alpha Centauri hadn't been enough to ensure that, this media scandal involving the freighters in the middle of a losing war that threatened to extinguish the species would surely do so.

Somehow, right now, she didn't feel the least bit oily.

"Is that Sam Devos or the president's chief of staff talking?" Eva pressed.

His gaze tightened. "Who are you, Eva? What happened to the team player who—"

"She's sitting right here. Think about *this* headline, Sam. BRAGG BRINGS HUMANITY'S PRODIGAL CHILDREN HOME IN OUR MOST DESPERATE HOUR. Think of the optics. Imagine how a handshake between the president and Sayyida al-Hurra would play. It'll knock the current scandal right off the teaser track. Pair this with Marcos's work on Sylvan Novus, and the narrative becomes, 'Piers Bragg is no warmongering president, no matter what his detractors say. This is a president who cares about people.'"

However much bullshit that might actually be.

As Eva had ticked off the political benefits one by one, Devos became pensive. He was calculating the upside for himself. When he opened his mouth again, it felt like another, perhaps milder form of "no" was coming. So, Eva spoke first.

"Let's open backchannel talks. We can make this happen, and fast track it. Everyone can win here."

There. Peace with honor. No actual agreement. Just agreement to talk about the possibility of agreeing down the line.

Devos's shoulders drew back, but his tone was conciliatory. "The president will never go for it. And everyone *never* wins, Eva. You know that."

"What I know is, everyone is about to lose. *Everything*. It's time to think outside the box, Sam. The president's a businessman. He'll get that."

Eyes shifting in consideration, Devos took a breath. Then, another. "I'll take it to him."

"That's all I'm asking, Sam."

"No, it's not. Not by a longshot."

He moved to cut the feed, but she preempted him.

"And Sam," she said. He hesitated, his expression full of impotent resentment. "Sorry about the 'shut up' thing before." She wasn't sorry at all, but it was important that he believe she was. The power balance needed to be restored, if nowhere else but in Sam's mind.

He nodded curtly. "It's a tough time for everyone. Don't give it a second thought."

And after the feed faded, she didn't. But Eva Park did smile broadly. Then she made herself a tall, stiff drink and sipped it in the luxurious quiet of her private quarters.

20
INTERVENTION

A SMALL STORAGE hold now served as the *Junkyard Dog*'s modest sickbay. Minimally suited to that role, it was close and uncomfortable if you were conscious. A far cry, Alice reflected, from the advanced medical facility they were headed to on Tarsus Research Station.

Cinnamon Gauss lay in the sole medbed, a converted crew bunk. They'd outfitted it with Cinnamon's personal mattress from her quarters, thinking its familiarity with her body shape would make her more comfortable. When they discovered the Kick hidden inside, Torque had exploded with anger. Alice wasn't sure whom she was madder at—Cinnamon for using, herself for missing the signs of it, or Alice for finding the stash and, thereby, making Torque aware of Cinnamon's inconvenient truth.

But that had been hours ago, and Torque's fury had guttered out. Now, like Alice, she stood vigil over Cinnamon's sickbed, the two of them alone with their silent fears.

"We used it on Ionia," Torque muttered. She whispered it, as though speaking might somehow interrupt Cinnamon's healing process.

Alice flicked her eyes up, gauging the big woman's mood. "What?"

Torque took Cinnamon's hand in her own. Alice thought it caring, at first, but then Torque lifted it and spread the fingers apart so Alice could see. Stick marks in the webbing of skin between the index and second fingers of Cinnamon's right hand. Even Alice knew them as the sign of drug addiction. Torque then held up her own hand, flattened it and spread her fingers. Alice saw similar prick marks, but almost invisible, almost healed.

"Sometimes, it was hard to wind down off, to rest, after what we had to do for Blackmore," Torque said. "We used the Kick to ... to stop feeling anything about it." Then, defensively, as if she'd just admitted more than she'd intended: "We both used it as a last resort. An absolute last resort."

There was a pang in Alice's left palm. Real or imagined, she wasn't sure. Or that it mattered. "I understand."

Abruptly, Torque said, "I want to go back there."

Alice was confused. "What, where?"

"Ionia. Smash Bello over the head like he did Cinn. But he won't have to worry about bleeding to death inside his skull. I'll just wake him up and shoot him."

Ah, Alice thought. That answered Torque's question before about how Cinnamon had come to be injured in the first place. And she'd been suffering this whole time, ever since they left Ionia?

"I just wished she would've come to me!" Torque said, her voice cracking. "If she was hurt and needed that stuff..."

Alice knew several reasons why Cinnamon hadn't. There was the tension between them, whatever that was about. She could point out Cinnamon's independent streak, which Torque knew all too well. Or maybe Cinnamon hadn't wanted to show weakness, out of some misguided notion of being ship's captain and, therefore, supposedly invulnerable.

You noble idiot, Alice thought. "Remember what Ben said. You researched it yourself."

Torque glanced up at her, not understanding.

"The hematoma. How it can influence mood, judgment. I mean, what she said to me about Sylvan Novus ... that wasn't Cinnamon, not really."

"She didn't mean that, you know," Torque said. "She never would have said something so crass had she been in her right mind."

"My point exactly."

Torque offered her a slight but grateful smile.

"I just wish we could do more for her," Alice said. "I'm afraid—I'm afraid we're not gonna reach Tarsus in time."

"We need a real fucking sickbay on the *Dog*." It'd almost become a kind of mantra for Torque these last few hours. "But your idea was a good one. Gal will get us there."

Alice nodded. Several of Desi's components were wired in with the *Junkyard Dog*'s diagnostic equipment, which had been pilfered and patched together from a dozen different salvage jobs. She'd half-convinced herself that such a jury-rigged system couldn't possibly provide valid or reliable readings. That what they showed was likely inaccurate and misleading. But Desi's state-of-the-art biosensors—though designed for battlefield triage, not clinical treatment—appeared to be in perfect working order. And all the wishing in the world couldn't explain away the prognosis.

Cinnamon was dying. Her status slowly worsening in downward trending, single-digit increments. The only cure was to relieve the increasing pressure caused by the clotting blood filling the space between Cinnamon's brain and skull and, of course, to stop the bleeding itself. Drugs could only alleviate the symptoms. It was Gal who suggested that's what Cinnamon had been doing with the Kick, an opinion that had finally popped the balloon of Torque's anger.

Around them, the ship shuddered, hard enough that Alice grabbed the edge of the medbed for balance. The hull hummed, resonant in its resistance against whatever Gal was flying them through. The humming faded into the familiar drone of forward thrust.

Torque's eyes rolled upward toward the ceiling. "Likely just turbulence."

"How likely?" Alice wondered.

Torque shrugged. "The quickest route to Strigoth isn't the smoothest."

Alice didn't doubt that. But her old guilt had returned with the knowledge that being assaulted on Ionia while trying to hide her is what had put Cinnamon's life in jeopardy. She'd put all of them in jeopardy by simply being here.

"None of this would have happened if it weren't for me," she said.

"Don't start that crap again," Torque said, then held up a hand. "I didn't mean that to sound so harsh. It's just that ... I've told you before, Alice. We've all made our own decisions to be here. Cinnamon, too. For you to keep harping on that ... it's cruel, in its own way. Understand?"

She didn't really, but Alice accepted what Torque had said at face value. It's the only way Torque ever said anything. It's how you knew it was true.

"I'm sorry," she said. "I won't say it again."

"Good."

They settled back into silence. But still, the old guilt lurked in Alice.

"Maybe I can help her."

Torque gave her a wary look. "What do you mean?"

Alice had no idea what she meant, not really. She had a power she didn't understand, an ability that made no sense to anyone other than Andre Korsakov. But she could make things move. Manipulate them. Change their shape even, like the bent fork in the Bell Jar. But she'd never used her power on a person before. Not to heal, anyway. The image of Korsakov, his spine pressed painfully concave against the Jar's ceiling, popped into her head. Alice chased it away. The one time she'd been asked to use her power for healing—beneath Drake's World, as Ben's friend Bricker lay dying? Only one thought had come to mind then.

Everyone dies.

Which would be true for Cinnamon too, one day. But maybe that didn't have to be today.

"Oh, no," Torque said, reading Alice's intent. "No, no, *no*. That's *way* too dangerous, Alice."

Alice inhaled sharply. "On Drake's World, I might have helped a man. He died, Torque. And I didn't even *try*. But I tell myself when I think about that—I didn't know what I could do, then."

"Do you know you can do this now?"

"No," Alice replied. "I don't."

She suddenly felt a tall presence behind her in the claustrophobic space—Light Without Shadow, hunched and glowing with that eerie, silver translucence of his species.

"Louie?" Torque said.

He didn't try to enter the hold. Instead, he projected the trade window Alice had seen once before, when he'd revealed the Skane fleet chasing the Arcœnum across Alliance space.

In the window, a small human child stood beside a roughly flowing river. She struggled to lift a heavy stone. A second being, an Arcœnum, appeared beside her. He bent down, lending first one, then another, then all four of his clawed hands to the task. Together, the girl and the Arcœnum lifted the stone. The English translation appeared below the image.

LET ME HELP.

They stared at the screen, which played its message over again. Then a new image appeared, showing Alice and Torque in the sickbay and Louie waking in the central compartment. He was explaining how he'd come to be there.

LOUD THOUGHTS.

The image changed again, became Cinnamon laughing. Smiling. Being Cinnamon. Or who Cinnamon used to be.

FRIEND.

"How?" Torque whispered to Alice. "You said you don't even know how you'd—"

"On Tarsus, I learned to plug into things," Alice said. She formulated the words as she spoke, but it was more like remembering and reporting. Following breadcrumbs of knowledge to an explanation. "I visualized connection and I just ... I see something the way I want to see it, and then it just *is*. Forks bend. Chairs levitate." She left out the part about attacking Korsakov.

"Forks?" Torque said. "Chairs? Alice, we're talking about rooting around inside Cinnamon's head!"

Light Without Shadow projected the image of the girl beside the river again, along with her multi-armed companion. Together, they lifted the stone.

LET ME HELP.

"But how?" Torque said to him.

A machete appeared on the screen between them, its blade long, thick, and meant for unsubtle hacking work. But then it shrank, became a medical scalpel.

FOCUS. CONTROL.

"You can help guide me?" Alice asked.

Light Without Shadow effected what approximated a human bow.

But Torque only shook her head. "It's too risky—"

"We might not make it in time," Alice said. She was firm. Determined. Confident that, with Louie's help, she could save her friend. His friend too, she knew now. "Let me do this, big sister."

Torque gave her a look. Half hopeful. Half resentful that Alice was asking for her blessing.

Alice said, "I have to try."

The *Dog* shook again. The motion rocked Cinnamon in her bed, in spite of the straps holding her down.

"Sorry guys," Gal's voice came over shipwide. *"Slowed us down a bit, but we're through it now."*

Torque reached out and took Alice's thin forearm in her firm grip. "Fine. Just ... be careful, yeah?"

Alice nodded and turned to her friend's slight, sleeping form. Above Cinnamon, a monitor displayed her vital signs. Another showed a scan of Cinnamon's skull with a dark region Desi identified as the hematoma sitting on her brain. Alice located that region of Cinnamon's skull and rested her hand on it.

"You've helped me so much. Now, it's my turn." She looked at Torque. "It's less distracting when I close my eyes. Can you tell me what Louie is saying?"

"Yeah."

After one last look at the hematoma on the monitor, Alice closed her eyes. She fixed the oblong image in her mind's eye. It was vaguely egg-shaped, and Alice imagined she could feel it as pressure inside her friend's head. She rested her hand on Cinnamon's stubbly skull over the location of the cloudlike clot. She gave form to her ability in her imagination, stretching out with her own life heat as a balm of loving intent. She shaped its purpose to pass healing from her own body into Cinnamon's.

"He's starting," Torque said.

Alice felt Light Without Shadow enter her mind. Another presence, but not intrusive. A second consciousness, but not invasive. A friend come to visit. A teacher come to guide.

"I can feel him."

"Is it... weird?" Torque asked.

"No," Alice said. "No, it's soothing, actually. It feels almost like I'm floating in my own head."

She was the little girl by the river. But instead of a stone, it was Cinnamon lying on the ground beside her. Little Girl Alice stroked her head. Behind her, Louie kneeled and took Alice's head in two of his hands, her shoulders in the other two.

Everything changed.

Her mind expanded.

Alice gasped.

It was like the breakthrough she'd had in the Bell Jar, before Korsakov saddled her with the shroud. And then she was inside Cinnamon's head. As though Alice had stepped into a museum of the mind that smelled like Cinnamon. Felt like her. *Was* her. There were vast rooms and tiny alcoves and artifacts and images from a thousand different moments in Cinnamon's life. Alice passed by rooms, glimpsing scenes like a friendly voyeur, curious but respectful. Cinnamon's grandfather, Joe Gauss, smiling at the dinner table with Cinnamon, a dour-faced teenager, before the orange spikes. Through another open doorway: Torque and the rest of the crew of the *Junkyard Dog*, younger, carousing in a bar that might have been the Swashbuckler's Leap. Another room, and for a moment, Alice thought something had gone wrong because she was back aboard the *Archimedes*. But not seeing things from her own perspective; rather, seeing herself for the first time through Cinnamon's eyes. Seeing the startled, fearful Alice Keller who'd just fled Strigothian space. Cinnamon's memory from when she'd boarded the yacht to retrieve Alice and provide her safe passage home to Alpha Centauri.

"He says this is all surface memory," Torque said. "He says he needs to go deeper."

Alice swallowed and stared down a suddenly extensive, very dark hallway. "Okay."

She stood on top of a rocky hill. There was no river now. No Louie. Only a starlit sky shining inside a faint, violet hue. Drake's World.

"He's using elements from your own memory. He says it should make it easier."

Her eyes shut, Alice nodded. She wasn't sure that was true, using the Terror Planet to help Cinnamon. But she'd committed to this, and Louie would know best, wouldn't he?

"Get ready, he says."

A large cloud appeared in the distance. It began to move toward her high on the hill, or she'd begun to rush toward it. Distinctions like that didn't seem to matter much in this twilight realm between conscious reality and unconscious memory. On Drake's World, the clouds had been white, catching and focusing the royal shading in the atmosphere. This cloud was dark, its color unfamiliar to the planet's palette, but its shape Alice recognized—like an ovular, black egg. The cloud now hovered directly overhead, blotting out the sky. It was all Alice could see.

"Start in the center, he says," Torque said. "See *through* to the stars beyond. Whatever that means."

Alice began by imagining a pinhole of starlight in the center of the darkness. And that grew to become a fingertip of shining silver. She concentrated harder, and the fingertip became a fist. Inside it, Alice fancied she could see a glimmer of the first of the three sister moons rising over Drake's World. The hole was big enough now that she could see the curve of that moon, and then the stars twinkling around its corona.

"Holy crap," Torque gasped. "I think you're doing it."

Alice raised her hands. Like she'd done in the Bell Jar. Like she'd done in the dungeon beneath Drake's World to protect herself and Ben from the avalanche that had crushed his friend. She was determined that no friends would die here today.

"I really think you're doing it!"

The hole expanded, burning off the inner edges of the blackness surrounding it, the opening blooming wider than the width of her outstretched arms. Its rate of expansion doubled, tripled, quintupled. Wider, faster it opened, beyond the base of the hill on which she stood. And before Alice realized it, the cloud had dissipated, leaving only the purple haze of the clear sky over Drake's World. She stood alone on the hilltop again, the sister moons ascending, competing with the silver light of a thousand stars.

In an instant, it all disappeared. Alice cried out at the sudden absence of beauty around her. And reeled at how she, of all people, could have come to think of Drake's World as something beautiful again.

But she was back on the smaller, green hill now of Louie's projection, the rushing river having calmed to a slow-flowing stream. Cinnamon lay on the ground beside her, breathing shallow but strong. Light Without Shadow released his hold on Alice and backed away.

Alice opened her eyes. What she saw in that dingy, cramped space of the makeshift medical room was more astonishing than all she'd just experienced.

Torque, her eyes shining with tears and smiling. She nodded to the second monitor. "You did it." Her voice held no trace of fear now. Only wonder and gratitude.

The scan of Cinnamon's head was empty where the clotted

cloud had hung before. Only fringes of it remained, still black but a mere shadowy halo of its former self. The bulk of the clot was gone.

A bucket appeared in the trade window. From a hole in the bottom of the bucket, a finger's width of water trickled.

NOT CURED.

The immediate danger was past, but the problem remained. Cinnamon was still leaking blood into her brainpan.

"Can we go back in?" Alice asked. "Can we—"

The scalpel reappeared in Louie's window, then bloated into the machete.

TOO DELICATE.

"It's okay," Torque said. "You've done enough. You both have. Now, we just need to get her to Strigoth."

Though disappointed she couldn't do more, Alice turned to Louie. "Thank you," she said. "Thank you so—"

Then she couldn't speak. Couldn't breathe, Torque was hugging her so fiercely. "You did it, little sister! You did it."

And Alice didn't mind. Either the stifling hug or the nickname she'd come to resent. Both felt like home to her. Home, with family. Loved.

The ship's alarm blared.

"Hold on down there, everyone," Ben Stone announced. *"We've got company."*

21
CAT AND MOUSE

THE ACKNOWLEDGMENT from Torque at Cinnamon's bedside sounded strangely upbeat. But focused as he was on the ship's hazy tactical readings, Ben had little time to notice.

"Engines off," Gal announced. "Switching to batteries."

The old trick, played again. Tucked inside the cavernous mouth of a semi-hollow asteroid, most conventional sensors can't find you. The thick, iron-nickel skin protected the ship from sensors in exactly the same way regolith rock had protected the first astronauts on Earth's moon from life-threatening radiation during solar storms. Powering down the TLD's reactor and relying on batteries to run the ship reduced to almost nil the likelihood enemy sensors could detect the *Dog* inside the cavern. The ionized gas and dust of the Triangle, particularly thick in this region, nearly guaranteed it.

"Any indication they saw us before we bolted?" Gal asked.

"With all the interference in this damned nebula, there's no way to know," Ben said.

"Come on, Adonis," Gal said, "make me feel better."

He really wished she'd stop calling him that.

"I really wish you'd stop calling me that."

"Mmm. You know, I believe in wishing for what you want."

Ben grimaced. "What the hell does that mean?"

"I figure if I call you Adonis long enough, maybe you'll reward me."

"Maybe I'll...?" Ben's ears grew hot. "Do you ever think of *anything* else?"

"Says the *man*," Gal snorted. Then, more thoughtfully: "You mean, like, different positions?"

The sound of heavy boots stomping forward from aft came as a relief.

"Sit-rep?" Torque requested, entering the cockpit.

"There's a ship out there," Ben said. "Profile pinged scout sized. Skane, maybe."

Torque stepped down to the co-pilot's chair. "Maybe?"

"Hard to tell at that distance. Sensors—"

"Yeah, I know. Unreliable in the Triangle." Torque tried to fit herself into a seat better shaped to Cinnamon Gauss's less-sizable butt.

"How's Cinnamon?" Gal asked.

"Better, actually."

"Better?" Ben regarded Torque over his shoulder and felt the crick in his neck already starting. Whoever designed this cruelly austere cockpit obviously couldn't have cared less about crew comfort. "How so?"

"Alice intervened. Louie helped."

"Louie—he's awake?" Ben asked. Part of him wanted to pull his sidearm and rush to Cinnamon's sickbed. "Alice is still there with the Archie now? Alone?"

"It's fine," Torque sighed.

"Alice intervened?" Gal said. "How?"

"Later. We have more pressing matters." Torque gazed out the window at their rocky hiding place. "We can't just sit here forever. Cinnamon needs a real hospital with real doctors."

Ben watched his tactical screen. The Skane ship, if that's what it was, could be anywhere out there. He popped his harness and crouched his way forward to the pilot well.

"Hi, stud," Gal said.

Ignoring her, Ben stared at the dusty, magenta fog outside. Outside the asteroid, only a handful of the brightest stars were visible. The natural rock formations helping to hide the ship looked like jagged teeth.

His display pinged behind him. Ben turned just in time to catch a blip before it winked out. Every now and then, their scout-sized friend reappeared on sensors, only to pop out again just as quickly. It gave them an inconstant but better-than-nothing sounding of the other's location relative to their own.

"That ship is getting closer," Gal said.

"They can't see us in here," Ben assured her. "No way."

Torque grunted her lack of belief in that statement. She keyed the engineering channel.

"Moze, how long can we stay on batteries only?"

There was a crackle from the other end of the connection. *"A full day, maybe a little longer. We can prioritize systems if we need to. Make that longer."*

Torque nodded. "Thanks. Since it's offline anyway, use the time to make sure the TLD is a hundred percent, yeah?"

"Never been a hundred percent. You know that. But I'll run some diagnostics. Engineering out."

"A day or longer if we turn out the lights? We can't wait that long," Gal said. "Unless Alice can *cure* Cinnamon—"

"Last resort only," Torque said, her tone negative. "Not sure if it'd be cure or kill."

"Fine, then, what?" Ben said.

The cockpit grew quiet.

Ping.

And then it was gone again.

But the blip had appeared closer than the last time.

"For now, we wait," Torque said. "Alice and Desi can monitor Cinn. We'll see where things stand in an hour."

No one said anything in response. Even Ben had to acknowledge it was the best bad option they had.

"I don't know how, but they can see us," Torque insisted.

"You don't know that for sure," Ben shot back. But he understood her conclusion.

The ping had continued its cat-and-mouse game with the *Dog*'s sensors. Maybe it was one ship popping up, Ben thought. Maybe it was ten different ships, each appearing only briefly, obscured by the Triangle's ionized interference. But each time it showed up again, the ship—or ships—drew closer. Torque's hour deadline had passed two hours earlier.

"It's a recon pattern," Ben said. "Not a beeline."

"A recon pattern that's homing in on this asteroid."

"There's no way they can know we're here!"

"No way they could know we're here based on *our* understanding of their command of technology."

"What—"

"Think about it, Stone," Torque said. "If the roles were reversed, you'd be right. Our sensors would be useless, especially with our quarry's engines off. But if it *is* the Skane... We have no idea what their tech is capable of. You saw how they ate Fleet's lunch in Alpha-C."

"Guys!" Gal exclaimed, as though corralling two unruly children. "You're focusing on the wrong thing in your little debate."

Her quarreling shipmates looked at her expectantly.

Ben said, "What do you mean?"

"Every minute we stay here is a minute Cinnamon can't afford," Gal said. "Alice bought her some time, but—at some point, we're gonna have to make a run for it."

"And I say sooner rather than later," Torque agreed.

Ben's screen remained clear. He knew they were right. Eventually, they'd have to chance it.

There was a plinking behind them, almost like the tinkling of a glass windchime in a light breeze. Ben turned and found Light Without Shadow worming his lithe but lengthy shape through the hatchway. He resisted the urge to put his hand on his sidearm.

Torque had heard the Archie's approach too. "Louie? Everything okay down there?"

Ben watched the screen appear that he'd seen once before. It projected an image of Cinnamon, strapped into her medbed, apparently asleep. Alice sat beside her, holding her hand.

SHE RESTS, read the caption below the image.

The screen wiped, then presented an exterior of the *Junkyard Dog* in the mouth of the asteroid. Her engines ignited, slagging the rock directly astern; then, out the rocky maw she flew.

LEAVE NOW.

"He wants us to vamoose," Gal said. "And that makes it three to one, chief."

It took a moment for Ben to understand she was talking to him. "First, this isn't a democracy. And second, the Archie wouldn't get a vote if it were."

Gal clucked her tongue. "First, his name is Louie. And second, this is the longest we've gone with no sightings."

Well, she was right about that. The tactical screen was clear, save for the features of the Triangle around them. No blip, no ship. The countdown clock he'd set up to measure the interval between sightings showed two minutes, thirty seconds.

"Shit," he exhaled. "Maybe it *is* gone."

"And third," Torque said, "when Cinnamon's under the weather, I'm in charge of this ship. Not you—*Captain.*" She flipped a switch. "Moze, fire up the engines. Prep for TLD jump."

The engineer's soft drawl came back to them. *"Aye. Gimme five. I've got to bring the drive back online."*

"Cold start...?"

"Yeah."

"Shit."

"Yeah. Dangerous. I've got to put the load on the system gradually or we risk—"

"Yeah, yeah, I know." Torque sighed, accepting the immutability of translight physics. "Just—make it fast."

"Uh, well, it's kinda the point not *to go fast—"*

"Handle it, Moze!" Torque barked. There was silence from engineering. "Sorry. Do your best."

Moze's answer was patient. *"Will do. Gimme five."*

Torque switched channels. "Alice, double-check that Cinn is secure, then do the same for yourself. Ride's about to get bumpy again."

"Okay."

She turned to Light Without Shadow. "Better strap in, Louie."

The Arcœnum gave a nod that stretched for half its body length, then headed aft.

"Ease us off the rock with thrusters," Torque told Gal. "As soon as we're out of this cave, jump us."

The navigator nodded.

While everyone prepped for departure, Ben stared at his screen, waiting for any sign the scout ship was still around. His stomach became a little lighter as the *Junkyard Dog* repulsed its landing struts from the asteroid. At fifteen seconds shy of five minutes, Moze gave the go-ahead, and the *Dog* edged between the upper and lower jaws of rock and into the cloudy open space of the Triangle.

"Alrighty, then," Gal said, "jumping in—"

The ship's proximity alarm blared. At tactical, multiple signals appeared.

"Incoming!" Ben yelled, his hands racing to bring up the fire control window. There was a shearing sound that thrummed along the hull, metal tearing metal.

On Ben's console, the ship's two-dimensional profile flashed red in two spots aft near the engines, where the strikes had hit. He punched the controls to deploy the ship's dorsal and ventral turrets, and with agonizing slowness, they began to emerge from the *Dog*'s hull. The grind of the hydraulic systems deploying them whined, cringing Ben's spine.

"Come on, come on, come on!" He repeated it like a prayer.

"There she is!" Gal pointed forward. "I'm getting us out of—"

"Don't engage the TLD!" Moze's screech came over the intercom, as frantic as Ben had ever heard her. *"Whatever the hell just hit us ruptured a main line. I can bypass—"*

"Hurry up!" Torque urged her. "Gal, I'm taking thruster control. You navigate."

"Aye!"

The point-defense turrets had finally, fully deployed. Ben set fire to automatic, and immediately they began to spray space around the *Dog*, intercepting a second brace of enemy fire.

"Jesus!" Torque shouted. "Hold on, people!"

Ben stole a glance over his shoulder, the crick biting his neck but ignored. Just ahead of them in the pinkish fog he thought he could make out the remote but unmistakable arachnoid form of a Skane vessel. But, at this distance? Must be his imagination...

Torque kicked in the starboard thrusters and began evasive maneuvers, applying power to the sublight engines. Done manually rather than relying on the computer, which itself depended on sensors, her efforts felt clumsy. The *Dog* flew as if drunk. But they were able to gain distance from the enemy ship anyway. The turrets spat their slugs as the Skane ship fired again, and it was clear now the aliens were targeting the *Dog*'s engines.

Trying to disable, not destroy us? Ben wondered. But his surprise was sidelined by Torque's performing another jerky maneuver. Ben's stomach lurched in response.

"Kinda hard to make this bypass with all these g-forces!" Moze complained.

"Deploying missiles," Ben said, working his controls.

"You'll never hit them," Torque growled, forcing a hard turn to port.

"Get us jumped and I won't have to," Ben shouted to Torque's back. He brought up a joystick that gave him fingertip control of the missile launcher, and the targeting reticle on the tactical screen obeyed his adjustments. He hadn't seen such an old-fashioned controller since piloting basics prior to OCS.

"They're gaining," Gal reported.

"Thanks, I assumed that," Torque snarked back.

"Keep her steady," Ben said, hovering his thumb over the fire button. He had no way of ensuring accuracy. Usually, the targeting computer did that for him. If he hit the Skane ship, it'd be blind damned luck. Man, he could use a drink. He squashed the thought. Releasing a breath as though he were on the firing range, Ben thumbed the fire button. "Missile one away." It streaked away from the *Dog*'s port-aft dorsal tube. The missile's avatar on his screen streaked toward the scout ship, then right on past. "Fuck."

"I'm not worried, stud," Gal called out. "I believe in you!"

If only that were enough, Ben thought. He needed targeting assistance. Torque was right. He had almost no chance of hitting anything this way. He might as well be shooting out the rear of the *Dog* with his sidearm.

The point-defense cannons sputtered again at the incoming fire. Ben's quick glance at the ammo counter showed only twenty-eight percent ammunition remained. After that, whatever the hell the Skane were shooting at them would slice right through.

He lined up on the intermittent sensor return, tried to discern a pattern, then decided all he had was his gut. After a sweeping maneuver by Torque upward and starboard, he called again, "Steady as she goes!" One last breath in as their course straightened, then "Missile two away!"

And another miss.

"Goddamn it!"

The PDCs showed seventeen percent. There had to be some way for him...

Something had niggled at him, ever since realizing he hadn't fired missiles with a joystick since basic training. The entire purpose of one four-week course was to teach Marines how to fight effectively without the aid of technology. Power cells failed. Electrical systems short-circuited. Sometimes all a Marine had was training, opportunity, and guts.

The PDCs had a tracer option. Each slug could be tracked on infrared, as well as in the visual spectrum. The Alliance Ground Forces still used tracers to teach Marines about wind resistance and the limits of momentum in gravity, and to basically instill in them a little humility to offset the machismo encouraged by the rock-and-rolling automatic weapon in their hands. Some modern Fleet vessels relied on targeting systems so advanced, their point-defense systems didn't include a tracer option anymore. But given how outdated most of the *Dog*'s systems were, he was almost sure...

There it was! One small, unassuming button on the fire

control panel. He could use the tracers to light up the target and line up the missile. Maybe. With luck. A lot of it.

Ben engaged the tracer option just as the Skane let loose with another brace of the circular, saw-like projectiles that had Moze working overtime. The point-defense turrets automatically intercepted them. He watched the enemy fire wink out on his screen. The *Dog*'s PDC ammo counter read twelve percent reserves.

"Let them get closer!" Ben called over his shoulder at Torque.

"What?"

"Let them get closer!"

"You're crazy!" cried Gal.

"Just do it!" Ben craned his neck around to find Torque staring at him, as though evaluating Gal's diagnosis. "You believe in me, remember?"

She held his gaze a moment, then said, "Reducing thrust. Hurry it up, Stone!"

Nodding, he turned back to the aft camera view. Turret ammo read seven percent. He switched off auto-defensive fire. If the Skane opened up on them again before he was able to fire …

"Straight course," Ben said, "let them fall in behind us."

"That'll put us under their guns!"

"Trust me, damn it!"

Torque made a frustrated sound. "Steady as she goes, aye! Moze, where the hell is translight?"

Ben didn't hear the reply. In the aft camera, the Skane scout ship had jumped suddenly forward when Torque reduced thrust. With his left hand, Ben sprayed a straight path behind the *Dog* with tracer fire. The PDC rounds were small enough that the Skane ignored them, which was just fine with Ben. The straighter they came, the easier the shot would be.

The tracers painted a path to the pursuing Skane ship. He gripped the joystick in his right hand. *Just a little luck,* he prayed inside his head. *Just this once.*

Ben didn't expect an answer, but he got one anyway.

You dumbass, your whole damned life has been lucky. Bricker, ever the drill sergeant, even in death. *Now shoot, Shit-box. Shoot!*

Ben exhaled. His right thumb pressed the button.

"Missile three away!"

The Skane turned at the last moment, but the missile found its mark broadside of the round ship's main hull, impacting with a furious, devastating explosion.

"Tag, motherfucker!" Ben shouted.

The cockpit filled with celebration and loud promises from Gal for Ben's choice of sexual favors.

The Skane's momentum pushed through the explosion, still in pursuit. Panic leaped into Ben's throat, and he girded himself to launch the *Dog*'s sole remaining missile. As his thumb hovered over the fire button, the spider-like craft listed sharply to port and fell off astern quickly when Torque reengaged the sublight engines.

Over the intercom, Moze sang out: *"Fixed! Go, Gal, go!"*

And the *Junkyard Dog* jumped away.

22
THE HANGMAN

"BUT DEVOS SEEMS POSITIVELY DISPOSED?" Sayyida asked.

Eva was careful in how she answered. She didn't want to lie, and she didn't want to build false hope.

"The backchannel negotiations are going well," she said. Then in her mind, like a kid crossing her fingers behind her back: *For certain values of "well."*

Sayyida's expression was patient but optimistic.

Typically mercurial in his reaction to reconciliation with New Nassau, Piers Bragg—according to his chief of staff—had been enthusiastic at first. Eva hadn't taken Devos's word for that; she'd confirmed Bragg's mood in private, one-on-one conversations with Leo. That's how she knew he'd cooled to lukewarm on the idea. His enthusiasm, apparently, depended on whom the president had talked to last. If that were Devos, the president would acknowledge the public relations value of bringing home humanity's "prodigal children," as Eva had called them. But it was a different story if he'd recently spoken with a congressional leader in the hip pocket of interstellar business, which begrudged any goodwill shown the pirates who'd raided shipping lanes for decades. Understandable, Eva supposed, but short-sighted when the fate of the species hung in the balance.

"How's the handoff to Joe going?" Sayyida asked Toma.

"All but complete," the colonel said. "Marshal Gauss and his deputies have essentially reassumed their pre-occupation duties. With some operational support from the 214th."

"Any resistance to the additional regulations?" Eva wondered.

Toma made a dismissive gesture. "Some, but nothing significant. My personal read on it: the colony is settling into the new normal."

Eva quipped, "The *new* new normal, you mean."

"Right."

Sayyida said, "I'm grateful for your willingness to hand over Private Matisse to Joe. Would have been easy for you to claim jurisdiction there."

"Oh," Toma said, "he'll face sanctions under the Uniform Code of Military Conduct, too. But if this is going to work"—she gestured at the walls of the room and the colony beyond—"then, everyone has to play by the same rules."

Eva had kept the story out of her reports to Devos. It was a small enough incident that she could justify doing so. You never knew what tiny burr of an irritant would set the president off, and subjecting an Alliance Marine—particularly a member of Bragg's Own Battalion—to local justice, no matter how well deserved, was a good candidate. But Private Elias Matisse had gotten drunk in spite of Toma's standing prohibition against imbibing mood-altering substances of any kind, then attempted to force himself on one of the locals. Her brothers intervened and ended up in the infirmary, and it'd taken two of his fellow Marines to finally subdue Matisse. He now sat in the New Nassau brig awaiting trial for sexual assault.

It wasn't nothing, especially to the woman, and Toma had handled it hand-in-glove with Gauss. Local justice first. By the time Matisse was prosecuted by the Marines, the question of reconciliation would have been decided long before. Assuming any of them lived that long. The cooperation over the Matisse incident was emblematic of the synergy developing between Sayyida al-Hurra's civilian management and Bathsheba Toma's military rule.

"This is going well," Toma observed.

"Yes," Sayyida nodded. "Joe Gauss agrees. He says he thought there'd be more hiccups, but your command staff has been nothing but professional."

"That's good to hear, but that's not what I meant." Toma circled her index finger to indicate the three of them. "This, I mean. I had my doubts at first. Was more comfortable, if I'm being honest, with military occupation than the idea of a joint ... whatever this is."

"Even with the daily headaches?" Eva asked with a jab of sarcasm.

Toma's brow furrowed. "Even then. At least, making all the decisions myself, I was confident in them."

Sayyida adopted an offended expression and found an amused reflection of it on Eva's face. "And now?"

Sheba Toma put up a placating hand, a grin playing at the corners of her mouth. "Oh, that's my point. A few weeks ago, I would never have thought this possible. Wouldn't have agreed to it, that's for damned sure. But the peace is holding. And that we're all sitting here ... well, Eva, I've got to give you the credit for, literally, bringing us all to the table."

"Hear-hear!" Sayyida enthused, slapping the table with her palm.

Oh no, Eva thought, *not this again*. She felt warmth in her cheeks. Her conscience demurred the credit and certainly the praise, but secretly—deep down in that private place where Little Girl Eva still jumped to be first in line for her teacher's vacuum alert drills and dreaded her Fleet father's booming voice when she hadn't done her chores—down there, she felt proud, a little taller within her own skin. As though she'd grown into clothing that had once been too big for her but now fit nicely. Like a kind of armor made just for her.

"Thanks," she said, and hoped they left it at that.

"Communicatio. Politica. Militaris." Toma said each word precisely.

"What?" Sayyida asked, puzzled.

The grin trying to secure the beachhead of Toma's mouth finally declared victory. "It's Latin. I was just thinking of Marshal Gauss comparing us to the Roman Triumvirate. Communications. Politics. Military. Each of us, one third of that greater whole."

Eva smiled. "Sisters are doing it for themselves."

All of them, even Toma, laughed aloud. There wasn't a hint of mockery to it. It almost sounded musical, in fact.

After a companionable silence, Sayyida said, "This is exactly what he wanted, you know."

Eva ventured quietly, "Your father?"

"Yes," Sayyida said. "Cooperation toward a more positive future. This would have made him very happy."

"I admired your father," Toma said. "It probably wasn't always obvious, and it took a while to take hold. But, despite his past, I admired him." Before she could say anything further, she touched her neck just below her right ear.

"Go, Major." Toma's easy friendliness hardened back into her more familiar, military bearing. "We're on our way."

"What is it?" Sayyida asked.

Toma had already risen from the table and was headed for the C&C. "The Skane are back."

Eva had become used to the red and green icons populating the tactical map. Lately, there'd hardly been any blue symbols representing pirate vessels, other than thosc flying with permission between the coves, and no green icons at all, which would signify Alliance ships. Needed elsewhere for the war and with the pirates reined in, few Fleet vessels plied the spaceways of the Malvian Triangle. So the clusters of ships Eva saw on the map when she entered the C&C were more enemy than friendly.

She and Sayyida stood to one side, giving Sheba Toma space to command her officers. Though the Marines were no longer considered occupiers, Sayyida had agreed that Toma should retain military command of New Nassau, at least for the present.

Eva didn't recognize the stellar features shown in two dimensions on the grid. She'd become accustomed to the map of New Nassau's home region with its overlapping swaths of pinkish-orange and yellow representing the ionized clouds of overlapping nebulae in the Triangle. The sector on the wall was largely empty space, with small spheres representing what she supposed were distant planets. In the middle of the map was a green hexagon labeled "GS."

"Situation, Major?"

The duty officer turned to make his report. "We're monitoring comms traffic from Third Sector Fleet."

"Admiral Thorne's command?" Eva said.

Toma turned and gave her a curt look strongly suggesting she stay in her lane.

"Yes, ma'am," the major confirmed. "A Skane fleet jumped into the system near Covenant, and Admiral Thorne's Third Fleet has engaged them."

Covenant—the planet in The Frontier that had lent its name to the peace treaty signed by the Alliance and Arcanus Collective ending the Specter War. The region's most populated planet and the seat of Alliance power—and the world that now, effectively, served as the unofficial capitol of the sector. Over the past two generations, The Frontier had come to symbolize the potential for Alliance-Arcœnum cooperation as a zone of profitable trade between the two species. And Covenant was its hub.

"Not the same Skane force that retreated from Sylvan Novus?" Toma speculated.

"No, ma'am. Too soon. I mean..."

"Spit it out, Major."

"Skane command of subspace is significant, Colonel, we've learned that much. Our knowledge of the extent to which they control it, however, is limited. But based on intelligence provided posthumously by Admiral Ferris from the battle? I'd say *no*. That fleet was fragmented and retreating. This one—"

"—seems fresh and whole," Toma finishing for him as she scanned the map.

"Yes, ma'am."

Eva could see the reason she'd reached that conclusion. The red icons were far more numerous than the total of reported ships fleeing Alpha Centauri after Ferris's flagship rammed the Skane command vessel, destroying it. Wherever those Skane ships were now, it seemed unlikely they'd already reached The Frontier. So, this must be a new and substantial Skane attack force.

"There's chatter about a group of starships on the way from Sol, ma'am, but they won't reach Admiral Thorne in time." The comms officer hesitated, then said, "Current casualties list coming through now."

"Speakers," Toma told her communications officer. When

the man didn't move, only eyed Eva and Sayyida, Toma nodded at them. "I'm authorizing them. Let's hear it."

The comms officer, a lieutenant, engaged the intercom.

"—lost the Shenandoah,*"* a woman reported. She sounded young to Eva. Either there was a tremolo in her voice, or subspace interference was making it sound shaky. *"Heart of* Zapata *and the* Armstrong *are disabled and burning. Admiral Thorne's* Legio IX Hispana *is redeploying with the remains of Third Sector Fleet to defend Gibral—"*

The transmission ended abruptly.

"Lieutenant?" queried Toma.

"Cut off at the source, ma'am."

The major said, "Jammed?"

"No, sir. Just—gone."

Eva released a breath. She'd recognized one of the ships named in the report, the *Shenandoah.* A destroyer that had formed part of the escort fleet sent with the *Terre* to retrieve the freighters. Had the woman been reporting from that ship? Had Eva met her in passing, only to forget her name five seconds after learning it? If the ships that had been under Commodore Crawley's command were now under Thorne's in defense of The Frontier, just how much did the Alliance have left?

And that grim question led to inspiration. To an idea that was every bit as absurd as it was promising. And all desperate gamble.

Eva took Sayyida aside while Toma and her command staff observed the battle. She pulled her back into the conference room and waited till the door walled them off from the C&C.

Sayyida said, "What is it?"

Eva wanted to make the obvious argument—that New Nassau had a duty, an existential imperative that demanded the colony help its fellow human beings. But she also knew the history between the pirates and Thorne the man. She kept her sales pitch short.

"I think I know a way to seal the deal with the Bragg Administration."

"Okay."

"Launch everything you've got."

Sayyida stared at her. "What do you mean?"

"Every ship. *Now*. Launch everything you've got and help Third Fleet."

Sayyida al-Hurra's expression set like hexacrete. "Help Malcolm Thorne? *The Hangman*? You can't be serious."

Eva said nothing, which was more effective than saying anything.

The commander of New Nassau scoffed and turned away. She began pacing the room. "Do you know how many of us he spaced? Recorded the executions and tightbeamed them into the Triangle as warnings? I wouldn't help that man die sooner, if I thought his suffering could last a little longer!"

"And yet, you were willing to make a deal with him before," Eva said, snatching at anything that might have the slightest chance of convincing Sayyida. "When you wanted to hand over Alice Keller."

Whirling to face Eva, Sayyida yelled, "That wasn't helping him! That was helping *us*!"

The emotion in the room buzzed electrically between them. Eva let it wash over her and fade into the walls, holding fast to Sayyida's gaze, white hot with fury. She knew it wasn't really directed at her, but at a history of perceived injustices perpetrated by the man Eva now suggested Sayyida should save from disaster. But time was short.

"This was always part of the deal, Sayyida," Eva said. "There were always going to be small reconciliations making the larger one possible. You know that."

"But this—"

"There's no time for this to be personal!" Eva hadn't meant to shout. But she didn't regret it either, even when Sayyida drew herself up, preparing to return fire. Eva spoke first, and deliberately subdued, so Sayyida would have to strain to hear. "We're all in this together. Every single one of us. We don't get to decide whom we help. Every human loss is a loss for all of us. One less person to fight for all of us." She took one step, then another until she stood before Sayyida. When Eva reached out a hand, she was heartened that Sayyida didn't shrink away. "We're all in this together."

Sayyida al-Hurra didn't respond. Her eyes focused on Eva's. Maybe looking for a different solution there. Anything else but what Eva was proposing. "The Captains Council, they'll never approve—"

"You have to try," Eva said. "What would your father do?"

At first, Sayyida flushed with outrage. How dare Eva evoke her father's memory as such blatant manipulation? But then the anger left her eyes, replaced by a kind of wise melancholy.

The door disappeared into the wall. It was the major, coming to fetch them. "The colonel needs you in the C&C," he said.

Eva gave Sayyida's arm a final squeeze, and the two women joined the third member of their Triumvirate in front of the tactical map.

As they'd walked in, the dark baritone of a commanding voice met them. "*—Thorne, commanding the* Legio IX Hispana. *I'm ordering the withdrawal of Third Fleet from The Frontier until such time as we can reorganize for a counterstrike. Acknowledge, Command.*"

"Thorne's lost a third of his ships," Toma reported. "He's retreating."

Sayyida released a long breath, as though she'd been holding it all her life. "Never thought I'd hear those words," she murmured. "'Thorne's retreating.'"

"He has little choice," the major said. "The Skane surprise attack was overwhelming. Some of Third Fleet's ships were even caught in port and destroyed before they could get under way. They didn't have a chance."

"He's practicing the tried-and-true military strategy of living to fight another day," Eva observed.

Toma nodded. "Better to launch a counter-attack tomorrow, when circumstances are maybe more favorable, than to lose everything today."

On the map, Thorne's green ship icons were scattered but sweeping in a shared arc toward the same, obvious destination: the Malvian Triangle.

Eva looked at Sayyida, who must have felt her eyes because she turned to face them straight on.

"This is your chance, Sayyida," Eva urged.

"We'd never reach them in time." Sayyida responded quietly, as though afraid a secret might get out. "Even if I could persuade the council, we'd never—"

"It doesn't matter," Eva said. To Sayyida's widening eyes, Eva amended, "Of course it matters—you ought to help them. But symbolically—how can Bragg say no if you at least *try*? New Nassau won't be just the place where the pirates live anymore. It'll be the place where the heroes live who tried to help save their greatest enemy—*former* enemy."

"For however long we're all still here," Sayyida said.

"Exactly."

Toma approached them. "What are you two whispering about? You're making my people more nervous than they already are. Not to mention me."

"I'm going to order all our ships into space," Sayyida said flatly, and with purpose. "I need you to let me do it."

Toma traded looks with first Sayyida, then Eva. Whether by telepathy or a tactical expert's learned insight, she now appeared to know exactly what they'd been whispering about. "I guess it's not my place to say 'no' anymore, now is it?"

"What about the Captains Council?" Eva said.

Moving to the comms officer, Sayyida said, "We don't have time for that. I'll explain why we're launching *after* we launch. Then we'll see just how much weight my word carries, I suppose. Or if I'm, you know, assassinated."

"Lieutenant," Toma said, addressing the communications officer, "give the commander whatever assistance she needs." To Eva: "I sure hope this works."

Eva watched Sayyida marshal herself to the task she found so personally repugnant. "Don't we all."

23
CHANGE OF HEART

"AND THERE WAS EVEN one still in the tubes," Gal told Cinnamon. "So we're not totally defenseless. Gonna need a full restock for the turrets, though."

Cinnamon Gauss scrunched her face in pain. It appeared sudden and acute, and completely tied to Gal's report. "It's gonna cost me a fortune to refit the *Dog*."

"Hey, remember," Moze said, "that Marine's rich. He's the one who missed. *Twice*. Make *him* pay."

"Now, there's an idea," Cinnamon said through a savory smile.

Gal and Moze stood each to one side of the medbed, summoned by Alice after Cinnamon had regained consciousness. Once Gal had briefed her on their near-destruction, she'd launched a series of questions at them related to the ship's status and their current heading. Told of Ben's inventive firing solution against the Skane, Cinnamon had even expressed a passing admiration for his tactical prowess.

That's how they knew she was still ill, Moze quipped.

"I haven't rewarded him yet," Gal said nonchalantly. "I think it's hard for him to choose."

Alice shot her a curious, piercing look.

"Pun intended?" squawked Cinnamon.

"Always!" Gal said.

"We're on approach to Strigoth," Torque said on shipwide. *"I need my navigator back up here."*

Moze thumbed the intercom. "Acknowledged. We're both headed back to stations."

"Won't be long now, Cap," Gal said with a final squeeze of Cinnamon's hand. "They'll have you fixed right up."

Cinnamon gave her a tired thumbs up. Moze made a mock salute and followed Gal out the door, leaving her captain alone with Alice.

"I hear you and Louie tag-teamed me," Cinnamon croaked from a throat roughed up by too much unconscious mouth breathing.

"I'll have to tell you all about it sometime. But you look like you could use some rest."

"Eh. I could sleep, I guess."

"I thought I might go up top. I know it might sound funny, but I'm actually looking forward to seeing Strigoth again."

"Sure," Cinnamon yawned. "You've done enough guard duty here."

"Ah, no problem. Before I go, is there anything I can do for..."

But Cinnamon's eyelids had already fluttered shut. Confident now that her friend and the ship were out of immediate danger, Alice headed up to the cockpit. She really did want to watch the approach to Tarsus Station.

"—and state your business. We do not receive unscheduled visits here. This is a private research facility. Now fuck right-the-hell off, or I'll blow you out of space."

Walking from amidships to the cockpit, Alice could hear a vigorous conversation in progress between Ben and a man whose voice she recognized but had never met. She'd never even learned his name in the three years she'd been on Strigoth.

"And I'm telling you, dockmaster, we have an emergency situation here. We have an injured crewmember and a damaged ship." Ben had that quality of command in his voice again, the one Alice had rarely heard one-on-one. It somehow made her feel safe and edgy at the same time.

"Not my problem, shipmaster."

Ben muted the channel. "Can you believe this guy?"

"I can," Alice said, standing in the doorway. Torque and Gal nodded greeting to her from up front, concern painting their faces. Ben grumbled something incoherent but stuffed with four-letter words.

"I don't suppose getting you to speak to him would help?" he asked.

Alice made a face. Considering how much Ian had wanted her off Strigoth in the first place, she doubted she could offer anything to improve their chances of docking at the station. "If anything, he might close the channel."

"Well, then, it's on to plan B." Unmuting, Ben said, "Dockmaster, let me present you with some facts. One: my name is Captain Marcus Ferris. Two: I'm a commissioned Marine officer in the Alliance Ground Forces. Three: This is a time of war. It's obvious you're unwilling to render aid out of the goodness of your civilian heart. I state that for the official record of this exchange. I am, therefore, invoking Article V, Subsection B, Paragraph 1.3 of the Military-Civilian Wartime Cooperation Act. You are legally bound to comply with my request for safe harbor. So—under pain of prosecution for treason, not to mention a hefty fine—I am *ordering* you to stand down your defenses and open your port to this vessel. Failure to do so will be reported to both Fleet Command and civilian authorities, and this facility will not only be shut down, but every single goddamned one of its occupants prosecuted to the fullest extent of civilian and *military* law. *As traitors.* Do you have a favorite wall? We'll be glad to accommodate your final request to line you up in front of it *before we shoot you.* Oh, and did I mention the fine?"

Ben muted again.

Alice, Torque, and Gal all stared at him in amazement.

Torque finally ventured, "Who the hell is Marcus Ferris? And was any of that true?"

Ben shrugged. "Maybe the guy really *does* have a favorite wall?"

She rolled her eyes. "You'd make a fair pirate, Stone."

"No need to be insulting, now."

"There's no such thing as a Military-Civilian Wartime Cooperation Act," Gal observed.

"So?" Ben quirked an eyebrow. "I'm betting he doesn't know that."

"Easily researched," Torque said. "That's what they do here: *research.* Damn it, Stone, if you just lied our way out of a chance to dock—"

"Shipmaster," came the reply after the extended delay, *"did you say your name was Ferris?"*

Ben winked arrogantly at his *Dog* mates. "I did," he replied to Tarsus, affecting the innocence of a child. "But, sir, I don't know what that—"

"Related to the Admiral Ferris of Alpha Centauri? The woman who saved that system?"

Ben paused an appropriate amount of time for a mourning

relative. He counted it off on one handful of fingers. Then, injecting a dash of pride to spice up the main course of difficult disclosure, he said, "She was my aunt."

"I don't know about any 'cooperation act,' but if you're the nephew of that woman, Mister Secord says you can bring your ship in. I'm transmitting a nav path now on a secure channel. Welcome to Tarsus Research Station."

The channel cut off.

"You're shameless," Torque muttered, shaking her head. "Using that woman's name like that."

"Would you rather we shoot our way to a berth?" Ben asked. "And it worked, didn't it?"

"I didn't say I disapproved," Torque added, "exactly."

Beaming at Ben, Gal spurted, "A shameless name-whore!"

Ben made a face. "That's funny coming from a nymphomaniacal pilot named Mango."

"You're even sexier now, Adonis, you know that?"

Alice glared at their flirty banter.

"Fly the ship, *Mango*," Torque said. "We're burning starlight."

Ben looked over his shoulder at Alice, a big, proud smile curling his cheeks. When he saw her sour face, his own expression cratered like someone had jacked up the artificial gravity.

"God, it's like one huge, round, rocky piece of shit," Gal commented as Strigoth dominated the forward window.

With a lengthy, wilting scowl at Ben, Alice said, "Professor Korsakov came here to avoid people."

"Good choice of planets, then!" Gal enthused. She confirmed to Torque, "They've slaved our nav. Ten minutes to dockside."

"Come on, Stone," Torque said, rising from the co-pilot's seat. "Let's get Cinnamon prepped for transfer."

Alice stood aside as they passed, an oddity already occupying her thoughts. The dockmaster had checked with "Mister Secord" before granting them permission to dock. Andre Korsakov had always personally approved any visitors to Tarsus Station, especially unscheduled ones. So, why would the dockmaster need to check with Ian?

"Ian Secord."

From her position hidden at the top of the ramp, Alice heard Ian introduce himself to Ben and Torque, who'd escorted Cinnamon's medbed down. Alice couldn't help herself; she had to sneak a peek. Edging one eye around the ramp's hydraulic strut, she took it all in. Nervousness and nostalgia twisted together as a curdling mixture in her stomach. The antiseptic brightness of Tarsus Station's lighting, the sanitized pattern of the deck. Torque and Ben stood with their backs to her, an unconscious Cinnamon hovering horizontal between them.

And Ian. His hair was longer, the cast of his face seeming older than the few, intervening months should account for. He looked taller.

"Marcus Ferris," Ben said.

"I don't think so," Ian replied. "You're Captain Ben Stone. The Hero of Canis III."

Alice tensed. The way Ian had said it was like a detective revealing a suspect's blatant dissembling.

"Okay," was all Ben said. He spread his hands. "You got me."

"You have a rather famous face, Captain. And there's no such thing as a Military-Civilian Wartime Cooperation Act. But I give you credit for ingenuity. And trading on Admiral Ferris's sacrifice? Brazen."

"Our friend is in a bad way," Torque interjected. "She needs your help."

Nodding, Ian said, "I'm glad to provide it." Alice relaxed. "In exchange for some information."

There was a long silence. Alice watched Ben adjust his hands, placing them on his hips. To Ian, it'd probably appeared innocuous. Like a person expressing indignation through body language. But she'd been around Ben long enough to know it was actually a Marine locating his gun hand closer to his weapon.

"This woman is dying," Ben said, "and you want to extort trade for aid?"

Ian raised his hands. "I just need to know where Alice Keller is."

Her eyes widened. Why? Ian had practically hated her by the time she'd fled Strigoth. Couldn't wait to get rid of her. Maybe he was angling to sell her to Bragg. Or Sayyida al-Hurra, who'd *then* sell her to Bragg. Alice shrank back against the cold metal of the strut.

"The girl from the documentary?" Ben said, feigning ignorance. "Why would I know where she is?"

"This is wasting time," Torque said. "Cinnamon needs—"

Ian did a double-take. "Did you say Cinnamon? Cinnamon Gauss?"

"Yeah, Mister Secord," Torque said. "We've never met, but I know you've had past dealings with Cinnamon."

Looking down at the thin woman on the floating medbed, Ian seemed shocked. "She looks so different from her calls. Never actually met her in person. The last time we spoke was to cut the deal to get Alice off the *Archimedes*."

Torque and Ben exchanged a look.

"Yeah," Torque said, "that sounds right."

Her skin tingling, Alice sensed a shifting happening inside her—it felt like the pieces of her life, finally coming together.

"I don't mean Alice any harm," Ian said. "Quite the contrary. I'm concerned for her welfare is all."

"Yeah, well, we have more immediate concerns," Ben said, "for our friend here."

Alice stood up. She couldn't explain why, couldn't begin to guess, but she was absolutely certain she was meant to be here now. In this place, at this time. As though Fate were showing her the way. She took a step down the ramp.

Ben heard and turned toward her. "No, wait!"

But Alice kept coming. She saw Ian see her, his face lighting up with first surprise, then delight. His expression was something she'd wanted to see—she'd *wished* to see—when she'd still lived here, when she'd still been in love here. Or, at least, in lust. By the time Alice stepped off the ramp and onto the deck, Ian had moved past a bristling Ben Stone to greet her.

"Alice!"

God, the look on his face! Where had it been a few months before?

Ian Secord wrapped her in his arms and pulled her close. He pressed her body against his.

Fate could be cruel, too.

"Hi, Ian," Alice said and let herself melt into his embrace. She returned it hesitantly, as though hugging him any harder might break the spell surrounding his happiness at seeing her.

"I'm so glad you're okay!" He'd spoken the words into her hair, his breath warm and full of affection. And for her, long-ago abandoned fantasies they could be anything more than friends stirred in her memory. "Zoey will be over the moon."

After a long moment that felt all too short to Alice, Ian withdrew and looked at her. They stared at one another a moment, and Alice wasn't sure anymore what she wanted to see in his face. What she found there was the relief of one friend at another's safe return. Just that alone, and nothing more.

And that, Alice thought with some sadness, might be for the best.

Ben cleared his throat. "Glad we could make this reunion happen. Now, about our friend...?"

Ian directed the station's medical staff to prep Cinnamon for immediate surgery. He wasn't a surgeon himself but would oversee the operation. Questions from the attending surgeon about the partial blood clot *reforming* on Cinnamon's brain in a manner that didn't jibe with their timeline for the originating injury were politely shrugged away. Meanwhile, Torque began assessing the damage to the *Junkyard Dog* with Moze and the station's chief engineer. No mention was made of Louie, who continued his half-squatting hibernation inside. And no station personnel were allowed to board the *Dog* for any reason.

That left Ben, Gal, and Alice observing Cinnamon's surgery through a broad, cantilevered window from a theater-like room a floor above. For Alice, seeing Zoey again had been just as surprising and pleasant. Like Ian, Zoey had experienced a change of heart and was regretful at how she'd treated Alice. There was a darker corner of Alice's psyche that took some satisfaction in that. But mostly she was just relieved that somehow Zoey and Ian had worked past their fear of her. It gave Alice confidence that maybe she wasn't the monster she sometimes feared she was.

They'd been viewing the procedure for half an hour, mostly in silence, and Gal was getting restless. She constantly attempted to engage Ben in polite, in-front-of-other-people conversation, which he answered with as few words as possible.

Alice's need for distraction from watching the surgeon poke around inside Cinnamon's skull led her to the question she'd been reluctant to ask since they'd arrived.

"Where's Professor Korsakov?"

Zoey tensed, though surely she must have known Alice would wonder. "He's in the observation room."

Alice stared at the side of Zoey's face. "The observation room?"

"We converted it for him." Zoey stated it matter-of-factly, as though narrating a procedure like the one occurring on the table below.

Alice regarded her a moment. "Zoey, what's going on? Ian is in charge of the station now, isn't he? What's happened to Korsakov?"

"He's..." Zoey appeared to work to find the right words. "He's not well."

"Is he sick?"

Sighing, Zoey said, "Mentally, yes."

"Hey," Alice said, "look at me. What's happened?"

Again, the young woman took a moment to formulate her response. "When you left... he didn't take it well."

"I'm sure he was angry."

"At first, yes, but that was the least of it. He..." Zoey looked Alice in the eye. "He's currently on anti-psychotics and mood stabilizers. Alice, it's like all his mental control is gone. He pretty much lays on that slab all day. Just keeps saying 'They're coming. They're coming.'"

"Who? Who's coming?"

"Ian thinks he means the military. We discovered ... Alice, we discovered some things in his personal data files. We didn't mean to snoop, we were looking for a way to help him, to understand what was happening to him. But what we found..." She leaned over close, whispered, "Most of our support funding the last three years has been coming directly from the Bragg Administration. Can you believe it?"

That feeling of teetering on a precipice—the gut-level certainty that answers were nearer, yet still out of reach—tickled Alice's insides again. Could her leaving Strigoth really have been upsetting enough to push Korsakov over the edge?

"I want to see him, Zoey. I *need* to see him."

Zoey seemed to shrink a little. "I'm not sure that'd be a good idea."

"Neither am I."

Alice turned to find Ben, who'd spoken, and Gal staring at her. They'd been listening in. She guessed she couldn't blame them.

"Well," Alice answered him, "it's not your decision." She turned back to her newest old friend. "I need to see him, Zoey."

"Okay, well... I'll speak to Ian and see—"

"Now," Alice said.

There was a hint of the old fear in Zoey's eyes at Alice's commanding tone. But then her expression changed, seemed to acknowledge Alice's right to see Korsakov.

"Yes, I guess you do. There's so much you don't know, Alice. But you deserve to know." Zoey rose to her feet. "Come on, then."

"Alice—" Ben warned.

"Watch over Cinnamon," Alice said. "I'll be back."

24

GENIUS IN MADNESS

THE OBSERVATION ROOM was located across the facility from the medical lab. The walk was long, quiet, and tense. Alice's growing anxiety wasn't just about seeing Korsakov again. As it now apparently served him, the bleak, bare room had been her first "home" on Tarsus Research Station. Her first testing lab before the Bell Jar; a kind of prototype for it, in fact. Once the door slipped into the wall, the bubble of her fear popped.

The room's design, though familiar, now reminded her of the stacked apartments in the Havens in New Nassau, an association reinforced by the single, transparent wall that gave the room its eponymous title. When Alice had first arrived on Strigoth, it'd felt like being in a voyeuristic prison cell, or single-occupant ant farm. Korsakov had quickly determined this simple room to be insufficient, and so he'd moved her sessions to the more sophisticated lab with its advanced monitoring equipment. He'd eventually constructed her canary's cage, the Bell Jar, with its advanced subspace sensor web.

Though short, her time in this room had made an impression on Alice. She'd felt like a prisoner under glass, if a pampered one. She'd always credited the visits from Morgan

Henry and his insistence on getting her out of there as often as possible to the cafeteria or the rec center with keeping her sane in those first days in a strange new place.

Seeing Korsakov in his present state pushed all that away. He lay curled in a ball on the white slab bench, his back to the clear wall between them. Dressed in one of the station's standard technician jump suits, he appeared to be asleep. His hair was long and looked dirty, gray with age and poor hygiene. Dark stains had spread from the underarms of his jumpsuit. How changed he was in so short a time!

Alice was reminded that she too had changed. No longer a fourteen-year-old girl, newly recovered from an alien world and spirited away from pursuers in secret to hide on a backwater planet. She was older, now, wiser. And, perhaps most importantly of all in this particular room, on the outside looking in.

"He's on a standard regimen of trioxadone and lethozenapine," Zoey said. "Anti-psychotics to mollify the effects of the break. He's calm—most of the time."

"Break?" Only part of Alice was listening. She stood and stared, enthralled at how far the man who'd pushed her so hard had fallen. He'd sometimes seemed like an angry god to her back then, the absolute, omniscient ruler of everything and everyone on Strigoth. And now, he appeared only a sick old man who couldn't even rule the kingdom of his own mind.

"At first, like you said, he was angry. Threatened to ruin Ian's career for helping you. Everyone gave him a wide berth. We thought he'd calm down. But then—after a few days—he changed. Started obsessing, saying over and over, 'They're coming.' The medical staff didn't know what to do. He's the boss, right? But eventually he became violent, and when no one else would step up and take control, Ian did." Zoey's face became pained. "Trying to get Korsakov under control ... it was horrible—you have no idea. Eventually, Ian and the interns decided to keep him sedated. Placed him here in isolation. With the meds, he's fairly docile."

"Oh, Professor," Alice whispered. The shell of a man lying on the slab was a far cry from the domineering, Russian-cursing ogre he'd become after Morgan Henry had passed away.

She wasn't ready to forgive him—not for any of it. Not by a long shot. But as tough as he'd been on her, he'd also been kind at times. Like at Morgan's bedside, when he'd urged her to stay a little longer in case Morgan might sense her pulling away in his final moments of unconscious life. Korsakov had been a father to her, if sometimes a cruel one, who'd provided Alice food, shelter, and a safe place to hide. He and Morgan had sometimes seemed like one father split in two, in fact, with Morgan supporting and encouraging, and Korsakov challenging her. Without Andre Korsakov pushing her to develop her abilities, Alice found herself thinking, Cinnamon might have perished before ever reaching Strigoth. They might all have died, for that matter, on the rooftop of the Swashbuckler's Leap.

"I'd like to talk to him," Alice said. She stepped forward and touched the transparent wall.

"Oh, Alice, I don't know," Zoey said. "He's calm. Sleeping. I don't think it would be a good idea..."

The intercom between the outer room and the observation cell was off. But it was like Korsakov had heard them anyway. Maybe sensed that someone was there. He unfolded himself from his fetal position, and turned his head toward them. It took him a moment to recognize Alice.

His eyes, she thought. Alice recognized the look in them. She'd seen it in the mirror on bad days, when she wanted nothing more than to cut again. *It's almost like they've seen too much.*

Korsakov jerked his body up and launched himself at the transparent wall. Alice felt hands on her, Zoey's hands, pulling her back. He pressed himself against the clear plastinium, his palms, his cheek, his mouth stretching grotesquely, his rheumy, sidelong gaze unblinking and wild.

"I think we need to assess his dose," Zoey stated with no humor whatsoever.

Korsakov made an attempt to focus and pressed the intercom button on his side of the wall. "Are you here, Alice?" he whispered. "Is that really you? Are you really here?"

"I'll get the tech down here," Zoey said.

"No, wait, don't. It's not like he can get through." Alice freed herself of the other's grasp and took a single, tentative step forward. "I'm here, Professor."

Korsakov released a breath. He slid down the wall but never took his eyes off her. "Thank goodness. Maybe there's still time. Maybe it's not too late."

"Too late?" she said. Maybe it was dangerous to talk to him. Maybe it would only feed his delusional state of mind. "Too late for what?"

"They're..." But Korsakov seemed to lose his train of thought. He looked away at a distant something only he could see. Slowly, he got back to his feet, then began to pad shiftlessly around the observation room, eyes darting left and right, fingers fluttering, his hold on reality clearly tenuous. Alice looked to the door, confirmed it was locked.

"It must be lonely in there," she said.

Korsakov halted, about-faced quickly, stared hard at her like he used to when she'd failed a test. "Solitude sometimes is best society." Alice had no idea what that meant, and the professor's focus went slack again. He resumed his roaming, becoming agitated. "They're coming. I'm so glad you're here! They're coming. Still time? Still time. Still time!" He stopped at the slab jutting from the wall, crawled back onto it, and lay on his side, turning his back to them again. "Still time," he muttered, as though singing himself tunelessly to sleep. "Still time..."

"Alice."

She turned to find Ben standing in the hallway. "Secord says he has something to show us. Cinnamon's surgery will take a few more hours. Might as well use the time."

"Okay." She offered Zoey a nod of gratitude, then turned back to Korsakov. How sad he was now. A tyrant turned street beggar. A genius, whose mind had existed on a plane levels of magnitude beyond the norm. But that mind now only an island, surrounded by stormy seas of madness.

Maybe she could help him, like she'd helped Cinnamon. Maybe with Louie's help—

"Alice," Ben urged. "Come on."

Nodding, she walked to the doorway, thinking, *It's just so sad.*

"We didn't come in here to spy on the professor," Ian said. He sat at Korsakov's minimalist smartdesk with its multiple monitors, just like Alice had found Korsakov when she'd come to apologize for attacking him in the Bell Jar. When she'd seen him talking to *them*—the Skane. "We came in looking for something to help. To explain what might have happened to him."

It wasn't so much what Ian said as the tremor rumbling beneath it. He sounded disappointed. Frightened. Zoey, standing behind him, put a hand on his shoulder.

"What did you find?" Ben asked.

While Ian called up data records, Zoey spoke. "Evidence of unspeakable crimes, Captain." She chanced a glance at Alice. "And even how we'd become complicit in them."

Alice was confused.

"Unknowingly," Ian was quick to add.

"Does that make it any better?" Zoey snapped.

Not venturing an opinion, Ian said, "Korsakov held all this on encrypted drives here in his quarters, off-network. To avoid detection, I suppose."

He pulled up still images on one screen, captures of various testing sessions with Alice in the Bell Jar. She was struck again by how different she looked in them. Her shoulders hunched. In one close-up shot, Alice's face showed a grimace of half anguish and half fury. A log of subspace messages populated a second monitor. A third displayed a list of personal diary entries organized by date.

"Come closer," Zoey said to Alice. "You need to see."

Ben took a step but when Alice didn't follow, he turned to look at her. "Alice?"

"I don't know if I want to see," she said. Ben started to say something, but he didn't get the chance. "But I need to."

"Obviously, I won't make you review all of this material," Ian said. "Combing through it, piecing the story together—that took weeks."

"Hit the highlights," Ben growled, peering at the log.

"First, Alice," Ian said, "you were brought here by Admiral Stone to protect you, right? Specifically, from Piers Bragg. The admiral assumed he'd want to exploit you as a living, breathing reason for incarcerating the Psyckers. Your life would be over, he thought, at least as long as Bragg was president."

"And Morgan stayed with you to ensure that didn't happen," Zoey added.

Alice nodded. "Yes."

"You're telling us what we already know," Ben said.

"I'm telling you," Ian said, "for context. Because it happened anyway."

Ben frowned. "What do you mean?"

"Shortly after Alice arrived, Professor Korsakov reached out to the administration," Ian said. "He wanted to study Alice, to add to his lifelong research into the mysteries of subspace. Doctor Henry shared data from brain scans he conducted on the *Rubicon*. They fascinated Korsakov. And after Admiral Stone described what happened with you on Drake's World, Captain ... well, to say he was intrigued is an understatement. He found a like mind in President Bragg."

"How is that possible?" Ben asked. "Bragg is an avowed hater of the Archies and their mind-control ability. He dog-whistled his way to power by stoking old fears of them. 'Humans First!' and all that shit. Why would he team up with Korsakov to..."

Alice looked to Ben expectantly. "What?"

"Do you see, Captain?" Ian prompted.

"He saw her military value," Ben muttered. He closed his eyes as, at last, he understood Piers Bragg's fascination with Alice Keller. "Operation Fire with Fire."

"Right," Zoey said.

"What's Operation Fire with Fire?" Alice asked. "Will someone please tell me what the hell is going on?"

"Zoey, you said earlier that the Bragg Administration had been funding Korsakov for, what, three years?" At Zoey's nod of confirmation, Ben sighed. "Bragg paid Korsakov to develop your power, Alice. As an ace-in-the-hole. To use against the Archies."

Alice looked from Ben to the screens to Ian to Zoey. "But he hates the Arcœnum—their power, I mean. He's afraid of it, right?"

Ian said, "Not exactly. He hates the threat their power poses."

"That's not exactly right either," Ben said. "What Bragg really hates is that *he* doesn't have that power." He stared meaningfully at Alice. "With you—a human with fully developed psychokinetic abilities under his control—he would."

"Korsakov was desperate for funding," Ian said. "His old family money, which built this place, was running out. So when you came here, Alice, he saw an opportunity."

Her skin was growing hot. Was she embarrassed at feeling so used? Angry at Korsakov for doing it? Or mad at herself for being ignorant of something she couldn't possibly have known?

"That sonofabitch," Ben said.

"He contacted the administration privately. Offered to sell you to them."

Alice blinked. "What?"

"It was a kind of hostage negotiation at first," Zoey said. "To make you even more valuable, he told Bragg about his research—that your actions saving Captain Stone on Drake's World proved his theory that direct manipulation of subspace was possible."

"He was talking out of his ass," Ian said. "In that moment, anyway."

"Driving up the price?" Ben suggested.

"Right." Ian paused and took a breath. Alice wasn't sure what she was feeling now. Anything? Numb. Detached from herself. Or wanting to be. Her left palm pulsed. Ian went on, "Then Bragg shared the military footage from that event."

"That was top secret!" Ben said.

Ian looked at him with the sympathy one offers a child who hasn't learned life's harder lessons yet.

"Never mind," Ben said.

"The footage convinced Korsakov he actually *was* right about you," Zoey said. "He suggested to Bragg that, covertly, they restart the Operation Fire with Fire initiative. With himself in charge, of course."

"And the offer to trade you for a lump sum turned into a

request for yearly funding to study you instead." Ian switched out the still images from the lab for electronic credit transfers. "Note when the transactions begin."

Alice closed her eyes and swallowed. Her throat was dry.

Ian brought up a list of communiqués between Tarsus Station and the Citadel. "It's all there. Long story short: this was an off-book agreement funneling credits through grant funding directly between Bragg and Korsakov. Only Sam Devos, the president's chief of staff, seems to have known about it."

"That hypocrite," Ben said. "Out of one side of his mouth he's throwing kids' club members in jail, talking up the dangers of humans dithering with powers like the Arcœnum have; and out of the other he's making deals to develop Alice's abilities?"

"Have you ever known a politician who wasn't a hypocrite?" Zoey snarked.

Ian cleared his throat. "That's only half the story. This is where it gets fucking unconscionable."

"*This* is where?" Ben said incredulously.

"Korsakov was working both sides of the street," Zoey said. "Hedging his bets."

Despite feeling overwhelmed by all she'd learned, that gut feeling of answers coming closer returned to Alice. Her unconscious mind, it seemed, had already made the connection.

"I saw him talking to the shadow-spiders," Alice said. "The Skane, I mean."

"That would be the other side of the street," Ian said. "Alice, you might want to sit down for this."

She reached out and forcefully swung Ian's chair around. "Just tell me."

"It's a lot to take in—" Zoey began.

"Just tell me!" Alice shouted. Ben put his hands on her shoulders and she shrugged him off. Still, she managed to calm her voice down. "Please..."

"Your ability?" Ian said, clearly nervous. "The Skane gave it to you."

Alice looked from him to Zoey. "What? Why?" She'd wanted answers, more than anything. For three years she'd pursued them. Now, she wasn't sure she wanted them anymore.

"We have no idea," Zoey said. "But we know they were responsible for the downing of your ship on Drake's World. They took you from the wreckage and..."

"And what?" Ben demanded.

"Reprogrammed your mind," Zoey whispered. "Doctor Henry found some signs of that when he examined you on the *Rubicon*, though he couldn't understand his findings. It was like your brain was too young for your age, he told the professor. And your amnesia—"

"'Reprogrammed' isn't exactly accurate," Ian said. "I'd characterize it as—"

"Who gives a fuck how you'd 'characterize' it?" Ben challenged him. "Alice, my God..."

"What happened to my family?" Alice asked. "Where are my parents and brother?"

Admonished, Ian considered his next words carefully. "Again, we don't know. But the professor's logs and exchanges with the Skane make it pretty clear they gave you your ability."

"That sonofabitch," Ben said again. "That *treasonous* sonofabitch. Working with the enemy?"

"We're still only at the beginning," Zoey said. "There's more."

"A lot more," Ian said. "You haven't heard the worst of it."

"Jesus Christ," Ben said. "What else has this asshole done? Dealing with the president to exploit Alice, dealing with the Skane to undermine his own species..."

Alice moved to a second chair at the console and sat down. Inside she felt herself hollowing out. Emptying of all feeling.

Dissociating. The pity she'd felt for Korsakov earlier was gone. Dried up and blown away. Whatever feeling remained to her existed only as an itch she couldn't scratch, located solely in her left palm.

She gathered herself, letting the information Ian and Zoey had shared sink in. No time now to process it. No time to even begin to understand it. But in a few hours, Cinnamon would be coming out of surgery, and Alice wanted to be there then and able to focus on her. So, now was the time to hear it all. Get it over with. Rip off the bandage and hope the entire arm doesn't come off with it.

"Tell me," she said, looking down at the old scars from cutting. She had a sudden, all-consuming need to make them new again. "Tell me everything."

25

RUN, GUN, RINSE, REPEAT

"STILL NO ACKNOWLEDGMENT FROM COMMAND?" Rear Admiral Malcolm Thorne asked.

Through the drifting haze of burnt circuitry, Thorne's communications officer shook his head, hunched his shoulders in a shrug of uncertainty. "Sent multiple times, sir. No way to know for sure if—"

"Understood, Lieutenant. Send, fleetwide: All vessels in Third Fleet to make for the Malvian Triangle at best possible speed. Exceptions: *Gladius*, *Serpent's Fury*, *Shandong*, *Requiem*. They're to form a battle wing with *Hispana* and provide a rearguard to cover the rest of 3F's retreat. Make sure each ship acknowledges the order."

"Aye, Admiral."

"So, we're leaving Gibraltar to her fate, then?" his first officer, Commander Meriweather asked. It wasn't accusatory. More like a request for permission to be okay with the decision.

"Only temporarily," Thorne replied. "We'll be back."

Although, frankly, he had no way of knowing that for sure. What was left of Fleet's assets were spread thin. The newest ship, *Covenant*, was screaming at flank speed from Sol Sector with every ship that could keep up with her, but she certainly wouldn't be here in time to help decide this engagement. Alpha-C's remaining fleet was holding in place and helping with civilian recovery and would have taken weeks to reach them in any case. Hence, the hold order. While the Skane, on the other hand, seemed to have no shortage of ships and personnel they treated like cannon fodder.

And so Third Fleet ran. It went against Thorne's grain to retreat, but his was the only effective fighting force in The Frontier, and the unrelenting Skane assault was quickly eroding that particular description. Third Sector Fleet lost three ships in the surprise attack on Gibraltar Station before they'd even known the Skane were in the system. The *Cavour* and *Trinity*, destroyed in port, had taken out the Fleet docking facility in orbit of Covenant's second moon. Thorne had ordered all ships into space within moments of the starships exploding in their slips. That Third Fleet had as many ships left as it did was a testament to her captains' bravery and Thorne's strategic resilience.

"Admiral, the Skane fleet is splitting," his tactical officer reported. "The smaller force is attempting to interdict our ships now bound for the Triangle. But the bulk of their fleet is changing course—for Gibraltar Station."

"Thank you, Mister Abraham." Tactically what he would have done, Thorne thought. Chase the gnats away while securing the strategic asset. Although, why the Skane would want—or need—the station was anyone's guess. A central command point for further operations? Maybe just a goddamned trophy for drinks with their spider friends... "Can someone please evacuate all this damned smoke?"

A muffled acceptance of the order was followed by the hiss of the atmospheric regulators, which slowed, stopped, and reversed. After a few moments, the acrid, ticklish scent in

Thorne's nostrils began to subside. Someone else thought to restore lighting to the extent it could be restored, washing away the battle-blood red with a fritzing but more natural silver hue of normal operations. Why had anyone ever thought such cues necessary to alert personnel once a battle was started, Thorne wondered. Klaxons blaring, scarlet light pulsing—like, without them, the crew might be unaware death was about to breach the hull and squeeze the life from their lungs?

"Status of the covering force, Mister Meriweather?"

"Forming up on our portside now, Admiral. *Requiem*, however—"

"On-screen," Thorne said, "and enlarge."

The Fleet fighter carrier *Requiem* had been headed under its battle wing commander's orders to support the attempt to prevent the Skane from boarding Gibraltar Station. Now the station was being abandoned, and Thorne's fleetwide retreat command was easy enough for smaller destroyers and frigates to follow. They could turn their smaller-massed vessels relatively quickly, that lithe maneuverability part of their design. Carriers like the *Requiem* typically freighted multiple fighter wings and, in wartime, a full complement of Alliance Ground Forces Marines with all their ground assault armor, dropships, and other combat machinery in addition to the officers and enlisted needed to maintain the ship. More massive, heavier, and with more breakable moving parts, carriers needed longer to change course, looking like nothing so much as a sleek, gray leviathan coming about in a wide, sweeping arc against the backdrop of a black ocean. The laws of physics exposed *Requiem* to the Skane while her escort vessels already burned for the Triangle on their admiral's orders. Smelling easy prey, two medium-sized Skane vessels detached from the main hunter-killer force, headed for the carrier.

"Helm, intercept course for the lead Skane vessel of that

duo bearing down on the *Requiem*," Thorne said. "Let's try to keep her from living up to her name."

"Intercept course, aye," the helmswoman answered.

"Comm, transmit to *Requiem*," Thorne continued. "Launch all fighters. They are not, I repeat, *not* to engage. They're to make with all speed for the Triangle with the rest of 3F."

"Aye, Admiral."

"Thirty seconds to weapons range," Meriweather reported.

Thorne acknowledged, "Very well. Switch to proximity tactical."

The image of space on the main screen transformed to a near-view of their smaller battle-within-the-battle. A central green icon labeled "R" for *Requiem* moved slowly toward their battle group of four ships, each labeled with short-hand of their own. Two red icons representing the enemy angled like predator birds for the lonely R on-screen.

They'd be lucky to escape with half the fleet into the Triangle. And then what? Well, not suffer immediate death, anyway. Not instant destruction. He was loath to apply Tasha Ferris's brave but ultimately losing tactic of ramming the Skane. It had been an act of desperation, an understandable one while cities on Sylvan Novus burned. But Fleet couldn't trade ships one-for-one and hope to win in the end. The Skane had the advantage of numbers. And so—much as it irked Thorne to run, much as the sacrifice of Gibraltar Station, short term or not, infuriated him—they'd have to retreat, retrench, and reevaluate to launch a counter-strike. To be able to do that, the priority was to survive. It'd be easy to play hero and attack the Skane till his last PDC slug, his last missile, his last ship's hull for ramming were all spent. But that would be a complete waste of life and materiel. As a boy, his father, a miner on Monolith, had always cautioned Mal Thorne to think with the big head, not his dick like his rowdy school friends often did, especially when they were showing off for one another. He was glad of that lesson now.

"Incoming!"

"Evasive," Thorne said calmly.

Legio IX Hispana, the flagship of Third Sector Fleet, hulled over and arced wide to starboard, her gravimetric compensators easily securing her crew's stomachs. The Skane projectiles, what everyone called "ninjas" since Alpha-C, spun toward the *Hispana*, most intercepted and destroyed by her point-defense cannons. One of the weapons penetrated that countermeasure, and Thorne imagined he could feel the damage to the *Hispana* like a knife in his own side.

"Damage report."

"The ninja hit the main power couplings on Deck Thirty-Two," Meriweather reported. "Engineering already trying to re-route."

"Very well," Thorne acknowledged.

On-screen, a green icon winked out.

"Lost *Gladius*, sir," Abraham said. The grim report was followed by one of the red icons disappearing as well.

We can't keep it up, Thorne thought again. *We haven't the numbers*.

"Admiral, I have an idea."

Thorne turned expectantly to Alison Hale, his science officer. His lover.

"Pathfinder, sir!" she exclaimed.

Meriweather's forehead wrinkled. "How, Commander?"

"I can use the algorithms to create false sensor returns," she said, her explanation gaining speed as she gave it. "We can reverse what we normally do, you know? Instead of projecting potential pathways mathematically to track a ship, we can—"

"Nuts and bolts, Commander," Thorne urged her. They didn't have time for a science lesson.

"Use our comms array, overload whatever sensor returns they're using to navigate and target," she said.

"Overload—with fake signals?" Meriweather said, beginning to understand.

"Aye, sir."

"But we don't know how the Skane use subspace for navigation *or* targeting," the comms officer observed.

"With that much data flooding subspace, it won't matter," Hale said.

"You know that for sure?" Meriweather asked.

"No, sir," she said, her confidence not the least bit diminished. "One way to find out."

"Sir," Abraham reported at tactical, "the *Fury*'s weapons are offline, but she managed to knock out the second Skane vessel first." But his report only sounded half finished.

"Have *Fury* make for the Triangle," Thorne said. "Now what's the bad news?"

"A second enemy interdiction force is headed this way. Ten ships. ETA: one minute."

"Close enough to prevent our entering the Triangle?"

"Aye, sir."

How confident they must be of winning the station, Thorne thought. To release that many ships to pick off we few stragglers.

"Comms, order our escorts to stick with the *Requiem* all the way into the nebula. We'll cover their retreat with *Hispana*. Mister Abraham, gin up a targeting solution for that incoming force."

Thorne's orders were acknowledged at duty stations.

"Commander Hale," Thorne said, addressing her formally as he always did whenever they were in public, "work with communications to implement your plan."

"Aye, sir," she acknowledged.

"Bring us about, helm. Aim us straight at that lead Skane vessel."

"Aye, Admiral. Course one-one-two mark—"

"Admiral!" Abraham interrupted. "New signatures emerging from the Triangle. They look like ... oh, God, Admiral."

"Spit it out, Mister Abraham."

"It's a whole fleet of pirates, Admiral." Abraham cast a bleak, I-should-have-lived-a-better-life look at Thorne.

On-screen, Thorne watched ten red icons appear from the Triangle on an intercept course for *Requiem* and her escorts. The carrier had appeared likely to outrun the pursuing Skane and pass into the sanctuary of the nebula, especially with *Hispana* running interference for her, but now she and the others were caught between two hostile forces. They'd surely be cut to pieces. More and more pirate vessels crept onto the screen as red symbols. There were a baker's dozen, then a score, then more.

Unlike most ship's captains he knew, Malcolm Thorne wasn't superstitious. He considered such magical thinking a waste of brain cells, a flaw in the armor of morale that invited defeat. But maybe, just maybe, Fleet shouldn't have named his ship after the Roman legion lost somewhere in Britain in the second century AD.

So much for reclaiming that particular piece of bad luck for the good guys, Thorne thought.

What he said was, "Shit."

"Three ships, Commander. All burning hard for the Triangle."

On the bridge of the *Shark's Tooth*, Captain Joshua Mattei acknowledged the report from his tactical officer. Sayyida al-

Hurra stood next to him, confident in her choice of Mattei to captain the mission's command vessel. She knew he was still plagued by his betrayal of his Fleet comrades when Eva Park had been taken from *L'Esprit de la Terre* all those months ago, despite assurances from Sayyida that he'd done what he had to for New Nassau to survive. Leading the rescue mission to save as many of them as possible might heal that wound inside him. Knowing what was running through Mattei's mind was easy enough because she knew Mattei. But what must the Hangman be thinking as he saw the pirate armada emerge from the nebula?

Or feeling, more likely... Despair? A sense of universal justice come to roost on his head like a vulture? Or maybe impotent anger that all his efforts to demoralize her people by spacing them, one after another, had come to naught? Sayyida allowed herself a few moments to revel in the satisfaction of *schadenfreude* for any or all of those possibilities. But there was no time for such self-indulgence, so she cut short her musing and addressed Mattei's communications officer.

"Transmit, the friendship message, all frequencies. Let's see if they believe it."

Eva Park and Sheba Toma had crafted the message together as an exercise in diplomacy and discipline. It was short and to the point and coded correctly, which was Sheba's contribution. Eva had branded it with her stamp of approval and authority as the Bragg Administration's official representative to New Nassau. Sayyida estimated a fifty-fifty chance Thorne would accept it as genuine and in earnest, which were pretty good odds, now that she thought about it.

"Pass to *Emasculator*, *Shrieking Ex*, and *Storm of Hades*—perform a quick jump in a fast arc around their portside," Mattei ordered his comms officer. "Let's give the spiders something new to shoot at."

"Run, gun, rinse, repeat?" said the tactical officer, referring to the hit-hard-and-retreat-fast tactic the pirates had employed for decades to minimize damage to their own ships.

"It's worked well enough against Fleet over the years," Mattei said with no small measure of irony lining his dry tone. "Maybe it'll work *for* 'em, too."

The three ships effected their maneuver, jumping ahead of the rest of the pirate fleet to meet the fleeing carrier and her escorts.

Sayyida had scrambled two dozen ships from New Nassau and her satellites. It was like they'd been ready for liftoff and merely awaiting her order, though she knew that wasn't the case. But they'd been grounded for so long, she suspected, that their crews had run, not walked, to their duty stations. Her explanation of the mission to their captains had met with some resistance, especially when they'd learned whom they were headed to save. But, like their commander, each had weighed their loathing for the Hangman against the moral necessity to stick by their own species, and common sense had won out.

"Enemy fighters—sorry, Captain, Fleet fighters—have entered the Triangle," reported the tactical officer.

Mattei nodded as the man at communications said, "Hail coming in from the *Legio IX Hispana*. What a godawful name for a starship."

"Stow the commentary," Mattei said. "Put them on—"

"Sir," the officer interrupted reluctantly, "the hail is directed to the commander."

Mattei shared a look with Sayyida, then nodded. "Put him through."

Thorne's worn face appeared on the main screen. He straightened up immediately. The Hangman didn't look so scary when it was his neck in the noose, Sayyida noted.

"This is Rear Admiral Malcolm—"

"We know who you are," Sayyida said. "You've listened to the friendship message?"

Thorne appeared to smell something foul, then remember others could see his expression. "We're verifying its legitimacy now," he said, glancing off-screen. Whatever he saw there seemed to reassure him. "I recognize you too, Sayyida al-Hurra. I've been after your father for a long time."

"And never caught him."

"Maybe after the war—"

"He's dead," Sayyida said. "And might I suggest we set aside the posturing for another day? By now, from the message, you've verified Colonel Toma's personal code and you have Eva Park's endorsement. We'll provide safe passage for you and your fleet into the Triangle. Many of your ships are already under our protection."

"Protection?" Thorne said. A generous interpretation would consider his tone dubious at best. "Or capture?"

"Captain," the tactical officer said, precluding her response, "the Skane are breaking off. Should I have *Emasculator* and the others pursue?"

"No, recall them," Mattei answered. "Have them fall in behind the *Hispana* ... assuming, that is, that Admiral Thorne won't shoot at them?"

"Beggars can't be choosers, Miss al-Hurra," Thorne said, addressing her instead of Mattei.

"I'll interpret that, Admiral, to mean that you'd prefer cooperating with pirates to being blown out of space by aliens. And for the record—it's *Commander* al-Hurra. You'll follow my orders while under my protection. Agreed?"

Thorne eyed her coldly but knew when to fight and went to yield. He had, in fact, already proven that once today with the Skane, and now did so again with a much older enemy.

"As you say, Commander. We'll follow you."

26
SKELETON KEY

"DIARY ENTRY 8,512: *January 15th. I've decided to bring Circe back to life. Alice's failure to develop beyond parlor tricks, and those unpredictably random in their expression, will not sit well with my benefactor. And now, with the other interested party—I've had no choice in their involvement, it's true, for had I said no ... but, no matter. As I always do, I've managed to turn threat into opportunity. And Circe will give me control over* both *parties.*"

Ian turned off the playback. Hearing Korsakov's voice, so calm and deliberative—it was like all her time away from Strigoth simply disappeared. She still felt empty inside, but also expectant, as though waiting on bad news she was sure was coming. It was a strange, sickly combination of anxious awareness and floating detachment from what was happening around her.

"Who's 'Circe'?" Ben asked. "And how's he going to bring her back to life?"

"Not who, what," Zoey said. "It's what Korsakov named an old project from decades ago."

"It's what finally got him kicked out of the scientific community," said Ian. "He was part of an academic team on Earth manipulating human DNA to eradicate diseases and disorders. Cancer, diabetes, dementia. When he was my age, Andre Korsakov was considered one of the brighter lights in protein synthesis, which is how proteins are made that regulate the way DNA—"

Ben held up a hand. "I appreciate that you've already waded through all this and are presenting the highlights. But could you highlight the highlights?"

Ian eyed him. "I'm dumbing it down as much as I can."

Ignoring the implied slight, Ben changed tacks. "So, why was he kicked out?"

"Because he thought he knew better," Alice whispered. Like Ben, she might not understand all the scientific hoodoo, but she knew Andre Korsakov. He always thought he knew better. "Because he wouldn't play by the rules."

Zoey nodded. "Right."

"The point of all genetic manipulation research for the past five hundred years has been to improve the human species," Ian said. "To help us live longer. Be healthier."

"Okay," Ben said.

"Korsakov started wondering about the other direction." Ian's stern gaze seemed how a priest might look trying to explain to a child what a heretic was. "What would happen if, rather than manipulating cells to make them healthier, you—"

"—changed them to make them sick," Alice said.

"In a nutshell, yes."

"I can see why that would put him on the outs with the scientific community," Ben said. "Ethics. Morals. You know—the little things."

"Why?" Alice asked. Despite all she'd learned, despite her growing loathing for Andre Korsakov projected backward over the past three years, assembling the puzzle of what must have driven the man crazy was helping to ground her in the now.

"What would make a person even think about that kind of thing?"

"Originally, when he was our age," Ian said, "it was scientific curiosity, if you believe his diary. Questionable, maybe, from a moral standpoint, but a valid enough approach from a purely empirical perspective. Great discoveries are sometimes made by turning the study question on its head."

"So, he began modeling how to corrupt organisms from the inside-out," Zoey said.

Ben said, "Setting aside how nutty that makes him, Alice asks a good question: Why?"

"I'm surprised you don't see it."

Eyes narrowing, Ben snarked, "Dumb it down for me a little more, won't you?"

"Would you guys stop?" Zoey said. "Jesus." She stretched over Korsakov's console and pointed at the date of the diary entry Ian had just played. "See this? It's a little under two years ago. He didn't bring Circe back online as a project until then."

"So?"

"He did so," Zoey continued, "because Bragg was pressing him to make faster progress with you, Alice. Korsakov was afraid the secret grant money would dry up, and he needed something else to offer the administration to keep them friendly."

"So he brings back the old project that got him blacklisted," Ben stated. Alice still didn't get it, but a light was coming on in his eyes. "A genetic bio-weapon? Well, he sure picked the right president to sell it to."

"The dawning of knowledge is a powerful thing, huh?" Ian said.

Ben let the sarcasm pass. "Korsakov thought if Bragg ever *really* got tired of waiting around for Alice's power to develop, he'd have this in his back pocket to sell to the administration. A bioweapon to use against the Archies. Keep that grant money flowing."

Zoey nodded. "And not just against the Arcœnum. You heard him mention 'the other interested party'? Guess who's coming to dinner..."

"The Skane," Ben breathed. "So, he also brought Circe back online as an insurance policy against them?" He saw the confirmation in Zoey's expression and continued, "He was working both sides of the street, all right!"

"All *three* sides, if you think about it," Ian said. "Working Bragg twice with Alice and the Circe project; and then having Circe in-hand should the Skane become a problem."

"I'll give him this," Ben said, "for a crazy guy, he's brilliant."

Alice stared at him, appalled.

"I'm just saying," Ben defended himself. "Anything that can help us against the Skane." He moved on to the elephant-in-the-room question. "Did he ever finish Project Circe?"

Ian exchanged a look with Zoey. They both turned to Alice.

She glanced at first Ian, then Zoey. Her brain was way past drowning, now. And she wanted nothing to do with the feeling of dread beginning to chill her from the inside. It was like old knowledge creeping forward through the quicksand muck of reluctant memory. Her discussion with Ben about how it felt to be haunted tickled at the fringes of her conscious mind. She hadn't really understood what he'd meant about the ghosts of his dead comrades. That he saw them, but couldn't be sure they were there. This, she decided, felt very much like an old ghost coming back to terrorize her. It was like she could feel the chilly presence of a bony finger near the nape of her neck.

"I still don't understand what this has to do with me."

"Alice, it has everything to do with you," Ian said, almost apologetically. "Everything." He reached forward and engaged a control on the console to scrub forward to another of Korsakov's personal logs. "I'll show you how."

"Diary Entry 8,689: July 7th. I've finally perfected the parsing algorithm! Not only can I understand their clicks and taps and respond in simple terms to them, I can now have significant conversations! I can even translate complex concepts back to them in their own percussive language—in real time!"

Ian paused the playback.

"The Skane. He's talking about the shadow-spiders," Alice said, confirming it. It was something she'd known already. Something she'd witnessed firsthand.

"Yes," Ian said.

She glanced over at Ben to find him deep in thought. "But he's been able to do that for—"

"Not at this level," Ian said. He pushed play.

"I've gone back through recorded exchanges, applied the enhanced translation algorithm. As hoped, I've learned how Alice gained her ability."

Ian stopped again.

"How?" she whispered.

"Yeah," Ben said, "that start-stop thing is really annoying. Skip to the end, would you?"

Ian gave him a scornful look. "This is not something that can be rushed. Trust me."

Ben said nothing.

"To 'skip to the end,'" Ian said, "Korsakov was able to confirm that the anomalies revealed by Morgan Henry's scans on the *Rubicon* were evidence that the Skane had manipulated your brain, Alice. Suppressed old memory, rewrote the way you produce brainwaves. They gave you the ability to pair the normal brainwave patterns we've known about for centuries with their subspace counterparts."

Ben appeared lost again.

"Remember the professor's theory, Alice?" Zoey said. "That each wave in normal space has its subspace shadow? For example, the alpha has its omega."

Staring at each of them, one after the other, Ben said, "What the hell are you talk—"

"The Godwave," Alice said.

"Yes!" Ian's voice held the excitement of discovery. "And he was right!"

"Okay, maybe I was wrong before," Ben sighed. "Slow down a bit. What is this Godwave?"

"It's why I can do things," Alice said. "It's why I can make things move." She sighed, blinked slowly, and met Ben's perplexed expression with a deep, tired gaze. "It's how I helped Cinnamon."

"Somehow," Ian said, "the Skane turned *on* the ability in Alice's brain to pair the alpha wave with its omega shadow. This gave her a raw form of telekinesis. *Telekinesis* is the ability to manipulate—"

"I know what telekinesis is," Ben interrupted. "But why give the ability to Alice?"

Ian turned to her. "Alice, I think you were like a skeleton key."

"A what?"

"A skeleton key. In ancient houses on Earth with a lot of rooms, the locksmith would always provide a skeleton key—one key to fit all the locks, in case the owner ever lost the original door key. Your DNA is like that for humanity, Alice."

She was growing frustrated again. "I don't understand!"

"Your DNA," Ian continued, "it had the necessary precursors to unlock the potential for human telekinesis."

Ben's face was curious. "But why would the Skane do that? Just to prove it could be done?"

Ian shrugged. "*That* we haven't been able to figure out, yet. But there's more, here."

"Of course there is," Ben sighed.

Ian pushed play.

"And the translation algorithm is only the second most-important breakthrough of this week!" Korsakov's excited voice burst from the speaker as if he were a child running downstairs on Christmas morning. *"Circe is ready for her next phase! I've determined a way of tagging the unique human-leukocyte antigen complex of the subject. This solves the problem of secondary infection by targeting Circe at a single being via its unique HLA complex. The likelihood that two unrelated individuals share the same HLA complex is less than one in a hundred thousand, so the potential for inadvertently infecting myself or other research staff is negligible."* Korsakov had calmed himself, as though gathering his resolve to proceed. *"Thirty years. I have to say, there were times when my faith in myself wavered. But patience, persistence, and dedication have paid off! With previous validation of the Circe viral model to ninety-six-point-eight percent surety, real-world trials can now safely begin."*

Ian paused again.

"Real-world trials?" Alice whispered. She shivered when the ghost's fingertip brushed nearer her neck.

Ian opened his mouth to continue, but Ben spoke instead.

"This Circe virus can be targeted to DNA, right? Signatured to a species?"

Ian nodded. "It's what makes it weaponizable. But a sample of DNA is needed to tweak the virus to a specific species."

"So Korsakov *did* finish," Ben said. "And it works?"

Zoey let out a painful gasp that sounded a lot like grief.

"Yes, it works," Ian said simply.

"What kind of real-world trials?" Alice pressed.

But Ben barreled forward. "You know what this means? We can defeat the Skane! If we can determine a delivery mechanism—"

"You can't be serious!" Zoey was disbelieving. "You have no idea what Korsakov has done!"

"Sure I do," Ben returned, just as passionately. "That crazy, traitorous bastard has given us a way to save the species!"

"Save us why?" Alice asked. She'd spoken so softly and yet so forcefully that everyone turned to her. "When we're capable of what Korsakov has done?"

"Let's debate the morality later," Ben said. "Kill the Skane now!"

"Oh, Alice," Zoey said, "you still don't even know—"

"Know?" Alice said. "Know what? What else could there possibly be...?"

Ian shut his eyes briefly, then engaged the diary recording again.

"I once called Morgan Henry 'friend,'" said Korsakov, his tone almost regretful. *"But he has stymied me with Alice at every turn. Every time I near a breakthrough, he gets in the way. Now, I've determined a way to advance both projects at the same time. God will understand."*

There was a shuffling sound on the recording, as though Korsakov were steeling himself to perform an unwelcome task.

"Oh, no," Ben said.

Past the ability to think, certainly past feeling, Alice queried, "Ben?"

"Stop the playback," Ben demanded. "Stop it now!"

Zoey reached a finger toward the panel, but Ian intercepted her. "She needs to hear this, you said it yourself."

"Turn it off!" Ben shouted.

"Ben!" Alice cried out. "What's—"

Ben lunged forward, and a one-sided struggle with Ian

began, the Marine captain easily shoving the scientist out of the chair. But Korsakov had already begun speaking again.

"I will introduce Circe to Henry tomorrow. He's due for a monthly B-12 injection. I can attach the virus as a rider to the vitamin. Then, we will monitor the progress of the disease."

Movement ceased. There was a single, hissing sob from Zoey, though Korsakov's treachery, his murderous act against his "friend," was obviously not new knowledge to her. Ben seethed, hunched over, knuckles white with fury as he grasped the console.

Ian lay on the floor, perhaps afraid to move, or perhaps unwilling to. Quietly, he said, "I'm so sorry, Alice."

She sat in the chair, eyes wide, unable to feel—anything. Half-convinced she'd wake from a terrible, perverse dream. A nightmare that tried to make sense of all the twisting tendrils of her life's path, a nightmare worse than anything she'd suffered on Drake's World. Waking on the *Seeker*, afraid and alone, the loss of her family, the heart-stopping terror of the shadow-spiders. The rescue by Ben, the torture in Korsakov's Bell Jar, and Morgan's strange wasting disease and death...

No longer a mystery now. As the depths of Andre Korsakov's betrayal hit her, Alice's mind abruptly focused, sharpened.

No, not Morgan's death. Morgan's murder.

Her face grew cold. Her palms tingled. A chill skittered across her skin on electric feet. Like the heralding breeze of a winter touching the edges of her soul. Determination laced its cold fingers together, crystallizing around her heart. Steeling her for action.

"Alice..." Ben stood up straight. His expression of sadness and worry for her almost broke through the fury that was building. Almost. "I know this is horrible. Morg Henry was a friend of mine, too—for my whole life. But I see that look on your face. I know that look. You can't—"

Alice heard him saying words but didn't comprehend them. They were just noise.

He killed Morgan.

Murdered him.

Took him from me.

Each thought, accompanied by an action.

Standing up from her chair.

Staring at Ben's mouth but not hearing him.

Stepping toward the door.

"Zoey," Ian whispered. "Get the shroud. Captain, you'd better—"

But Alice didn't wait for them to act. She'd spent her whole life—her whole *new* life—letting outside forces push her in one direction or another. Now, she'd decide, and no one else. No one would stop her.

No one can *stop me.*

Ben reached out a hand, but Alice slipped past him.

"We need him, Alice!" he cried out.

He stopped moving suddenly, was locked into place. They all were. Unharmed but unable to move.

"Don't kill him, Alice!" Ben shouted. "He can help us beat the Skane!"

Exiting Korsakov's quarters, Alice heard him but wasn't listening. They were all calling after her, trying to stop her, but it was all just noise.

She'd decide what came next.

27
THE STRUGGLE

"GET UP," Alice said. Her thumb slid off the intercom button, leaving the channel open.

Inside her was void. As though there existed within only cold vacuum for Andre Korsakov where her sense of self, her emotional center, had been.

With his back to her, the professor lay motionless in his fetal cocoon.

"I said, get up."

Outside the door, Ben and Ian shouted. Alice had released them from their paralysis and locked herself in with Korsakov. She could hear their attempts to gain entry, bypassing this and trying to force that. They wouldn't succeed.

Korsakov finally moved. Like a hibernating mammal in winter, sluggish with the memory of how muscles worked. Abruptly, he turned and rolled in one swift motion into a sitting position. He'd shaved. His hair was cut. How had he managed that in the short span since she'd since last seen him? Except for the simple technician fatigues he wore, he seemed almost his old self. A bit thinner, maybe.

"I thought earlier must have been a dream," he said. "For once, I'm glad to see I was wrong."

"You lied to me," Alice said. "Everything was a lie. You murdered Morgan."

Korsakov stood smoothly. The wrinkles in his jumpsuit stretched out. "'Murder' is a word fat with judgment. You of all people, Alice, should refrain from such pedestrian concerns."

Her raw hatred growing for Korsakov as he spoke, she walked to the window-wall. "Is that your strategy? To make us seem similar? To justify your *murder of Morgan* by making us, what, outsiders together?"

Korsakov stepped forward too. One step, two, until he stood mirroring her.

"But we are similar, Alice," he said. "Both gifted amongst the steaming herd of banal humanity. Both obligated by our talents to ignore the rules that keep the rest of the cattle in line. You and I have a holy calling. To ignore it would be to ignore the will of God."

"You're crazy," Alice said. "You're insane."

Korsakov shrugged. "Do you know the definition of insanity, Alice?"

"I'm looking at it."

His lips broadened with a smile. "Clever, if a bit predictable. But at least you avoided that tired, old cliché about repetitive action." He dropped his hands to his sides and stood arrow-straight, like a soldier enduring inspection. "The definition of insanity is whatever the cattle say it is. Because they don't understand the exceptions to themselves. Because their so-called morality can't possibly endorse what they term 'aberrant behavior.' Cattle need classifications to keep the nightmares away in the waking hours of the day. They need to feel in control of the fragile illusion of their so-called reality."

"You're just babbling bullshit," Alice hissed. Every time he spoke, every time that conceited tone issued from his throat, she felt an irresistible impulse to cut it off. Along with his air. "I asked you a question."

"So you did."

"Well?"

Korsakov waggled his head back and forth, considering. From the corridor, the pleading and pounding continued, filling the momentary silence.

"They're right, you know," Korsakov said.

"What? Who?"

"I know how to stop the Skane."

"I don't care," Alice said.

"I don't believe you."

"I don't care about that, either. Tell me why you murdered Morgan Henry!" There was a popping sound, then a cracking. Between them, a small break the size of a human hand appeared in the wall. Alice forced herself to calm down. *Not yet. Not yet.*

"Ah, there it is," Korsakov said, staring at the fracture. "Proof I'm right—again! You've transcended yourself, Alice. You've become all I knew you could be. I'm so proud of you—"

Alice felt her power swelling, like vomit clawing its way up her throat. It needed to go somewhere. Her right hand lifted, formed a clamp. Her fingers grasped air as if it were a solid thing. Andre Korsakov's head jerked up. His teeth clacked together. The veins of his neck stood out, as she constricted his airway.

"Will you ... murder *me*, then?" he gasped. "Answers..."

Alice blinked. "What did you say?"

She released him, and Korsakov fell to his knees.

"I have the answers you seek," he rasped, tasting air again. "I know what happened on Drake's World."

It was like the door had been transformed. Become just another part of the wall with useless lines around its edge once marking where an actual door had been.

"Is there no other way into this room?" Ben Stone asked, hoarse from shouting.

Ian Secord reclined against the wall, massaging his hand. "No. This is the only door."

Ben studied the exposed manual override panel. He needed Moze down here. But no, it wasn't a mechanical problem. Alice was holding the door locked.

The facility's alarm rang out. The lighting around them snapped from the bright white of normal operations to the red of crisis.

"What's that?"

Ian answered, "No idea."

"Hey Adonis," Ben heard in his ear.

"Gal?"

Ian looked at him funny, and Ben stepped away.

"Our friends are back. The creepy ones."

Ben glanced backward at Ian, then decided now was not the time for need-to-know. "The scout?"

"Yep. And headed this way."

"ETA?"

"Minutes, max," Gal said. *"Outer edge of the system."*

"Ship's status?"

There was a pause while Gal looped Moze and Torque into the channel.

"We're not done refitting but we're spaceworthy," Moze said. *"But it's gonna take me longer than we have to put all the pieces back together."*

"Get started," Ben said. "We need to have a backup plan. You're it."

"Backup plan?" Torque asked, irritated. *"What's Plan A?"*

"Just put Humpty Dumpty back together again," Ben said. "We've got our own problems down here."

Another pause, and then Torque said, *"Moze, put it all back together. Do your load testing on the fly, if you can safely."*

"Now that that's settled," Ben said, "Plan A is that someone needs to reassemble Desi, too."

Silence littered with a bit of static.

"I'm your girl, stud. I'm the only one without both hands full."

Leave it to Gal Galatz to sound lewd with a life-or-death threat approaching at translight speed.

"I'll turn on instruct mode," Ben said. "Desi herself can help you. But she needs your hands."

"Folding tabs into slots?" Gal said. *"My favorite pastime!"*

"And set a clock on that scout ship. Put it on the public address system, or whatever they have here."

"Will do," Gal said. "Dog *out."*

Ben turned to Ian, who stood with an impatient, expectant look on his face.

"I heard half of that. The Skane are coming here?"

"A scout ship, in a few minutes."

The young scientist's face went slack for a moment, but Ben had to give him credit. His fear response passed quickly.

"We have formidable defenses here."

"I'm sure you do." Ben replied to be kind. But he'd seen their defenses. Analyzed them while the dockmaster was playing his game of chicken as the *Dog* entered the system. The meager defense platforms of Tarsus Research Station might make a poorly armed pirate think twice before venturing too closely, but they'd be easily handled by the Skane. They needed to be ready to repel invaders. "What kind of personal weapons do you have?"

Ian stared blankly. "We're a research facility." He appeared oblivious at just how naïve he sounded. "We don't have soldiers here."

"Well, you've got *one*." Ben clapped Ian on the shoulder. "Time to Alamo up, egghead."

"You know what happened..." Alice's cheeks flushed with rage.

Korsakov got back to his feet. But despite his expression of bravado, his attitude reflected earlier in his ramrod posture was diminished. They both knew why.

"You *knew* the whole time!" Alice shouted.

"Not the whole time. But in my exchanges with the aliens, I came to understand."

The lights switched from ambient to siren red. The station alert erupted from hidden speakers.

Korsakov cocked his head. "Proximity alarm. By the sequence of the clarion, it sounds like a hostile ship has entered the system." He'd spoken normally, but Alice could barely hear him. With a thought, she muted the noise. Korsakov looked at her somberly. "They're coming."

She eyed him coldly. "But not to save you."

Flatly, he answered, "No."

"Eleven minutes, thirty seconds to alien incursion."

The auto-countdown came without urgency, in a flat, dispassionate tone.

"And my family?" Alice pressed. "Did you ever really look for them?"

"I did!" Korsakov's enthusiasm sprang back to life. "I thought, there might be three more out there just like her! Alas, what happened to them remains a mystery."

Alice assumed that was likely a lie, if only because Andre Korsakov had spoken the words.

The tiny cuts in the window-wall crept outward like icy fingers.

"But here's what you really want to know, Alice," Korsakov said. "You were to be a wedge. Between the Alliance and the Arcœnum."

"A wedge? What does that mean?" Knowing that what he said was most likely untrue didn't deter Alice from wanting to hear it. Maybe there were nuggets of truth she could mine from it later. After he was dead. "Explain."

Korsakov stood up straighter, as though addressing a conference of his peers. "The aliens—"

"They're called the Skane," Alice said.

"Are they? I never felt the need to name them. But, as you say. The *Skane* are a species driven to conquer. To exterminate competition in the universe; to take worlds and resources, and propagate across space. Not for any reason we can understand; in fact, there's no *reason* to it at all that I've been able to determine. No evaluative process. No cost-benefit analysis. They're like intelligent, space-faring locusts: moving, stripping, leaving nothing useful behind when they move on. Unfettered by morality, unhindered by any sense of responsibility to a power greater than themselves. They simply exist to continue existing. And to *expand*."

"Why does that have anything to do with—"

"Historically," he interrupted, "Drake's World was a platform for studying the region around it. For decades, scientists looked up, focused especially on the Red Scar Nebula. Marcus Keller was different."

Alice's ears perked up. "My father? Different how?"

Korsakov's smile was almost admiring, if an aspiring god can be said to admire a mere mortal. "Marcus Keller looked *down*. He studied Drake's World itself. Its various species. Its ecological diversity. Most significantly for you, its underworld."

Korsakov's expression became pensive. "I surmise that your father's otherwise empirical interests threatened to expose a forward outpost of the Skane. They've prepared for decades to conquer this region of space—that much I gleaned from my conversations with them. In you, they found a weapon to help them do so."

"Me?" Despite her boiling anger, it came out quiet as the squeak of a fieldmouse. "You mean my abilities?"

"Indirectly, yes." Korsakov began pacing the length of the splintered wall between them. "The aliens, for all their superficial barbarity, are quite intelligent. Lingering paranoia of Arcœnum mind-control from the previous war catapulted Piers Bragg into power. In you, the Skane discovered the potential to unlock similar abilities inside humans..." He swung around, excited. "Can you imagine, Alice? The power to pull apart, remap, *remake* your DNA to give you control over *subspace*. The power of a god to bend reality to your will!"

"You're lying," Alice said, not nearly so convinced as she made it sound. She reached up to touch her temple. She couldn't remember having the scar before she'd woken aboard the *Seeker*. But then, Alice couldn't remember much before she'd awakened, only incomplete snippets of emotional memory tied to her family. When she noticed him watching her stroke the old wound, Alice jerked her hand back down. "You always lie!"

"I'm not lying now."

"If the Skane gave me this power, why would they hunt me? Try to kill me?"

"Hunt you?" Korsakov appeared genuinely puzzled. "*Kill* you?"

"In the dungeon! The caves below Drake's World. I barely got away from them!"

Understanding lit up Korsakov's face. "Oh, you thought...

No, no, no. They weren't pursuing you, Alice. They were *protecting* you."

Now it was she who didn't understand. "What do you mean? Protecting me from what?"

"Anything," Korsakov replied. "Everything. Protecting you, and driving you forward."

"Driving me..." Then, their minds synced. "Toward the surface. Toward Ben!"

Korsakov nodded. "So the Alliance would pick you up."

Alice wanted to protest, but it all rang true. She'd never understood how she'd outrun the shadow-spiders in the caves. Now, she knew, they'd never intended to catch her. But Korsakov's supposed connecting of the dots only raised more questions.

"You said 'indirectly' before—that the Skane used me *indirectly* to invade. How did giving me this ... this power, how did that help them?"

Resuming lecture mode, the professor faced her straight on. "One way or another, your exhibiting genuine psychokinetic ability would make it easier for them to conquer. Would the Arcœnum see you as a weapon developed by a hostile Alliance president in preparation for a war he all but promised in his campaign? Or would a hostile Alliance president, predisposed to believe the Arcœnum would pervert a human by giving her their own mind-control ability, see you as the ultimate infiltrator for the enemy? Remember his paranoia of the Psyckers? You would serve as the proof that he was right to lock them up! Either way—whichever species instigated the war, with you as the catalyst—the other would naturally respond as they must. And once both sides were weakened..."

"The Skane would attack," Alice said. "After Sirius, after the new war began there—"

"The Skane decided to strike," Korsakov said.

"Ten minutes to alien incursion," announced the automated countdown.

"You still haven't answered my question," Alice said. "Tell me *why*."

"Why? Why what?"

"Why you murdered Morgan!"

"Oh, that." Korsakov made a dismissive gesture. "I had to make progress with you, Alice. And I needed a test subject for my research—"

As he spoke with couldn't-care-less detachment, Alice raised her hands again. Both opened, and Andre Korsakov lifted from the floor. His hands flew to his neck, trying to counter the invisible force once again stopping his ability to breathe.

The fractures in the plastinium between them extended with an almost imperceptible *ssskrick* sound. Alice moved in closer, dozens of her own reflections advancing back at her.

"What will be gained if you choose this?" Marcus Keller asked in her head. Her father's scientist voice, as dispassionate as Korsakov, as detached as she herself felt.

He deserves to die. He's a monster. He murdered Morgan!

Korsakov's face grew more and more red. Blood, trapped in his skull from the pressure.

"And what will you lose?"

Not her father's voice, but Morgan Henry's. Gruff with affection. Prickly but patient.

I miss you so much!

The cracks in the plastinium stretched to the walls now, a thousand deadly knives waiting to be released outward.

"Answer my question, kid."

Korsakov kicked at the air, his feet angled down, seeking floor. His face, purple.

I—I don't know... He deserves to die!

"He does," Morgan admitted in that I'll-grant-your-point-but way of his. *"But do you have the right to take his life?"*

If not me, who?

Fixed on Alice, Korsakov's eyes were no longer smug. Only fearful of the unknown. An aspiring god coming into the unwelcome knowledge that even gods can die.

"Not for you to know, maybe." Alice heard the shrug in Morgan's voice. *"But you don't need me to tell you that, do you? I think you know."*

"Don't spoil the test now, Alice," Marcus Keller said. *"We almost have the final results."*

Her eyes flooded. With tears, with memories, with longing for all she'd lost. With absolute hatred for the amoral human being whose life she was ready to take away. With the struggle inside herself, the need to make sure Andre Korsakov never harmed anyone, ever again. And if she took upon herself the right to judge and execute Andre Korsakov, what would that make her if not an aspiring god, cast in his own image?

You of all people, Alice, should refrain from such pedestrian concerns.

Her skin tingled with gooseflesh. Her hands fell to her sides.

Korsakov dropped to the floor.

The resonant hum in the plastinium faded, leaving a broken but still-standing window between them.

"Five minutes to alien incursion," said the automated countdown.

28
DEVIL'S DUTY

A VAGUE RUMBLING CAME from inside the station's walls. The sound reminded Ben of an Old Earth war vid, when distant shelling unnerves the hero and his comrades, soon to receive their own dose of it.

"What's that?" Ian asked.

"Bombardment." Ben's lack of familiarity with Tarsus Station prevented him from estimating what the Skane were hitting. "Softening up your defenses."

"Mister Secord, please respond," said a voice Ben recognized. But this time, the man spoke with far less attitude. Far more fear.

Ian engaged the wall comms. "Go ahead."

"The attackers took out our pulse cannons," the dockmaster said. *"Thankfully, they didn't hit atmospheric."*

Ben held up a finger and Ian asked the dockmaster to hold on.

"Is there a secure part of this facility?" Ben asked. "With extra shielding? Heavy blast doors? Anyplace like that?"

"Sure, medical is double-shielded against radiation. And

there's a secondary facility below that, a strike-rated bunker. We call it the basement."

"That's your Alamo chapel," Ben said.

"My what—?"

"Get everyone in there. And keep trying to reach Alice. We need Korsakov alive, Ian. We can't win this thing without him."

Ian stared down the long, empty corridor leading to the medical wing but didn't move. Ben didn't blame him. "What are you gonna do?" Ian asked.

"Stand in their way," Ben said firmly. "The sooner you go, the safer you'll be. Once they breach..."

"*Breach*?"

"Ian, order your people to meet you in medical, and hurry. And tell the dockmaster to restore normal lights! I can't see jack shit with all this red."

If he had Desi, it wouldn't matter. But he didn't have Desi. Yet.

Ian walked, not hurriedly, toward the medical section while talking with the dockmaster. He held Ben's gaze, as though eye contact were a rope keeping him from falling.

Ben called after him, "And don't forget Cinnamon if you have to retreat to the basement!"

The scientist nodded before disappearing around the corner. In the moment that followed, Ben felt very alone, very naked with only his sidearm and two magazines of ammunition. The stationwide attention alert sounded.

"This is the dockmaster. All personnel are to proceed to medical on Mister Secord's orders. Leave personal belongings behind. Repeat: all personnel are to proceed to medical, Mister Secord's orders."

The lights around Ben snapped back to normal luminescence. At least he wouldn't have to fight half-blind. The exposed wall panel tempted him to try and break into the observation room again. But Ben's mission had changed with the Skane preparing to board the station. He had multiple priorities vying for one Marine captain's operational abilities to meet them. It was then, in the thorny silence after the announcement, that Ben felt the presence coalesce behind him.

"Been a long time," he said, turning to meet it.

Bricker shrugged his ghostly shoulders. *Been busy.*

"Where are the scouts?"

I imagine they're prepping to board the station at its weakest point. I'd guess that to be—

"Not the Skane scouts. Baqri and DeSoto."

Oh, them. They're what kept me busy. But I got 'em up the hill, finally.

"Heaven?"

The shrug again. *Let's just say they mustered out. Moved on.*

"Care to brief me on what that means, Sergeant?"

Nope. Not on my duty roster.

"Convenient."

Beggars can't be choosers, L-T.

"Captain now, actually."

Well, shit my britches. Will wonders never cease?

"What are you still doing floating around here?"

Checking off things that are *on my duty roster.* Bricker twirled a see-through index finger at the facility around them. *So, what's your mission plan?*

Bricker asked it conversationally. Like they were standing at one of those tri-cornered tables in Fort Leyte's Rumor Mill, shooting the shit over tepid beer.

"Kill the enemy," Ben said, "before they kill me."

I see you paid attention in advanced tactics. Mission details?

"Not a clue. Hard to plan for an enemy you know nothing about." Ben pulled his pistol, double-checked it was in working order. Dropped the magazine, reassured himself it was full, popped it back in.

You should clean that more often, Bricker critiqued.

Ben grinned at the ghost with a glibness he didn't feel. "That's what *she* said."

The station's inflectionless female emulator stated, *"Two minutes to alien incursion."*

Bricker's ghostly eyes roamed the ceiling. *A hundred twenty seconds until he's watching his innards spill onto the deck, and he's making jokes. Shitbox, in case you missed this mission-critical detail, time's short.*

"It usually is. And that's *Captain* Shitbox to you, Sergeant Slaughtered." Ben holstered his sidearm. His palm left the grips slick with sweat. "And I see the afterlife hasn't improved your attitude at all."

Miracles are in short supply all over, Bricker grunted. *Just remember what I told you before.*

Frowning, Ben asked, "What was that again?"

Fucking officers. The spirit clucked his spirited tongue. *My tour's almost over in this deployment, boy. I can't keep wiping your ass for you!*

Seeing Bricker's body, crushed beyond saving, buried under the rockfall below Drake's World landed on Ben with all the weight of memory. But then, he remembered. "A Drop Marine's first duty is to fight for those who can't fight for themselves."

Bricker grunted. *Now, see? That wasn't so hard.*

Ben leered at the gray ghost. "She *never* said that."

The smartassery helped keep the emotion deep in his gut, where it was useful. Kept him from vomiting it against the wall and making a mess that reeked of his terror.

The specter sighed a breath of air he wasn't actually breathing. *These poor bastard eggheads are doomed.* He straightened up at attention as though hearing something Ben couldn't. *Gotta go, Shitbox.*

"I've got one for you," Ben said.

No time. The pale shadow of the grizzled sergeant already seemed thinner. *If you're late for reveille up there, there's hell to pay—*

"Are you real?"

Bricker's ghost stopped talking, open-mouthed, as if he wanted to answer but couldn't. Maybe wasn't allowed to. But before he'd faded altogether, Ben heard his own question answered with another.

Does it matter?

The thought hung like a whiff of pleasant memory in Ben's mind. An eyeblink later, and he stood alone again outside the observation room.

The stationwide hail sounded. *"This is the dockmaster! We've got a breach in—"*

There was a scathing, spine-raking sound like metal grinding metal. Then, static. Then, nothing but the fear of what was coming drawing up Ben's balls. He wrangled the fear, held onto it tightly, sculpted it into motivation. Just like he'd been taught.

Marines run, he thought, quoting his boot camp sergeant's sly twist of words. *But* toward *the danger. Never away.*

"Station breach," reported the alert system in its automated, passionless tone. *"Station breach."* The channel died at the source.

What, strategically, would the Skane be after? Alice? Korsakov? Tarsus Station itself?

"Gal," Ben pressed the skin below his right ear and let that question percolate in his hindbrain. "How's Desi coming along?"

"Gal's a little busy," Torque replied. *"Almost assembled. We'll be down ASAP."*

"We?"

"You think I'm gonna sit this one out?" Torque sounded offended.

"Fine. Meet me in Korsakov's quarters. Sending a ping. That's where they'll head, I think."

Ben loathed leaving Alice unguarded, but just lately, she'd shown she could take care of herself. And this time, the girl wasn't the mission. The Skane were here for something. And the most strategically significant thing on the station, even more important than Alice and her abilities, was Korsakov's research. Isolated on encrypted drives in his quarters. Maybe the Skane wanted it for themselves. To create a countermeasure to its threat, maybe even weaponize it against the Alliance. Ben couldn't let that happen.

So he stepped off for Korsakov's quarters, the fluttering fear in his belly shaping into something useful: inspiration to live. To preserve the research, to protect Alice and Secord and his staff, and the whole damned species, when it came down to it. *Hell, even Korsakov,* Ben thought, his fast walk becoming a quick march. To protect even those who *could* fight for themselves, like the *Dog*'s crew. If he did his job right, they wouldn't have to. From the back of his mind came the ghostly echo of Bricker's dearly departed voice.

Watch your six, Captain Shitbox, sir.

Drop Marine Captain Ben Stone kneeled, pistol braced, wedged in the open doorway connecting the corridor and the outer library of Korsakov's personal suite, reviewing mission-critical specifics. His pistol ammunition was limited. No rapid-fire, vid-hero bullshit. Targeted, single shots. Panic meant failure. Primary defensive position in the doorway; fallback position at Korsakov's office, where the final dead man's switch option was ready to go. Check, check, and check.

He heard them before he saw them.

Tap-tap-tap.

The rapid-fire advance of their sharp, blade-like gait on the bone-white station decking. Ben tried to parse their advance, tried to estimate their number, but it was impossible. How many legs did they have? And how many of those were dedicated to mobility? Could be one Skane. Could be a dozen.

My stomach votes for one.

There were two. One up top, one below. Shadow followed by substance as they took a hard right from the T-junction at the end of the corridor. Skittering like spiders, black as space, eye-like knobs dotted over core bodies. Extended, claw-like legs curved downward like scythes propelling them forward.

The Skane look just like their ships, Ben thought, holding his fire.

Trigger discipline.

The corridor was long and his ammo limited.

They covered the distance quickly.

Target discipline.

Ben exhaled. He fired at the lead Skane scurrying along the ceiling, plugging it center mass. There were more of the bone-scraping screeches he'd heard when the dockmaster died.

Well, they can be hurt. And there was hope in that.

Neither of the Skane stopped. There was no time for fear to take hold of Ben. His psyche switched to autopilot. Focused his vision. Nothing mattered but the two targets rushing at him from the killing zone of the corridor.

Ben squeezed off another round, then another, methodical

and controlled, and the first Skane warrior dropped to the floor, still moving but less mobile. Wounded.

Careless of its comrade, the second Skane didn't waver, just kept on coming. Ben dropped his aim, popped three successive, quick rounds as it charged him. But the alien had learned, dodging impossibly fast. *Almost phasing*, Ben thought. One round hit, two missed. It didn't slow at all.

The first Skane crawled forward, intent on reaching him.

Both squealed what might be pain or a challenge or both, and Ben emptied his weapon into the faster alien. More spine-gripping screaming, and the closest Skane's dodge diminished.

But both still came on.

When they were ten meters away, Ben pulled back inside Korsakov's quarters. The door *shunked* into the wall, and he slammed his palm over the lock, engaging the emergency seal.

A sharp *thunk!* impacted the outside. Backing away, Ben dropped the empty magazine from his pistol, replaced it, nearly tumbling backward over a couch in the library.

Multiple blows pounded the door. The second alien, joining the first. The polysteel dented inward, if barely. Another series of impacts, and the dent became deeper. Ben continued his retrograde until he reached the second doorway leading to Korsakov's wall of monitors and computer banks. At the station where Ian had sat not so long ago, revealing the extent of Korsakov's betrayal—of Alice, of all of humanity—the cursor flashed patiently, waiting for Ben's voice command.

DELETE ALL DATA? Y/N

This is where he'd make his last stand. And if the Skane got through, if all hope was lost, he'd decided it was better to delete Korsakov's research than let it fall into the hands of the enemy.

A shriek erupted from the control panel of the outer door. A smaller version of the wheel-like ninjas the Skane had sent against the *Junkyard Dog* embedded itself in Korsakov's bookcase. It had sliced through the door's control panel, shorting out the lock.

"Where's that goddamned armor!" Ben shouted into comms. "Torque!"

No answer. The outer door cracked but didn't open. Both Skane, moving with difficulty but moving, grabbed it with their reaper-like legs and tore it open with a vicious shearing of resistant metal. Ben took aim and fired once, twice, three times at the lead warrior as it plunged through the opening. It jerked with the impact of the slugs, writhed, and fell to the floor. The second alien grabbed the first, lifted it up, pushed forward. Heedless, ruthless, it used its writhing comrade as protection and lurched across the room. Every shot from Ben's pistol hit the body of the still-squirming shield.

"You want Korsakov's magic virus?" he snarled. "Come and take it!"

Then, the alien shield stopped moving. Stopped screaming. The second Skane maintained its meticulous, tortured advance, holding up its dead comrade for cover.

Three rounds left. Ben was tempted to charge. Maybe the warrior would drop the Skane corpse to meet him. Maybe he'd get a lucky shot in a vital organ and have one last chance at killing it before he ran out of ammo. But if he left cover and wasn't lucky, if the Skane got past him, Korsakov's research...

A leg showed itself. Ben adjusted his aim and fired once. The warrior screeched, halted, cowered down behind its corpse-shield.

"Computer," Ben said, gathering himself to charge before fear paralyzed him altogether. "Proceed with—"

Two loud concussions filled the room. So deafening, Ben's ears clouded over. Instinctively he ducked, thinking something had exploded. Had he completed the delete order to the computer? A quick glance behind him revealed the cursor, still flashing. Looking forward again, he saw the most beautiful sight he'd ever seen.

Torque strode through the twisted doorway, shucking shells from her shotgun. The second Skane screamed, dark ichor jutting from its core. So, they could bleed! Black, like everything else about them. The Skane turned on Torque, exposing its flank to Ben. He stood up, took careful aim as it rose on its hindmost legs and demonstrated at Torque, who leveled her shotgun. Together—pirate and Marine, shotgun and sidearm—they unloaded their weapons at the same time. The Skane warrior split in two, cut apart by the fire, its shrill challenge cut short in a cloud of black mist.

"Now, that was a fucking entrance!" Ben enthused, his grin wide. He thought he might just run over and kiss the big lug of a woman.

Torque's face was anything but triumphant. In fact, she looked downright grave. "Don't get your undies all sticky, Stone," she rumbled, reloading. "More bad guys are on the way."

"More?" Ben said stupidly. His ears were still flooded. Maybe he'd heard her wrong. "More than two?" He looked down at the open slide of his sidearm indicating it was empty. And that had been his second magazine. He watched, mute, as Torque pulled two fresh shells from the bandolier slung across her torso like a beauty queen's banner.

"Moze took control of station lockdown protocols and managed to slow them down by closing off pressure doors. But yeah, they're coming."

Like he'd jabbed a field stim into his thigh, Ben's tactical training kicked back in, fixed him toward the coming fight. He looked around, searching for anything that might make a decent weapon. Korsakov was fond of antiques, or antique re-creations at least, and Ben spotted a small wooden table in the reading nook of the library. He picked it up and threw it as hard as he could against the wall. It smashed into three pieces, and he grabbed up the stoutest, sharpest one. Turning it on end, Ben made a quick assessment of the cross-section: compacted, polymered wood 3D printed to represent five-hundred year-old, upper-crust furniture. Solid enough to make a respectable club.

Better than his bare hands, anyway.

Over comms, Gal sent, *"Armor's headed your way, homing in on your location. ETA two minutes!"*

Examining the door's ruined state, Torque answered, "Make sure Moze opens those pressure doors for Desi, or all she'll find is two corpses full of spider holes."

"Copy that!"

29
ALAMO UP

"THEY'RE COMING," Torque said.

But Ben could hear the *click-clack-click* of their bladed feet. Torque tumbled the library's couch over to make a barricade, then pulled two shells from her bandolier to hold in her left hand for faster reload. Ben positioned himself to one side of the door for ambush, pressing against the far wall, hoping he was outside the scatter pattern of Torque's side-by-side.

The *tap-tap-tap* of the enemy stopped just outside the mangled door. Ben and Torque shared an anxious, curious look. An object whirred into the room almost too fast to see, then stuck itself with a shearing thunk into the wall opposite the door.

Ben recognized a grenade when he saw one.

"Cover!"

No explosion followed, but pain stabbed through the middle of Ben's skull. His vision flashed orange and blurred. His inner ear failed, and he collapsed dizzy to his knees.

The effect began to fade quickly but left both humans helpless. The first Skane warrior wedged its bulk into the doorway.

Ben's vision cleared. He didn't see Torque. The warrior focused its attention on him.

Ben felt drunk with vertigo. His limbs were slow to respond. Standing was a fantasy, and he tried to crab backward, made awkward by the club in his hand, to put distance between himself and the enemy. The alien yanked its last leg from the ripped metal of the door and came at him. Fighting to regain equilibrium, Ben scampered clumsily away until his back hit the wall. Torque reappeared, using the couch to right herself. She leveled her scattergun at a second warrior crawling in from the corridor. The first Skane charged at Ben.

On your feet, Marine!

Torque's shotgun boomed once, eliciting choppy shrieks from the second warrior. Wounded, but not down, and now clear of the doorway and charging the source of its pain. The first Skane was on top of Ben now, and he twisted to avoid a scything limb aimed at his stomach. He offered a weak back-hand riposte with the table leg, and it bounced off the alien appendage, sending a reverse shock of kinetic energy up his arm.

Ben scrambled along the wall—*I'm fucked, I'm fucked, I'm fucked*—and finally managed to hunch to his unsteady feet. A second *boom!* of Torque's shotgun clotted his ears.

The first Skane chittered eagerly, closing the distance to him again. Imagining DeSoto and Baqri ambushed, speared from behind with no chance to defend themselves, lit a furious fire in Ben's belly. He somehow dodged a series of slashing attempts to cut him in two. But he was so focused on his enemy he stumbled over a chair, and Ben fell backward onto his ass. The Skane mounted the overturned chair and raised two of its bladed limbs over him, preparing to strike.

Ben tried again to clamber backward. The chair! His foot was caught in the fucking chair!

The shotgun blasted once. The Skane looming over him jerked, screamed, rounded on Torque. A second blast shook its swollen body, and black blood covered Ben in warm, clinging rain. He extracted his foot from the chair and yanked himself out of the way as the warrior collapsed.

Eyes wide, soaked in the warm blood of the alien, Ben looked to Torque to thank her, praise her, promise to give her children, only to find her now in a hand-to-hand struggle with the second warrior. It shrieked as it struck with taloned feet, barely deflected by Torque's shotgun, now reduced to a club itself. A strange scream then, not alien, and Ben recognized it as Torque's own roar of pain as the Skane speared her upper thigh. The strike went straight through the muscle and out the other side. Torque barely parried a second strike with the stock of her shotgun. The Skane pressed down; she resisted. A third leg rose into the air, its curved blade aiming at her head.

Ben shot to his feet, ignored a twisted ankle, charged. He howled a challenge that knew no language and needed none. The Skane brought its killing blow down, and Torque lurched aside at the last moment, crying out as the embedded limb twisted in her thigh. The Skane penetrated her shoulder, and Torque's roar filled the room. Ben hammered down with his club, aiming for the eye-like lumps. He swung over and over again, clubbing at the Skane until something cracked, gave way. Not the alien's body, but the table leg, splitting in two. Half of it rebounded, spun away into the room. But Ben double-gripped the thick splinter that remained and stabbed at the Skane, in and out, in and out, in and out. Ichor flowed, and the Skane's movements weakened, became more desperate.

Torque tried to help, but her position kept her from gaining leverage. What happened next, Ben would swear later to Alice, was the most incredible act of bravery he'd ever seen.

The Skane tried extracting its two limbs impaling Torque to

counter Ben's attack. But Torque dropped her shotgun, useless now, and grabbed both limbs to hold them in place. She screamed as the Skane pulled an inch out, then two from her flesh. The razor-like edges of its scythed legs flayed her grasping palms, and fresh blood flowed, red not black. A screeching, tearing sound came from the doorway, but Ben ignored it, stabbing, stabbing, stabbing, each wound he made answered by the alien's mad screams.

The room spun as he was abruptly snatched off the alien and pushed away. There came a sharp, mechanical whine, then one quick burst of Gatling fire and an eruption of black blood. The Skane jerked against the bullets riddling its body, then sagged, and became still in death. Ben righted himself, preparing to attack the new threat.

"May I be of further assistance?" Desi vocalized.

Blinking, exhausted, his nervous system humming inside him like an overclocked fusion drive, Ben stared gobsmacked at his combat armor as its glowing, right gauntlet spun down from action.

"Triage mode," he croaked. "Help her!"

"Acknowledged," Desi said, turning her attention to the unconscious Torque, who hung above the floor, suspended in the dead alien's talons.

"I'm disappointed in you, Alice." Korsakov rasped, his throat coarse as sandpaper. Weak, he could only prop up on one elbow. "Glad to be alive, to be sure—but disappointed."

Her veins were on fire. Her ability coursed through Alice, seeking release. It was like that moment in the Bell Jar before Korsakov had shrouded her power, when all color, sound, sight, smell, touch fused into a single sensation of connection with the universe. Alice strode back and forth outside the cracked window, nervous energy fueling her gait, something scratching at the edge of conscious thought.

"You're not worth my pain," she said aloud.

"Now *that's* how a god thinks!" Korsakov smiled. He gently, carefully rose to his feet. "There's hope for you after all, child."

Alice whirled, her eyes blazing with hatred. She stalked toward the starburst pattern of the wall. A thousand Alices drew nearer in a thousand scattered reflections, their expressions a skewed spectrum of human emotion.

"You must *want* to die," she hissed, very tempted to grant him that wish. Again. The universe seemed to demand it of her. Finish Korsakov, once and for all.

The look on his face was ambivalent. "*Want* might be a bit strong..."

"Station breach." Then again, before the warning stopped short. *"Station breach."*

The notion knocking at the back of her mind became clearer.

My friends.

Cinnamon, lying prostrate and helpless in her bed. Ben and Torque, no doubt arming themselves somewhere, intent on keeping her safe, no matter the cost. And Gal and Moze and Ian and Zoey...

"Well," Korsakov said, darting his gaze at the silent intercom, "they're here."

Alice watched as the smugness on his face became something else. A kind of resignation that passed through fear first. She turned away from him and opened the door to the corridor.

"Wait," Korsakov said, "where are you going? We're not finished, Alice."

"I'm finished with you," she said, striding away. "My friends need me."

"Your friends?" Korsakov laughed. "The Skane will take care of your *friends*. What do you think you can do against *them*?"

"Whatever I can," Alice called back.

"Oh, by all means, try, Alice." Korsakov's laughter curdled, becoming feral and foul. Its mockery followed Alice long past hearing. "Try! Try! Try!"

"It's nice to have you back, Captain," Desi said. *"Analysis, eighty percent complete."*

"It's nice to be back," Ben muttered while he waited. Funny thing was, he meant it. Having Desi wrapped around him like a second skin made him feel safe, no matter the echo-breathing, sweat-humid claustrophobia. He felt nigh-on invulnerable.

The staff cafeteria—what the station's signage insisted was really a "collaboration café"—was disturbing in its emptiness. All those empty tables and chairs. Armored up and ready for action, Ben was its sole occupant, and it was hard to shake the feeling that he was the last surviving human on Tarsus Station. He told himself that was just the psyche's way of scaring the living shit out of its human home, a defense mechanism to keep Ben alive. It was, so far, working brilliantly.

He'd followed Desi to medical to deliver the severely wounded Torque for treatment. Cinnamon Gauss, he learned, still slept in what Ian had called the basement below the main facility. As Ben, now encased in Desi's polysteel plating, prepared to duck through the doorway to leave, Ian had asked him where he was going.

"To take the fight to the enemy," he'd replied. "I'm tired of always playing defense."

Now that he had Desi, the tactical situation had changed.

With her security-overriding comms tie-in to Korsakov's console, he could remote-wipe the professor's research with a single command. That meant he could go on offense. But he needed space for that, to keep Desi's systems, designed for combat on an open planetary surface, from being rendered ineffectual in a tight space. The high-ceilinged, wide-spaced cafeteria provided that. It was also a common area the Skane had to pass through from the point of incursion to reach Korsakov's quarters. Time to give them a taste of top-shelf AGF Marine oo-rah and see how much they screamed then.

"Analysis complete," Desi announced. *"Your theory is sound, Captain."*

"Excellent."

Ben had conducted his own tactical analysis of events so far, then passed his thoughts over to Desi for evaluation. The Skane scout ship was still embedded in the station's side like a tick on a hound's hide. Their first assault had been analogous to a Marine scouting mission, feeling out interior defenses. Then they'd sent a second probe, clearing the way with the ninja but still only sending two warriors. They were being cautious. But after two defeats of limited personnel, Ben figured that prudent approach was past. He expected a full-on attack now. They'd throw every warrior they had left at securing Korsakov's research. And Desi had just endorsed that idea.

"You've got fast-movers inbound," Gal warned. Ben almost didn't recognize her voice without its usual flippancy. *"I think they've emptied their ship, Ben. There's half a dozen of the fuckers."*

Ben? No Adonis? No Stud Muffin?

She really must *be worried.*

But he had Desi.

"Acknowledged. Stay buttoned up on the *Dog*. I've got this."

They came all at once through the doorway on the far side

of the café—skittering along the deck, walls, ceiling. Still fighting in pairs, but three pairs now. Every one of them armed with ninjas this time.

As one, they hurled the sawblade projectiles at Ben. Desi's targeting computer was faster. Her armored legs launched him into the air, dodging, and Ben's insides hung on for the ride. Desi's Gatling guns opened up from both gauntlets, compensating for the physics of her evasion, snatching two ninjas from the air and tracking her fire back to one of the Skane warriors. It screeched once and died. A third ninja cut straight through the wall behind Ben's former location, a fourth was obliterated by Desi's second barrel. The two remaining ninjas banked, tracked, doubled-back like heat-seeking missiles. Desi turned, snatching one from the air lightning-fast and crushing it.

The sixth ninja hit home, ripping through her left gauntlet and shearing off the barrel of the Gatling gun. Then the Skane warriors were on Desi, finding purchase with their scything limbs. Desi swung, fought, bucked like a crazed horse, but the aliens glommed on as though glued. Their talons came down, glanced off the polysteel, but always seeking penetration. Desi reached overhead, then underneath, twisting and turning, and Ben shut his eyes to avoid being sick as the café whirled around him. The Skane ducked her attempts to snag them. Her left, ruined gauntlet caught one warrior, crushing its body in a sudden glut of blackened blood. Unable to pierce the polysteel with their legs, the warriors pulled more of the ninjas to use like carving knives, their subspace phasing slicing straight through Desi's plating. Warning lights flashed yellow, then orange, then red in Ben's heads-up display. Servos behind Desi's knees and at her articulated ankles failed, and the combat suit sprawled backward onto the floor. The aliens swarmed Ben, carving and cutting through his battlesuit.

"Multiple systems failures imminent," Desi announced in her maddeningly calm manner.

His HUD lighting up across the board, Ben shouted, "Manual control!"

"Acknowledged."

He tried to bring his remaining gauntlet with its Gatling gun around, but a Skane warrior sheared the short barrel off. Desi's safety protocols shut the compromised system down.

"Fuck!"

He reached for anything that yielded like flesh. The warriors evaded, one too slowly, and like Desi before, he grabbed it, crushed it, shrieking to its death. Two of the remaining warriors slashed furiously at the armor with the ninjas, and Desi's AI controls glared bright red. There was no audible warning from her now. She was incapable of issuing one.

All at once, the flurry of attacks ceased. The aliens held on but were unmoving, until Ben saw through his plastinium visor one of them rising over him. A slavering Skane, the unit's commander perhaps, afforded the privilege of the kill. Ben tried to swat it away, but it easily ducked his clumsy swing. The Skane's intention was clear as it raised two of its reaping limbs. The polysteel might be impenetrable to those legs, but the visor wasn't. Time slowed, even as Ben's thoughts raced. He was Private Israel again, alone in his armor with the maddened Arcœnum in this very same, triumphant posture, about to breach his helmet to the toxic atmosphere of Canis III. Why? Why? Israel's terror in death, the Archie's mad grief, both together and inseparable—Ben inhabited both emotions now. The calm admission of abject failure to complete his mission as a Marine, as a man, inflated to fill his gut.

The Skane levitated, screeching in protest, flew across the room and smashed into the wall.

"No! Leave him alone!"

The muffled shout was almost unrecognizable inside Ben's helmet.

Almost.

Alice?

One after another, the three aliens squatting over him rose and were flung against the walls. With barely enough of Desi's servos working to make it possible, Ben levered himself up.

Alice was standing, hands raised and gripping the empty air like claws, the café's scattered, broken tables and chairs strewn around her. The once pristine, white walls were now streaked in brackish blood, the crushed, contorted bodies of the Skane flung around the room in a random pattern of unrestrained rage. It seemed to Ben he existed inside the life-sized Rorschach image of a broken mind, exploded outward.

"Hi, Ben," Alice said as calmly as you please. She hovered over him, obscuring the horror painting the room around them. When he didn't answer immediately, just stared at her, she asked patiently, "Are you okay?"

Ben blinked once without speaking, then again. Three separate thoughts crowded their way into his conscious mind. First, he was still alive and whole. Second, this was the third time, if he'd kept proper count, that Alice had saved his life. And, following naturally on that, came the final thought that she was one badass motherfucker who no longer needed anyone else's protection. If she ever had.

"I am now." When she indicated she couldn't hear, he popped the release on his visor. "I am now."

Radiating down on him, her smile felt warm as fall sunshine.

30
CONFESSIONS AND RECONCILIATIONS

IT BEGAN as a dim awareness of not being dead. Not of being alive, exactly, but rather recognition of a series of sensory inputs. Burbling sounds. Gray light flitting with grayer shadows. A sinking sense of being inside her own heavy body.

It's not the Kick, Cinnamon knew. *Because I can fucking feel.*

She was lying in a bed, and she reached compulsively down to feel for the slit in the mattress. But it wasn't her mattress. No Kick to take the edge off.

Fear mixed with relief.

There was cross-talk, the murmuring techno-babble of medical consultation. Turning toward the voices, she saw amorphous blobs shrink and sharpen into several individuals dressed in straight-lined attire. They stood as a group around another bed nearby.

Something emerged from Cinnamon's mouth. It wasn't quite language. She swallowed to try again, wincing at the dryness in her throat. She croaked, "Hey."

One of the men turned. Young, attractive. Apparently in charge.

"Welcome back to the world."

He seemed familiar.

"Where am I?"

"Strigoth. Tarsus Research Station, specifically."

"Tarsus—?"

He walked over to her, setting his datapad aside. A young woman looked in Cinnamon's direction, then went back to her grim discussion with the people around the other bed.

"How's your head?" the man asked.

"I know you," Cinnamon said, squinting.

"Ian. Ian Secord."

Secord? The fog hemming in her ability to think was beginning to lift. *Tarsus*. Cinnamon reached up to find the bandage wrapping her head.

"Careful with that. The hole in your head is healing, but it's not healed yet."

"Hole?" After a moment, she repeated, "Ian Secord. The scientist's lackey?"

Cinnamon couldn't begin to interpret the range of emotions that passed over his face.

"Not anymore. Answer my question, Cinnamon. How's your head?"

"Throbbing. Feels like someone pumped it up with air."

He nodded. "That'll get better. You're very lucky, you know. Your people fought hard to get you here."

"My people—?"

The young woman walked over to join them, revealing the occupant in the other bed.

Torque!

Cinnamon tried to lift herself up, but nausea kept her horizontal.

"What's happened to her?" she gasped. "What's wrong with Torque?"

"First, stay in your bed," the woman said. "I'm Zoey, by the way."

"I don't care who you are. What happened to Torque?"

"Don't excite yourself, Miss Gauss," Zoey said. "That hole in your head—"

Cinnamon fought the queasiness, made herself sit up straighter. "I'll excite *you* in a minute, and the next person to mention the hole in my head is going to get a new one of their own. Now, tell me what's wrong with Torque!"

"She was in a fight," Ian said. "A bad one."

"A fight..."

"The Skane attacked the station," the woman said. "She and Captain Stone defended us."

"What's her condition?" Cinnamon pressed.

Zoey hesitated, looked at Ian.

Cinnamon's insides trembled with dread. Her heart hammered in her chest. She wanted the Kick, badly.

"She was ... injured," Zoey said.

"I got that! Prognosis!"

"Cinnamon," Ian said, moving between them, "calm yourself, or I'll sedate you."

"You key-tapping egghead, if you don't—"

"Grave," Zoey interrupted. "We're doing all we can for her, but she was stabbed, repeatedly. Her wounds were serious. She's lost a lot of—"

"Zoey," Ian warned.

"No, she wants to know, she can know!"

Ian stepped back, raising his hands in a let-it-be-on-your-head gesture. Zoey moved closer to Cinnamon, whose eyes were wide with worry.

"We don't know if she'll make it, Miss Gauss. That's the truth. But she has a remarkable constitution. Anyone else? Likely dead already. We're doing everything we can for her."

"You said that already," Cinnamon muttered, but her anger had melted into concern for Torque. She stared intently at Zoey for a moment, to see if she was lying for some reason about their doing all they could to help. It was one of the first skills she'd developed after losing her family to the rock phage. People telling her it would be all right when it wouldn't. People telling her she'd feel better over time, which she didn't. Only her grandfather had shot her straight. She could tell Zoey was shooting her straight now.

"Mister Secord," one of the med-geeks said, "Captain Stone is up top. He says it's safe to come up."

Ian nodded. "I have to go see what our status is. Zoey can answer any other questions you might have."

Cinnamon didn't respond. She lifted her hand to move Zoey aside so she could get a better look at Torque resting in the other bed. Her big hands lying atop the sheet were fat with bandages. Multiple tubes led from her body to the machines that beeped and pumped fluids into her. Even in sleep, Torque's typically jovial face appeared stretched by pain.

"Do you have any other questions?" Zoey asked gently.

"No."

"All right, then. I'm around if you do." Zoey turned to follow Ian.

"Wait!"

Zoey turned back.

"How long till I can get out of this bed?"

Shaking her head, Zoey said, "We've applied some rapid healing tech developed here on the station. It'll help your skull knit faster. So, you'll be up and around quicker than you might expect."

"Straight answer, goddamnit!"

Zoey's eyes hardened, then softened again. "A day or two. If what we just heard is right, we'll be moving you both to the proper facility upstairs soon."

"Thanks. You can go."

Dismissed, Zoey beat a fast retreat to join Ian and the rest of the staff standing in front of the lift. That left Cinnamon and Torque alone for the moment, one awake and painfully aware, the other unconscious and fighting for her life.

Cinnamon wanted more than anything to yank the damned tubes and monitoring sensors from her body, get up, and walk to Torque's bedside. But the other details—of the Skane, the fight, and the fact that she had no idea if Alice was all right—all of it convinced Cinnamon to remain in her bed. Some of that she could fill in from there. A day or two, the woman had said. A day, then, max. Then, she'd be back on her feet and no longer dependent on these half-wits for information.

She contented herself to watch Torque sleeping—only sleeping, Cinnamon reminded herself—her skin singing with emotion. Mostly guilt for Torque's injuries. *I should have been there*, Cinnamon cursed herself. *Torque, hell, even Stone—they shouldn't have had to fight alone.*

God, she needed the Kick.

But no. That had been the problem, hadn't it? First, on Ionia, a go-to for dreamless sleep. Then, aboard the *Dog*, a way out of admitting to herself that something physical was wrong. That Oromo's cracking her skull had done more than simply knock her out. It was dim, almost dream-like, but she remembered Alice sitting with her, trying to explain how her brain was bleeding onto itself.

Alice ... so, she'd been okay then, at least.

And all of that rancor. All that snark and hatred directed at Torque for making the deal with Oromo. For trading Blackmore's life for her own. Something inside Cinnamon had broken loose when that had hit home, what Torque had done.

Cinnamon looked at her now in that bed, bandaged, with death hovering over her like an impatient ferryman holding out a hand to help Torque aboard. With the Kick cleared out, Cinnamon understood now where the real anger had come from. She was angry at *herself*. At her own survival. Not for surviving Ionia. Blackmore's death in and of itself meant nothing to her. He'd earned his fate. No, she was angry at herself for surviving the phage that had taken her family. Somewhere inside, Cinnamon had decided long ago never to trade her life for another. It was just too hard on those left behind. And she'd used Torque's actions on Ionia as an excuse to exorcise that guilt by beating someone else up with it. The human psyche was a sadistic, self-loathing bastard sometimes.

"I'm sorry," Cinnamon whispered. Her insides shook. She felt her eyes filling up with how unfairly she'd treated her oldest, dearest friend. "I'm sorry, Torque. You didn't deserve that."

Her oldest, dearest friend didn't respond. The machines beeped. Torque's chest rose and fell.

"Keep doing that," Cinnamon said with a hint of her old, snide self. Roughly, she wiped her cheeks. "God, I was such a bitch." She could feel her head again. The heavy hammer pounding on the inside was back, and she hugged tightly to the discomfort. It was something she deserved. She'd own it.

She closed her eyes. No more Kick. Never again.

"I should be grateful, I know," she said. "You got me out. And you got Alice out. I should be grateful."

Cinnamon looked over at Torque again. She hadn't moved a muscle.

"Truth is, I don't do well with others doing things for me. When that fucking phage hit the colony ... why did it take my parents and my sister, and not me? I don't understand it."

She watched her friend breathe. Calmly, in and out.

"I can't lose you too."

Torque, the only person in the world besides her grandfather she'd trust with her life. And Torque had held that trust sacred, hadn't she? She'd done right by her, protected Cinnamon by making the deal with Oromo, and would have done so even if she'd known what Cinnamon's reaction would be afterward. That's what selfless love was.

"Thanks, big sister. Thanks for saving me. And Alice. And the others."

She suddenly felt very tired. Having burned themselves out, the emotions of the moment had left Cinnamon's body empty of energy.

"Don't leave me, bitch," she ordered her friend with the authority of a ship's captain. "Don't you leave me in my sleep."

Cinnamon hadn't expected an answer, but she got one. Unintelligible. But Torque's lips moved.

The need for rest abruptly vanished. "What? What did you say?" Cinnamon homed in her ears, listening past the beeps and dings and the low hum of the room's atmospheric processor.

"I won't," Torque groaned, "if you won't."

"Shit." Cinnamon's cheeks flushed with embarrassment. "You heard all that?"

For an answer, Torque's bandaged left hand rotated to the vertical, her thumb lifting to the ceiling.

"Shit."

"Deal or no deal?" mumbled Cinnamon's oldest, dearest friend.

With relief burning through her, Cinnamon couldn't keep the smile from her face. But it was okay that it was there. Torque's eyes were closed.

"Deal," she said, letting herself drift, after all, toward sleep.

Only to be wakened by a mechanical whine what seemed like mere moments later.

It came and it went.

Came and went.

Mechanical, grinding, like someone had forgotten to lubricate the locking mechanism of a ship's hatch and kept opening and closing the goddamned thing. It annoyed the shit out of her. Caring medical staff my...

Cinnamon opened her eyes to unfamiliar surroundings. Bright, silver lighting. White walls. She'd been transferred to a proper medical bed, could hear the slow pinging of the heart monitor. Voices muttered around her in cloudy, medical lingo.

The whining came and went again.

Came and went.

She turned her head, preparing to unload a brace of curses, and stopped short when she recognized the back armor plating of Ben Stone's battlesuit. Scarred, ripped, listing like a vessel with damaged portside stabilizers. He was talking to Secord. When Stone moved an arm to make a point, the whine sounded again. Not a hatch, then. The servomechanism articulating the armor's joints.

"What the hell happened to you?" Cinnamon asked.

Both men turned, Ben's effort a grinding of hydraulics in dire need of repair. When he limped to her bedside with Secord, he sounded like a robotic, peg-legged pirate.

"Had a little dust-up with the Skane," Stone said. "You don't look so good yourself."

"Fuck you," she replied. "I have a hole in my head. Looks like you almost did."

"Yeah."

"How are you feeling, Cinnamon?" Secord asked.

"More awake," she allowed. "More alive."

"That's a start." Secord glanced at the medical readouts over her bed. "Pressure's better. I think you're out of the woods."

"Woods? What woods?"

"Sorry. Old saying. I was trained by ..." His face flattened. "Old instructors, old expressions, I guess."

She grunted empathy with that. "Stone? The Skane did that to your fancy Marine armor?"

He nodded. "The local threat has been neutralized, but yeah, some significant damage to Desi, and—"

"Cinn!" Alice bounded across the room from the doorway, with the woman, Zoey, following behind. "You're awake!"

At seeing Alice, a tension Cinnamon hadn't known she'd been holding released inside her. Loosened the space between her shoulder blades.

"Hey, little sister," she said. Alice grabbed her hand, and in the shared touch, there was something new, something more substantial for Cinnamon. A feeling of gratitude behind the greeting. A memory of them holding hands during Cinnamon's delirium aboard the *Junkyard Dog*. She'd always felt protective of Alice, ever since that day she'd boarded the *Archimedes* and saw the frightened look on the face of the teenage girl who had no idea what the stranger with spiked, orange hair and double-slung sidearms intended to do with her. Their entire relationship had grown from that seed, with Cinnamon making it her personal mission to shield Alice Keller from harm, from even worrying about harm, if she'd anything to say about it. But now, after their time on the *Dog*, things felt different. More equalized, somehow. It wasn't something Cinnamon could explain or felt the need to. But whatever one-way mission she'd been on to safeguard Alice had evolved into a mutual responsibility to care for one another. It was, Cinnamon thought, something she could get used to.

"How are you feeling?" Alice asked.

"Like Moze has been trying to escape from my skull," Cinnamon complained. Gripping Alice's hand for leverage, she tried to sit up and see past the crowd gathering around her. The other bed was empty. "Where's Torque?"

Stone exchanged a look with Secord. His suit whined with the movement. Cinnamon's heart quick-flipped in her chest.

"Surgery," Secord said. "We had to go back in."

"What? Why? Can't you use that fast-healing miracle tech on her you used on me?"

"We did," Secord said. "The nano tech allowed us to go in faster than we could have otherwise, repair the damage. But her injuries were much more extensive than yours. Her body was violated with multiple wounds, internal hemorrhaging. Her recovery will be decidedly more complicated."

As she read his face, Cinnamon's heartrate refused to calm. "So she's not 'out of the woods' yet."

"Hey, Doc," Ben Stone advised, "read the room."

Abashed, Secord nodded. "Sorry. I slip into scientist mode sometimes and—"

"Don't sugarcoat it," Cinnamon interrupted. "Is she going to be okay or not?"

Another glance shared, this time with Alice. *Goddamn, can't you just for once give me a straight—*

"We think so. The nano tech is helping to support her natural recovery systems. We think we've sealed off all the internal bleeding." Secord shrugged. "Now, it's all about her will to live."

It was Cinnamon's turn to trade looks with Alice. Both smiled like mirror images of one another. Both burst out laughing. Cinnamon winced at the answering ache in her temple. Even Stone chuckled. His armor seemed to begrudge him doing it.

"Did I say something funny?" Secord asked.

"Hell, Doc," Cinnamon said, "if that's the case, she's so far out of the woods, she can't even see trees anymore."

Secord smiled then, too.

Leave it to Stone to bring the room down again.

"Soon as you're able, we need to catch up," he said. "The immediate danger is past, but there's a much bigger threat. And this facility holds the key to dealing with it."

"Yeah?" Cinnamon said.

"Yeah." Stone turned to Secord. "You said you needed a sample of DNA to tailor Circe to a particular species. There's plenty of that available down in the cafeteria."

"Who the hell is Circe?" Cinnamon asked.

"Like I said," Stone replied, "we need to catch up."

31
THE GREATER GOOD

SO, this might be her greatest test yet, Eva thought.

The busy, seemingly unregulated activity of the docks was like a projection of the thoughts storming around inside her head. Thorne's shuttle descended past the watching windows of the Havens, the Fleet pilot carefully navigating the controlled chaos of the pirate ships standing off in space outside the colony awaiting refit and repair. And behind them, Third Sector Fleet's vessels, second in line for the same. Joe Gauss had broken it down for Eva as they'd observed the battle from the command center: Third Fleet had been lucky to get away, much less with a third of its ships still spaceworthy, and those only thanks to New Nassau's intervention in covering their retreat. Eva's convincing Sayyida to help had saved a lot of lives, he'd assured her.

A shuttle that had ferried wounded Fleet personnel to the colony for treatment lifted off, emptying a slip for Thorne's command shuttle to occupy. Sayyida had extended her goodwill a step further without Eva even asking, allowing the overflow of injured from Alliance starships to be transported to New Nassau. That traffic had finally slowed, and it was time for the two commanders to meet in person.

Eva held her hands in front of her, fingers interlaced but flitting. She rose up and down on her toes like a teenage girl waiting on a prom date.

"Nervous?" Toma queried.

Thorne's command shuttle descended, extending its landing struts. Air erupted as the repulsors kept the small ship from gut-planting onto the landing pad. The wind washed over them, forcing Eva to raise her voice.

"Me? No. Not at all."

"Artificial gravity on that one-by-one square of deck plating not working properly, then?"

"I missed my morning workout. My calves need training."

"Ah." Toma waited until the shuttle settled its weight on the pad and spun its engines down. "Figured it was something like that."

Eva let her have the last word. She needed to focus. Where the hell was Sayyida? Thorne might take offense if she wasn't here to greet him. Military types, particularly senior officers, could be sticklers like that. Then again, her being here might be an affront to his admiral's sensibilities. Eva had no way of knowing, knew nothing about him really, that didn't come from rumor and reputation. Storied career officer. Hard ass. Brilliant innovator for some invention she couldn't remember the name of that made it easier to track pirates in the Malvian Triangle. And, oh yeah, hated as the Hangman. She had no idea who was about to step off that shuttle: agreeable ally or fanatical foe? And Sayyida, Eva guessed, was one caustic insult away from throwing Thorne and his command staff in the brig.

She side-eyed Toma. Would she let that happen? Eva's fingers fluttered faster, but she kept her feet flat on the deck.

The shuttle's hatch opened. The ramp extended but hadn't yet met the ground of New Nassau before boots *thunked* on metal. Thorne. Eva was struck first by the rugged good looks of a man in his late-forties. Most of the impression, she realized, came not from physical attributes, which were rather plain, but from the calm, total confidence the man exuded. This impression was reinforced by the fact that he'd had no Marines precede him. Rear Admiral Malcolm Thorne must feel he didn't need them. That smacked of a man used to wielding absolute power over his immediate environment. Or, perhaps, a man with a willful, even pathological disregard for danger.

Oh, this will *be fun.*

"Director Park," Thorne said, stepping onto New Nassau's deck. He glanced around briefly, and Eva wondered if he was assessing the facility's capacity or experiencing self-satisfaction in at last penetrating the inner sanctum of his enemy. Maybe both. He didn't offer to shake her hand in greeting. "It's good to see you well."

"Admiral," she acknowledged.

"Colonel Toma of the 214th Drop Marines, isn't it?" he said. "I'm familiar with your mission here."

"Yes, sir."

His eyes scanned Sheba top to bottom, taking their time. At first, Eva assumed he was merely being a chauvinistic cad. What Thorne said next, and the way he said it, made her wish his ogling had been that uncomplicated.

"You're out of uniform."

Sheba didn't fidget a millimeter. Marine discipline.

"Sir?"

"Where's your armor? The 214th is an occupying force in a colony peopled by thieves and cutthroats." Thorne looked around at the busy docks and the grimy, unkempt personnel performing their tasks. They wore the variety of garb that served as the anti-uniform of the common pirate. His mouth sported a frown when he again addressed Toma. "Any one of these people could knife you in the back."

"That's not going to happen, Admiral," Eva interjected. "Things here have ... evolved."

"Yes, so I've gathered from Colonel Toma's reports." Thorne shifted his attention to Eva with a if-you-were-under-my-command look in his eye.

While they'd exchanged greetings, such as they'd been, two other officers of senior rank, a woman and a man, had descended from the shuttle. Along with two Marines, their rifles pointed at the deck but slung ready to aim them elsewhere. The officers took up position behind Thorne, who made no effort to introduce them, as if he didn't plan to stay long enough to become acquainted. The Marines assumed mirrored guard positions at the foot of the ramp.

Nodding politely to each of the senior officers, Eva said, "Sometimes, Admiral, shared advantage trumps individual interest."

"I suppose, when the stakes are high enough, that's true," Thorne replied neutrally.

"Trust me," Sayyida al-Hurra said, walking up, "it took an existential threat to the species for me and my captains to do anything other than blow you out of space."

Thorne coolly turned to the sound of her voice. "Perhaps after we've tossed the Skane into the dustbin of history, you can try your luck."

Sayyida smiled tightly. Her hands were clasped behind her back. Funny, Eva thought, how body language spoke for you even when you were trying your damnedest to stay the fuck silent.

"I look forward to that," Sayyida said.

The commander and the admiral sized each other up. Neither extended a hand, despite the fact that they'd just shared a surprise if limited victory over the deadliest enemy mankind had ever faced. So, as usual, Eva did the hard work of making the compromise happen.

Rituals are important when it comes to preserving pride.

She extended a hand first to Thorne. "Now that Commander al-Hurra has joined us, I'd like to say on behalf of the Bragg Administration, congratulations on living to fight another day, Admiral."

Not quite reluctantly, Thorne took her hand in his. "Thank you, Miss Park."

Turning to Sayyida, Eva offered her the same hand. "And to you, Commander. For giving us a fighting chance to save humanity."

Eyeing Eva with a knowing suspicion at her sudden formality, Sayyida nevertheless shook her hand as well. "Another victory for you too, *Miss Park*," she said, injecting irony into her rare use of Eva's surname. She knew the game Eva was playing, and Eva knew she knew it. Thorne knew all that, too, and was likely amused by the playacting. And yet, Eva took heart in the fact that Sayyida was willing to play her part. As was Thorne, apparently.

The four of them stood, staring at each other like awkward strangers at a garden party where everyone had shown up armed. Neither Thorne nor Sayyida seemed inclined to offer the other a direct handshake of congratulations. Or, for that matter, any formal acknowledgment beyond I-agree-for-the-moment-not-to-kill-you-outright.

Well, Eva decided, sharing transactional DNA through the medium of her own palm would have to do. For now.

"Admiral," she said, "I'm sure you'd like to visit your wounded in the infirmary. Commander al-Hurra has had her medical staff prepare a complete report. Shall we?"

"Lead on," Thorne gestured, still staring at Sayyida.

Oh, I intend to, Eva thought.

Sayyida was seriously beginning to wonder if this marriage of necessity was going to work. If it even *should* work. She couldn't escape her loathing for Malcolm Thorne, even in the quiet refuge of her own quarters. Maybe she shouldn't have let Eva talk her into sending the fleet out in the first place. Maybe she should still incarcerate the man and try him for murder —*multiple* murders—if not kill him outright in the public square. He'd certainly done enough of that himself.

Well, she thought, *I suppose that's not exactly a priority*. Not with the Skane in the neighborhood.

The visit to the infirmary had passed without incident. Eva had put it first on the itinerary as a way, she'd told Sayyida, of disarming Thorne by showing him how New Nassau's medical staff were caring for his injured personnel. It had worked to a limited degree. The icy demeanor of Thorne and his staff had thawed only when they'd interacted with their injured comrades. In that context, the stick-up-his-ass adherence to the haughty distance of rank relaxed a bit. Thorne had sat by bedsides, joking with his younger, wounded subordinates about the positive impact their battle scars should have on their dating lives. He'd inquired—in a whispered but earnest tone—as to their treatment. And he'd walked away from the tour seemingly reassured by their answers.

Afterward, Colonel Toma announced she would escort him to his local quarters, as per the itinerary. Sayyida had assigned him and his officers rooms in the command wing, not uncoincidentally the most secure part of New Nassau. They wouldn't be here long, just long enough for Eva Park to propose a formal partnership against the Skane. His departure couldn't come soon enough for Sayyida.

The chime came requesting access to her quarters. Sighing,

Sayyida again lamented, if only briefly, her inability to set her worries aside for even a moment's peace. Daily, her admiration for her father grew. His ability to maintain his famously even-keeled attitude with such seeming ease was not something she'd apparently inherited.

"Come."

The door swept aside, and to her surprise, Joe Gauss stood there. She wasn't sure whom she'd been expecting. Eva, maybe, come to take her temperature on how the tour had gone. But not him.

"Apologies, Commander, for the late hour." He stepped inside, and the door shut behind him.

"Joe," Sayyida said with a tired smile, "you were a second father to me. Here, at least, no titles. Okay?"

He nodded.

"What can I do for you?"

Joe shuffled, one foot to the other. Hell, Thorne's visit was even getting to him, Sayyida thought. A former quartermaster to her father aboard the *Nicomo's Luck*, who'd said "no" a hundred times for every one grumbled "yes." And now a chief marshal whose job description, while a bit more exacting, followed basically the same tenet.

"Joe?"

"I hesitate to burden you with this, ma'am."

"And yet," she said, trying to make it lighthearted, "you're here."

He flinched. He shuffled again.

Jesus. What is it he's carried on his shoulders into my quarters?

"Some of my men have heard rumors. Tantamount to plans."

"Plans about what?"

"Our guest."

Oh. That. Sayyida was surprised to hear it had taken this long. She was surprised someone hadn't rushed Thorne's shuttle as soon as he'd stepped dockside. Or tried to shoot the shuttle down before it'd even landed.

"Go on."

"Nothing sure, mind you," he said, backpedaling. "Just rumors."

Sayyida regarded him. "I'm sure you can handle it, Joe. I suppose I could talk to Colonel Toma about assigning Marines to act as adjuncts to your—"

"That won't be necessary," Gauss said quickly, sounding offended. "We just got our badges back. We surrender them the first time there's a possible crisis and..." He left it at that.

Sayyida nodded understanding. She waited, her patience draining. She wanted her space back, but the chief marshal was obviously *reluctant* to leave. Or was reluctant the wrong word?

"Something else, Joe?"

He cleared his throat. "You can't trust the Hangman."

Ah, here we are. The real reason for his visit.

"You've never been one to waste time stating the obvious," she said.

Joe moved into the room. One step, then two. "Maybe we shouldn't stifle the rumors I mentioned."

She exhaled. Inhaled. Exhaled again. "You're suggesting we let nature take its course?"

He wasn't looking at her. Then, he was. "Something like that."

"I'm surprised to hear this coming from you," Sayyida said.

"It's not exactly a recommended course of action—"

"Isn't it?"

His eyes drifted away again. "You're disappointed."

"Not at all. Think I haven't thought the same thing? The

Hangman's here. In range. *At our mercy.* We outnumber him. When the hell's the last time that was ever the case?"

Joe turned, took a step, then a second, turned back, made eye contact again. "Never."

"So," she said, rising to her feet, "we can be exactly what he expects us to be—untrustworthy, back-stabbing murderers—or we can be something else. Something better."

He was nodding. "Your father aspired to that. Believed in those high-minded ideals. But he's dead now. And not everyone's as honorable as that."

"Hardly anyone, in my experience," Sayyida said, drawing closer to him. She saw it, now. The heavy burden of his job that had shaped his shoulders, more curved now in old age. From a lifetime of saying no, when it would have been so much easier to say yes. But not for him. For Joe Gauss, the harder course was usually the better one. Less internal strife that way. Her father had taught her that. And more than once, Hadrian al-Hurra told her, he'd been taught the same lesson by a crusty old quartermaster determined to instruct an idealistic, young, up-and-coming ship's officer in the crueler ways of the universe.

Never make a decision you can't be proud of when explaining it to your children.

"Still," Joe sighed, "I suppose *not* killing Thorne is the right thing to do. For the greater good"—his tone turned gritty—"and all that crap."

He made to turn away, but Sayyida stopped him with a light touch. He turned back with a surprised, open expression. She gathered him into a hug and, slowly, the old marshal allowed it. Returned it.

"Keep the peace, Joe," she whispered to him. "It's what my father would have wanted."

Gauss nodded against her, then pulled away, flashed a brief smile of solidarity to her and retreated to the door. It opened and he hesitated, as though evaluating the veracity of what she'd said to make sure that allowing Thorne to continue breathing was truly the right course of action. But at his core, Joe Gauss was a man driven by an obsession for balance. Justice, not expediency, was his guiding star. Malcolm Thorne—the Hangman—walking the corridors of New Nassau as a free man grated on him. As it did all of them. Went against everything justice demanded. But was necessary to have a chance in hell of defeating the Skane and saving them all.

"Right," he said and left.

32
ALIEN AUTOPSY

"FASCINATING!"

She'd said it so often in the past two days, Sadie Abara, MD, Ph.D., had turned the word into a punctuation mark. "I'd need years of study just to begin to understand them. There's so much about the *human* brain we don't know, and we've studied *that* for centuries."

Ben offered an indulgent, rictus grin. Patience was getting harder to maintain. Not only because of all the muscle aches—so deep it had seeped into his bones—from being beaten nearly to death in his own armor, but because Abara had been at her gruesome work for two days. With little to show for it, so far as he could see.

The spherical body lay sprawled across two autopsy tables, its deadly, sword-like appendages hanging down, petrified now with rigor mortis. Abara stared at the Skane corpse with the anxious curiosity of the brilliant scientist she was. She'd insisted on meticulously revealing the alien's innards, peeling back the black layers of epidermis. Slicing deeper—slowly—to penetrate the dermal layers, taking samples, and diligently labeling them. Once she'd identified the brain, she'd slowed the process down even more, despite Ben's reminding her that time was of the essence. When Abara had threatened to throw him out of her autopsy room, he'd almost lost it altogether.

Right, not fast. His grandfather's words aimed at some long-forgotten school project when Ben was a teenager. *Life, not death,* he shot back while Abara did her work. At a teeth-chattering 4 degrees Celsius to retard decomposition, the chilly room wasn't helping his aching body one bit. Ben glanced up at Alice, who'd opted to remain in the observation room on the upper floor, where they'd watched Gauss's procedure. She stared down, seemingly bored and—ugh, fascinated—at the same time. And warm, no doubt.

"Now, this is interesting," Abara was saying.

Not 'fascinating?' Ben jabbed as Ian angled for a better view.

"See how developed the limbic lobe—or limbic system if you prefer—is compared to the frontal? Outsized, compared to our own proportions. I mean, assuming I'm even seeing what I think I'm seeing."

"Mmm," Ian said. "Might account for the Skane's animal-like behavior?"

"Mmm," Abara agreed. "Maybe."

"Explain," Ben said, gooseflesh rippling over his skin.

"Doctor Secord?" Abara prompted, clearly engrossed in the dissection process.

"The frontal lobe of the human brain is responsible for executive decision-making," Ian explained. "The limbic region is associated with instinctive, emotional responses. Humans use their thinking center, the frontal lobe, to regulate their baser instincts. Metaphorically, that tracks with the human ability to rule our emotions with conscious, considered thought."

"As I've tried to tell my teenage son," Abara remarked.

"Exactly," Ian said. To Ben's raised eyebrow, he explained,

"The frontal lobe is notoriously underdeveloped in teenagers, which explains their penchant for taking risks. Doing what they *feel* instead of the smart thing. By their mid-twenties, that's brought into balance through natural development."

Explains a lot, Ben thought. *Something to share with the old man the next time I see him.*

"And look at this..." Abara said, grabbing one of her retractors.

Oh, Jesus.

The doctor tugged back a thin layer of grayish gristle. Pulling it produced a wet, tearing sound that made Ben want to vomit.

"Is that the pineal gland?" Ian asked.

"My God, it's huge," Abara observed. She peeled the surrounding subdermal layer away to reveal more of the creature's brain. "*Fascinating*."

"Something significant about that?" Ben managed, staring deliberately at Abara's rapt expression and not the alien horror show unfolding in front of him.

"Who knows?" Abara answered. She continued her painfully slow examination.

Ben felt the sudden urge to take her into a headlock until she said something useful.

"Korsakov would think so," Ian said.

Ben's limbic impulse was overruled by his frontal lobe hearing something potentially valuable. "How so?"

Ian jerked his head to one side, and the two men stepped away from Abara.

"In Korsakov's diaries, he talks a lot about the pineal gland in humans as a possible conductor for human telekinesis," Ian explained. "He believes it's the organ through which those with real abilities, like Alice, channel their power. Somehow, the pineal gland—he believes—allows them to harness regular brain-waves in tandem with their shadows."

"His Godwave."

"Right."

"Any proof of that?"

Ian's face scrunched up. "Not exactly. That's what he was trying to document through his experiments with Alice."

"But Korsakov thought this gland was important?"

Ian nodded. "For centuries it's been speculated—and I emphasize that word—that the pineal gland is the focusing mechanism for supernatural power. Even the home of the human soul—the source of who we are beyond our physical selves. It's all over Earth's old religions. Sometimes depicted as an additional, or third eye. You might have heard it called 'the mind's eye.' In Buddhism, the third-eye chakra is associated with clairvoyance and intuition—having a sixth sense of things. Ever had déjà vu or the sudden urge to check on a loved one you fear is in danger? A Buddhist would say that's your third eye opening to see into the metaphysical. Hindus believe humans can achieve spiritual enlightenment by cultivating the third eye, represented by an actual eye in the middle of the forehead in images of Lord Shiva. Christianity is more obscure, but the concept is there if you look for it. Ancient Egyptians had the Eye of Horus, which some believe is actually a rough sketch of the region of the brain containing the pineal gland."

Ben took it all in. "So, it's a religious thing. You seem to know a lot about it."

"Only because it's all over Korsakov's journals. And, I admit, I became a bit captivated with the concept myself when we were scouring his files. The idea that there's knowledge beyond what we already know is what keeps us research-types in the lab into the wee hours. You'd be surprised how much in science actually involves a happy accident; or a leap of faith beyond what the raw data shows. And speaking of science, the role of the pineal gland in humans isn't solely a topic for theologians."

"No?"

"No. Philosophers have wondered about its function, too. Korsakov admired René Descartes for many reasons, including his belief that the gland is the seat of the human soul. And we know—from science—the gland serves an everyday role for humans unlike, say, the appendix. It helps regulate the sleep cycle. Your eyes take in light and, when there's not enough, the pineal gland produces melatonin, making you sleepy. It also produces N, N-dimethyltryptamine—or DMT—a hallucinogen."

"Really? A hallucinogen?"

"Yes. Associated in the literature with dreaming, even near-death experiences. Rats, for example, have been shown to produce DMT when they're about to die. Korsakov theorized that our nighttime dreaming is a glimpse into that enhanced reality. I did a little research of my own after reading his journals. Some believe—and here we come full circle back to religion—that the gland and its mysteries are the key to heaven's gate."

Ben was shaking his head and doing his best to tune out the occasional eruptions of "Fascinating!" behind him. He said, "This sounds like a lot of mumbo-jumbo to me."

Ian shrugged again. "We can't entirely discount the anecdotal histories we can distill from the religious texts, but that's not evidence we can empirically analyze, either. Without objective data proving the gland's supposed role as a conduit to what we'd call the supernatural, we can't lend any weight to its role in doing that, scientifically speaking."

"Scientifically speaking," Ben repeated. "And that's what

Korsakov was searching for with Alice: objective data that proved his theories."

"Precisely."

The high-pitched whine of a robotic bone saw spun up, only to bog down as the teeth cut into alien skull. Ben did his best to ignore it.

"Ben?"

Startled, he turned to find Alice standing next to them. She'd been there for a while, he realized, listening to Ian's lecture. Abara finished her cutting work, and the saw powered down.

"Could that be where my abilities come from?" Alice asked, terrified and hopeful at the same time. "Maybe that's what the Skane did to me—somehow 'turned on' this gland thing." Her gaze narrowed. "Opened up my 'third eye.'"

Ben reined in his frustration from the past few days before responding. "Alice, Ian is right. There's no real basis for that belief, or anything related to what your pineal gland does for you—well, beyond helping you fall asleep and maybe giving you a hallucination of heaven before you die."

Her expression became as chilly as the air in the room.

"How do you know it's a hallucination?" she said.

And another question, gravelly and grumbling, from farther back in his head.

Does it matter?

She addressed Ian. "You said sometimes science requires a leap of faith."

"Yes, but there are leaps, and there are *leaps*. The kind of leap I'm talking about is based on hypotheses with inductive evidence pointing in a general direction, demanding provability."

"But we have that, don't we?" Alice said. "Different cultures, different religions, but basically coming to the same conclusion. You said thc Egyptians even had a diagram! You're describing the essence of the empirical method my father taught me. Recreating an experiment to achieve the same results."

"But Alice," Ian said, "there's no repeated 'experiment' here to prove a theory. Just religious treatises and philosophical suppositions. There's no objective evidence of extraordinary human abilities—"

With a sharp intake of breath, Ian lifted straight up into the air. Carefully, and only a few inches.

Alice quirked an eyebrow. "You were saying?"

"Alice," Ben cautioned, "put him down."

Ian's feet found the floor again.

"Sorry. I couldn't resist."

Ian swallowed hard. "It's not *your* ability I doubt, Alice. Far from it. But the source of it? There's just not enough physical evidence—"

"Korsakov's crazy, but he's a genius too," Alice stated. "So much of what he believed about subspace turned out to be true. You said yourself that he was fascinated by the pineal gland. Maybe his belief in its importance is true, too..."

Ian was ready but reluctant to argue his case further that no scientist would make a leap of faith across so wide a chasm.

"Fascinating!" Abara's enthusiasm made them all look in her direction. "Ian, you're going to want to see this."

"What'd you find, Sadie?" Ian led them back to the table.

"Maybe something," she said. "Maybe nothing."

Ben held the cursing inside. His body ached. His mind was starting to as well.

Abara had removed part of the Skane's skull and cut away much of the brain matter to better access its penial gland. "It's amazing how similar brain constructs are across species. Even between alien species and humans, it seems. But, as when comparing humans and Earth animals, there are variations in the brain's composition—some slight, some significant."

"Like the different sizes of the frontal and limbic regions in the Skane compared to humans."

"Exactly. And look here..."

Abara reached in with her gloved hands and pulled out the alien's pineal gland. She'd severed it from the rest of the brain. It was shaped like a large clove of garlic.

"See?"

Wincing at the moist, *shlooping* sound the organ made as the doctor pried it apart, Ben peered at the black-and-gray matter hesitantly. "What am I looking at?"

"A structure not totally unlike our own, but much more sophisticated."

"Okay," he said. "So what?"

Alice stood beside him, shaming Ben's squeamishness with how unfazed she seemed by Abara's messy display. He noticed Alice was shivering, though, and drawing closer to him.

"What does that tell you, Doctor?" she asked.

"Oh, I have no idea," Abara said. "But it's fascinating, isn't it?"

The desire to put her in a stranglehold until she blacked out for being so glib was nearly overwhelming. Sometimes the limbic region, while socially impractical, was actually quite satisfying, Ben thought.

"But Andre had ideas about how the pineal gland might act as a control center for your abilities, Alice. I don't know if you know this, but the gland has a storied history as a kind of center for magic powers—"

"We're familiar, Sadie," Ian said. "The professor was intrigued by the possibilities."

"Indeed he was. See these striations?" The scientist held up the organ. It squelched, producing clear fluid as Abara's thumbs pressed and pulled to reveal the gland's inner contours. The cranial fluid dripped onto the reflective metal of the autopsy table in long, syrupy streams. "Korsakov posited a structure similar to this as necessary for subspace manipulation. And there's something familiar about my preliminary neurological scans I can't quite put my finger on..." Abara trailed off, trying to pin down that particular piece of elusive knowledge.

Ben elbowed past his queasiness. "Are you saying you've found evidence that Korsakov was right? That the penial gland really *is* the ... magic organ ... for controlling subspace?"

"I'm saying nothing of the sort," Abara said, outwardly aghast at the suggestion. "I'm merely pointing out how fascinating it is that—"

"Thank you, Doctor," Ian said. "Please do continue your examination."

Nodding, Abara was quite happy to return to performing her work rather than attempt to explain it.

"Convinced yet?" Alice said leadingly, drawing the two men aside again.

"Not even close," Ian stated. "Could be coincidence. Could be a lucky guess on Korsakov's part."

"Or maybe Alice is right," Ben said. Despite Ian's exasperated, don't-encourage-her expression, he continued, "We've got nothing else to go on, right? Maybe Abara will find more. Maybe not. But for now, we have a lot of anecdotal evidence, Korsakov's own assumptions—the doctor's 'striations'—and Morgan Henry's discovery aboard the *Rubicon*. That Alice's brain had been—what, rebooted? Maybe unlocking the potential of her penial gland was part of that."

"You're making huge leaps of logic there, Captain," Ian cautioned.

"Or leaps of faith?" Alice said.

"Alice—" Ian began.

"No," Ben said, "she's right. Sometimes you just have to roll the dice."

Ian sighed. "Even if all that's true, so what?"

"So what?" Ben repeated, incredulous. "So, we'd know how the Skane control subspace. We weaponize that knowledge."

Ian's forehead furrowed. "And how would we do that?"

"Well, that's the question, isn't it?" Ben said. "And your department, I believe, Doc."

Ian sat down. He massaged the bridge of his nose with thumb and forefinger. "Captain Stone, forget the penial gland for a moment. The only scientifically viable path forward I can see involves Project Circe—developing a strain of the virus that killed Morgan Henry, aimed at the Skane genome." With an apologetic glance, he said, "Sorry, Alice, to bring up Doctor Henry's death."

"It's okay."

To Ben: "But as I've tried to explain, you can't simply whip up a virus. Even with the Skane DNA we have now to experiment with, we'd have to build models, run simulations, and maybe—*maybe*—finally we'd develop a virus with a reasonable chance of infecting them. That process would take months at the very least. But then, how would we replicate it in volume? Deliver it across the quadrant? By the time we could do all that, the Skane will have finished us off. It's impossible!"

Ben got to his feet. He didn't intend to appear menacing, but his jaw was set hard. "Marines do the impossible every day, Doctor."

Ian glared up at him a moment, then stood as well to level the playing field. "That might work with the grunts, Captain, but science can't be bullied into action."

Ben advanced a step as if to test that theory.

Ian didn't back off.

"Stop it," Alice said. "Just—stop." Angry and exhausted, both men turned to look at her. "Please, both of you, just *stop*."

Ben backed off a step. With a huff, Ian retook his seat.

"I'm going to look at Korsakov's journals again," she said. Alice held out her hand, palm up. "Ian, I need your security badge."

"Uh. Sure." He handed it over.

"Alice," Ben said, "I don't know if that's a good idea. Those files need to stay secured—"

"Know anyone better able to protect them?"

He shut up.

"Now, I'm going to do something that will maybe be productive," she said, staring first at Ben, then Ian. "I suggest you two do the same."

Before either could argue or make excuses or even apologize, Alice spun on her heel and left the autopsy room.

33
THE MOTE IN ALICE'S EYE

THIS SHOULD HAVE BEEN EASIER, Alice thought. Why did everything in life take so much goddamned effort?

She wished Korsakov were still on-station. She could make him help them, couldn't she? She could feel her powerful fingers wrapping around his neck, imposing compliance without even touching him. But with that vicious thought came the guilt for indulging it, and the image of Korsakov hanging over the floor faded. Hell, he might even *want* to help them, if it meant protecting himself from the Skane.

But Korsakov was no longer on Tarsus. He'd fled while Torque and Ben fought to save everyone from the invaders. How hard had it been for Korsakov to shatter the cracked containment wall? Not very, apparently. A calculation of its fragility, then a kick in just the right spot? Or had it only taken a single flick of his finger?

More guilt as Alice realized how, unwittingly or not, she'd helped him escape. If irony had an odor, she thought, that's what it'd smell like. It had been her rage, after all, her lack of control that had fractured the wall in the first place. And the Skane ship had gone missing, too. Had Korsakov figured out how to pilot it himself? It wasn't beyond the realm of possibility. Ben thought the Skane had sent the last of their warriors against him, that the ship had been sitting empty—but maybe not. Maybe there'd been one Skane left aboard. Had Korsakov talked to it, somehow convinced it to help him escape? In the aftermath of the skirmish, with the station's medical staff fighting for Torque's life and Desi inoperable, no one had thought to secure the ship. Now, both it and Korsakov were gone. An extensive search of the station had proven that. And with no other ship than the *Junkyard Dog* he could have left on...

Two plus two.

Gal had tracked the Skane ship's flight but Ben, unaware at the time that Korsakov must be aboard, and had decided to let the alien vessel go. The under-crewed *Dog* had been in no shape to attempt to stop it. Once they'd realized what had happened, Ben was furious. Who knew what kind of deal the mad scientist might make with the enemy? Time mattered more than ever now, and Alice could understand why Ben was so impatient with Abara's painstaking examination of the alien corpse. Still, she didn't see how two cocks pecking at each other in a barnyard would help. So she'd left Ben and Ian to their cockfighting, and here she sat staring up at the monitors displaying all that evidence of Korsakov's deranged ambitions. His exchanges with the Bragg Administration. His daily diaries of discovery. Her own image, staring back at her, helpless, from the Bell Jar.

But Alice wasn't helpless anymore. And she wanted answers. That seemed to be her perennial state these days—frustrated and full of questions. Needing them answered.

Need first.

She'd been tempted to search for anything related to her family. But Alice was almost sure he'd been telling the truth about knowing nothing about their whereabouts. So she shook off her meditation on their recent bad luck and got back on task. Time to try another keyword combination.

"Computer, new search parameters: *alien, subspace, pineal, gland.*"

A long list of returns populated on-screen.

"Computer, display only journal entries."

The resulting list seemed hardly to have shortened, since the volume of files still ran off the bottom of the display. How could she winnow down the results, make this search manageable? She had to think like Korsakov. That thought sent a chill through her. But, Alice told herself, she didn't have to *be* like him—she'd already shown she could step back from that precipice, hadn't she?

You just have to think like a self-obsessed, narcissistic, demigod wannabe—and you should find what you're looking for.

Those things were all true of him, but not how he saw himself. Above all, Korsakov thought he was a man misunderstood, didn't he? Or not understood at all by "the rest of the cattle" of humanity. A brilliant, once-in-a-generation genius who held himself above the "pedestrian concerns" of humanity, who deserved not only recognition but *veneration.* By his colleagues in the scientific community. By all mankind. A man meant to be more than a man, whose destiny had been predetermined by "the will of God." He even called his great discovery the Godwave.

Wow. And I thought I *had issues.*

But, Alice supposed, that name followed on naturally from the rest. Not just because Korsakov was obsessed by his own sense of self-importance but because religion itself had pointed to the abilities he wanted to prove existed.

Enlightenment. Self-knowledge. Opening the secrets of the universe to the interpretation of the human soul. Boiled down, wasn't that just another way of plugging into ultimate power?

To know God's intent for you? All you had to do was open your so-called third eye. And if you could know the mind of God, how much further then to take the crown for yourself?

"Computer, delimit search returns with new parameters: *soul, third eye.*"

A single journal record remained.

"Play."

"Diary Entry 8,444: November 8th. I've always thought of the human soul as less a physical (or even spiritual) thing, and more as the seat of human potential. Of our power over ourselves, our own destinies. What we aspire, in our brighter hours, to be—in short, more than who we are. *Knowing ourselves in a way that denies any other being's power over us. So, in that sense, Descartes and I agree on the soul's ultimate significance. If the pineal gland is the seat of the soul and the key to unlocking human telekinesis—and through it, power over subspace—what wonders of human potential are there yet to discover! We have only to unblind our third eye to see it..."*

Alice grimaced. More of Korsakov's ravings. This wasn't helpful at all!

An irritant made her blink, and she rubbed at her right eye. An eyelash. A mote of dust flitting through the air. The more she rubbed, the more it felt like there was a rock in there. Alice opened her eye, blinked. Still there. She wiped at it again, hard, driven by annoyance. Her eye squished in protest. When she stopped again to see if she'd gotten rid of the irritant, orange stars burst across her vision. Still there.

Damn it!

She blinked and rubbed, blinked and rubbed.

"Damn it!"

How would she find the answer if she was too blind to see?

Alice stopped rubbing.

Eyes could be blinded.

"Maybe even third eyes," she mumbled.

Her irritated eye clamped shut like a leering pirate, Alice jumped up so quickly, she knocked the chair over behind her.

Ignoring the amused stares of the staff she dashed past, Alice ran all the way back to the autopsy room. She almost ran into the door, but it slipped aside just in time to let her pass.

"I know what we can do!"

The room was empty. The autopsy table still held its grisly specimen, but now sewn up in a body bag. The room temperature, set for cold storage, seemed even chillier without its animated, arguing human occupants. Where was everyone?

Irritated, Alice inserted Ian's security badge into the computer. "Locate Director Secord and Captain Stone," she said.

"Director Secord and Captain Stone are in the testing facility."

"Thanks."

"You're welcome."

Alice swept out of the room, down the corridor, and to the section of the station her muscle memory knew so well. She spied a technician whose name she couldn't remember, towel draped around his neck, exiting the small rec facility where she'd tried to outrun her grief for Morgan Henry. She passed the hallway branching off to the living quarters where she'd spent so many nights engaging in romantic adventures and plotting Korsakov's demise. *If only...* By the time Alice reached the testing lab, she was breathing hard.

The door opened, and she leaped inside for take two.

"I know what we can do!"

Ian and Ben turned wearily as she entered. Ian sat, a glass

one-quarter full of amber liquid resting on the computer console. Ben was perched next to him, the glass he was holding half-full of something clear.

"Hi, Alice," Ben said.

She straightened up, disappointed at their lackadaisical reaction to her announcement. Then, the glass in his hand registered.

"That's not...?"

"Water," Ben said. He raised his drink as if to toast his own sobriety, then waggled it. Ice tinkled against the sides of the glass, as though that somehow proved the contents weren't alcoholic. Alice took his word for it.

"Where's Doctor Abara?"

"Sleeping. Finally," Ian said. He took a swig from his own glass and winced slightly.

Definitely not water.

"We're just here commiserating," Ben said. "Trying to clear our heads a little."

"What do you know?" Ian asked.

"What?"

"You said you know what we can do..."

"Oh!" Alice's face lit up again. "I know how we can defeat the Skane!"

Both men regarded her evenly. Neither joined her in her enthusiasm. Neither even roused from their lounging.

"What happened to your eye?" Ben asked, peering more closely at her. "Looks red."

"That's just it!" Alice came closer, determined to infect them with her excitement. "Ian, remember the shroud?"

He regarded her. Took another drink. "Alice..." He paused, amended his tone to be less patronizing. "There's no way to make a shroud big enough—"

"No, that's not what I mean."

"What's this 'shroud'?" Ben wondered.

Ian's irritation grew. "It doesn't matter! It's like the virus solution, which isn't really a solution, because it's not doable."

"You're not listening to me!" Alice insisted. This wasn't going at all like she'd planned. "Why won't anyone ever just *listen* to me?"

Had there been an amplification of her voice? It'd seemed to fill the room. Was that her ability expressing her annoyance? Or just her imagination?

"You're right," Ben said, setting his glass down. With a glare at Ian, he said, "We'll shut up. Go ahead."

"Thank you," she breathed. "To answer your question, Ben, it's over there." She pointed at the Bell Jar, still standing in the center of the testing facility. A web of connected, button-sized electrodes dotted its otherwise transparent surface.

"What's it do?"

"Korsakov invented it to mute her ability," Ian explained. "Those emitters produce inverse waves that counter her command of subspace."

Ben blinked. "Okay. But we can't build one big enough to encompass the galaxy, so—"

"My point exactly," Ian said.

"*My* point in bringing it up," Alice interrupted, "is that we just have to figure out a way to stop the Skane from controlling subspace, right?"

"Right," Ben said.

"But we don't just deaden them, like the shroud did me." She paused dramatically. "We kill the ability altogether."

"Alice—" Ian began.

Ben raised his hand to stop him. Puzzled but attentive, he asked, "And how would we do that?"

"Well," Alice said, eyebrows wagging, "Ian said it's like a third eye, right? The penial gland. It's like a focal lens, only not for concentrating light. For connecting to a higher plane of existence. Maybe even for controlling subspace."

"So lore, and Andre Korsakov, would have you believe," Ian said tentatively, disdain creeping back into his voice. "But what does that have to do with—"

"What happens when you look at the sun too long?" she asked.

Ian said, "Blindness."

Alice looked from him to Ben. "So—let's blind the Skane."

Both men stared at her. Ian with weary bewilderment. Ben with increased interest.

"What if we could use subspace like sunlight?" Alice wondered. "Overwhelm the Skane's pineal gland, maybe even burn it out like too much sunlight does to our retina?"

"You're talking about solar retinopathy, which is usually not permanent," Ian said. "But we're not even sure the pineal gland is how the Skane *control* subspace. We're so far off in La-La Land here—"

"But we have good circumstantial evidence," Ben stated. Alice could tell he was trying to assemble the clues in a way that pointed to hope. "Abara's findings provide that. And Korsakov's theories—La-La Land, maybe, but proven where Alice is concerned, right? We could make the reasonable argument, couldn't we, Doc, that we know the *likely* way the Skane control subspace?"

Ian shook his head. "Without proper testing, re-testing, under observably objective conditions—"

"Doc, for once in your life, think with the little head."

That image made Alice giggle. Her own fatigue had started to catch up to her, was making her giddy.

"Do what now?" Ian said.

"Forget it. Point is, sometimes you just gotta go with your gut."

"Use your limbic lobe," Alice said.

Ben chuckled. "Yeah, that. Blind them, huh?"

Alice beamed at him.

"What if we could do that using subspace itself?" Ben said. "Like using sunlight to inflict blindness. Too much of a good thing, as it were."

The space over Ian's nose crinkled. "What do you mean?"

"We don't have the time to deploy a traditional viral weapon, right? And this shroud thing—never mind. But what if we could send a subspace signal across a wide spectrum. So strong, it would corrupt—or disrupt—the organ itself? Maybe even burn it out?"

Ian stared at him. "Now, how would we do—"

"Just answer my question!"

Rolling his eyes, Ian said, "Your guess is as good as mine, Captain. But I suppose, if you could somehow overwhelm the Skane's ability to process or manipulate subspace, even for a short time, everything they rely on it for would be compromised. Maybe even the conduit connecting individuals to the species hive mind."

"In the Marines, Doc," Ben said, "we call that a significant tactical advantage."

Ian sighed. "Even if you could somehow 'short out' the Skane's gland with a subspace surge like blinding the human eye with a sunburst, how could you possibly do so across stellar space? You'd need a huge communications array of massive power to conduct that kind of signal."

Ben smiled and winked at Alice. "So happens, I know just where we can find one."

34
MEETINGS AND MISLEADINGS

EVA PARK LIFTED her cup of sweetened coffee to her lips, thought better of the added dose of caffeine, but followed through with a fake sip anyway to avoid appearing indecisive. More energy in the room was maybe not what was needed. Still, optics were important.

She set the cup back down on the round conference table. The glacial atmosphere they'd experienced dockside when Thorne arrived was back. The tension in the room crackled. Thorne sat erect as a statue as though his Fleet uniform had too much starch. Bathsheba Toma seemed, for her, nervous, which was to say she appeared only slightly less stiff than Thorne. Sayyida darted her gaze at Eva, who took the cue for what it was.

Someone has to get this show on the road.

"Thank you all for coming," Eva said. "We have much to discuss."

Thorne shifted in his chair. "Oh," he said, "we had a choice in the matter? I was under the impression that attendance was a condition of my parole."

To her credit, Sayyida made no response.

"You're not under arrest here, Admiral," Eva assured him. "I've brought us here to talk about an alliance."

"You still haven't thanked me," Sayyida said, her gaze leveled at Thorne.

He turned to her. "Thanked you?"

"For saving your ass."

Thorne merely stared.

"It would be nice, Admiral, if we could start off on a positive note," Eva said.

Thorne nodded and tapped the table with an index finger. "You're right." He seemed to relax, just a bit. Almost to Toma level. "Without your intervention, Commander al-Hurra, many more lives would have been lost. The Admiralty is grateful for your—"

"The Admiralty?" scoffed Sayyida.

Thorne took a breath, then released it, not as a sigh of surrender but as acknowledgment. "I'm grateful," he said simply. "As a leader in wartime, nothing is more precious to me than the lives of those who serve under my command." His eyes found Sayyida again. "A position, I'm sure, you can appreciate"—belatedly, he added—"Commander."

Sayyida smiled, ever so slightly. Not in victory, Eva thought, but in relief.

"I can," Sayyida said.

The room went quiet again, but the tension seemed to have, if not dissipated entirely, at least subsided.

"And now that we've crossed that bridge," Thorne said, sounding almost amiable, "might I suggest we get to the real purpose of this meeting?"

"Agreed," Sayyida said.

Well, I suppose that's a start, Eva thought, reaching out for a generous sip of her coffee.

"Yes," she said. "I'm no military strategist, but here's what—"

Thorne raised a hand as though in a classroom. Eva halted mid-sentence. "Admiral?"

"Here's the way forward," he said. "I will have Commanders Hale and Meriweather inventory the pirates' ships—class, ordnance, spaceworthiness, et cetera. Once we have that accounting, we'll formulate a battle plan to retake Gibraltar Station and secure Third Sector."

A tight explanation of a simple plan. An entirely unacceptable one. Eva knew what was coming even before it came.

"You must be joking," Sayyida said. Both hands gripped the table's edge. The naturally dark pigment of her skin grew paler at the knuckles. "Turn over intelligence on all New Nassau's fleet assets to you?"

Thorne regarded her coolly, his rod-straight posture back. "How am I to construct a plan of attack without a proper understanding of the resources at my command?"

Sayyida's eyes flared wide. "*Your* command?"

The admiral spread his hands to the room as if to ask, see what I'm forced to deal with? "I am the senior Fleet officer with the most experience—"

"My people will never follow orders from the Hangman," Sayyida said.

The space between Eva's shoulder blades abruptly tightened. "Admiral, Commander, if you'd just—"

"You people need to stop this."

Eva ceased the plea she'd been formulating. All eyes turned to Sheba Toma.

"Colonel?" Thorne said. "You have something to say?"

"I do, sir," Toma said. Despite acknowledging his rank, there was only the minimally required deference in her tone. "This colony is boiling again. It's already suffered through three major traumas recently. The people here had barely gotten used to a battalion of AGF Marines patrolling their corridors in battle-suits. There was nearly a civil war over the idea of reconciling with the Alliance, then their leader was murdered by a teenage boy in pathological puppy love. The three of us—Director Park, Commander al-Hurra, and myself—have managed to avoid the implosion of New Nassau by listening to all sides, risking inflaming passions when we had to, and compromising where we must. On top of all that, Sayyida set aside years of hatred—not to mention convincing the Captains Council to do the same—to put her people and ships in harm's way to save the man who's spent a large part of his career hunting her comrades. And you make demands of a colony that's once again boiling over with the most popular common notion it's held, collectively, since Hadrian al-Hurra was alive: namely, assassinating you!"

As Sheba's rant had ramped up, Eva had fought hard to keep a smile of admiration from her face. It wouldn't be appropriate. But it would have felt good, especially as Thorne's own expression had transitioned from indulgent to offended to reprimanding. Apparently out of steam, Sheba looked apologetically at Eva, clearly embarrassed at her outburst.

"I've talked with Joe Gauss about that particular threat already," Sayyida said, sounding remarkably subdued after Sheba's speech. "He has a handle on security."

"How reassuring," Thorne said sarcastically. Ignoring both Sheba's insubordinate lecture and the daggers Sayyida stared at him, he addressed Eva. "I'm willing to consider a temporary partnership with al-Hurra and her people."

"Like you have a choice," Sayyida said.

"However," he continued, as though she hadn't spoken, "this will be a Fleet operation with—let's call them auxiliary forces—*in support.*"

Sayyida clucked her tongue, and now Thorne did look at

her. "You mean," she said, "like Ancient Rome supplementing its legions with units of the newly conquered for front-line fodder? While your pretty Fleet vessels lob missiles from a safe distance?"

"I mean," Thorne said, each word pronounced precisely, "to lean into our respective strengths. Fleet training and discipline will lead the operation. Your less-capable forces—which, frankly, excel at running away with their outmoded weaponry tucked between their legs—will remain in a position that isn't vital to victory."

As Thorne spoke, Sayyida's face flushed darker. By the time he'd finished, her eyes shone with outrage.

"Without my *less-capable forces*, you'd be dead right now!"

"I didn't say your people are useless." Thorne spread his hands again, granting the point. "You're new to command, so let me impart some wisdom from someone with a bit more experience at it, *Commander* al-Hurra. Officers must divorce themselves from personal animus—toward one another or the duty required of them. Emotion mustn't color one's ability to objectively assess the strategic situation and do what's necessary to achieve victory. Nothing else matters."

An enthusiastic member of the Boys Club, Eva thought, that's what Malcolm Thorne was. She thrust aside her annoyance before she gave voice to what she was thinking.

"*You* lecturing *me*?" Sayyida demanded. "That's rich!"

"Perhaps," Toma said, still sounding contrite, "we should take a break and reconvene—"

"I should have known," Sayyida said. "I let you talk me into this, Eva, and it was a mistake."

"My case in point," Thorne said. "This is exactly the kind of—"

Thrusting her chair backward, Sayyida stood and, without saying another word, stalked from the room. Toma and Eva, who knew better than to try and prevent her exit, watched her go. Meanwhile, Thorne examined his regulation-length fingernails.

After a moment of heavy silence, Eva said, "You were out of line, Admiral. And you came into this room in bad faith."

Thorne regarded her. "The tide of this war resides entirely on the shoulders of this operation. If we are to turn that tide, we must stop the Skane here." He leaned forward and stabbed the table with his index finger. "Here! In this sector! We must counter-attack with the only effective fighting force this Alliance has left and retake Gibraltar Station. Leaving our future in the hands of a—"

"What 'operation,' Admiral?" Eva shot back. "You've just likely ensured there won't be any—"

"I'm still unconvinced how a bunch of—" Thorne began.

"Something I had to learn, Admiral," Toma broke in, "is that you must first respect these people, see things from their perspective. Respect becomes a basis for trust. And that, a foundation on which to build a mutually beneficial relationship."

Turning his cold gaze on Toma, Thorne said nothing. But evident was his disdain for the colonel's presuming yet again to critique her superior officer.

Eva cleared her throat. "This operation *will* happen. It has to. Let me remind you, Admiral, that the military answers to the civilian authority of the Office of the President of the Sol Alliance. And *I'm* that authority in New Nassau."

Thorne opened his mouth, thought better of whatever he was going to say, and closed it again.

"I'll agree to your terms if..." Eva waited for his surprise to pass. "...*if* you agree that Sayyida al-Hurra is your co-commander on this mission." She raised a hand to the protest Thorne was about to mount. "You will have *overall* command.

But the citizen captains of New Nassau will answer directly to Commander al-Hurra."

Thorne released a sympathetic breath. "That would never work, Miss Park. Effective commands can't work like a committee. In the heat of battle, orders can't be second-guessed. Or people *die*."

"But," Toma said, "orders can be delegated. If we establish a specific tactical objective within the overall strategy and assign that mission to Commander al-Hurra, the pirates can essentially act as an adjunct force—like you suggested, Admiral. Detached, under Commander al-Hurra's authority, assigned to achieve that objective—but under your operational command."

He regarded her thoughtfully, this time with less personal hostility. "All right." Eva perked up at that. She wondered if the reason for Thorne's agreement was his assumption that Sayyida would never go for it. "But I choose the mission for the adjunct force."

Eva looked to Sheba for her military assessment of that suggestion. The colonel gave the most surreptitious of nods.

"Deal," Eva said. Grabbing her cup, she downed it to the dregs. "Now, for the hard part."

Thorne and Toma looked to her with the obvious question.

"I have to convince Sayyida to come back to the table," she said.

"You picked a long day to reach out, Captain," Sheba said. She'd almost refused the communication request. But something about reconnecting, whatever she thought of his motivations in going AWOL, had intrigued her with the allure of a surprising nostalgia. "A lot going on here."

"Here too, Sheba," Ben Stone said. "Still, it's good to see your face."

Okay, now she *knew* something was wrong. After her failure to maintain personal discipline in the meeting to end all meetings, Sheba had retreated—strategically redeployed, that was—to her quarters to regroup. She'd found Stone's request waiting for her, previewed by the intriguing subject line A Second Chance for Success. And maximally encrypted, of course.

"Get to the point, Captain."

"My intel proved good before, yeah?" he said.

"On the Skane? Yeah." With Sayyida's earlier scolding of Thorne's ingratitude fresh in her mind, she added, "Thank you for that."

"My pleasure."

"You really killed ten of those things?"

He'd opened their conversation with a tactical briefing on the skirmish at Tarsus Research Station. She wasn't sure at first that she believed all the details, because, after all, it was Stone. She'd do a deep dive into his battlesuit logs later.

"Not by myself," he said. "I had help. Lots of it. But yeah, body count ten, Colonel. So far."

Well, she thought. *That was said with a refreshing lack of ego.*

Maybe the letch really had changed.

"I was thinking of the old days recently," Stone was saying. "Remember that simulation on the *Fannin*? The one with the Archie weapons cache?"

Oh, she remembered it. Dog Company had been assigned to secure a store of Archie weapons on a planet abandoned by the aliens. The cache promised to be a treasure trove of alien technology. The coast looked clear. Mission, simple enough. Drop the Marine units in a ring around the site, link up individual platoons on the flanks, and slowly tighten the perimeter, ensuring no enemy remained, until the cache was secured. All simulated, of course, in a holographic environment. The real purpose for the exercise was to test the character of young platoon lieutenants, a test Ben Stone had failed miserably. Instead of following his superiors' orders, he'd turned the exercise into a footrace to reach the site first, with company bragging rights the real prize at stake in his eyes. His selfish impulsiveness had earned Dog Company failing marks and the punishment that went along with it. But the real salt in the wound had been Colonel Josiah Strickland's debrief, wherein he'd praised Ben Stone's "initiative" in defying orders. It had grated on Toma then, as it did now, like fingernails screeching on a metal wall.

"I remember. What of it?"

"I'm sending you my thoughts on how we could have better executed the operation."

She heard the ping of the data packet log in after her system cleared it of viral infection. There was a starlike, black seal next to the datafile.

"This is why you contacted me, Stone?" she asked, perturbed. But the seal protecting the file was intriguing. Why would Stone use the strictest top-secret encryption available to protect a standard tactical simulation that anyone with a Marine manual could access?

"Just take a good hard look, Sheba," Ben said. "When we get back to base, we'll rock that simulation. Stone, out."

Sheba started to respond, but his image faded. Get back to base? The only thing awaiting Stone wherever they ended up was a court-martial. Despite her irritation, his message demanded a closer look. Sheba clicked on the data packet, entered her credentials. The schematic of the rendered alien planet loaded up.

Wait, what?

The geographic features for the simulated drop were correct, but the details of the operation itself were all wrong. Alien planet—check. Cache of weapons left behind by the Archies when they'd bugged out—check. Objective: seize the cache for analysis—check. But the specifics playing on her screen...

Instead of Dog Company's platoons dropping in a circle around the cache, then slowly drawing together until the objective was secured, they'd been dropped as a cohesive unit to establish a planetary "beachhead." Like the landing that had happened on Canis III. Simulated ships delivered a simulated company near—but not on—the simulated objective, the weapons cache. A second, smaller ship then dropped another, much smaller force between the landing zone and the objective. The second group darted forward toward the cache with all the mad-dash abandon of Stone's platoon in the actual simulation. Then, the playback ended.

Tactically, the plan made no sense, Sheba thought. And in almost no way that mattered was it representative of the original exercise. This was a landing meant to secure a secondary operation, with the 214th standing by, protecting it. What was Ben Stone playing at here?

"This is the dumbest fucking, most tactically unsound plan I've ever seen."

Just take a good hard look, Sheba.

A ping got her attention. There was another file piggybacked on the first, an executable application that unfolded itself onto her hard drive. The computer ran its virus scan, then had to run a second Black Seal-level of decryption for Sheba to gain access. She scanned the contents. Images of a dead Skane corpse flashed up at her. And there was a report plagued with medical terminology presented in excruciating detail from someone named Abara. The executive summary at the end summarized its findings, and Stone popped up again, dumbing down Abara's thesis but still sounding more like a biogenetic engineer than a Marine officer. After reviewing it all, Sheba realized, he was pitching an operation...

"Ben Stone, you crazy bastard."

The medical findings read like a Hail Mary fairy tale—could the Skane possibly be so vulnerable? But what the hell that had to do with...

When we get back to base, we'll rock that simulation.

It clicked. The objective wasn't an alien planet. It was a base. A base built on a rock.

As in, the Rock of Gibraltar.

The code was absurdly schoolboy simple. Classic Ben Stone.

Somehow Gibraltar Station held the key—buried in the obscure nomenclature of a genomic-level autopsy—to defeating the Skane. It sounded like pie-in-the-sky scientific voodoo to Sheba, but maybe the admiral's science officers could evaluate Abara's findings. If they held as much promise as Stone thought they did...

"You crazy bastard," she whispered again. It was also clear that Stone intended to lead the mission. That would be a non-starter for Thorne, she knew, and should be a non-starter for her, too. But whatever their contentious history, Sheba couldn't help but admire the size of Stone's, well, stones.

If you're right, Ben...

"Oo-rah, Captain. Oo-fucking-rah."

35
THE CAPTAINS COUNCIL

"BUT YOU'VE GOT her back on-board?" Sam Devos asked.

My, Eva thought, how times had changed. Devos appeared to have aged years since she'd first broached the topic of reconciliation. Back then, he'd been outraged at the suggestion. Negotiate with pirates? Have President Piers Bragg, the Mogul of Monolith, look so desperate as to offer clemency to generations of criminals?

Now, Devos seemed hungry for just that, starving for any political victory he could get his hands on. Bragg's public addresses had become self-pitying complaints of persecution by the interstellar Congress, now calling for his resignation. Reports of the fall of Gibraltar Station and, with it, access to The Frontier's resources were all over AllianceNet, as were the first glimpses of the terrifying Skane warships. No one likes a wartime president who loses. The only bright spot of news came from Sylvan Novus, where Miranda Marcos had turned rebuilding and rehabilitation into a well-oiled machine of mercy. She'd gone big not home, all right.

Leo had put it perfectly: the people of Sylvan Novus had fallen in love with Miranda Marcos because of what she did for them. That'd been easy since she was a homeworld girl, but that feeling had spread well beyond Alpha Centauri. By contrast, Bragg was becoming reviled for what, Alliance citizens had begun to realize, he'd done *to* them. Turned them in to scared losers-by-proxy too afraid for their own lives to expend much energy empathizing with his political troubles.

"Eva?"

"Sorry, drifted away for a moment. Yes, Commander al-Hurra is back on-board. It wasn't easy, but she's accepted the necessity of a split command. Along with the idea that we have to fight the Skane together, or lose to them separately."

"That's good," Devos said. "That's great."

"She addresses the Captains Council tonight. They didn't take her rescue of Admiral Thorne well for obvious reasons. But her moral authority is intact." Internally, Eva winced. She'd intended to state a fact, not to imply Bragg's position with his own constituency was much weaker.

"No, that's good," Sam said again, clearly oblivious to the inadvertent contrast. "We need this win, Eva."

We?

She was quite sure he meant the administration, not mankind. Eva didn't dwell on the difference. But Devos did.

"He's terrified of becoming a one-term president, you know? Of being drummed out of office. All because of those fucking alien spiders."

He went on like that for nearly a minute. Eva stopped listening but forced her face to exhibit concern. She needed Sam, so she projected sympathy.

"Eva?"

"I'm sorry. Lost focus again."

"I don't blame you," Devos said. "I haven't gotten much sleep lately either..."

Before he could spin up the pity party again, she said,

"You've studied the outline for reconciliation? I know it's a lot to cover and with everything going on—"

"Yeah, I've looked it over. I don't see any major concerns." He'd actually brightened a little, as he did lately, whenever the topic of reuniting the citizens of New Nassau with the greater Alliance came up. Different times, indeed. "We're transmitting a release on subspace tomorrow."

Eva tried to keep it off her face, but that bit of news pleasantly surprised her. Once it was public, the administration's commitment to bringing home New Nassau and her satellite communities would finally, *formally* be under way. The reconciliation initiative was at last worthy of a public-facing capital-R. Sayyida would be overjoyed to hear it. And it couldn't hurt to make that announcement to kick off what was sure to be a contentious Captains Council.

"Great," she said. "We'll hammer out the details on Covenant."

That too seemed to fill out the lines of Sam's war-weary face. "Yes. After we've defeated the bastard Skane," he said. "Together."

Nodding, Eva said, "Talk soon, Sam. I've got a meeting to prep Commander al-Hurra for."

"Good luck," he said, and it was sincere. "You've always had a magic touch for messaging, Eva. The president saw that a long time ago."

Eva offered him a smile. For one thing, she knew he needed it. For another, she knew he meant what he'd said, and she allowed herself a moment to enjoy the compliment.

"Stay healthy," she replied, and signed off.

The news that the Bragg Administration was set to publicly embrace reconciliation had indeed put Sayyida al-Hurra in a good mood. Joe Gauss had reacted with his usual gruff distrust, but even he'd let a smile slip through.

Several dozen ship captains talked among themselves in the well of the cargo hold, where all Captains Councils had been held since Sayyida's father was a young crewman. There was something democratizing about a hold, the place where the loot and credits were usually divvied up. No chairs, no conference tables. Just storage containers for seats and an open area below the upper-tier gantry, where a captain with a grievance might voice it.

Joe Gauss picked up a steel pipe for a gavel and banged it three times on the gantry railing. The ringing call-to-order carried over the heads of the small gathering below.

"Captains, please come to order," he said officially. "Commander al-Hurra wishes to address this council."

Sayyida approached the railing overlooking the hold. "Captains of New Nassau, I have good news. Tomorrow, Sol reckoning, the Bragg Administration will announce its intent to recognize our colony."

There was a moment of absorbing quiet.

"Ain't that big of 'em!" someone shouted.

A woman demanded to know, "Clemency?"

And a grumble from the back: "What they want for their side of the parlay?"

"Order, you bastards!" shouted Gauss, clanging his pipe. "Show a little respect for your commander. That goes for you lady bastards, too."

Laughter answered the chief marshal.

"Thank you, Joe," Sayyida said, letting the room settle. Maybe she should have expected suspicion rather than jubilation. All negotiation resulted in loss, and these men and women wanted to know what they'd gotten—and, more importantly, given up—for citizenship.

"Yes," she said, "there will be no deal without clemency. Full citizenship, with the right to come and go—or stay right here—as we please."

"Sounds too good to be true!"

"We're just starting the parlay." Sayyida's expression hardened. "But that won't matter if we don't stop the Skane."

At least the response to hearing the name of the alien enemy was right on target. Amid the passionate cursing, a tall man elbowed his way forward.

"Madame Commander, I have a motion to put before the council!"

Behind her, Sayyida heard a low, grumbling sigh from Joe. The man coming forward was Pete Cooper, known by the unfortunate moniker Poopdeck Pete.

Joe banged his pipe. "The floor isn't open to motions, Poopdeck."

"Call to a vote!" Cooper groused, with a stern look at Joe Gauss.

Sayyida made an effort to stand very still. Better to seem statue-like, with at least the appearance of composure, than let her shoulders sag. Her father's wisdom stiffened her spine. Democracy was hard, he'd taught her. Messy. That's why mobs preferred dictators who did their thinking for them.

"Very well," she said. "All in favor of hearing Captain Cooper's motion?"

Aye votes filled the room.

"Opposed?"

Only a smattering of *nays*.

She took a symbolic step backward. "You have the floor, Captain."

"The Hangman walks among us." Cooper launched into his

prepared remarks. The captains standing in the well of the lower level made way for him. Others, sitting down, slapped the polysteel containers beneath them. "The council demands justice!"

An uproar of voices filled the hold. Cooper encouraged it with broad gestures of his lanky arms. It took a moment for Joe's ringing gavel to be heard over the clamor.

"You speak for the whole council now, Poopdeck?" Joe said.

Cooper rounded on him. "You of all people ought to agree with me, Marshal! You're a 'man of justice.' We've butted heads over the years, but that much I gotta grant. Where's the justice in feeding, warming, hell even taking orders from the Hangman!"

More uproar. More banging of Gauss's gavel.

"It's the need for justice that's set this course for me," Joe said, his voice low.

Cooper had to crane an ear to hear. "What's that?"

"I said, it's *justice* what's set my course for me!"

There was Joe, Sayyida thought, as good in public as his personal, private word. As if she'd expected anything less. Even if the darker angels of his nature agreed with Pete Cooper.

"Justice is simple enough. We've got the Hangman," Cooper said. "We oughta hang him!"

Sayyida's skin prickled when the hold erupted with agreement. She was losing control of the room.

Joe rang his pipe against the gantry. "That kind of small thinking is what's kept you small, Poopdeck."

Someone guffawed from the other side of the room. Cooper's strutting became stilted.

"I understand," Sayyida said, stepping forward. "I understand your desire for a reckoning with Malcolm Thorne. I share it."

"Prove it!" a woman shouted. "I lost my husband to that butcher. My son ain't got no father now!"

Mary Werner. Thorne had spaced her husband, Alix, half a dozen years earlier. Tightbeamed it into the Triangle as a warning, like he always did.

"That's true, Mary," Sayyida said. "I know it's not the same, but I also know a little about how it feels to lose a father. May I say my peace?" She awaited Werner's permission, a tactical decision on Sayyida's part she thought Eva Park would appreciate. The widowed mother granted it with a grudging nod. "Your son has suffered a terrible loss. And under any other circumstances, I'd be prosecuting the Hangman's trial myself. But we all face losing loved ones now. Some of us already have." She addressed the larger crowd, who'd elected her their captain of captains. "The Skane murdered tens of thousands on Sylvan Novus. Her largest cities are burning. They've routed Fleet from The Frontier and taken Gibraltar Station. Sol is sending the last of its ships to join what remains of Thorne's battle group. Humanity, ladies and gentlemen, is hanging by a thread."

She ended with the prepared line, which she hoped didn't sound prepared, by staring straight at Pete Cooper. He opened his mouth.

"I know this is asking a lot," Sayyida said before he could speak. The crowd's anger simmered but stayed on a low boil. "But we all must sacrifice now. Not merely in blood and treasure, but in what we're willing to swallow to see *true* justice done. Justice for an entire species with one foot out the airlock."

There was more dissent. Incoherent and hateful. But aimed at alien murderers, not human ones.

"A good captain—I know I don't have to tell you—looks to the health of her crew, first and foremost. Why?" Sayyida rested on the railing and waited.

The captains in the hold quieted down.

"Your commander asked you a question!" Joe Gauss shouted.

Mary Werner said, "Because without the crew, the captain commands nothing. And no one."

"Without the crew, there is no ship," a man added.

Sayyida nodded. "I am captain of this colony. Duly elected by popular consent of this very electorate. And you have every right to *un*-elect me if you disagree with the course I've set."

"What?"

"No one said anything—"

"Commander," Cooper stuttered, "I wasn't suggesting—"

"If we're to sail through this storm," Sayyida interrupted, lifting her voice above the muttering crowd, "then this is our course! If anyone can see a better way to safe harbor, I'll open the floor to them."

A hush fell over the room. Soft and absolute. When no one spoke, Sayyida continued.

"Our alliance with the Hangman may be unholy, but unholier still is our fate without it. Now, will you withdraw your motion so we can proceed?" She stared straight at Pete Cooper as she asked the question.

Murmuring anger came again from the far side of the hold. Confusion, bordering on outrage. But strangely subdued.

What now? Sayyida wondered.

Boots rang on the deck, punctuating the crowd's grumbling. Measured, slow, purposeful boots. A chant picked up the pace they made.

"Hang him."

Whispered, at first, then louder.

"Hang him. Hang him. Hang him."

Fists pounded palms, keeping time with the chant.

"Hang him. Hang him. Hang him."

Yet no one touched Malcolm Thorne as he passed among

them. In fact, the captains parted for him as they had for Pete Cooper. But unlike Cooper, Thorne wasn't satisfied to stand among them. He stepped up to the gantry to stand beside Sayyida al-Hurra.

What's he doing here? she shouted in her head. She'd almost had them!

"I request permission to address this assembly," Thorne said to Sayyida.

"Hang him!" Cooper shouted.

The council took up the chant again.

Thorne turned to regard Cooper, and after a brief staring contest, Poopdeck Pete glanced away. It was like a signal to the rest of the room, and the cries for Thorne's summary execution dried up. Thorne looked again at Sayyida, who nodded her permission for him to speak.

To his jury of judges, the admiral said, "You don't want me here. And I don't want to be here. But here I stand."

There was no answer to that from the well below.

"I heard our shared situation likened to a ship in a storm. And all of you as part of the crew of the ship—what shall we call it, Commander?" Thorne glanced at Sayyida, who remained placid but attentive. "The *SS Hope of Mankind*, perhaps. Well, that's appropriate enough, I suppose." Thorne placed his hands behind his back. Spread his feet apart. Jutted out his chin. "I don't know what the future will be like after we kick the Skane's ass."

There was a dash of laughter at that. It quickly subsided, as though the person realized they shouldn't be laughing at anything the Hangman said.

"I doubt I'll like that future much," Thorne continued, his meaning clear. Amnesty was as unjust to him as his continued breathing was to them. "But I'd like there to be one, nevertheless."

"We don't trust you!" Cooper shouted.

"Well, Captain, I don't trust you either. Which is why you'll report to Commander al-Hurra and not to me. But if we combine our strength, we may yet live to fight another day."

Cooper grunted. "Can I fight *you*, then, on that day?"

Thorne gestured nonchalantly. "You might have to fight others for the privilege first."

There was more laughter, and it was easier now. What the Hangman had done wasn't forgotten, and certainly not forgiven. But adjudicating justice, for now, could be deferred.

Thorne returned the meeting's control to Sayyida.

"Do you agree to set your motion aside for now, Captain Cooper?" she asked.

Cooper looked around, assessing his waning support. "Aye."

"Then I'll introduce the motion I came here to," she said. "A motion to sail the fleet in support of retaking Gibraltar Station from the Skane. The terms are these: Third Sector Fleet will have overall command, supported by New Nassau's fleet. You and yours will report directly to me—and no one else." This last she said with a pointed look to Malcolm Thorne. Again he acknowledged her authority with a stiff bow of his head. "Discussion?"

No one raised a hand to protest.

"Very well, then, I call for the vote. All in favor?"

Slowly, one at a time, then in twos and threes: "Aye!"

"Opposed?"

There were one or two obstinate nays. So, not unanimous. But enough. More than enough.

"Motion carries," Joe Gauss announced, banging the pipe three times on the railing.

There were some small exclamations of approval, but most of the members of the Captains Council merely walked away mumbling to one another.

"Why the hell did you come here?" Sayyida hissed where only Thorne could hear.

"They needed to see me," Thorne said. "Needed to hear me. And I, them. I won't have commanders sailing under me who deny my authority over them. It courts disaster."

"You risked everything," she said.

"We're all risking everything, aren't we, Commander?" Thorne asked. "Besides, I waited for the right moment. You had them already."

His sideways praise surprised her. "I didn't come here tonight for you," Sayyida clarified. "I came here for everyone. *Else*."

Thorne nodded. "Of that, Commander al-Hurra, I have no doubt."

36

OPERATION ODYSSEUS

A 3D IMAGE of The Frontier hovered over the round table, rendered at extreme range. In the lower-right quadrant, the Triangle's outer edge was visible. In the middle hung the icon labeled "GS."

Commander Alison Hale said, "Run simulation."

Two score blue icons representing the pirate fleet sortied from the Malvian Triangle at two points—one high above the galactic plane, the other far below. Just as they began arcing toward one another, Hale pressed a button, and the virtual universe ceased movement.

"Thank you, Commander," Jack Meriweather said. As Thorne's XO and first officer, explaining the admiral's battle plan fell to him. "There are three phases. The first is *engagement*. Commander al-Hurra will engage the enemy with her two battle wings. Once we see how the Skane react, we begin phase two: Admiral Thorne's main thrust"—and here he nodded to Hale, who queued the simulation again. Third Sector Fleet's remaining fifteen vessels emerged from the Triangle at a point equidistant along the galactic horizon from the two pirate wings—"to penetrate the enemy battle line at their weakest point."

"Fast-forward a bit," Thorne ordered.

"Aye, Admiral," Hale said.

Eva shared a surreptitious look of amusement with Sayyida. It was cute the way the two taciturn officers acted in public. Necessary, she supposed. Appreciated even. But apparently even animated statues like Malcolm Thorne needed to feel close to someone. Needed to feel human. That fact reassured Eva. They could do this, she thought. They could pull this off.

The model scrubbed forward to half an hour later in simulated time. Hale zoomed in to the rear of Third Fleet and one hexagonal icon labeled "L9H/NL."

"Once the Skane fleet is neutralized," Meriweather explained, "phase three, the boarding action, begins. The *Navis Lusoria*, the dropship carrying Dog Company of the 214th, Bragg's Own Battalion, will exit the *Legio IX Hispana* and breach Gibraltar Station, establishing an ingress point *here*."

The model zoomed in so fast, Eva felt slightly nauseous. Angular renderings of allied and alien starships flew at her until a sudden stop at the hull lines of Gibraltar Station reminded her she'd had synthesized fish for lunch.

"Colonel?" Meriweather said.

Sheba Toma nodded. "Dog Company will breach the station at this cargo bay. Normally used for delivering supplies in bulk, it's big enough to accommodate the dropship's landing. Once we've pacified any Skane resistance, we'll head to main engineering two decks up to deactivate station defenses. We'll also secure environmental and communications. At that point, Captain Stone aboard the *Junkyard Dog*—"

"Hold that thought, Colonel," Thorne said. "Vital mission details *only*, at this point."

Sheba nodded again, her lips pursed. Eva empathized. Thorne's disregard for findings his own Fleet scientists seemed to agree with—that nullifying the Skane was at least worth a try

—grated on Toma, as it did Eva. Of the three of them, Sayyida had been most sympathetic to Thorne's assertion that unproven scientific theories were irrelevant to the plan to retake Gibraltar Station. Even if Stone were right, even if his plan worked, everything else had to go right first: beat the enemy fleet, secure the station, and give Stone—whom Thorne regularly named an AWOL traitor—the opportunity to prove it.

"Once we've neutralized the station's defenses," Toma continued, "the rest of the 214th and other Marine battalions from Fleet will land at strategic points around the station and pacify any remaining resistance."

Thorne said, "Questions?"

"I have one," Eva said. "What are we calling this thing?" The others in the room looked at her. "You military types love naming things like this. What's the—"

"Operation Odysseus," Sheba said quickly.

Thorne turned to look at her.

"Captain Stone's suggestion," she continued, as if already speaking on his behalf at the court-martial. "Secord's idea."

"Academics," Thorne said, and it wasn't a compliment. "Demonstrating their advanced degrees is like a fetish."

Hale, whose advanced degrees in the astrosciences had come in handy for the admiral more than once, tilted her head, her lips curling up in an intriguingly private way. "I like it."

Thorne didn't acknowledge that, or the semi-sultry way she'd said it.

"Why that name?" Sayyida asked.

Sheba glanced to Thorne, who rolled his eyes and nodded his permission for her to explain.

"In Greek mythology, Odysseus and his crew were coming back from the Trojan War. They were shipwrecked on an island with the Cyclops, a monster with a single eye in the middle of its forehead. The Cyclops trapped Odysseus's men in its cave and began to eat them. The survivors escaped by first blinding the monster with a spear."

Though a little brainy for her taste, Eva appreciated the allusion to Ben's plan to blind the Skane. "Clever," she said.

"If we might get back to the battle plan," Sayyida urged.

"Indeed," Thorne said. "To summarize: Commander al-Hurra will distract the Skane and, with luck, entice them to split their fleet to engage her. That should open a path for Third Fleet to punch its way through to the target. Colonel Toma will land her Marines, neutralize station defenses, and enable a larger landing by 3F's remaining Marine battalions."

"A tall order," Sayyida said. "But doable."

"With a name like Operation Odysseus, how could it fail?" Eva quipped.

No one laughed.

"Other details worth mentioning," Meriweather suggested.

"Please," prompted Thorne.

"Unlike at Alpha Centauri, the Skane haven't introduced a bombing campaign in The Frontier," Meriweather said. "Monolith, Ionia, even Covenant have remained unmolested."

Eva said, "So?"

"We think it means the Skane are stretched thin," Hale said. "Sylvan Novus was their attempt to break Alliance morale. It failed. We think taking Gibraltar Station is their attempt at establishing a foothold from which they can launch a local blitzkrieg. Fracture the Alliance by cutting off The Frontier, its greatest supplier of resources."

Eva nodded, running her own mind-simulation of the political fallout of losing The Frontier. Panic in Sol. And after the tragedy of Sylvan Novus, likely riots on Earth. Bragg would surely be run out of office then. Maybe the Sol Parliament, too. Meanwhile, the Skane would exploit the chaos and—well, so much for the SS *Hope of Mankind*.

Game over.

"That's why this mission is so important," Thorne said. "If we're right and the Skane are stretched thin, this may be our last, best chance to break the back of the invasion."

"Any word on that Sol fleet?" Eva asked. She could still see Earth's cities burning in her mind-sim.

"The *Covenant* is coming," Thorne said, "along with the *Monolith* and some of her escorts. The Admiralty is holding back the majority of the Sol Sector Fleet. For a last stand."

"When can we expect the *Covenant*?" Meriweather asked.

Thorne seemed reluctant to answer. Then: "Unknown. She went radio silent two days ago. We have a translight estimate, but..."

"Why radio silent?" Eva wondered.

"To keep the Skane guessing," Sheba said. "Interfleet comms are encrypted, but we can never be sure the Skane aren't listening." She regarded Eva calmly. "*Covenant* and her escorts are our last hole card to play in The Frontier."

"I wonder who they gave her to," Meriweather said. "Maybe Martin Crawley?"

Thorne shrugged. Uncharacteristic for him. Crawley, it seemed, was not his first choice to command the most powerful starship ever built. "He's a man who knows how to prioritize command decisions," he said with little enthusiasm.

Well, that was certainly true, Eva allowed. Whether those priorities were what was best—well, that was debatable. Martin Crawley, the fleet commander who'd escorted Bragg's Treasure Fleet full of lonsdaleite home from The Frontier, hadn't inspired her with much confidence. But that success might have earned him the *Covenant* as a plum command of honor. Bragg liked to reward those he considered loyal, to keep them that way.

"Anything else, sir?" Hale asked.

"Yes. I want to make one thing clear," Thorne said, "and this brings us back to Captain Stone's so-called mission." When he said Ben's name, Eva noticed, it was like he was spitting on the deck. "Stone is a traitor. He disobeyed a presidential directive." Thorne turned to Sheba Toma. "He's one of yours—or he was, anyway. This half-baked mission of his will in no way put at risk our larger goal of securing Gibraltar Station. Do I make myself clear?"

"Crystal, Admiral," she said.

"Let's keep things in perspective, people," Thorne continued. He looked to Sayyida first, who stared right back without blinking. Then, he looked to Hale and Meriweather. Then, Toma. Lastly, he graced Eva Park. "Our primary mission is to retake Gibraltar Station and deny its resources to the enemy. And if we have to destroy the station itself to do that, we will."

"And all the Fleet personnel aboard?" Eva challenged. It wasn't the first time this specific operational detail had come up. It was the mission failure protocol all of them liked least. Especially Thorne.

"As I've said before, Director Park," the admiral replied, clearly annoyed at rehashing a decision that had already been made. "The strategic necessity of denying the Skane the starbase outweighs the lives it might cost to do so." He held her eyes with his own, then returned to his overview. "Secondarily, as part of retaking the base, we destroy the Skane fleet. We still don't know what happened to the enemy who retreated from Sylvan Novus. And, for all we do know, there could be an even bigger Skane armada hiding out in subspace somewhere."

"But we can't worry about that," Sayyida said.

"No," Thorne agreed, "we can't. Mission focus, people. We go with what we know. Dismissed."

Medical felt crowded. That, Ben thought, was because it was.

Cinnamon and Alice stood on either side of Torque's bed, with Gal and Moze perched at the end like catchers at a G-ball game. Ben stood beside Alice, one hand on her shoulder in support. Saying goodbye to her big sister might be hardest for her of all of them.

In the far corner of the room, Light Without Shadow stood, slightly hunched to avoid knocking out the overhead light panel. On the opposite side—near the door and far away from the Arcœnum, Ben noted—were Ian and Zoey and Torque's attending physician.

"It kills me that I can't be in this fight," Torque said. Her voice had the mama bear's rumble in it. Her eyes were misty. "You'd better come back," she said to Cinnamon. "We have a lot to talk about." Then, to everyone: "That goes for *all of you*."

"Oh, we'll be back," Cinnamon promised. "The *Dog* always comes home, you know that."

"Someone called her 'one small ship' once," Torque warned. "Keep that in mind, Cinn. I'm not there to keep your more dangerous impulses in check."

"The woman who said that was a little drugged up and had a head injury when she said it," Cinnamon reminded her. She tapped the side of her newly healed skull. "All better now. Besides, it's always the smallest dogs who are fiercest, right?"

"Right, " Torque said with a feral grin.

"Don't worry," Ben said. "I'll keep her limbic lobe under control."

Torque stared at him. "What?"

He leered just a little, leaving her with the mystery. "Never mind."

Alice reached out and took Torque's hand. It was still bandaged, but more to encourage healing than staunch blood flow, the doctor had said. So, progress.

"Get well, big sister. I'm gonna need you down the road."

"Oo," Torque said, "that sounds intriguing."

"Get well first. Then we'll talk." Alice grinned and pulled away, taking Ben with her. The room began to clear, with spicy encouragement from Gal and warm wishes for a quick recovery from Moze. Once there was space, Light Without Shadow glided forward. Ben stopped in the doorway, the instinct to reach for his sidearm still strong.

"Hey, Louie," Torque said. "Haven't had a chance yet to say thank you. So, erm, thank you."

The ethereal alien made his elegant bow. On his translation screen, images of an animated Torque displayed. Torque with her shotgun, firing. Torque in the co-pilot's seat of the *Junkyard Dog*, shouting at something. Torque in a bar, putting down her shot glass and turning to face a loudmouthed patron making trouble.

She laughed and winced, placing one bandaged hand over her ribcage. "Don't make me laugh, Louie. Hurts."

The screen went dark.

"But yeah," she said. "I'll be back on my feet soon enough. Thanks to you and Alice."

Louie bowed again and, coming a little too close to Ben for comfort, drifted from the room.

"Hey, Stone," Torque said as he turned to follow. He looked back. "Bring them home, yeah? Don't let Cinnamon get herself killed."

He nodded. "That's the plan."

She grunted. "Desperate, is it? The plan, I mean."

"As they come."

"Good." Torque quirked an eyebrow. "Someone told me once that sometimes desperation is the difference between defeat and victory."

Recalling the memory they shared, Ben nodded. "You know it."

The *Junkyard Dog* looked like a patchwork quilt woven together from scrap metal.

"Will this thing even fly anymore?" Stone asked.

"She'll fly!" Moze said hotly. The grease stains painting her face where done in broader strokes than usual. She'd been in the *Dog*'s bowels, tightening every bolt, reinforcing every strut for the upcoming mission. "A blemish makes you appreciate a woman's inner beauty all the more."

"This 'woman' must have one hell of a personality," Ben said.

"Ben!" Alice scolded. "Haven't you outgrown yourself yet?"

"Stop insulting my ship, Stone," Cinnamon barked, hopping up the ramp. "Or you can float to that damned station."

But Ben was too focused on the tall Arcœnum coming toward him to shoot back. On the translation screen, Louie's image appeared beside Ben, Cinnamon, and Alice on what Ben assumed was Gibraltar Station. The alien had made himself a fourth member of their infiltration team.

"No," Ben said simply. He didn't want Louie at his back. He had enough to think about to accomplish the mission and keep his promise to Torque. He'd be distracted enough putting Alice in danger. But she'd certainly come in handy in the cafeteria. No arguing anymore that she couldn't look out for herself—and him too, come to think of it.

"Maybe Louie can help," she said.

"Alice—" Ben began.

"Remember how he helped with Torque."

Her reminder derailed Ben's argument. Expectations of the

alien's treachery aside, what had Louie done but proven his loyalty to Cinnamon and her crew? And what if they encountered something Ben's tactics, Cinnamon's pistols, and Alice's ability couldn't handle? Maybe having Louie along could make the difference. And too much—that was, *everything*—was riding on their success to voice regret later for an opportunity missed. Hell, if there even was a later.

If you're going to roll the dice, you might as well throw them to the end of the table.

"Fine. But he stays in front of me. *The whole time.*"

The image on Louie's screen showed them creeping along like jewel thieves in a corridor of the station, Louie in front of Ben.

"And remember," Ben said, "I'm in command of the team. *Period.* You don't follow my orders, I shoot you. Got that?"

The image morphed. Now the Louie avatar was walking away from Ben, who casually shot him in the back. Virtual Louie fell to his knees, then collapsed dead on the deck.

"Hey!" Ben said. "Not like that! I mean..."

Actually, if it did happen, it'd probably happen just like that.

Louie strode into the *Dog* after Cinnamon, leaving behind him the distinct impression that Ben had just become the butt of alien humor.

Ben jumped as he was clapped on the shoulder by Gal Galatz.

"Mount up, Adonis," she said, all toothy grin and dancing eyebrows. "Let's get this thing done so we can get on with the celebratory sex!"

She sprinted up the ramp as though by doing so she could hurry things along for everyone.

"Hey Ben," Alice said, "I've been meaning to ask—"

Ben said, "Don't. Just ... don't." He was in no mood for lurid suggestions; he got enough of those from Gal. Thinking better of his tone, he looked at the uncertain, half-hurt expression blooming on Alice's face. "Come on, kid. Like our oversexed pilot said, let's get this done."

He took her hand, and they climbed the ramp together. By the time they reached the top, Alice was smiling.

37
GHOST FLEET

SPACE WAS A VAST EMPTINESS. Perhaps a truism, Sayyida al-Hurra realized, but it felt even more so today than most.

Leading her battle wing aboard the *Shark's Tooth*, Sayyida wasn't sure what she'd expected to find when emerging from the Malvian Triangle. No, that wasn't quite true. She'd expected to find the Skane fleet that now controlled Gibraltar Station and, with it, the entire Frontier. She'd expected to find them deployed and waiting to slice through her two wings of ships with those goddamned spinning missiles that slipped through hulls using some kind of subspace sorcery.

Instead, she'd only found empty space. Sayyida wasn't sure which option was more distressing. With its ability to spin literal nothingness into doomsday, the human mind truly was a wonder.

"Message from *Dragonfire*," her comm officer, Yu, announced. "Captain Mattei for you, commander."

"I'll bet." She peered at the black velvet void on-screen. "Put him through."

"Not even a patrol?" Daniel Mattei said without greeting. "Seems odd."

"It does."

"Sensors are clear," he said. "Probe squadron?"

"Sure."

Mattei nodded, and the screen faded once again to show only interstellar space.

"Tactical," Sayyida said. She'd seen it scores—make that hundreds—of times before, but looking at all that void was making her inexplicably queasy.

"Aye-aye," acknowledged Ervin at tactical.

The screen flattened to a basic 2D sector map. The icons representing Daniel Mattei's battle wing, fifteen vessels of the pirate fleet, appeared on the left and led by *Dragonfire*. Sayyida's wing with seventeen ships was positioned on the right. Thirty-two vessels in all of every type, from two salvaged frigates mothballed by Fleet decades earlier, to converted cargo carriers, to pinnaces, barques, and even one unassuming luxury yacht captured as a prize when Cinnamon Gauss rescued Alice Keller in the Shallows. Redubbed *The Last Sip of Socrates*, she was now a fast reconnaissance vessel used for scouting.

In two dimensions, the display's two-dimensional layout appeared deceptively simple. In 3D space, the two wings of starships were actually equidistant from one another, the first above, the second below the relative horizon of the galactic plane. The plan was straightforward enough: attack the Skane from above and below and pull apart the enemy fleet as it turned to meet the two-pronged attack. Then, Thorne and Third Sector Fleet would push through the middle like a running back, carrying Sheba Toma's dropship forward like a football. Once Toma's company breached Gibraltar Station, it'd be a ship-to-ship slugfest until she'd taken the defensive systems offline and the rest of Third Fleet's Marines could land and secure the station. Then it'd still be a slugfest, but at least they'd have the station.

Simple, right? Sayyida thought, staring at her woefully

small, divided forces on-screen. Only, where were the Skane? As Mattei had alluded, any competent enemy would have maintained patrols near the Triangle after chasing Thorne into it.

"Captain Mattei is sending *Riftskimmer*, *Strumpet's Howl*, and *Socrates*," Yu reported.

Sayyida nodded. "Order *Emasculator*, *Shrieking Ex*, and *Storm of Hades* forward."

Yu acknowledged the order.

Maybe Fleet's analysis was right, Sayyida thought as each wing sent its three probe vessels forward. Maybe the Skane had overextended, thrown everything they had at kicking Thorne out of The Frontier and taking Gibraltar Station. Maybe the resistance of Fleet personnel aboard the station had been stiffer than expected, and the enemy was spending resources controlling it. The fact that the Skane hadn't bombed the Alliance's Frontier planets like they'd done Sylvan Novus was welcome, but militarily curious. Or, maybe self-evident—avoiding unnecessary collateral damage, preserving those planetside resources for themselves? Maybe Sylvan Novus was useless to them so far out and, therefore, expendable. Maybe they'd merely run out of supplies to make their spinning subspace bombs. Maybe, Sayyida chided herself, she should quit worrying about questions she had no answers to and focus on the task at hand.

She watched while the six vessels scouted ahead, moving farther away from the sanctuary of the Triangle and the security of the strength-in-numbers of their battle wings.

"Contact!" Yu announced. "Skane ships are ... appearing out of nowhere, Commander!"

Of course they are.

"Jumping in?" Sayyida said.

"I don't think so. No drive signatures." Yu was becoming increasingly anxious. "They're phasing out of subspace, I think. Popping up like ghosts, ma'am—"

"Just the facts, please," Sayyida replied calmly. That sonofabitch Thorne might be right about one thing. Military discipline could sometimes be in short supply among her pirate crews. Panic could kill them if they weren't careful, every bit as effectively as the Skane.

"Aye, Commander. Now, half a dozen ship groups, ma'am. Make that eight. Ten. More appearing..."

The forward tactical display began dotting with the red icons of the Skane fleet. As though a magician had pulled back a curtain revealing something that had been there all along. Which, of course, it had.

"Groups, you said?"

"Aye," replied Yu. "Dozens now, squadrons of three or four vessels. Loose formation. *Emasculator* and *Storm of Hades* are engaging."

Sayyida cursed. "They know better than that. Order them back!"

This was no time for run, gun, rinse, repeat. The job of the probe ships was to find the enemy, not to fight them.

Sure, bad morale could kill them. So could stupidity.

"Aye-aye. Captain Mattei for you, ma'am."

"Let's have him."

He appeared with an expression somewhere between relieved and hungry. "Well, we've found them. But this staggered formation of squadrons is strange. Usually they just swarm and overwhelm."

"Right," Sayyida said, "but the way they've positioned themselves doesn't change our mission. Pull your probes back. The engagement phase starts now."

"Aye, Commander. Mattei out."

"Ma'am," Yu said, her voice shaky, "*Emasculator* is destroyed. *Hades* is disabled. *Ex* is signaling she'll attempt a rescue—"

"No!" It went against every instinct to deny the captain of the *Ex*'s request that hadn't really been a request. Sayyida said again, "No. Order Captain Perez back."

"But Commander—"

"Do it!"

Behind Sayyida, Yu began issuing the order over subspace. She admired Perez of the *Shrieking Ex* for his loyalty to his fellow captain in distress. Under normal circumstances, a rescue attempt was the right thing to do. But these weren't normal circumstances. And they needed every ship they had for the fight in front of them.

Also gnawing at her—somehow the Skane had obscured their presence from sensors. When the probe ships got closer, they'd revealed themselves. And Sayyida, in her hubris, had questioned the Skane's competence? She resolved not to make the same mistake again.

"Start a continual data stream back to Third Fleet," she said to Yu. "I want Thorne aware of the Skane's ability to fool our sensors, even if we can't tell him why."

"Aye."

"Helm, order the wing forward. Mirror Captain Mattei's wing until the shooting starts. Tactical, zoom in and rotate along the z-axis. I need to see what's going on."

Her crew acknowledged. On the forward screen, the view accelerated inward, then turned ninety degrees. Left and right became up and down, letting her see the relative position of Mattei's vessels compared to her own and the numerous avatars showing the Skane squadrons, now dominating a line stretching center-screen. Both Sayyida's battle wing and Mattei's edged forward to engage. The prongs of the pirates' attack, beginning to close.

The Skane, so far, hadn't responded. Just sat there in their clumps of ships like hosts in a receiving line. On-screen, the *Shrieking Ex* and Mattei's own probe ships had nearly returned home to the fold.

"Give me fleetwide," Sayyida said.

A few manipulations of Yu's console, then the comm officer said, "You're on, ma'am."

"All ships, this is Commander Sayyida al-Hurra of New Nassau." Thorne and his people would be listening too. She hoped she remembered what Eva Park had written for her; or, at least, could paraphrase it well. "We've set aside our differences to fight together, Alliance and Separated. We residents of the Triangle call ourselves that no longer. We're all in this fight together. Today, we reclaim control of our future as a species. You might feel fear. *Use* it. *Channel it.* Forge it into anger. Remember Sylvan Novus! Fight for your children!" She paused to take a breath, and side-eyed Ervin at tactical. He was staring at her, with an expression that was either impressed or aghast. "Fight for all mankind's children, everywhere. Al-Hurra out."

Sayyida faced Ervin straight on and with a level gaze.

"Here we go."

Mattei's closer wing engaged the Skane first. *Dragonfire, Riftskimmer*, and *Strumpet's Howl* targeted the vessel on the far right of the enemy formation. The rest of his starships hung back, long-range tactical sensors overwatching the enemy, prepared to react to their reaction. The pirates' weaponry was two and three generations old compared to that of their Fleet allies, but pirate missiles still delivered destruction. They could still kill Skane ships and dart away to come 'round again.

Run, gun, rinse, repeat.

Ship battles have a natural gravity about them, Sayyida knew from long experience. Pirate captains are hunters by nature, and when one saw an opportunity, it was hard to ignore the instinct to pursue it. That was true of humans, anyway. She knew little of what motivated the Skane, but restraint didn't seem one of their virtues. And yet, here they sat, offering no answer to the pirates' initial attacks.

As she and Mattei picked at the far edges of the Skane formation, the hope was that enemy ships would drift outward from the center to meet them. When Thorne struck from the Triangle, his more powerful starships would hit their weakened center like Thor's hammer. Would it be enough? Well, that was the question now, wasn't it...

Only, the first part of the plan had already gone wrong. The Skane weren't drifting outward, lured by the pirates—weren't moving at all. Whatever enticed them to kill the *Emasculator* and disable the *Hades* before, their squadrons now appeared dormant. Unmoved by the destruction of two of their own as *Dragonfire* and her sister ships made their first pass.

It was unnerving.

"Coming into weapons range," Ervin reported. "The *Ex* and *Sorcerer's Apprentice* are launching."

"Add our voice to theirs," Sayyida growled.

Ervin zoomed the forward display to the targeted enemy ship. *Shark's Tooth* launched three missiles that arced in behind those of the *Ex* and *Apprentice*. One explosion, followed by a second. With the first Skane vessel destroyed, two of the *Tooth*'s missiles redirected to another in its group of three, and soon a second explosion followed the first.

With no reaction from the rest of the enemy.

Damned unnerving.

"Ours is not to reason why," Sayyida muttered under her breath.

Ervin asked, "Sorry, ma'am?"

"Nothing. Send to all ships in both wings: weapons free. Attack!"

Yu at communications relayed Sayyida's order to their wing and Mattei's, who'd already taken the initiative and fully committed his ships to the offensive. As though they'd heard her attack order themselves, the Skane ships began to pull back. In an ordered, controlled retreat as though each were an individual component in a single, massive vessel.

That fucking hive mind again.

The prongs of the pirate attack continued to close. Ervin pulled out the view again, and the enemy's retrograde began to slow. Then, it was like a bomb had detonated in the middle of the Skane formation. Their ships broke the discipline of their line, scattering outward to engage the pirates.

"It's working, ma'am," Ervin said.

"I can see that."

The Skane favored Mattei's lower wing for their heaviest response. But after one pass answering the pirates' attack, after two of Mattei's starships joined the *Emasculator* in death, the aliens broke off again.

What the hell are they doing?

It was like the Skane had lost all the viciousness, all the savagery they'd shown in Alpha-C. The token resistance they'd offered so far had resulted in a fairly even trade of lost ships. That was unexpected. Every move the Skane had made so far had been unexpected.

And then Sayyida realized what they were doing when she recognized the tactic unfolding on-screen. The Skane had adapted the pirates' own combat playbook against them. They'd played dead, then pulled back, then attacked, then pulled back again.

A wilier form of run, gun, rinse, repeat.

Hide, wait, retreat, attack.

Beyond unnerving.

"Captain Mattei is pursuing," Ervin reported. "The Skane are breaking off from us too, Commander."

On-screen, all across the theater of operations, the Skane were running. Something tickled in Sayyida's gut. A sixth sense of dread that the humans' plan had been accounted for in a larger plan not crafted by humans at all. The Skane retreat wasn't the sudden rout it was meant to look like, she was sure of it.

Sayyida turned to Yu. "Have Mattei recall his starships. Break off pursuit. Same with ours. Let's regroup."

Excepting the rough white noise of routine around her, the bridge of the *Shark's Tooth* fell silent.

"Ma'am?" Yu said.

"You heard me. Do it now."

Yu began transmitting.

"Commander!" Ervin said. "New signals!"

The tactical view pulled out to reveal a radius around them covering more than five hundred thousand kilometers in 3D space. One, five, ten, twenty red icons popped up. Ahead, behind, on the flanks, above and below. Fifty now, a hundred. They appeared so numerous that, at this distant view and with signals overlapping, they looked like a red cloud expanding, filling in all that space that had seemed so empty before. The red cloud bloomed like a new nebula forming around the still-exposed wings of the pirate fleet. Surrounding them.

The Skane squadrons were turning, coming back. Around the friendly icons on the tactical display, the cloud began to morph and move.

"Tactical, what the hell am I looking at?"

"Commander, they're ninjas!" Ervin replied. "Dozens ... hundreds. Homing in on—"

"Evasive maneuvers!" Sayyida shouted. "Yu, fleetwide! Evasive! Break off! Break off!"

Yu chattered quickly, her voice rising on a wave of adrenaline. Sayyida watched the main screen as first one, then a second of Mattei's ships disappeared. The ninjas striking, passing through their hulls, breaching engine containment, detonating ordnance.

"*Socrates* is gone," Ervin reported. "Now the *Howl*. Commander, the *Dragonfire* is—"

But Sayyida saw for herself when Mattei's ship winked out. This had been the Skane's plan all along. Lure them in with the appearance of weakness, retreat to pull them in farther—but all only a feint. A predator lying in wait, with its poisoned fangs masked, hidden inside the shadows of subspace. A spider in a hole, waiting for the precise moment to spring its deathtrap.

"Give me fleetwide," Sayyida told Yu. Her voice was strangely calm. As though she'd accepted that she was dead already, and that was okay. Because acceptance gave her focus.

The *Shark's Tooth* slammed hard to starboard, rolled, its railguns spitting slugs in a curving, twisting arc to intercept the ninjas now aiming for her hull. Sayyida gritted her teeth at the screen, fought the nausea clawing its way up her throat, waited out the brace of defensive fire till the ship's compensators caught up with physics and restored the artificial gravity.

"You're on," Yu said.

"All ships," Sayyida said, her tone still calm in the eye of the storm. "Break off. Retreat. We'll regroup in the Triangle. Repeat! Break—"

"Belay that order!" shouted another voice, a male voice,

commandeering the channel. "Commander al-Hurra, you will maintain contact with the enemy."

A hated voice.

Unmistakable.

Thorne.

38
WHAT MIGHT HAVE BEEN

ON THE BRIDGE of *Legio IX Hispana*, Malcolm Thorne felt the eyes of his command crew upon him. He considered ordering them to focus on their duties but knew they needed to see him calm and collected—unaffected by the clusterfuck ambush unfolding on-screen. Even if he could sense their collective disapproval of the order he'd just issued to Sayyida al-Hurra. Maybe especially then.

"Admiral," said Commander Meriweather, "shall I order Third Fleet forward?"

"Hold our position, Commander."

The communications officer cleared his throat. "Commander al-Hurra is hailing us, Admiral."

"Let's have her."

Sayyida al-Hurra appeared on-screen, her face paler than he remembered, though her expression remained cool. Icy, in fact.

"Thorne! Why did you countermand me?"

Not used to having his orders questioned, Thorne nevertheless indulged her. After all, she wasn't Fleet trained, as he himself had pointed out. "If you retreat now, you give the Skane the opportunity to reconsolidate their forces."

Al-Hurra lost the battle she'd been fighting to maintain her composure. "Reconsolidate? They're consolidated now, and killing us!"

Her image shook when *Shark's Tooth* took a hard hit.

"Commander, I need you to better coordinate your attack on the enemy fleet."

"Mattei is dead," she said, answering a question he hadn't asked. "Railguns are running low."

The screen scrambled again, freezing al-Hurra's scowl in place. Thorne could see it in the wide eyes, the stretched mouth, the gleam of spittle sheening her teeth—terror, though not of death, he suspected. Of failure. Of throwing her people's lives away. That, he realized, was a terror they shared.

Al-Hurra animated in mid-sentence: "—attack with Third Fleet. Open an escape route—"

"I can't do that, Commander," he said. "Not yet."

"We're being slaughtered!"

"We agreed to trust one another, Commander. Prove you're as good as your word. I recommend you pull Mattei's ships under your direct command and—"

"Fuck your recommendation," she barked, and cut the feed.

The silence that surrounded Thorne on the bridge was almost as heavy as the critical eyes had been before. Only the helmsman stared forward. His hands, Thorne noticed, poised ready to engage the *Hispana*'s translight drive and make the jump into the fray.

"Communications, any word from the *Covenant*?"

"Still radio silent, Admiral."

"Admiral, if I may—" Meriweather began.

"I understand the impulse to ride to the rescue," Thorne interrupted, "but if we go in too soon, we risk compromising the entire operation."

"She was right all along." At the science station,

Commander Alison Hale spoke quietly but critically. "You're using them as cannon fodder."

Thorne turned to look at her. Normally, in spite of hearing al-Hurra out, he'd never have indulged the same kind of blowback from his own officers. Not even from the woman he intended to marry once they left Fleet. But in this case, at this hour, he made the exception.

"I never sacrifice human life casually."

"But you knew the Skane would be waiting—or at least strongly suspected it. And you sent Commander al-Hurra's pirates out there to trip the trap."

"We'll all have to make sacrifices if we're to prevail, Commander," Thorne said, using her rank as a none-too subtle hint that she should save her reproval for after the battle, and privacy. "Our best chance for victory is to preserve as much of Fleet's superior firepower as possible, to use it as effectively as possible at just the right time. If that means Commander al-Hurra's forces make the enemy spend its offensive capability—"

"'Offensive capability?'" she said. "Mal, those people out there are dying!"

"To give mankind a chance!" Thorne shouted, his fist pounding the arm of the command chair. He reined his anger in quickly. This, he reminded himself, is why emotion had no place in orders given or followed. Only accomplishing the operational objective mattered. "Not only because I told them to. Because they have to."

Disappointed in himself for allowing the dissension in the first place, Thorne sighed. He should have shut Alison down before she'd gotten started. Doubt was like an infection—a virulent, rampant infection that undermined morale as surely as acid melting skin away from bone.

"Admiral," Abraham said at tactical, "Commander al-Hurra has lost half her ships, but the pirates are rallying."

"Status of those ninjas?" Thorne queried.

"Many of them are still operational," Abraham responded unhelpfully. "But many aren't."

"Sir," the communications officer cut in, "a single ping from *Covenant*! ETA, ten minutes."

Thorne exhaled quiet relief. Ten minutes, and Fleet's last, best hope would add its untested but substantial firepower to 3F's own. Maybe it would be enough. But he should still wait, he reasoned, let *Covenant* get closer. Not be moved by the sentiment around him or, if Thorne were being honest with himself, his own instinct to 'ride to the rescue.' Then again, ignoring his instincts usually led to worse outcomes than following them.

"Communications," Thorne said, "send to all ships. Stay tight. We are leaving the Triangle and engaging the Skane. To carriers *Requiem* and *Callisto*: launch all fighters. They're to sweep forward and clear any ninjas. I want a clean pathway straight to the station."

"Aye, Admiral."

"Helm, time to thrust the point of the spear at the enemy."

"Aye, sir!"

He could feel Alison's eyes on him, no less angry it turned out. *Some days, you just can't win.* He locked onto the hazy pink of the Triangle, now beginning to plow past *Hispana*'s bows. Through the cushion in the command chair, he could feel the hum of her engines from her forward thrust.

Maybe, Thorne pondered, *we'll have a chance to reclaim the honor of that lost legion after all.*

Abraham reported, "Thirty seconds to weapons range, Admiral."

"Understood. Commander Hale, the data the pirates sent

when the Skane first appeared—any idea how they evaded al-Hurra's sensors for so long?"

"I recognize some of the math it would take," Hale said, all-business now in expressing her expertise. "My theory is they learned from our using Pathfinder against them in the previous battle. Somehow reprogrammed its algorithms to project false returns—essentially to mirror empty space, make it look like nothing was there."

"So they turned our own technology against us," Thorne said. "How do we counter it?"

"Impossible to say, sir," Hale answered.

So they'd be trusting to luck again, Thorne thought. Rolling the dice that the Skane had no other tricks up their spidery sleeve. He much preferred the predictable probability of Alison Hale's algorithms.

"Sir," Abraham said, "al-Hurra's concentrating her attack on the far left of the enemy fleet. I recommend we aim for that as well and—"

"No," Thorne said. "We stick to the plan. Punch straight through the middle to Gibraltar Station. Destroyers *Irkutsk* and *Nanchang* to follow *Hispana* straight up the slot. Pass along my order to Commodore Messing—he's to take the bulk of Third Fleet and run interference against the Skane. We'll fight our way forward, but al-Hurra's on her own—make that crystal clear to Messing. His job is to keep the Skane off our back. Flank speed, helm."

A chorus of responses acknowledged Thorne's orders.

On the main screen, space was alive with combat. The perspective streaked upward as *Hispana* dived to avoid a mass of pursuing ninjas, her railguns spewing slugs to intercept the alien ordnance. *Hispana*'s proton cannons fired massive broadsides from her port and starboard batteries as she passed between two smaller Skane vessels. A flash of white and orange from the fore-starboard quarter signaled the explosion of an enemy ship. *Hispana*'s hull plating rattled with aftershocks.

"Tactical on-screen," Thorne said. "Show me Gibraltar."

The real-time display in front of them shifted to the sector map, then zoomed out. The station was still nearly two million kilometers away. A long gauntlet to run against so many Skane warships, even in a dreadnaught as capable as *Hispana*.

"*Covenant*'s position?" he requested.

"Still five minutes out, Admiral."

Moved from the Triangle too soon. Thorne had to make an active effort to stop the thought from peppering him with doubt. He'd made a decision. He'd live with it.

If I'm lucky.

Hispana rocked again, hit by offensive fire.

"I think they know where we're headed," quipped Meriweather.

"Aye," Abraham said. "Five Skane ships angling to cut us off. Commodore Messing is moving to intercept."

"Quarter speed," Thorne groused, annoyed at having to slow down. "Communications, get our escorts between *Hispana* and those incoming ships."

The display showed the balance of Third Fleet streaking past the three icons representing *Hispana*, *Irkutsk*, and *Nanchang*. The two destroyers maneuvered to cover *Hispana*'s starboard side facing the enemy vessels, as now, half a dozen in all, they bore down on Thorne's ship. The battle-within-a-battle appeared pre-determined. 3F's guns significantly outweighed the six enemy warships, and initially that weight carried the day as Messing destroyed two by concentrating his fire in the first exchange. Then *Irkutsk* lost her engines and exploded, disabling one of 3F's light cruisers to boot. Third Fleet tallied three ships lost to the Skane's six. But more enemy vessels, diverting from al-Hurra's depleted threat, were on their way.

"Resume flank speed," Thorne ordered. "*Covenant?*"

"Three minutes, Admiral."

He sternly eyed the changing landscape of the engagement unfolding on the forward screen. The Skane were abandoning the pirates. Meriweather was right. They'd finally clued in to the real purpose of the counterattack. The slugfest had become a running fight. A foot-pounding, face-pounding street brawl in space. Thorne engaged the comms key of his command chair.

"Toma, get your pilot ready to launch from the hangar bay."

"Aye, Admiral. Been kinda rough down here."

"It's about to get rougher. Thorne out."

"Sir," Meriweather said, "al-Hurra has disengaged. She's making for the Triangle with her remaining ships. The Skane are now fully committing against Messing."

Thorne was tempted to point out that al-Hurra and her pirates were doing what they did best—running. But they'd acquitted themselves better than he'd hoped. And running was part of the plan—run and hope at least a few of the hungrier Skane pursued. But the aliens weren't pursuing. Their one-track command structure had re-tasked every ship to interdict *Hispana*'s run for the station.

It all depended on Messing and 3F holding them off, just a little bit longer. On-screen, Gibraltar Station lay a mere half-million kilometers distant.

"Get me Messing," Thorne said.

The commodore's face, when it appeared, was grimy with sweat.

"Admiral. A little busy over here."

"I'll make it quick, Ewan. Consider yourself an independent command with one objective: exterminate the Skane fleet. No matter what happens to us. Understood?"

"Aye, sir."

"Good luck and Godspeed, Commodore."

"Incoming fire!" Abraham said.

Meriweather asked, "From the station?"

"Aye."

Well, Thorne thought, they couldn't have been *that* lucky. The Skane controlled the station's weapons systems. So much for the fantasy that maybe they hadn't learned to use them. Toma had her work cut out for her.

Hispana's point-defense cannons intercepted some of the station's incoming fire. Knocking out the missiles was the easy part. Gibraltar's heavy proton cannons would be harder to deal with. But for Toma to have a chance, for the dropship carrying Dog Company to survive the approach and land successfully, the *Hispana* would have to get very, very close—and well inside the effective range of station defenses.

The ship quaked. The first of Gibraltar's proton cannons, finding their mark.

"Evasive maneuvers—" Meriweather began.

"Belay that," Thorne said. "Maintain course."

Abraham reported, "Three hundred thousand kilometers to target."

"I've got to begin the deceleration burn," the helmsman said. "Or we'll shoot right past and leave the carrier hanging—"

"Do it," Thorne said.

At tactical, Abraham was reassuringly, perversely calm. If they lived through this, Thorne noted a commendation in his future. The distance to the icon labeled "GS" on-screen sped down its count from two hundred thousand kilometers.

"New tactical reading!" Abraham said.

Meriweather said, "*Covenant*?"

"Negative. It's coming from the station. From behind Gibraltar's shadow..."

Hispana jolted again.

"Show us," Thorne said.

Gibraltar Station appeared, her cannons pumping out enough firepower to vaporize smaller starships. Around the shadow of her profile, a large, nebulous, dark shape became visible. It was dotted with enough lights to remind Thorne of a large city viewed from low Earth orbit. Long, sword-like arms extended from the rounded body. They angled forward toward *Hispana*. Thorne knew a tactical array homing in on a target when he saw one.

"Mothership," Thorne said.

In the same moment, Meriweather said, "*Shelob*."

"Commander?"

Meriweather shrugged. "Gotta name it something better than 'mothership.'"

"Another new signal," Abraham reported. "Sir! It's *Covenant*!"

Thorne allowed himself half a moment of secret celebration. *Thank God*.

"Hail her and—"

But before the order was out of his mouth, an explosion occurred. The *Legio IX Hispana* dropped to sublight as decompression vented the ship's interior and dozens of personnel into space. The massive starship turned one complete rotation along its keel. Thorne blacked out, then experienced an erratic interval of fighting his way back to consciousness. Next thing he knew, he was on his hands and knees on the deck. The ship's alert sirens blasted around him. The bloody glare of secondary lighting flooded the bridge.

"Report!"

No one answered. "I said..." A quick look around the bridge stopped him. Meriweather was moving but still out of it. Splayed around the deck, injured or incapacitated like Abraham, none of his command crew could respond.

Thorne struggled to his feet as the artificial gravity stabilized. He staggered to the helm console. Fire control and translight were out. Offensive weapons, offline. The crew had only been saved from physics pasting them all over *Hispana*'s bulkheads by the ship's automated systems. Their forward motion continued to slow, making *Hispana* a ripe target for the Skane mothership and Gibraltar's big guns.

"Sir?" Meriweather was on his knees, trying to clear his head.

"Take tactical," Thorne said. *Nanchang* was gone. Meriweather's *Shelob* was headed straight for them, maneuvering between *Hispana* and the station—for now protecting Thorne's ship from Gibraltar's proton cannons by its positioning. Thirty-two thousand kilometers. They were almost close enough for Toma to make her run.

From communications, a voice was calling out. Almost recognizable, but not from *Hispana*. Martin Crawley on *Covenant*? Thorne focused on the scattered sound, watched as a familiar, feminine hand reached from below the communications console to accept the hail. Alison raised herself up, hair hanging loose, face streaked, a nasty gash on her temple.

Still lovely, Thorne thought.

"*Hispana*..." she said. "Aye."

"Hispana, Covenant. *Admiral Thorne?*"

Didn't sound like Crawley.

Too decisive. Too old.

Using the console for support against the ship's deceleration, Thorne dragged himself toward communications, nearly fell again when *Hispana* trembled violently. *Shelob*, spinning her ninjas outward. His ship's PDCs, Meriweather guiding them, answering with defiance.

"Thorne here," he said, bracing himself. His hand brushed Alison's, and for one, brief glorious moment they shared a look without the distance of rank separating them.

"Can't reach you before that spider-ship does," *Covenant*'s commander said.

"Forget us. Cover the running back."

"Acknowledged. Drop Toma and get clear, Admiral. That's an order."

Thorne identified the voice, then. And in the order given, also recognized the desire to preserve the lives of Fleet personnel he'd once so hotly accused the very same man of lacking.

"Admiral Stone," he said, "you're now in command of this operation. Thorne out."

He cut comms before Stone could reiterate his order, thereby perhaps preserving deniability for the record, then engaged the secured channel to the troop carrier. Thorne knew something Stone maybe didn't. They were almost inside the station's defensive perimeter. The *Legio IX Hispana* had to clear the mothership from its path, or the Skane would obliterate Toma's dropship and her Marines along with it.

Not on my watch.

"Colonel, I'm opening bay doors. Get ready to launch."

"Aye, Admiral."

He clapped off the blaring klaxon and stumbled back to the helm to right his ship and plot the straightest approach to Gibraltar Station. *Shelob* bore down on them.

At tactical, Meriweather said quietly, "Sir, we've got no weapons left beyond PDCs."

"We've got engines though," Thorne said. He opened the launch bay. "Commander," he said to Hale, "order Toma to launch. Do it now."

"Aye, sir," she said, her eyes lingering on his before she turned to give Toma her launch order.

"Ferris Maneuver?" asked Meriweather without a hint of fear.

Thorne grunted. "It's all we've got left."

His first officer nodded, released a long breath.

On-screen, the mothership launched a brace of ninjas. But the Skane had guessed Thorne's intent, and the huge vessel began a broad arc to port.

In the last moments when he still had sensors to guide him, Thorne adjusted his course, *Hispana*'s powerful sublight engines tracking the mothership, aiming for where she'd be, not where she was.

Ninjas ripped through *Hispana*'s hull. Fresh alarms sounded. The view on-screen snowed out, as though *Legio IX Hispana* were closing her eyes after committing herself to one final objective to complete her service life.

But Malcolm Thorne's eyes were wide open. He turned to find Alison Hale staring back at him.

Frightened, but resolved to share their final course together.

Still lovely.

Still in love.

What might have been...

39
BOARDING ACTION

"HOLY SHIT," muttered Ben.

It's stunning when a dreadnaught explodes. When it takes a Skane mothership with it, Ben thought, it's like a fucking supernova. The conflagration was so bright, it forced everyone in the cockpit of the *Junkyard Dog* to shade their eyes. The *Dog* helped by briefly auto-masking the pilot's window.

"Drop out of translight into this?" Gal said. The *Dog* pulled up hard, banking sharply starboard on a new heading away from Gibraltar Station. "Can we go back to the shithole planet?"

"No," Cinnamon frowned from the co-pilot's seat.

An alert flashed on Ben's panel. He expected it to be yet another plea from Alice wanting to join them from the central compartment, where Cinnamon had insisted she stay strapped in. But it wasn't Alice calling. It was the formal hail of a Fleet vessel, tightbeamed directly to the *Dog*.

"You gonna get that, Stone?" Gauss asked.

"Uh, yeah. *Junkyard Dog*, here. Who's this?"

So, he wasn't a comms officer. So, sue him.

"Junkyard Dog, *this is* Covenant. *Ben! Is that you?"*

Apparently, the woman running communications for Fleet's

most advanced starship wasn't much on protocol either. The vid connection was dicey.

Ben boosted the subspace gain. He hadn't recognized the hailer's voice, but when her image coalesced on-screen, he certainly recognized her face.

"Maria?" he said, stunned more by her face than the *Hispana*'s explosion.

Maria Hallett's beaming smile stared back at him. *"Aye, sir,"* she said, *"switching."*

If Ben was surprised before, he was shocked now.

"Gramps?"

Nick Stone's expression was grim but somehow welcoming at the same time. *"That's Grand Admiral of the Fleet Gramps to you. We'll have a reunion later, Ben. Have your pilot fall in behind* Covenant. *We'll shield you while Colonel Toma makes her run."*

"Aye," Ben answered reflexively. "Aye, Admiral."

*"*Covenant *out."*

Sheba Toma's teeth still ached with the echoes of *Hispana*'s destruction thrumming through the dropship. She realized she'd been clenching them since the launch. First, against the bone-rattling pounding of Thorne's ship exploding, then from the furious grief that followed. She tried to push the deaths of those one-thousand souls from her mind and focus. With willpower, she brought the wet, harsh, rapid breathing inside her helmet under control.

A strained conversation had just ended involving the pilot. Her tactical memory served up the main details. Orders from the *Covenant*, now in command of the op. The dropship, ordered to haul in close beneath the protective shadow of

Covenant's lower hull for the final approach to Gibraltar Station.

"Colonel," the pilot said, "*Covenant* is taking out the last of the station's batteries near the access point. She'll shield us as we go in."

"Copy that. ETA to ingress?"

"Two mikes."

"Solid copy."

That oughta be enough time, she heard in her head. Not her voice, but Harry Mitchell's. Her senior platoon leader, a kind of de facto role model when she'd first taken command of D-1 Platoon. Back then, almost against her own stubborn will, Sheba had internalized everything Mitchell said or did. She hadn't wanted to make a single mistake, and so she'd naturally looked to the company's Old Man to show her how it was done.

This'll be a dog fight, all right, Old Man Mitchell told her now. *Say something to your officers. Encourage them to rev up their grunts. Remember, teasing dogs only makes 'em meaner.*

And they'd need all the meanness they could muster, Sheba thought.

"Dog Company, sound off."

The platoon commanders did so, one after another.

"Sixty seconds to breach," Sheba said. She cast around inside herself for something inspiring to say, didn't find much that didn't sound fake or rehashed from the manual. The Mitchell in her mind was no help. So with as much *oo-rah* as she could: "Any final questions?"

Ever diligent about details, Victor Taikori asked, "*Weapons free the moment we drop? Double-checking.*" Taikori, now captain of the company, had slotted back into his old command of D-1 Platoon at the last minute when its lieutenant had taken ill. Last-minute substitutions were considered bad luck and tactically problematic, but Toma was glad to have him there anyway.

Turning slightly, she spotted his battlesuit down the line of strapped-in Marines. Couldn't see Taikori's eyes though his helmet at this angle, but she spoke to him like she could.

"Yes, but watch your fire. Could be Fleeters on the station will show up and help us secure the bay."

"Copy that."

"Be pretty hard to mistake even a Fleeter for one of those spider bastards," Osira Tso, commanding D-3 Platoon, said. *"Still no penetrating the Skane blackout of station communications?"*

"Negative. No way to know for sure if any personnel are even still alive," Sheba said.

"What if they are?" It took her a moment to recognize Marigold, D-2's green second lieutenant. The whole platoon had been replaced following the massacre on Canis III. More than once, Sheba had had to shut down others in Dog Company naming them "the ghost platoon." They'd never seen deployment in-country outside a simulator. She supposed that wasn't true, if you counted the occupation of New Nassau. Marigold said, *"What if the Skane use them as human shields?"*

It hit Sheba that he likely looked up to her as she had Mitchell. The thought both pleased and alarmed her.

Tso chimed in. *"Weapons free doesn't mean shoot anything that moves, Goldie. Keep your head, or the Skane are likely to take it."*

"Right," Marigold answered with nervous laughter.

The pilot miked in. *"Drop in ten."*

"Quick word to your commands," Sheba said. "Hold on. We're going in hot."

"Here we go, boys and girls." Quiet up to now, Dawson

Zwikker seized the common channel for all sixty groundpounders to hear. *"Wahhhhhhh-Hooooooo!"*

Sheba couldn't resist the smile that came. Zwikker had taken over as the D-Company troublemaker everyone loved to hate after Ben Stone's promotion to captain. Usually, he just annoyed Sheba in that old way too, but in these final moments before the boarding action, she appreciated his enthusiasm.

The dropship began to rattle and hum, superstructure stressing with extreme deceleration. The Marines' battlesuits protected them from most of the strain. Sheba didn't envy the pilots, who relied entirely on the shuttle's AG to keep from stroking out. Outside the windows, covering fire from the massive *Covenant* popped and flashed, clearing the flak coming from Gibraltar Station.

And somewhere out there was Ben Stone himself and his pirate friends with their crazy mission, waiting for Dog Company to do its job. Somehow, Sheba thought as the shuttle bucked around her, this wasn't how she'd seen her career going. The Martian recruiter hadn't said one goddamned thing about hurtling toward horrific death at the hands of an alien enemy.

See the galaxy, my ass.

"Go, go, go!"

Taikori and D-1 Platoon charged down the exit ramp to Gibraltar's deck. The unit's advanced scouts set up a perimeter, weapons hot, trigger discipline in force.

"Clear," Taikori reported. *"No heat sigs."*

Using the dropship's landing struts for cover in the largely empty cargo bay, D-1 set up to cover D-3, now pounding down the ramp to join them. Two of D-3's squads bolted for the tall main cargo door providing access to the station's interior. Tso's command squad jetted up to the second-story gantry for an overwatch position of the entire bay.

"Clear," he confirmed.

It went like that, smooth as silk, for ninety seconds. The remaining platoons of Dog Company formed up beneath the protective hull of the dropship, now powered down.

"Well," Marigold said, surveying the empty bay, *"that was easy."*

"Maybe they're too few to defend the station properly," suggested Zwikker. *"Can't be everywhere at once."*

"Maybe you should stay frosty and make sure your Marines do too," Toma warned. She accessed the station schematics on her heads-up display, then swiped it out to her platoon leaders. With eye movements, she highlighted the maintenance hatchway now being guarded by D-3. "Lieutenant Tso, get into the walls and secure the path to communications. We need to make contact inside, find out what's going on. Taikori, there's your access to engineering. Zwikker, environmental. I'll coordinate from here with D-5 and Marigold in reserve."

"Tight fit in that maintenance tube," Tso observed.

"Suck in your gut armor," Zwikker snarked back.

Tso turned to his squads to execute Sheba's infiltration order.

Ninjas spun into the bay from every door, hatch, and vent. One of Taikori's Marines shouted a warning too late. A ninja slammed into his suit, and his scream of pain filled the common channel as it sawed through the armor. The bay erupted with controlled chaos. Battlesuit targeting systems snapped online but too slowly. Three more Marines went down, the ninjas hitting strategic weak points in their armor.

A blend of rifle and gauntlet-mounted Gatling fire sprayed the cargo bay. Platoon leaders shouted over comms. Two other Marines went down under the onslaught of spinning discs.

Sheba's tactical system lit up like everyone else's, trying to keep up. The ninjas seemed to wink in and out of existence. On the gantry above, Tso managed to snag a disc from the air and crush it with his powered hand. The tactical systems had finally adjusted, sacrificing accuracy for speed, and after a minute or two of battlesuits dodging, grabbing, ducking, and firing, the few ninjas still airborne were destroyed. And four more Marines were down, dead or disabled.

Ten, in all. A fifth of Dog Company, in less than ten seconds.

"Check your buddy!" Taikori yelled over the common channel. *"Make sure autodocs are working!"*

"Get the wounded aboard the dropship," Sheba ordered. "Marigold, you're on triage duty. Tso, Taikori, secure those access—"

A loud thumping, shearing sound came from the ceiling. It echoed in the near-empty bay, then Sheba realized the tearing came from multiple locations at once. On the gantry above, Tso pointed at something higher up. She snapped on her tac lens, and the ceiling lit with a green glow as a square of plating tumbled to the deck.

"Heads up!" Sheba shouted.

Other plates loosened—no, were pounded from their fastenings. Shadows dropped through where they'd been, thick shadows with limbs jutting outward, shining like burnished scythes. Tso opened up on the first Skane, riddling its body with Gatling rounds, black blood raining over his comrades below. The warrior impacted the deck heavily and attempted to right itself with only two of its legs still mobile. Multiple targeting lasers homed in, ending its screech of defiance in a rapid crossfire.

More shrieking Skane leaped from the ceiling. Two landed on Tso's scaffold above Sheba's position, engaging his squad.

One warrior landed on the back of a private to her left, its sickle legs arcing down, sawing at the man's battlesuit. The Marine jerked up his gauntlet and cut the alien in half at point-blank range. Pitch-black blood slung across Sheba's armor.

Comms screamed with Marines cursing, fighting, killing. The surprise attack by so savage an enemy in so small a space threatened to break morale. Officers worked to rein in the panicky comms traffic. And that infernal shrieking of the Skane... Sheba almost turned off her exterior audio just to be rid of it. A second warrior pounced on the young man next to her, and she leaped to his side, grabbing the Skane's flailing, knife-like legs in her powered gloves and ripping them from its body. The private brought his gauntlet into its gut and unloaded a spray of Gatling fire as before. The warrior slumped to the deck.

And just like that, the anarchy of the attack was over. The bay was a writhing mass of prostrate bodies. There were Skane shrieking and scrambling on the deck, and more Marines down. But combat was done. Sheba resisted the after-images that tried to impose themselves on the cargo bay, of the canyon littered with bodies on Canis III. This wasn't that. Most of the dead and dying were Skane—most.

"Dog Actual, respond."

The dropship pilot. Before Sheba could answer, another voice took control of the channel.

"Exterminate those bastards!"

The voice, so raw and brutal—if his ID hadn't flashed on her HUD, Sheba would never have known it was Victor Taikori. Once the baby of their cohort of platoon leaders, so shy and reserved and ill-fitting as a Marine officer. His voice, now soaked in hate and devoid of mercy. In answer, intermittent fire burst around the bay as Marines executed the remaining Skane wounded.

"Dog Actual, respond."

Sheba miked in to answer the pilot.

"Dog Actual. Go for Toma."

"We've been ordered to lift off, Colonel. Get your Marines away from the ship."

Not unexpected. But in the wake of the attack, not exactly welcome either.

You'll leave us stranded, she wanted to say. The slight, scared little girl on Mars she'd once been, pulling scraps out of refuse bins and brawling with bigger, brattier kids for whatever she'd found—Sheba felt a twinge of terror at the thought of being abandoned here. The Marine she'd become thrust that fear aside.

"We have wounded."

"You have two minutes to get them aboard and we're out."

"Acknowledged." On the common channel, she ordered Marigold and Zwikker to have their squads prep the wounded for evac ASAP. This wasn't over. She'd carefully studied Stone's after-action report of the skirmish on Strigoth. The Skane would hit them again. Unless the 214th attacked first.

"Tso, set overwatch on that ceiling. And Taikori, secure those vents! This was a probe. They'll be back."

"Solid copy," both veterans acknowledged.

Sheba surveyed the room. Marigold and Zwikker did their work as delicately as they could. Normally stoic Marines moaned as their battlesuits triaged their pain to the best of their ability. Stone had warned her that ninjas could cut through power armor as easily as the hull of a starship. He'd warned of the ferocity of their reaping limbs, churning until they cracked a battlesuit's visor and speared human skull. But she'd only half-believed the details. Not because she thought Stone was lying or aggrandizing his battle report. She was past that expectation of him now. No, she'd only half-believed him because she hadn't wanted to, hadn't seen it with her own eyes. Couldn't quite grasp, despite Stone's own battle footage giving evidence to his testimony, that such rampant, mindless savagery existed in the universe. Even after Canis III, even after the Arcœnum attack on Fort Leyte, it still hardly registered as reality in the grown-up consciousness of the little girl who'd clawed her way from the Martian slums.

But now she'd seen it with her own eyes. Now Sheba believed.

With the wounded loaded and its lift-off pad clear, the dropship fired up repulsors and slipped from the cargo bay. It had just cleared Sheba's field of view when another ship appeared in its place. A battered pinnace that hadn't seen a decent service year since before Sheba was born. Patched with ill-fitting, unmatching polysteel plates and seemingly too bulky to enter the bay. But someone was making the attempt anyway.

"Back up!" she ordered.

Sheba's Marines gave the vessel a wide berth as, carefully and inch by inch, it slipped into the tight space. With a flush of air-powered relief, the ugly ship settled onto the deck where the dropship had been.

The hatch opened, and Ben Stone was first down the ramp. Sheba surprised herself at how glad she was to see him. The carnage around her must have affected her more than she thought. Then, she forgot all that when the Arcœnum showed up in the pinnace's hatchway. Sheba brought up her battle rifle and covered the trigger with her index finger.

Unthinking instinct, that.

"Trigger discipline!" Stone shouted to the bay as he made straight for her, one soothing hand raised. "I can explain."

"Hold fire," Sheba told her Marines before activating her external vocalizer. "You'd better, Captain. And it'd better be good."

40

A DUNGEON OF DEEP CLOSETS

HE'D BEEN SO focused on Toma and her reaction to Louie, Ben hadn't noticed the carnage in the cargo bay. He noticed it now. Top to bottom, the military gray of the deck and walls was streaked with red and black. As though a blind artist with a giant brush had gone mad.

A Marine moved to aid one of his comrades and slipped in the slick. Ben's stomach knotted against the gore. There was more black than red, at least. But it was more than the blood that threatened to make him sick. It was knowing what was coming for Toma, the notifications she'd have to make. The depth of loss you discover for people as you try your damndest to make a death notice sound heroic. People who died under your command but whom you hardly knew. The sinking sadness of the families, and knowing there's not a goddamned thing you can do to soften the blow.

Why?

The question from the abandoned Archie scientist-turned-avenger on Canis III. The same question from Private Israel's corpse in the canyon on that planet. From Bricker and DeSoto and Baqri, the dead of Drake's World. Ben saw none of them now, and that was a mercy, but he heard the furious echo of their chorus in his head. The dead demanding answers.

"*Stone,*" Toma barked. "Explain yourself. And this mind-raper with you."

She'd spoken to Ben, but Sheba Toma hadn't taken her eye —or aim—off the Arcœnum with him.

"His name's Louie," Ben said. "Light Without Shadow." He took a moment to tell the ghosts in his head to shut the fuck up. He needed to concentrate. He had to make Toma understand. "I told you about him before."

"You're stalling, Captain."

"No," he said, taking a step forward, putting himself between Toma and Louie. "No, I'm not." Gauss was getting antsy on the ramp behind him. This could quickly spin out of control. "Light Without Shadow is the Arcanus Collective's trade ambassador to New Nassau," he continued, leaning on the facts. "He's who gave us the intel on the Skane, remember? And he's been helping us these past few months."

"Helping you avoid the president's order, you mean," Toma said. She was looking at Alice now. "Aiding and abetting—"

"That was my call," Cinnamon Gauss said. "Unlawful orders are meant to be ignored. Doesn't your Marine manual say something about that?"

Toma shifted her gaze to Cinnamon but didn't move her rifle off Louie. "You're Gauss," she said. "Joe's daughter?" Grunting, she said, "I see the resemblance."

"Granddaughter. So if you know who I am, and you know my grandfather, you also know you'd best lower that rat-killer. Before someone gets hurt."

"Someone's already been hurt," Toma replied. Her eyes found Ben again. "Remember Sirius? Remember the dead of Fort Leyte?"

"I assume you've kept up with current events," Ben said,

refusing the bait. "You know we're allies now, Alliance and Arcœnum, after Alpha Centauri. Stand down your Marines, Sheba."

"How can you forget that easily, Stone?"

"I haven't forgotten anything," Ben said, "but that's for the politicians to work out. Assuming, that is, humans and Archies are still around to haggle over the whys and wherefores later."

Toma stared hard at him. "I haven't missed you, Stone." But she lowered her rifle and ordered her Marines to stand down.

"Louie is our friend," Alice said, edging past Cinnamon to the station's deck. "That's all you need to know."

Ben experienced the unsettling certainty that an unstoppable force was about to meet an immovable object.

"So, this is the infamous Alice Keller," Toma said. "I admit, you don't look like a threat to the Alliance. I've seen the threat, and you don't look anything like it."

To Ben's amusement, Alice stuck out a hand. To his amazement, Toma moved her rifle to her off-hand and took it.

"I've heard a lot about you," Alice said. "Travel takes a while in The Frontier. Lots of time for stories. Ben thinks very highly of you."

To his embarrassment, Ben spluttered a thin denial that had little resemblance to cohesive language.

"Louie's fight is our fight now," Alice said.

Toma's eyes narrowed. "I don't know what you mean, Miss Keller."

"Like I said, there's lots of time in space to talk. Louie told me how the Skane hit Arcanus first. That fleet that helped out in Alpha-C? Those were the refugees. All that's left of the Arcœnum. They attacked your fort in Sirius because they went there to colonize—again—and found humans already there. They were searching for a new home. *Are* searching for a new home. They're desperate to survive. So desperate that the

Arcœnum listened to the human descendants of those they captured in the Specter War now living with them. When their fleet arrived in Sirius, it was the humans among them who convinced Louie's people to attack."

"I don't believe that for a second," Toma said. "And I don't have time for this now, Miss Keller."

"It doesn't matter what you believe," Cinnamon said, descending the ramp to stand beside Alice. She indicated the two Marines still injured on the deck. "We can help those men."

"They can't be moved yet," Victor Taikori said as he approached. "Their autodocs are still stabilizing them." Taikori acknowledged Ben with a terse nod. "Colonel, we still have two full platoons including yours, three others understrength. Respectfully, suggest we take the fight to them—"

Toma held up a hand. "Get with Tso and Zwikker. We'll deprioritize environmental and communications and focus on taking the most direct route to engineering. Get control of the other systems from there." She nodded to the massive cargo door. "I want the two full-strength platoons driving forward, with the partials as escorts."

"Leave the bay unguarded?" Taikori asked, unsure.

"Don't have the manpower to hold it. If we don't take engineering and, by that, this station, having Marines at the beachhead won't matter. Understood?"

"Yes, ma'am!"

"Get to it." She turned her attention to Ben. "As for you—"

"You were made for this, Sheba," Ben said, stopping her order-giving in its tracks. "Command isn't a promotion track for you. It's a destiny."

Alice smiled and crossed her arms. "Told ya."

At a momentary loss for words, Toma just looked at Ben. Likely, he figured, trying to suss out the veiled smartassery in the compliment he'd just given her. That was the thing about being a liar and a fuck-up. Even when you said something from the heart, people almost always assumed it was just more bullshit.

"As I was saying," Toma said, "you're on your own, Ben, with this mission of yours. I can't spare anyone to guard you."

"Didn't expect you to," he said.

"Where's your battlesuit?"

"Battered, beaten. Desi was too damaged to fix in the time we had."

"They only help so much, the suits, against them." Toma indicated the two Marines still on the deck. "But they're better than nothing."

"I don't have 'nothing,'" Ben said. He jerked a thumb at his comrades. "I have them. Trust me, they're better than armor."

Toma's gaze skittered over Alice and Cinnamon, lingered again on Light Without Shadow. "Sounds like he thinks a lot of you, too," she said to Alice.

Alice's smile widened.

Ben asked, "How do we get to communications from here?"

Sheba pointed across the bay to a door ringed in rivets and sealed with a pressure lock. "That's your entry point. Safer in the walls, I think. Here..." She pulled up, then swiped the station's schematics to his handheld tracker. "Maintenance corridor. Straight on till you come to the ladder. Climb two levels. Back out into the main corridor and a straight shot to the control room. Minimal exposure that way. But watch your six. These fuckers crawl through walls too."

"Thanks." Ben motioned toward one of the combat rifles lying on the deck. "Mind if I..."

"Take it," Toma said. "Take a couple extra magazines, too. Private Haig ... he doesn't need them anymore."

After a few kind words of encouragement to their wounded

owner, Ben claimed the combat rifle and extra magazines from the wounded Marine.

"Newer model?" he said to Toma, impressed. "Over-and-under. Grenade launcher!"

"Use it in good health," Toma said. Ben shuffled his new acquisition around awkwardly and shook her extended hand.

"Good luck, Captain. Oh, and be aware—the Skane can mask their bio-signatures somehow. Same as they can hide from starship sensors."

"I guess I'll know 'em when I see 'em."

"You will." She nodded a final farewell, then moved off to plan her counter-attack.

"Come on, people," Ben said. "We're burning starlight."

One of the colonel's Marines sealed the door of the maintenance corridor behind them with a plasma torch. "Yeah, to avoid exposing our six," Ben explained when Alice asked if trapping them inside the walls was really necessary.

The memory of hiding with Ben inside the wall on Ionia rushed back. She'd felt something else then, something personal and pleasant, being in such tight quarters with him. But tucked inside the dark closeness of the accessway with Cinnamon and Louie along for company felt quite different. Fearful. Fear of the air, which inhaled heavier than she thought it should. Fear of the pitch-black darkness. Fear of the distant noises Alice could hear echoing from deep within the aging space station.

Ben snapped on the combat light beneath the barrel of the rifle and flashed it around them. "Tight in here. Humid."

"Maybe the Skane changed the environmental settings," Cinnamon said.

"Maybe they like it this way," Alice added, thinking of the

underground of Drake's World, which had always seemed to have a misty quality to the air.

After a few moments' searching, Ben asked, "Anyone see a light switch?"

"Hang on." Cinnamon brushed past him, igniting her own torch. Shadows hopped and bobbed, stretched and disappeared as she searched for a control. Alice told herself the shadows weren't alive, not like they'd been on the Terror Planet. They were just metal wall and deck reflecting and blocking the light.

"Here we go." Cinnamon flipped a switch.

Nothing happened.

Ben cleared his throat. "Sure that's it?"

Even in the sub-glare of two jittering light sources, Alice could see her scowl. "Yeah. Pirate, remember? I'm used to crawling around dead hulks looking for salvage." Cinnamon made a noise of annoyance. "Must be something wrong with the power. Blown fuse. Something." She turned the switch on and off, as though trying to convince it to work.

"Maybe the Skane like it dark in the tunnels too," Alice said. *Just like on Drake's World.*

Ben grunted. "Well, we have our lights. Louie, it's a little tight in here. I know what I said before about always staying in front of me, but bring up the rear anyway. Cinnamon, stick with Alice. Make sure you light her path. Don't want anyone tumbling down an access ladder."

"Aye-aye, Captain Stone, sir," Cinnamon said with a sting.

"Thank goodness." Ben pointed his barrel light forward. "Hadn't heard the trademark snark in a while. Thought you were going soft on me."

"Go dry-fuck yourself, Stone."

Even in the dim of the accessway, Alice noticed his grin. Hearing them biting at one another—as distressing as it'd been on Ionia was somehow reassuring in their present situation.

Reminded her she wasn't alone. So, not like Drake's World at all.

The narrow passageway stretched forward well past what the lights could show, with smaller, work alcoves branching off along the way. For accessing the plumbing or computer network or AG controls, Alice guessed. Metallic surfaces flashed and disappeared again whenever Ben and Cinn cast around their torches. System lights blinked around them, though emitting little ambient glow. It was like walking through a dank, deep vault with tinier, hidden vaults all around.

Darkness hides things.

The old wisdom, made new again. Alice expected a Skane to leap out at her at any moment. Her heart raced with the fear of it.

Tap-tap.

She froze, and her racing heart skipped a beat. There was a heavy, looming presence behind her. Light Without Shadow, nearly bumping into her in the dark.

Cinnamon turned back. "Alice?"

"Did you hear that?" she whispered, her voice trembling.

"Hear wh—"

A groan of metal rolled through the walls around them. As though someone had taken each end of Gibraltar Station in a colossal hand and twisted the structure along its axis like taffy.

"It's just the hull expanding and contracting with pressure," Cinnamon said. "Nothing to worry about."

"That's not what I meant."

Louie placed a reassuring, spirit-light appendage on Alice's shoulder, and she nearly jumped out of her skin.

Three concussions boomed distantly, reverberating in the walls.

"That's Toma," Ben said, his gaze following the halo of his

rifle light as he cast it around them. "Grenades. She's making her move on engineering."

Alice's eyes followed Ben's light. "That's not it either."

Tap-tap-tap.

"*That.*"

But it was farther away now, and followed by more structural moaning from deeper inside the walls. A rapid series of short bursts—Alice recognized the rifle fire—that followed more grenade blasts.

"Louie, watch our six," Ben said.

The Arcœnum removed his clawed hand from Alice and shifted in place to comply. Even that slight movement echoed in the narrow corridor. Alice winced, afraid he'd given away their location.

Ben removed the tracker from his belt and checked their location. "Not far to the ladder. Come on, folks."

They crept forward, Ben's strides becoming longer, more confident. They reached the way up in short order.

"Okay, we climb this for two levels and we're on the comms deck. I'll go first," Ben said, pointing his rifle barrel up for a quick sweep. "Then I want Louie. Then Alice. Cinnamon, you're batting clean-up."

Murmurs of acknowledgment, and Ben mounted the access ladder, his light bobbling as he climbed. Louie stepped on behind him, and Alice found herself envying his six clawed limbs. Her palms were slick with sweat, her muscles loose and weak. It was just fear, she told herself. Fear and a need for all this to be over.

"Alice," Cinnamon prompted her. "Your turn."

She wiped her palms on her clothes, then grabbed the ladder with both hands.

"I'm stepping off here," Ben whispered from far above.

In less than a minute, they stood together beside him in

another maintenance corridor that ran perpendicular to the one two levels below. The sounds of battle, remote and furious, thumped in the walls. Alice supposed she should take heart in that. It meant Toma's Marines were still alive. Still killing Skane.

"Okay, there's an exit door," Ben said. "Straight ahead. From there, it'll be a short walk to communications."

With Ben leading, they made their way to the large door, a bookend to the one they'd accessed in the cargo bay. He motioned Louie and Alice to stand back, then had Cinnamon take up a flanking position opposite him. With a nod to her, Ben tapped the control to unseal the door, then spun the lock wheel counter-clockwise. The seal light phased from red to green.

"Here we go, people."

The door opened onto a broad, main corridor. Someone had engaged the station's emergency lighting while they'd been skulking through the walls. The hallway appeared murky, red, and empty.

"Come on," Ben said, snapping off his combat light. His steps were cautious but quick, and he pointed toward a reinforced doorway at the end of the lengthy corridor. "That's communications."

They'd made fifteen, maybe twenty steps before the Skane attacked.

41
HELPING HANDS

"GET BEHIND ME!" Ben yelled, drawing a bead on the lead warrior.

At the far end of the corridor, his target and two other Skane charged. Ben's index finger had just cleared the rifle's trigger guard when a banshee wailed behind him. Cinnamon Gauss darted past, drawing a pistol with each hand. Her steps were quick but smooth, providing a stable platform for steady aim.

"Goddamnit, I said—"

But the sharp reports of Cinnamon's gunfire overruled him, one shot after another, one hand aiming and firing, then the next as she walked straight at the enemy. Ben released a breath, retargeted the closest warrior not blocked by Cinnamon. It was turning to meet her threat, jerking and shrieking as her methodical step-and-fire routine hit home. Ben fired a controlled burst, and together they took it down.

The other Skane didn't waver. There were two sharp snaps —*click-click!*—as Cinnamon dry-fired. She dropped the pistols and pulled...

A knife? A fucking knife?

"Come on, spider-fuckers!" Cinnamon shouted.

The two warriors screeched triumph and charged. One scampered up the wall and onto the ceiling, while the other came straight at her along the deck.

Ben aimed at the lead attacker, pumped three rounds into it, stopped. He had a better option. No time to think. Thinking would get Cinnamon dead. He pumped the wider under-barrel of the combat rifle once.

It would be damned close.

Cinnamon stood in place, settling her weight into her heels, still screaming deadly defiance and waving the knife. Ben exhaled, pulled the trigger, and a grenade launched from the lower barrel. The lead warrior had almost reached the pirate captain, shrieking, its taloned legs churning like bladed pistons, when the grenade impacted behind it. The explosion rocked the corridor, ripping into deck and wall and ceiling. Cinnamon was blown backward. In the space of three sharp breaths from Ben, the haze began to settle. Both the Skane were down, the one behind motionless, the other that had almost reached Cinnamon, screaming and scraping its half-severed limbs, fighting to rise. Ben took two brief steps forward, aimed his rifle, and shot. The struggling warrior ceased moving.

"What are you trying to do, get me killed?" shouted Cinnamon. She was already crawling forward again, seeking her pistols, lost somewhere in the debris and alien viscera.

"Doing a pretty good job of that yourself!" Ben snapped.

"What?" she shouted back, her voice strained overly loud. She grabbed the one pistol she could find.

The blast had been close. Might have clouded her ears. "Forget it—"

"There's more!" Alice said, sprinting forward.

Cinnamon half-kneeled on the messy deck, was focused on loading. She hadn't heard Alice's warning. Alice pointed past her through the foggy air of the after-battle, and Ben yelled at her to stop running. A single Skane warrior emerged from the haze, almost on top of Cinnamon. She could only stop and stare at the sudden threat, her pistol not yet functional, her knife forgotten on the deck. The warrior reared up on its hind limbs, poised to strike with bladed legs. Ben shouldered his rifle. Alice was in the way.

As the Skane's feet came down, Alice raised one hand. The warrior screeched, its attack halted, its bladed feet paralyzed but ready to impale Cinnamon. She shirked off her shock, jerked the pistol up, fired twice. The Skane above her jerked with the impact of the slugs but fought to spear her with its paralyzed limbs.

Two more warriors dashed out from the comms room.

"Fall back!" Ben ordered, attempting to angle a straight shot on the Skane struggling over Cinnamon. "Fall back!"

Her pistol empty again, the pirate scrambled backward toward Alice. Shouted at her something impossible to hear. But Alice stood solid as a stone wall, murderous intent etched in every line of her face. She balled up her reaching fist, and the Skane imploded. Crushed beneath the force of the Godwave, its bones cracking, its black blood bursting outward to paint the gray metal corridor.

"Alice, fall back!" Ben said as Cinnamon, finally on her feet, backstepped. Ben rushed forward, intent on covering Alice's retreat, and tripped over a warrior's corpse. He dropped to a knee, converted the stumble into a prostrate firing position, took aim at the lead warrior of the two bearing down on Alice.

Another group of four warriors appeared behind the two. The castaway girl still refused to move.

"Alice!"

Ben plugged the lead Skane with a single targeted shot, was amazed when it fell to a streaking stop. Light Without Shadow sprinted by him in a silver-white blur. With no time to worry at the Archie's intentions, Ben focused on the four Skane that had just appeared.

"No!" Cinnamon shouted.

Ben thought she was warning him not to fire, trying to protect Alice, but then saw the warrior scrambling toward the girl and knew Cinnamon's terror as his own. Alice rose, and it seemed she'd levitated herself into the air to avoid the charging warrior. But it was Light Without Shadow, who'd grabbed her from behind, then turned in one graceful motion and tossed her backward. Alice slid toward Ben in the blood of the slain. Ben centered himself, aimed well past Louie, and launched his second grenade.

The lead Skane warrior and Arcœnum slammed together, ancient enemies joined once more in mortal combat. One shrieking its bone-raking battle cry, the other entirely silent, four thin claws fending off churning, piercing limbs. The grenade thumped straight into one of the four charging warriors, embedded itself, and there was a half-breath of doubt before the explosion tore the Skane apart, sending shattered bone fragments into the other three, the force of the blast throwing them against the walls.

Ben's ears rang with the explosion, a cloudy, high-pitched, overpowering tone that flooded him with vertigo. He staggered, half-turned to see Cinnamon shouting, though he couldn't hear her. Alice was pointing again, her mouth open in a scream, and he turned to find Louie and the Skane, still locked together. One, now two scything limbs slipped past Louie's defenses, spearing his body. The ringing in Ben's head changed pitch, and he realized it wasn't a physical sound but a psychic scream gouging a trough through the middle of his mind. It was Private Israel begging for his life in the canyon on Canis III, but also the abandoned Archie in the interrogation cell, screaming as gravity crushed him—both at the same time. Louie's agony was excruciating. Ben felt only its echo, yet still he nearly blacked out from the pain. The warrior withdrew its talons from Louie's body, repositioned itself to strike again.

Cinnamon raced past Ben, shouting, screaming, cursing, but Ben could hear none of it. Could barely see what his eyes were showing him through the red haze of Louie's shared suffering. She fan-fired her pistol once, twice, five times, six. The warrior jerked backward, riddled with slugs. Then Alice was there, grabbing Louie, dragging his heavy body away from the Skane, holding on to him, trying to hold him up. But Louie shrugged her off, pushed past her to the warrior, which now lay twitching, shrieking on the ground. Louie reached for it, and with the claws of his limbs that could still function, ripped two of the eye-like bulbs from its body. The Skane gave a final shudder of defiance, then stopped moving.

Light Without Shadow stood alone over his dead foe, pale fluid streaming from heavy wounds, and arced his head up at the black-spattered ceiling tiles. He made no sound, but a white-hot roar stabbed at Ben's consciousness. A psychic cry of victory yes, but also of anguish, of justice served for the homeworld in Arcanus that no longer existed.

Then, the Arcœnum collapsed and was still.

Alice dropped to her knees beside Louie. How could she help him? His wounds leaked freely. His exoskeleton had protected him, or it could have been much worse.

"Is he alive?" Ben asked in a straining voice.

She turned anguished eyes to him, found he wasn't doing well either. "I don't—I think so, I—"

"Move aside, Stone," Cinnamon said. She kneeled next to Alice, examined Louie, then rolled him over to access the controls of his exoskeleton. "He's alive. His suit protected him—mostly." She tapped a series of buttons in sequence.

"What are you doing?" Ben asked.

"It's a version of your autodoc. Not as sophisticated, I don't think. I've never actually used one."

"Are you sure you know—"

Before Alice completed her question, Cinnamon grabbed a rip in her own shirt, yanked it free and made it into a tourniquet. She wrapped it above the worst of Louie's wounds. A beep from the exoskeleton sounded, and Cinnamon nodded, satisfied. "He's stable."

"We need to get moving," Ben said, with a nod toward the door at the end of the corridor. "They'll be back."

"How do we carry him?" Cinnamon asked. "We can't leave him here."

Alice stood up. "I'll carry him."

"You?" Ben said. "He must weigh—"

Light Without Shadow rose into mid-air. As though he were resting, horizontal, on an invisible evac bed.

"Oh," Ben said, "right."

They made their way through Skane bodies to the end of the corridor. The placard over the door read ARRAY MAIN CONTROL.

"This is the place," Ben said, readying his rifle. He nodded to Cinnamon.

"Likely sealed, you know," she said. "Lockdown in a crisis."

Ben made a try-it-anyway gesture.

With a pistol filling her off-hand, Cinnamon touched the lock control. The door opened.

"Huh," snorted Cinnamon.

The comms control room for Gibraltar Station stood empty.

Ben swept in quickly, covering left, covering right, targeting eye guiding the rifle barrel.

"Clear." With a credulous expression, he stood up straight. "Huh."

Cinnamon leaped through the doorway, pistols sweeping the room.

"Well, this is unexpected," Ben said. "The bunch that jumped us must have been the team assigned to this room."

Cinnamon snapped, "You don't know that, Stone. The whole station could be headed here now." And, with the voice of experience: "Never trust easy."

"True," Ben answered, "but don't spit in the face of luck, either. Seal that door." He moved to a large control console in the center of the room, surveyed it, touched a button. The panels lit up. Ben adjusted a frequency scanner until he found what he was looking for.

"—coming to your aid," said a voice. Female, exhausted. Steadfast. *"ETA, five minutes."*

"Acknowledged. We'll hold them. Covenant *out."*

"That's Sayyida al-Hurra," Cinnamon said.

"And my grandfather." Ben's face, elated a moment before at their apparent good fortune, now appeared grim. He brought the viewscreen on the console to life, and it populated with tactical icons. The starship battle outside the station was still unfolding. There were far fewer friendlies than when the *Dog* had first arrived. And plenty of Skane remained, outnumbering them. *Covenant* and the rest of Third Sector Fleet fought away from the station, waiting on Toma to take control of the defensive systems. A separate, smaller group of ships—al-Hurra and her pirates—converged on a point between the two. "Looks like they're getting ready to make a last stand." He got Alice's attention. "We don't have long. Come here."

She floated Light Without Shadow to where Ben stood, then lowered him tenderly to the deck. "What do you need me to do?"

"For the moment, just listen," Ben said. "Knowing how this works might help you with..." He waved his hand. "Whatever it is you're going to do."

Yes, Alice thought, *whatever that is*. They'd been so focused on getting here, she realized she had no idea what came next. Could she simply will away the Skane's ability to control subspace? And how would that work exactly...?

"Do you know how this works?" Cinnamon asked Ben.

Ben shrugged. "More or less."

"More or less?"

"Communications is core to, well, the corps," Ben said. "I know the basics."

"The basics."

It was obvious how Cinnamon rated Ben's comms expertise. Without another word, she took up overwatch on the main door.

"So, how does it work?" Alice asked.

"Crash course," Ben said. "The reason I picked Gibraltar Station is because it's the central node for the Alliance's subspace network. Connects Sol to The Frontier, Alpha Centauri, Sirius—anywhere Fleet goes. The network is crucial, both for navigation and communication."

"Okay..." Alice said, trying to keep only the essentials and immediately discard the rest.

"As the central link in that chain, Gibraltar has the most powerful array next to Earth's own. That's why it's so important strategically. Lose Gibraltar, lose the network beyond The Frontier. The array is powered by the same tech behind translight drives. Understand?"

"Sorta..."

Ben went on. "In interstellar crises, the EP protocol—"

"EP?"

"Emergency Priority. The EP protocol takes precedence over

everything else on the civilian network—entertainment, personal messages, even navigation logging. The signal acts as a single, multi-frequency alert across the entire subspace spectrum."

"Is all this blah-blah really necessary, Stone?" Cinnamon said, her gaze still on the door.

"I have no idea!" he answered, exasperated. "I'm just trying to help her—"

"Help faster," said the pirate captain.

"You want me to send a ... what, a command?" Alice said. "As an emergency priority signal. A command that 'blinds' the Skane."

"Exactly. Burn out the Skane's ability to 'see' in subspace." He made a mumbo-jumbo gesture again. "However you do what it is you do."

"That's a vast distance to send any signal," Cinnamon said. "How do you make sure it doesn't degrade? How do you keep it secure?"

"Military-grade beamforming," Ben said, "with boosters from network satellites combined with threaded banding for security. I've actually given this some thought, you know."

"Threaded banding can be hacked, given enough time," Cinnamon said, still challenging. "How do you make sure the Skane don't cut through the encrypted shield frequencies wrapped around the core signal and corrupt it? How do you even know the Skane will pick up on—"

"Stop!"

Both captains turned to Alice.

Over the speakers, the drama unfolding outside the station began its final act. The remaining Alliance and pirate vessels had merged into a single fighting force, and the vastly outnumbered human fleet now prepared its last-ditch offensive against the Skane.

“Please,” she said. “Just ... just make it work, Ben. I’ll do the rest.”

“Right.” Muting the speakers, Ben sat down at the console.

I have no idea what I’m doing.

Alice wracked her brain, thinking, *thinking*.

But that was just it. That first time her ability had manifested, when she’d diverted the boulders on Drake’s World. Then with the avalanche below ground when she’d saved herself and Ben. And with Korsakov when she hadn’t meant to hurt him—and even when she had back on Strigoth—Alice hadn’t put any thought into it at all.

She’d simply acted.

On instinct.

“Comms array online,” Ben said. “I’m programming the security frequencies now. Almost there, Alice.”

Alice touched the side of her forehead and the almost-forgotten scar there. Evidence of what had been done to her. Her defining feature that first time she’d seen her reflection in the window of the *Seeker*. Now, hardly noticeable. Like her power, an indelible part of who she was.

I can do this, she thought. *I* need *to do this*.

If only to reclaim that piece of herself she’d lost to the Skane. They’d thought to use her as a wedge between human and Arcœnum, Korsakov had said, to enflame the paranoia, one for the other, and weaken both. What sweet poetic justice it would be now to wield the Skane’s own weapon against them. And yet how...?

Something pawed at her leg. Alice glanced down to see Louie’s clawed hand reaching up. On his chest, the window displayed an image-in-motion Alice recognized. The girl beside the river, trying to lift the heavy rock alone.

LET ME HELP.

The way he’d helped save Cinnamon. Alice hadn’t known

what she was doing then either. Been on the brink of despair at her own ignorance of how to help her friend. But Louie had lent her focus. Together, they'd made it work.

The servos of his exoskeleton whirred as Louie first sat up, then stood behind her. His slack body a mere passenger in the suit that lifted him. He placed one uninjured hand on Alice's shoulder as he had before on the *Junkyard Dog*.

"We're ready," Ben said.

"So are we." Alice's voice was deeper, more resonant. As though she spoke for the both of them with one voice. Perhaps she did.

42
THREAD AND FLAG

"I'M GOING to transmit the EP break-in signal," Ben said. "It'll disrupt all civilian comms traffic with a test pattern. And all that will do is hijack the subspace network for a few seconds. Cinnamon's right—I don't even know for sure if the Skane will pick it up or be affected in any way by it. But that's your opportunity, Alice."

"I understand," she said.

"Transmitting in five..."

She could feel Louie come into her consciousness.

"Four..."

Like an old friend she hadn't seen in a long time, sitting beside her on a park bench. On Sylvan Novus, maybe, before the attack.

"Three..."

The day was sunny, and a light breeze cooled her skin. Louie wasn't injured. His mental energy, his spirit of being, remained vibrant. Pure and uncompromised.

"Two..."

Serenity surrounded her. Alice's mind sat back into itself, got comfortable. Seemed to exhale, to relax, as though her psyche had lungs.

"One."

Everything changed.

Her mind expanded.

Alice gasped.

She grew beyond the limits of the walls around her. Found herself outside the station, encompassing it. She was the mind's eye of the universe, looking down on a child's toy. The subspace signal extended in all directions. Like a billion silvery threads, sunspires of energy discrete and divergent at the same time. Alice remained unmoving at the source but also followed the signal in all of its infinite directions across the vastness of interstellar space. She existed now in the subspace realm, where speed, time, and space had fundamentally different meaning.

Other toys—satellites, starships, space stations—flitted by too fast to count, though each registered with Alice, were easily recognized, categorized, and filed away. Planets and star systems unfolded as though she'd always been a witness to their existence, each a masterwork of precision set in motion by a master maker of the infinite. Civilizations rose and fell, lived and died. Evolved to the pinnacle of achievement, then withered, buried under the sands of time, all in the blink of her cosmic eye.

I SHOW YOU THIS SO THAT YOU KNOW HOW SPECIAL YOU ARE. IN ALL THE ÆTHER, HOW COMPLETELY UNIQUE.

Light Without Shadow, speaking in her mind.

Speaking!

IN THE REALM OF DREAMS, ALL THINGS ARE POSSIBLE. DREAMS ARE WHERE THE CREATED ASPIRE TO BE THE CREATOR.

It's so beautiful, she said to her friend sitting with her on the bench. *Everything, everywhere is—*

CONNECTED. IN BALANCE.

"Like the synchronized parts of a complex mechanism," Marcus Keller said in her mind, a scientist understanding at last a fundamental truth. *The* fundamental truth. "Everything dependent on everything else to work as it should."

Alice considered that. The dreadful cost of what she had to do dawned upon her. She wanted to stop. But she needed to finish.

I have to sever one of those connections. I have to stop the Skane.

YES.

But the Skane are part of this ... this tapestry of the universe.

YES.

As if conjured by her deliberation, the enormity of all that Alice was seeing shrank in on itself, until only a single Skane stood before her. Like a museum display, motionless and without sound. Seemingly, without life.

This is the Skane, she said. *All of them.*

YES.

But now that she had seen all there was to see, all at once, doubt shadowed illumination. Not uncertainty that she could accomplish what she'd set out to do; she *knew* she could do that now. And it would be easy—frighteningly simple, in fact. But whether or not she *should* accomplish it. That was the question. Even after all the Skane had done, all the lives they had ended. All the lives they appeared destined to end—without her intervention.

Andre Korsakov appeared beside the specimen that was the Skane. A professor standing next to the object of his lecture. "You of all people, Alice, should refrain from such pedestrian concerns."

And if I pull on this thread...

Light Without Shadow said, THE BALANCE WILL CHANGE.

And if I don't, humanity will die. Your people, too.

THE BALANCE WILL CHANGE.

Korsakov watched her think, his expression shrewd, his eyes eager. Alice knew he was only in her mind, a construct of guilt or expectation of failure, and did her best to ignore him. She focused on Light Without Shadow, who stood beside her in the clarity of his being, awaiting her decision.

But the balance changes all the time. Predators kill prey. Disease takes children. Suns explode, eating their own young and all life on them. And yet, when the balance changes, it achieves a new balance. Everything that happens tends toward the equilibrium of existence. Makes opportunity for some. Forces tragedy on others.

YES.

Maybe I don't have to end the Skane, like they intend to end us. I could just sever their ability to think as one mind.

THE BALANCE WILL CHANGE.

Alice reached inside the round core of the Skane. She felt past the brain matter she'd seen Abara cut through, until she held the source of its power over subspace in the scarred palm of her ethereal hand.

So, all we can do is what we believe to be right. And hope that we are.

YES.

Alice pulled the thread.

"Why'd you stop?" Ben demanded angrily. "Alice?"

She heard him, but she also saw him from behind, bending over her, one hand gripping her shoulder. Alice hovered above him and her own body. Louie lay on the deck again beside the console, unmoving. And Cinnamon merely stared at them all, her expression open with fearful hope. Alice registered all this, and then once again settled into herself. The heaviness of returning to her body dragged at her, the connection to Louie and everything else cut off by the cage of her own consciousness. Alice felt diminished, less-than, an insignificant speck in the continuum of all she'd just experienced.

I show you this so that you know how special you are. In all the æther, how completely unique.

So, not insignificant after all. Certainly, not alone.

Individual but connected.

Unique and necessary.

A vital part of the universal masterwork.

Alice had to fight to force her eyes open. Lifting their lids was like the labor of Atlas raising the world on his shoulders. But not lonely—not anymore.

"Why'd you stop?" Ben asked again. "Time is too short!"

Alice almost laughed at that. "It's done," she said.

Ben opened his mouth, closed it again.

Cinnamon asked his question for him. "What do you mean 'it's done'? You just started, Alice. You just closed your eyes."

Ben turned to the console, brought the running report from the fleet back up on the speakers. Voices, anxious; the sounds of battle, furious. But Alice wasn't listening. Inside her head she heard Korsakov's laughter, and his judgment. His satisfaction at his own genius being proven once again. In pulling the thread, Alice had finally become what he'd always wanted her to be.

Transcendent over the moral repercussions of her actions.

A higher being with a greater purpose.

A god.

"Listen!" Ben said.

"—almost adrift," Sayyida al-Hurra said. *"Totally uncoordinated."*

"All ships, concentrate on your nearest targets," ordered Nick Stone. *"Best to strike while the iron's hot."*

Ben dialed down the feed when the cheering from a dozen ships threatened to overwhelm the volume. "Look!"

Alice looked. On-screen, the friendlies moved against the Skane ships. Even in the abstract of the tactical map, the alien vessels appeared uncoordinated, almost aimless. Slowly, one after another, as the humans pressed their advantage, the Skane ships disappeared.

I'm so proud of you, Korsakov said in her mind.

Alice noted, by its absence, that the masochistic, self-hating part of her psyche didn't add "child." Her mind-Korsakov's acknowledgment of her growth. A nod to her ascendance to the tier of the divine.

Then words she'd heard recently popped into her head. Something Toma had said to Ben when they'd landed on the station. She'd said it smarmy and chiding, as an old frenemy's biting barb, familiar but with no real animus behind it. When Alice thought it to Korsakov, she meant it quite literally.

Go dry-fuck yourself. I haven't ascended to anything.

So—her battles with self-uncertainty weren't over. There'd always be some suspicion that she wasn't good enough, didn't quite measure up to what Alice Keller expected of herself. And apparently, that self-doubt would express itself in the Russian-accented, belittling voice of Andre Korsakov. But maybe that was a good thing. A necessary thing. The absence of it, and the conceit of self-pride that would fill up that space... Well, wasn't that how Andre Korsakovs were born?

Korsakov's obsession, Alice understood now, was with power itself. Getting it. Having it. Wielding it. The only god that mattered to Andre Korsakov was power itself. And, like all gods, power preferred to be worshipped in its own image.

As Ben and Cinnamon cheered the victory being won

beyond the station's walls, Alice knelt beside Light Without Shadow. The indicators on his exoskeleton seemed positive. He appeared in a restful slumber, a more active version of the hibernation state he'd inhabited for so long aboard the *Junkyard Dog*. Alice touched his arm and felt life there.

But it's not about the power, is it? That's what you were trying to show me. It's about the person who holds it. How they use it.

And she was a good person. With all her flaws, she was a good person worthy of herself.

Alice Keller knew that now.

"D-1 is pinned down." Sheba did her best to keep her voice steady. "Daws, you're up."

"Solid copy," said Dawson Zwikker. *"Help's on the way, Vicky!"*

"Goldie, seal the door. Plasma torch."

"Copy, ma'am."

It'd been a grueling fight from the cargo bay, a brutal sequence of covering advances that required vigilance in every direction. Sheba had never before considered how many ambush points a station corridor could have, and her Marines lost another ten casualties learning the lesson of caution. Despite her better instincts, she'd ordered the casualties left where they lay, trusting to their autodocs to care for them. All eyes, all rifles pointed forward. If they didn't take Gibraltar Station's engineering complex, tending to the wounded now wouldn't matter later.

That hard decision had paid off. They'd breached the door and established a foothold in engineering. But the Skane hadn't relented, hadn't given a foot of deck for free, and were now pressing Victor Taikori's D-1 Platoon, trying to eject Dog Company again from the heart of the station. Sheba monitored her HUD as Zwikker's Marines advanced in two's to reach them.

"Don't dawdle, Daws," Taikori said. *"They're all around us. And we're dry."*

Sheba's skin went cold. She checked her own ammunition count. Gatlings almost empty. Rifle on its last magazine. Grenades long gone, not that she could have used them here. One blast—hell, one bullet—holing the reactor core mix-housing or a containment vat, and it was sayonara Gibraltar.

"Ammunition low here too, Colonel," Osira Tso said, confirming her fear.

A thought—not quite a plan—tickled Sheba's hindbrain. Something Ben Stone might have come up with, which made her question its value on principle. Something out of a history book. Something so absurd... Then again, there was that old saying about desperate times and desperate measures.

There was a short burst of rifle fire followed by celebration as Taikori and Zwikker linked up. And then a lull as the Marines took a breath and Sheba made a decision. They had to do something. While they still had *some* ammunition. While they still had enough Marines to secure engineering.

But how to coordinate an attack against an enemy that's surrounding you? What do you do, charge in all directions?

"Colonel!" Marigold called. *"Up top!"*

Sheba followed his armored finger pointing toward a gantry. A Skane warrior had dropped onto it from the ceiling, followed by another. She brought her rifle up, then checked her fire. Both warriors stood, mute and motionless. Had they been human, she'd think them disoriented, confused. The first warrior scurried to the second and stabbed it twice through its swollen body.

What the hell?

More Skane appeared, wandering out from cover all around engineering with that same clueless detachment. One bumped into a turbine, then steadied itself. Another began to run erratically around the center of the room as if attached by a tether to a stake in the deck.

The warrior that murdered its fellow Skane leaped down from the gantry. It noticed one of Zwikker's Marines and charged. A crossfire cut it in half.

"What's happening?" Marigold asked in wonder. *"Colonel?"*

Stone. Had to be. The crazy sonofabitch had been right.

Sheba turned up the Fleet channel. There was cheering, disbelief, and cool-headed orders from ship captains to attack the Skane vessels no longer fighting back. Like ducks in a shooting gallery. That archaic phrase came through on subspace more than once.

Sheba miked in to her Marines. "Dog Company, this is Dog Actual. Engage the enemy. Take them down!"

"Kill the bastards!" Taikori shouted over the common channel.

And they did.

Dog Company secured engineering without a single additional casualty. Reports from around the station indicated the Fleet personnel who'd been locked down by the Skane were fighting back with anything they had at hand. Gibraltar Station was quickly coming back under friendly control.

Toma detached Marigold and Tso with their largely intact units to secure the wounded they'd left behind and get them to the nearest sickbay. And then she took an incoming call.

"Yes, Grand Admiral," she said to the *Covenant*'s commander. "All weapons systems disabled."

Nick Stone nodded. She could see the face of the young man he used to be. The face his grandson would grow into as he aged. It was a good face, she had to admit, when attached to good character.

"Acknowledged, Colonel," Stone said. *"First thing—I'll drop the rest of the 214th to relieve you."*

"Solid copy," Sheba said, relief flooding her aching muscles. The adrenaline had worn off. What she wouldn't give for a semi-soft bunk and about twelve hours of rack time. "Oh, Admiral, I'd like to run an idea by you."

"Sure, Colonel," Nick Stone said. *"Go ahead."*

"A favor, eh?" Ben said from the communications array main control room. *"And what do I get in return?"*

"How about I speak on your behalf at the court-martial?"

His face fell, but she knew acting when she saw it. "Thanks, no. I'd prefer to avoid the firing squad." Ben leaned over the station's comms console. "Okay, you've got the civilian channels. With Admiral Gramps relaying via military frequencies, you should have anyone and everyone who can hear. Emergency priority in three..."

Clearing her throat, Sheba stood up straighter. Her forehead felt slick, but she resisted the temptation to wipe it clean. They should see the blood, see the sweat. Her throat, on the other hand, felt dry as a desert.

"You're on."

"Attention, all ships and stations," Sheba said, addressing all mankind. "This is Lieutenant Colonel Bathsheba Toma, Commander of the 214th Battalion, First Drop Division, Alliance Ground Forces. I'm pleased to report that Gibraltar Station is once again in Alliance hands."

On every screen in the sector and beyond, on every HUD display of every Marine, across the entirety of the civilian AllianceNet, her resolute expression was replaced by the virtual image of a waving rectangle. The flag of the Alliance, with the orange star of Sol on the right and the orange/yellow binary star of Alpha Centauri on the left.

Raised over Gibraltar Station once again.

43
COVENANT

ALICE HAD NEVER VISITED the so-called Jewel of The Frontier.

But from this distance, Covenant certainly looked the part. As though someone had poured green and blue paint on the floor, then rolled a ball through it. The alternating bands of verdant land mass and deep blue oceans ringed the planet, spotted above with white clouds. Were he here, Marcus Keller would already be lecturing on the planet's ideal ecosystem as a rich farming world.

"It's beautiful," Alice said, leaning into the *Dog*'s cockpit from the doorway.

"Most planets are," Cinnamon dryly observed, "from afar."

"Not Strigoth," Alice snarked.

"You know the old saying about Covenant?" Ben's tone carried a romantic quality. "'As pretty as Earth from a distance. As beautiful as Sylvan Novus close up.'"

"Mmmm," Alice replied dreamily. "Sounds about right."

Cinnamon shifted uncomfortably in the co-pilot's seat. "Not sure why we need to be here."

"How could we miss it?" asked Alice. "It's such a historic occasion!"

"Plus, we're on a diplomatic mission," Ben said. "Gotta deliver the new Archie ambassador for his crowning ceremony. Even Bragg can't argue with that appointment now, not after everything that's happened. And with the armistice in place, the Interstellar Exchange is already skyrocketing."

Cinnamon's opinion of Ben's political insight was less than enthusiastic. All the Fleet vessels and Marines in one place made her nervous.

"Plus-plus," Gal added, grinning, "I'm looking forward to some fun downtime." She glanced to the tactical station and worked her eyebrows at Ben. "Followed by uptime. Followed by—"

"My dance card is full," Ben interjected. "Vertical or otherwise."

Gal made a huffing sound. Alice only smiled. Whereas once Gal's overtures annoyed her, now they only amused her. She knew Ben had no interest in the randy pilot.

There was a buzzing sound ambling forward from amidships. She'd get used to hearing it, Alice figured, just about the time her big sister no longer needed the support to move around.

"I hate this thing," Torque groused as Alice stepped aside for her. Adding the exosuit to Torque's already considerable bulk made for closer quarters than ever in the cockpit. "Hate, hate, *hate* it."

Cinnamon suggested, "You could go back to the medbed on Strigoth. You'd heal faster."

The mama bear growled her mama bear growl. "I'm good, thanks."

Ahead of the *Junkyard Dog*, Covenant now filled half the forward window.

"Pretty planet," Torque said.

Ben smiled. "You know the old saying about Covenant—"

"We all know it, Stone," Cinnamon sighed.

The snarking exchange, now with fifty percent less snark, urged Alice's smile a tiny bit wider. Everything good seemed to be happening, all at once. The Alliance and Arcœnum coming together on Covenant, not only to formally end the hostilities grown cold under the Skane threat, but also to establish a new trade agreement between the two powers. Louie becoming an ambassador to the Alliance for his people... It was hard not to feel like the whole of the universe was made of warm sunlight. Alice wasn't sure she trusted that feeling, but she was sure she wanted to. Her eyes found Ben. The future seemed so bright to her now. The thought felt more like a wish, really.

He caught her staring at him. "What?"

"Nothing. Just thinking ahead."

He seemed to consider that. "You sure about what comes after this? Your plans, I mean?"

She looked at him, gauging his expression. Less worry there than there used to be. But not a total lack of it. A little worry was okay, Alice decided. Meant she was cared for. Loved, even.

"I'm sure," she said. "Are you?"

"Well, I don't have a lot of say in that," he replied.

"But you do. You don't have to go down there."

"Well, I kinda do."

The bosun's whistle announced a hail. Cinnamon put it on speakers.

"Junkyard Dog," said Covenant's dockmaster, *"you are cleared for docking. Surrender your navigational control for dockside guidance. Welcome to the Jewel of The Frontier."*

Gal acknowledged, turning the ship over to the directional signal from the planet.

"They just call it that, Gauss," Ben said. "There's not an actual jewel here for you to steal."

Cinnamon regarded him coolly as the ship's course adjusted.

"This ship still needs a lot of repairs before we go anywhere else," she said. "I hear you're rolling in credits."

"If it'll keep you from getting us all arrested, I'll see what I can do."

"Well, that takes all the fun out of robbing the rich," Torque said.

"Company manners, just for once?" Ben implored. "I'm already facing one court-martial."

"They'll take you over my lithe, supple, dead body!" Gal exclaimed.

Ben shared a look with Alice.

These people, his said.

Family, hers replied. *Whatcha gonna do?*

Eva's toe wouldn't stop tapping. She'd even refused the perfectly dressed coffee she'd been offered more than once by the overworked wait staff.

But she had to give the trade minister credit. Neither the reception's elegance nor its upbeat atmosphere could be credibly criticized. Bright lights, immaculately set tables times forty, uniformed military everywhere, tux-and-tails, and a horde's worth of jewelry on shameless display... The minister himself was overseeing the final arrangements on the dais at the front of the room, making sure no one would sit too closely to anyone they couldn't stomach for a couple of hours.

Well, that'll be a challenge.

What with Piers Bragg, Sayyida al-Hurra, the new Arcœnum appointee ambassador, Light Without Shadow, not to mention all the CEOs and higher-tier military leadership to be accommodated? It promised to be an interesting evening. One of the anxious staff happened by who wasn't carrying coffee. Eva snatched the mystery cocktail from the tray with a practiced hand.

A stir at the main door got her attention, and she was delighted to see a friendly face entering. Sayyida, who'd traded in her austere commander's uniform for a formal gown more appropriate to the occasion. Her dark skin was luminous against the bone-white dress, and she wore jewelry around her neck that, while no doubt unimpressive to the well-to-do of Covenant's elite, got the job done. Joe Gauss accompanied her, clean-shaven and looking unsure where to place his foot to find the next step. His star, positioned not on his hip as usual but over his left breast, fronted a simple uniform of tan and brown. Sayyida spied Eva, offered her a low-key wave, and made a beeline.

"Thank God," Eva said. "I hate parties where I hardly know anyone."

"My thoughts exactly," Sayyida said.

Gauss groused, "Some party."

"Here for security?" Eva asked.

"That, and I heard there's free booze."

As though on cue, the waitress appeared at his elbow. Joe swiped two cocktails from the tray and thanked the woman.

Reaching, Sayyida said, "Nice of you to—"

"Not for you," Joe said, swigging the first one down. Before the waitress could get away, he placed the empty glass back on her tray.

"And I thought *I* was nervous," Eva said.

"It's all these Fleeters and ground-pounders." Joe took a sip from his second glass. "The back of my neck itches."

"No sightings yet?" Sayyida asked.

"He'd never enter before you did," Eva snorted.

"Of course. Decorum must be maintained." Sayyida's sarcasm seemed to inspire Joe to take another swig.

"What *is* this stuff?" he asked. "I've had better hooch from a still."

"It's free," Eva reminded him.

"Ah, right. Tastes like it."

The trade minister on the dais tapped a glass with a fork.

"Ladies and gentlemen!" He *clink-clink-clinked* the glass till he had their attention. "The President of the Sol Alliance!"

All eyes turned to the main door. Synthesized trumpets sounded, drowning out the polite applause from the assembled guests. Three cams hovered over the entryway, ready to capture Piers Bragg's entrance. Two Marines, their armor gleaming with the gold-over-blue style of the president's Tokyo estate, marched in and flanked the doorway. Bragg walked through, and the local power players jostled one another to shake his hand.

Despite the pomp, Eva thought, the way they received him seemed positively subdued. Smiles, yes, the occasional good wishes or half-joke as he made his way down the line. But once he'd passed them, the smiles faded and the palm-shadowed whispers began.

"Maybe that's his natural pallor," Joe said. "But he looks like a bride who's having second thoughts."

"Too late for that," Sayyida observed. "I hope."

"Trust me," Eva said, "it's way too late for that."

The president made his way over to them, Sam Devos right behind, those damned cams hovering everywhere. As Bragg grew closer, Eva noticed he'd begun growing his hair out again, like he'd worn it during the campaign. *Like Samson, mustering his strength before the big bout.* Evidence for her theory that this peace conference was not only that, but also the first stop on the president's reelection campaign. A long shot, that, though ousting an incumbent president is never easy, even an unpopular one like Bragg. But if the rumors were true, and the opposition party was courting Miranda Marcos to oppose him in the election, there might just be—

"Eva! Best-looking advisor I ever had," Bragg said with a broad smile. "No offense, Sam."

"None taken, sir," Devos responded. "Eva."

"Sam." She turned to Bragg. "Sir, if I may—"

"Wait, wait, wait!" A man of modest height interjected himself between them. "One moment, while..." He directed the cams to new positions to capture the historic meeting. "Now. Please proceed."

"Don't mind him," Bragg said. "Zack's just here to document things."

And with that dismissal, the man faded again into the background.

Patiently, Eva resumed her introduction. "Sir, this is Commander Sayyida al-Hurra of New Nassau."

Bragg reached out a hand, which Sayyida took in her own. "Commander al-Hurra," the president said formally. "So nice to finally meet you in person. And, may I say, you're the best-looking colony leader I've ever met."

Sayyida accepted the compliment with grace, though Eva wanted to punch Bragg for his perfectly predictable Boys Club comment.

"You ain't bad looking yourself." Sticking out his own hand, Joe Gauss introduced himself to the president.

"Yes, well," Bragg said, shaking perfunctorily and quickly disengaging, "I'm heartened to be bringing our wayward children home, Miss al-Hurra. And, I understand, you've decided to accept my appointment as governor of the colony, once all the details of reconciliation are finalized." The way he said it left no room for speculation as to who would be in charge, once all those details were set.

Sayyida, as before, smiled indulgently at the president. Ignoring the hook trying to catch a thank-you, she said, "It will be my continued privilege to serve the people of New Nassau."

The man of modest height interrupted again. "Folks, can I get a face-on shot?"

Bragg and Sayyida moved to stand side by side. Sam Devos craned his head around. "I think we're missing someone ... ah, there she is."

Eva spotted her too. Bathsheba Toma in her dress uniform, sans armor, walking toward them.

"I'm not sure this is necessary, Mister President," Sheba said, nodding a greeting to Eva and the others.

"Nonsense, nonsense!" Bragg insisted. "You're in the shot, and that's an order. Eva, you too. Marshal, I think we can do without you, if you don't mind."

Gauss caught Eva's eyes with a caustic roll of his own, but moved away. Zack placed Eva and Sayyida, the two shortest subjects, in the middle, with Bragg and Toma on either end.

"Okay, now hold that a moment. Let's look like we like each other, folks, okay?"

A few snaps later, and Zack disappeared again.

"I trust your travel from the Triangle was uneventful?" said Bragg. Then, with a gleam, "No pirate troubles, I hope."

Sayyida again took the president's ham-handedness in stride. "Not this trip, sir, no."

"Good, good," he said, peering intently at the dais. "Looks like a good spread." His expression soured slightly before recovering its plastic optimism. An Arcœnum assistant was overseeing preparations for the ambassador. "Never forget," murmured Bragg.

"Sir?" Eva said.

"Fort Leyte," Bragg said. "Lost a lot of good people on Canis III. Josiah Strickland..." He shook his head. "I'm still not sure about extending this temporary détente with the Arcœnum—"

"Wasn't it the humans now living with the Arcœnum that suggested they attack Canis III in Sirius?" Sayyida asked. She'd said it in such a way as to imply she wasn't quite sure what she'd heard was true. "After being evicted from Arcanus by the Skane?"

"That is mere *rumor*." Bragg said the word like it tasted foul. "I can't imagine any human ever—"

"But, of course," Sam Devos said, stepping forward, "there are lots of things to work out still. Lots of ... history to reconcile. That's what this peace conference is all about, yes?"

"Exactly," Eva agreed.

"Yes, well," Bragg said, "I look forward to exploring our new economic opportunities with the Arcanus Collective."

Scripted. Rehearsed. And expressed with the body language of a hostage.

A hostage to circumstances, that's for sure, Eva thought.

Time for a course correction. "Congratulations on the promotion to full colonel, Sheba," Eva said. "Well deserved!"

"Agreed," Sayyida said. "I couldn't have asked for a better partner in keeping the peace."

Ugh. These damned scripted lines. Always sound so fake.

Even if Eva had scripted that one for Sayyida herself.

Bragg was ladling his own praise onto Sheba, but Eva hardly heard him. Leo Byrne had just arrived. They spotted one another at the same time, and his face lit up like a mirror of her own. That smile. Those dimples. That fluttery feeling in her stomach.

"—no finer commander for Bragg's Own Battalion," the president was saying. "The Hero of Gibraltar Station!"

"I think that might already be taken," Leo said, approaching at a fast gait. He positioned himself to stand next to Eva, and it was all she could do not to reach out and take his hand. Their relationship was still, ostensibly, a secret.

Fucking decorum.

"Nonsense!" Bragg said. "It's a new era. We need new heroes to meet it. Besides, the 'Stone brand' has become somewhat tarnished of late. I'm sure you'll live up to the confidence I'm showing in you, Colonel, with your next assignment."

"Sir?" Sheba said.

"Your next assignment with the 214th. You mean Sam hasn't told you yet?"

Eva glanced at Sam, who said, "No, sir, I haven't had the opportunity."

"Oh, well then, let me give you the good news!" Bragg placed one hand on Sheba Toma's shoulder and offered her the other. Sheba took it without thinking. "You're going after that traitor—eh, what's his name, Kormanov?"

"Korsakov, sir," Sam supplied helpfully.

As if you didn't know, Eva thought. *You disingenuous bastard.*

"Korsakov, yes! You're going to bring him back to face trial, Colonel. His crimes ... simply unconscionable." His face a portrait of moral outrage, Bragg said it loud enough for the cams to pick up over the growing clamor. "And now hiding among the Skane somewhere..."

"At least they've been neutered," Sam said.

"So far as we know. We still have no idea about that fleet in Alpha-C, right? It simply disappeared? We have no idea—" Sayyida broke off, reading the room around her. No one needed to be reminded of the unknowns. This was a happy occasion.

As if she hadn't spoken, the president drew Sheba in with his hand still clasped in hers. "Make no mistake, finding the professor and assessing the remaining Skane threat are also your next opportunity for advancement, Colonel Toma." What came next was said *sotto voce,* though Eva was close enough to hear. "Don't fuck it up."

"Thank you, Mister President," Sheba said. Her gaze tossed to Eva added, *I think.*

The trade minister rang the fork against the glass again. "Ladies and gentlemen, I'd like to invite our distinguished guests to join me up here. And ask you all to please find your seats. It's time to make history!"

Bragg and his entourage took their leave.

"Commander?" Joe said, motioning after them.

As Sayyida followed the president, Eva could see her mouthing the words to the speech she'd written for her.

"Guess we ought to sit too," Sheba said.

Joe Gauss led them to a table at the front of the room. Leo pulled Eva's chair out for her, then sat down next to her, just two colleagues sharing in their boss's victory lap.

"I'm going to miss New Nassau, I think," Toma said as she watched Sayyida mount the stage.

Eva found that a startling pronouncement. She was tempted to offer a tart response, then found she sympathized with the sentiment. Giving Sheba a hard time about it would feel too much like hypocrisy.

"How long's this backslapping festival gonna last?" Joe asked, grabbing another drink from a passing tray.

Eva said, "I made Sayyida's speech as short as I could."

"The shorter, the better," Joe observed.

"As someone who has to write the damned things," Leo said, "I couldn't agree more." Eva eyed him hungrily as he smiled at someone at the next table. When he was sure no one was looking, Leo looked at Eva and dipped his hand beneath the table cloth to find her thigh. "I'll reward you later."

44
THE FUTURE

IT WAS an odd thing to stand in a roomful of people and wonder why he hadn't been arrested yet. Odd, maybe, because it'd been a long time since Ben's unhealthy relationship with formal receptions had been a concern.

"Sayyida did well," Torque said, gesturing toward the dais of milling dignitaries with a whine of her exosuit. "Bragg's speech, on the other hand..."

"Shorter's always better," Cinnamon declared, face dour with contempt. Like the others, she was watching the glad-handing at the front of the room, skeptical of how long cooperation would last.

Louie, Ben noticed, seemed to exist in his own lonely bubble as the humans on-stage spoke only to one another. *Clan cohesion.* But no sooner had that assumption snuck into his thoughts than Sayyida al-Hurra took her leave of Piers Bragg and approached the Arcœnum.

"Your grandpapa's headed this way," Cinnamon said.

Ben followed her gaze to see Nick Stone carefully descending the stage. He wondered if it was age or the weight of the medals on his dress uniform making him stoop slightly as he gripped the railing.

"So's yours," Alice said.

Joe Gauss made his way toward them through the crowd. As did Bathsheba Toma, accompanied by two Marines wearing that godawful blue-and-gold armor.

Well, this is it then, Ben thought. *So much for the reprieve.*

His gaze landed on the empty dinner plate on the table. For a last meal, it'd been palatable, especially after eating expired military rations on the *Junkyard Dog* for so long. Still, rubber chicken was rubber chicken.

"Ben!"

He turned just in time to receive Maria Hallett in a warm hug. The medals adorning her bosom, still impressive at seventy-eight, scratched at the rough weave of his civilian tunic.

"Back in action, huh?" Ben said, indicating the uniform.

"Oh, no," she replied, separating for a good look at him. "One mission, and one mission only. That was the deal Nick made."

"Deal?"

Raising a covert hand to her mouth, Maria whispered, "Bragg begged him to come back to command *Covenant*."

"Nobody better qualified," Ben said.

"That, and if we won—*when* we won," Maria corrected herself, "he could grab onto your grandfather's popular coattails one more time."

"Ah, optics," Ben sighed. "Well, I'm not surprised he said yes, I guess. No one more patriotic than Admiral Gramps."

"Actually, there were a few conditions," Maria said. "And, like I said, it was a one-time only deal."

"Again."

"Right."

"Can I get in here?"

Maria stepped aside, and there was Nick Stone, his face lighting up at the sight of his grandson. Ben couldn't quite fathom why he'd be so happy, with Toma on her way to arrest Ben. But he did his best to be in a good humor for the old man's sake.

"Congratulations on your victory," Ben said as Stone pulled him into another hug. In front of the others, he was slightly embarrassed in a way he hadn't been with Maria. Like a child dropped off for his first day at school and wanting nothing more than to be an orphan as his mother sheds a tear. Clearing his throat, Ben asked, "But did you have to upstage Bragg?"

"*Our* victory," Stone said. "And it wasn't my fault I was a few minutes late. *Covenant* needed my attention, as I informed the president. More important than any high-falutin'—"

Leaning in like a conspirator, Maria said, "He totally was late to show up Bragg."

"Maria..." Stone said.

"Well, it's true!"

"Admiral Stone!" Alice pushed Ben aside to demand a hug of her own. "It's so good to see you!"

"Hello, Alice," Stone said. "God, you've grown!"

"You've shrunk. You look great!"

"Farm living," Maria explained. "He has to work for his dinner."

The admiral took a moment amid the hubbub around them to look deeply into the eyes of the young woman once known as the castaway girl. Leaning in close again, he said, "Morg would be very proud of you, Alice. He *is* proud of you."

"Thanks," she said, her eyes glistening. "Thanks so much for everything—to both of you."

Cinnamon cleared her throat in that hands-near-weapons way.

"Captain Stone," came the voice of authority. Bathsheba

Toma, resplendent in her formal dress uniform, had arrived with her armored escorts.

"Sheba," Ben acknowledged. "So, this is it."

"I suppose so." Turning to his grandfather she said, "Grand Admiral, General Bradshaw passed the word." Nick Stone nodded in return.

"Look, can we just get on with this?" asked Ben. "The suspense is killing me."

"Very well," Sheba said, facing Ben straight on. "Captain Benjamin Stone, you are hereby formally and dishonorably discharged from the Alliance Ground Forces of the Sol Alliance. These two Marines will escort you to retrieve your battlesuit and any other weaponry or gear you may retain in your possession that belongs to the AGF."

Ben gaped at her. "What?"

"Shall I repeat—"

"I'm not under arrest?" he asked.

"You've finally gotten yourself drummed out of the corps," Stone said with faux disappointment. "Congratulations."

"I don't understand—"

"Half-listening as usual," Sheba said.

Nick Stone made a clucking sound. "He was always like that."

"Sometimes even fell asleep in mission briefings." Sheba shook her head. "So embarrassing."

"You people are horrible!" Maria scolded. She pushed past Sheba and took Ben by the shoulders. "In light of your contribution on Gibraltar Station, the formal charge of desertion is dropped. But the AGF can't have a famous disobeyer of presidential orders for a poster boy. So—you're fired."

Fired. But not a firing squad? Well ... that was better then, Ben thought.

Devil's luck, grumbled a ghost from somewhere.

"You can thank your grandfather for that, Stone," Sheba said. "Only way he'd keep the rank beyond the needs of the battle, he told President Bragg."

"But I'm giving it back after this bloody conference," Nick Stone insisted.

"Oh, Ben, that's fantastic!" Alice said. "Now, we don't have to sneak you out!"

Ben just looked at her. "You were planning to sneak me out?"

Sheba Toma turned to Alice, whose bright-eyed wiliness, faced with the colonel's serious expression, banked its fire. Sheba said, "As for you..."

Cinnamon's hands went to her beltline, thumbs hooked but loose. Torque's exosuit whined a bit as she centered herself.

Sheba noticed, but chose to ignore them. "The *habeas corpus* order is lifted—evidenced by the fact that you weren't taken into custody as soon as you landed. President Bragg thanks you for the part you played in defeating the Skane."

Alice's face lit up again, though Ben's bullshit meter pinged suddenly into the red.

"Why would he do that?" he asked. "After all that effort looking for her, after Korsakov and... Why would Bragg—"

"If you haven't noticed lately," said a new voice, "his popularity is in the shitter."

Sheba stepped aside, and there was a new-old face Ben hadn't seen in a while. Alongside a face he'd never seen.

"Eva!"

They embraced briefly, and she introduced him to the man with her. "My fiancé, Leo Byrne."

If Ben was surprised by that revelation, Byrne appeared flabbergasted by it. But delight quickly replaced the shocked look on his face.

"Glad to meet you, Captain Stone," Leo managed to say.

"Just *Mister* Stone, now," Sheba stated.

"Yeah, about that, and Alice—"

Eva interrupted, "Your grandfather convinced the president that throwing you into hard labor on Monolith and incarcerating Miss Keller in another lab wouldn't garner many helpful headlines. So, this is the compromise. But I wouldn't hang around too long, in case he changes his mind." She turned to Nick Stone. "Congratulations on your reinstatement, Grand Admiral."

"It's very temporary," Stone was quick to say. "As soon as the formal treaty with the Arcœnum is signed, I'm headed back to Iowa." He grimaced and scratched at one arm. "I think I'm allergic to these new uniforms."

"Come on! Come on!"

The high-pitched order came in a voice Ben hadn't heard since Canis III.

Cams surrounded the party. Zack the Director pushed a scowling Cinnamon aside, thought better of attempting the same with the huge woman in the exosuit, and motioned for the rest of them to gather.

"This is perfect. Perfect! Even the lighting in here is good."

One of his assistants began arranging them for the image the director wanted to capture.

"No, no, a little to the right," Zack complained. "I want that dais and the flags in the background. Get it right! I'd like you in the shot too, Miss Park. Mister Byrne, we don't need you I'm afraid."

It looked to Ben like it was against her better judgment, but Eva complied, moving to stand beside the rest of them. "Looks like I get to be in all the family photos today," she muttered.

"You sure you want me in it?" Ben asked, thinking of his dubious status as halfway back to being considered a hero, but with a dishonorable discharge on his permanent record.

"Good point," Zack allowed. "We'll do one with, one without—always good to have options, right? For now, squeeze in. And come on, people, perk up! This is for the history books!"

"More likely a campaign ad," grumbled Eva.

Nick Stone manufactured a smile. "An old friend of mine would say 'same difference.'"

Alice nestled in close to Ben. It felt nice. And not at all crowded.

"All right now everyone, look here, please. Altogether, now: 'Peace treaty!'"

Next to angry sex with a willing ex, reunion sex might be the best sex of all.

In the sated afterglow of her ravenous coupling with Leo, the revelation snuck into Eva's brain like a shadowy secret slipped to her by a wicked spirit. She watched with pleasure her lover's buttocks flexing as he walked away from the bed.

"You've been working out."

"I figured I'd need my stamina when I finally got to see you in person again," he quipped, halting at the mini-bar. "Plus, stress relief. Which lately I've had a lot of. Stress, that is."

"I bet."

"Bragg is getting desperate. Blaming everyone for his troubles but the man responsible."

But Eva was only half-listening to the old lament. In the soft, tawny lighting of her quarters, Leo's skin glistened a light bronze. Like a statue from antiquity, excepting the slight paunch of male belly fat ringing his middle. She found herself grateful for that Achilles gut. It made Leo, a man perfect for Eva, slightly less than perfect. Made him someone she maybe deserved after all.

"You caught me by surprise at the reception with the pronouncement of our new 'status,'" he said, dropping ice in one glass, then a second. "Pleasantly so, but still..."

"When I can't surprise you is when we need to strongly consider divorce."

"Divorce?" He poured amber liquid from a carafe. "We aren't even married yet."

"Yet." She stretched out the word. "Is that—?"

"Mars Shinshu's Iwai 25," he said, turning around and holding both glasses high. He was nearly perfect from the front, too. To hell with whether she deserved him or not. She'd take him anyway. From now on.

"Here, on this planet?" Eva sat up, anticipating the warm burning down her throat. "How did you—"

"I'm the bloody head speechwriter for the bloody president of the bloody Alliance," he said, padding back across the plush carpet. "I know people." Handing her the glass of her favorite whiskey, he sat on the bed beside her. "Also, Covenant is well stocked with high-end liquor."

"Mmmm," she said taking a lavishly decadent first sip. "Maybe we should honeymoon here."

Holding his glass up to stare at the twinkling liquid inside, he said, "We'd never leave the room."

"I'm pretty sure that's true wherever we go."

Leo leered at her and they touched glasses. "To the future." He took a long swallow. "And now that we've survived existential Armageddon, I'd like to talk about *our* future."

Funny, that. She'd been thinking the same thing.

Leo took another swig. "I've told Bragg that, once this ceremony is over and the treaty is signed, I'm resigning from the administration."

She watched his face, not quite believing him. Delighted, since his decision might dovetail with her own plans. But also, wary that their respective concepts of their future together might crash right into each other.

"Are you sure, Leo? You live for the fight."

"Maybe once. Not so much now. Not Bragg's fight, anyway."

And that simple statement changed everything. Made Eva think maybe they were on the same page after all.

"I've had some thoughts too. About the future."

"Yeah? What'd you have in mind?" Leo snuggled up next to her on the bed, banking the pillows so they could sit propped up, naked skin touching naked skin. His voice settled back into the low purr of a post-coital, near-dreamy, soul-relaxed state. "I know! After the honeymoon lovefest, how about a two-week hike up Mount Oku-Hotaka! Or maybe Yari? Fuji, maybe..."

"Not exactly what I had in mind," Eva said. She took a big swig of liquid courage. "But it'll be a hell of a climb, that's for sure."

"I don't give a good goddamn what the rate sheet says! We're guests of the president! We berth for free!"

They could hear Cinnamon's cursing echo all the way from the cockpit straight down the *Dog*'s ramp. Passersby on the dock hurried their step along.

"'Guests of the president'?" Ben said. "That might be stretching it a bit."

"Hello," Alice said slyly, "pirate."

"Someone called?" The whir of Torque's exosuit announced her approach. "Locals still trying to get Cinnamon to pay the slip fee?"

"Seems so," Ben said.

"Well, we just got our slates blanked," Torque said. "I'd better get in there before—"

"Hey," Alice said, reaching out to intercept the big woman, "are you sure you're up to this?"

"Secord says I'm almost well enough to put the suit aside. Should be out of it by the time we get there."

Alice gave her arm a squeeze and let her go. "I appreciate you coming along, big sister."

Torque brightened. "Wouldn't miss it! Now, I need to do an intervention before Cinn gets us all arrested." She quick-stepped up the ramp.

"Ready to go?"

Alice thought Ben was talking to her, then turned to find Moze and Gal. The engineer carried a load of refit equipment, and Gal had a big sloppy grin on her face.

"Got the last of the backup components right here," Moze said. "Good to go. Thanks for the bankroll, Ben. We've never had a patron before."

"Might entitle you to extra crew benefits," Gal said suggestively. Waving him after them as they mounted the ramp, she said, "Come on Captain Stud Muffin, we've got at least five minutes before—"

"I'll pass, but thanks," Ben said. "And I'm not a captain anymore."

Gal shrugged as she followed Moze into the *Dog*. "Plain old Stud Muffin it is, then."

"Finally!" came Cinnamon's voice again. "Someone with some common sense!"

"Looks like she got her way—again," Alice said.

"Sounds like we're ready to lift off." Ben offered her his hand, but Alice hesitated, seeing the tall, silver Arcœnum who'd appeared across the bay. Louie raised four of his six long, lanky arms in silent farewell. She was tempted to run across the deck, to hell with his new ambassador's rank, and throw her arms around him. Instead, she simply raised her left hand and waved in return. When he departed to attend to his new duties, Alice found herself feeling the slightest bit sad. But she'd see him again. And she had duties of her own to take care of.

"Alice, this is your charter!" Cinnamon, summoning her aboard. "We're burning starlight!"

Ben lightly touched her arm. "No need to rake all this up again. We can go anywhere we want, you know."

"Yeah, I know," Alice said. "But I need to find out what happened to them. At least to try. Figure the best place to start is where it all started."

"Alrighty, then," Ben nodded. "Drake's World it is."

He took her hand, and together they headed up the ramp and into the *Junkyard Dog*.

EPILOGUE

TWO YEARS LATER

EXCERPT OF A SPEECH *written by Eva Park-Byrne and Leo Byrne. Given by Miranda Marcos on the steps of the reconstructed planetary capitol building of Sylvan Novus, upon the occasion of accepting her party's nomination to run for President of the Sol Alliance.*

...Some may ask what I, Miranda Marcos, can possibly understand about public service. How has my life as a daughter of wealth and privilege prepared me for it? Having never wanted for anything growing up, you might ask of me, how can I understand what the average citizen needs?

Excellent questions. My all-inclusive answer is this. Over these past few years—as an advocate for the Psyckers, unjustly incarcerated, and for the survivors of Sylvan Novus—I've received an education. I've dug through rubble with my bare hands to reach the buried. I've lobbied lawmakers for relief funds until they released them. I've comforted mothers cradling their dead babies in their arms. These experiences have been the crucible of my character. They've molded the person I was into the person I am—someone who does the right thing because it's the right thing to do.

Character, it's been said, is what we do when no one else is watching. Nowhere is this need for holding oneself accountable greater than in those we elect to public office. We look to our leaders to protect the people today and guide the ship of state through the unknowns of tomorrow. To more than merely represent us—to inspire us to look beyond the demands of daily life and envision a future we'd be proud to bequeath to our children. Leaders should lead—by example. And yet, all too often, our leaders disappoint us. They exemplify the privileged and unaccountable, entrenched in wielding power for its own sake. But elected officials were once known as "public servants." How much better off might we be today if that were still a common notion?

After a disaster strikes we often see the noblest aspects of humanity's character. Neighbors helping neighbors rebuild. Politicians living up to the potential of the faith vested in them. We saw it here on Sylvan Novus as we pulled together to first rescue, then recover loved ones. Even former political adversaries put aside their differences in common cause. Why is it, I ask you, that tragedy must strike before we unclench the fist of petty conflict and offer one another a helping hand?

Consider this: the Skane studied mankind, manipulated us, and exploited our paranoia toward the Arcœnum. They nearly succeeded in not only conquering, but exterminating both species. But we avoided annihilation by reaching out, if with understandable caution, to our former enemy—and that leap of faith has proven out. Ask the businesses booming in The Frontier. Ask the scientists discovering groundbreaking interventions in medicine. Ask yourself.

As you consider casting your vote in the next election, I ask you to challenge yourself before supporting any party—including mine. What does the party believe in beyond the flag-waving, beyond its own brand? What is the quality of the candidate's character? What do they believe in? And most importantly of all, what do *you* believe in?

Piers Bragg is right about one thing. Humanity needs one vision—not of ideology or platform, but of *what it wants to be as a species*. His is a vision that divides us, twisted by prejudice and corrupted by self-interest. My vision for mankind embraces the belief that we are more than the sum of our meaner desires. If you believe we need each other; that we're stronger together than apart; that the misty cords of union which bind us are critical to our survival—then I ask for your support in the next election.

Ladies and gentlemen, the Skane nearly determined our fate for us. Can we now meet this moment of fierce urgency, together, and chart that course for ourselves?

AFTERWORD AND ACKNOWLEDGMENTS

I began writing *War for Empire* back in 2020 PCT. (Pre-COVID Time.) Once the routine of the pandemic settled in and the whole world hadn't zombified, I thought my productivity would ramp way up. All this time at home and the Internet still worked... But nope—like a lot of people I holed up in my house with my wife and my dogs, did a lot of navel-gazing, reinvented how I worked for the day job, and wondered if Nostradamus had maybe been right after all.

After the new normal became "the weird but whatever normal," I walked the dogs a lot and learned I could get away with wearing walking shorts on work calls as long as I previewed my camera before connecting. What I didn't do was get more productive with my fiction writing. But now, as 2023 begins, the trilogy is done.

And I had a lot of help finishing it. First and foremost, as always, my wife Alison read sections as I completed them and offered excellent insights on all aspects of the story. More than that, she helped me better understand the workings of the human brain, which especially influenced Alice's character.

Most importantly of all, her unflagging love and support for my writing encourages me more than anything else to keep at it. And we didn't kill one another during COVID lockdown, so there's that.

I pitched the story to Aethon Books way back in 2019, and they've patiently waited for me to finish it. Rhett C. Bruno and Steve Beaulieu—the principles at Aethon, and two of my best friends in the writer community—are nothing but supportive during the creative process. As authors themselves, they understand the challenges of producing emotion, action, and "strange new worlds" from the relatively tiny space between a writer's ears.

Speaking of ears, I have to give a shout-out to Garrett Michael Brown, the narrator for the series audiobooks. His nuanced performance brings such life to the characters and excitement to the action—I was blown away when I heard him. From Alice's visceral rebirth and Ben's lecherous conduct early on to Nick's unassuming heroism and Eva's discovery of what she's all about, Garrett imbued each with a unique voice, elevating the prose into something special. If you haven't had a chance to listen to the audio yet, consider giving it a try. You won't be sorry.

Rob Salerno, Aethon's editor, worked on all three books and made them measurably better for you. I appreciate not only Rob's expertise in correcting grammar and mechanics, but also his mindfulness in how the story hits the reader. Appropriateness of phraseology, consistency of characterization, etc.—Rob saved me from a number of Oops! moments, so you can thank him for fewer speed bumps along your reading journey.

My writer friend and gaming buddy Christopher Boore built an interstellar map to help me keep straight where events took place. Jon Frater, also a writing buddy and science guy extraordinaire, was instrumental in helping me understand multiple technical areas, including DNA-level diseases and the physics of space travel. My good friend Elena Giorgi—author, photographer, and former researcher at Los Alamos National Laboratory—helped me construct Morg Henry's fictional disease and why it was, essentially, incurable within the confines of my story. And Yvonne Baum, my sis-in-law and a medical doctor, clued me in to how Cinnamon's subdural hematoma might manifest.

Rick Partlow, U.S. Army veteran—and if you haven't heard of him, you must not read much military science fiction, because he's a top-tier seller in the genre—gave me early feedback on how I represented the 214th Drop Marines. Likewise, my nephew, U.S. Marine Major Alec Pourteau, supplied tactical expertise and "this is how it actually is" wisdom for the 214th's inner workings. Any liberties regarding how Marines do what they do are entirely mine and owing to the needs of the story. Also, it's set 500 years from now, so...

I'd be remiss if I failed to mention the influence on this trilogy of Jon Meacham, professor of history (and expert in presidential history), Pulitzer-Prize winner, and *New York Times*-bestselling author. Meacham is not only knowledgeable, he's also an eloquent writer and speaker. He turns history into riveting storytelling about what motivates humans—especially U.S. presidents—to act the way they do. His books *And There Was Light: Abraham Lincoln and the American Struggle* and, especially, *The Soul of America: The Battle for Our Better Angels*, are inspiring, hopeful examinations of how presidential character can lead a nation—born of conflicts inherent in its own character—in embattled times. Miranda's sentiments expressed in the epilogue owe a lot to Mister Meacham's scholarship.

And thank you, dear reader, for gifting me your time in reading this series. Time is one resource all of us share in rather limited supply. I very much appreciate you spending yours on my story. I hope you enjoyed it.

Chris Pourteau
College Station, Texas

THANK YOU FOR READING INVASION!

WE HOPE you enjoyed it as much as we enjoyed bringing it to you. We just wanted to take a moment to encourage you to review the book. Follow this link: Invasion to be directed to the book's Amazon product page to leave your review.

Every review helps further the author's reach and, ultimately, helps them continue writing fantastic books for us all to enjoy.

You can also join our non-spam mailing list by visiting www.subscribepage.com/AethonReadersGroup and never miss out on future releases. You'll also receive three full books completely Free as our thanks to you.

Facebook | Instagram | Twitter | Website

Want to discuss our books with other readers and even the authors? Join our Discord server today and be a part of the Aethon community.

Also in series:

War for Empire
Legacy
Warpath
Invasion

Looking for more great Science Fiction?

A lone soldier is gifted the power to save humanity. When a training exercise at a classified research facility goes awry, Joe Kovacs loses much more than his eyesight. He loses his career. He can't lead one of the military's top spec-ops teams if he can't see. A decision with consequences. Joe's only shot at getting his life back lies in the hands of an anonymous 'shadow' scientist. The offer is risky, an experimental implant that may or may not work. He jumps at the chance, but quickly learns the device does more than restore his sight. Much more. There's no going back. Joe begins seeing strange flashes. Ghosts of images, overlaid atop his own vision. Actions he could have taken but didn't. Worse, the visions are increasing in scope and frequency. Believing he's going mad, he confronts the scientist, only to discover the implant's shocking origin. Nothing is as it seems, and all the possible futures Joe can now see point to a system-wide conspiracy that will shift the balance of power for hundreds of years. Joe's visions hold the key to stopping it… if he can learn to control them in time. **Don't miss this exciting new Military Science Fiction Series that will make you not only question just what it means to be human, but also if there is ever a "right" side. It's perfect for fans of Halo, Rick Partlow (Drop Trooper), Jeffery H. Haskell (Grimm's War), and Joshua Dalzelle (Black Fleet Saga).**

Get Homecoming Now!

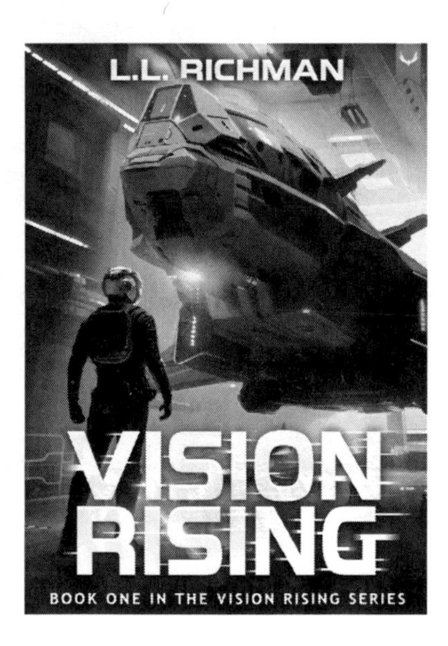
L.L. RICHMAN
VISION
RISING
BOOK ONE IN THE VISION RISING SERIES

A lone soldier is gifted the power to save humanity. When a training exercise at a classified research facility goes awry, Joe Kovacs loses much more than his eyesight. He loses his career. He can't lead one of the military's top spec-ops teams if he can't see. A decision with consequences. Joe's only shot at getting his life back lies in the hands of an anonymous 'shadow' scientist. The offer is risky, an experimental implant that may or may not work. He jumps at the chance, but quickly learns the device does more than restore his sight. Much more. There's no going back. Joe begins seeing strange flashes. Ghosts of images, overlaid atop his own vision. Actions he could have taken but didn't. Worse, the visions are increasing in scope and frequency. Believing he's going mad, he confronts the scientist, only to discover the implant's shocking origin. Nothing is as it seems, and all the possible futures Joe can now see point to a system-wide conspiracy that will shift the balance of power for hundreds of years. Joe's visions hold the key to stopping it... if he can learn to control them in time. **Don't miss this exciting new Military Science Fiction Series that will make you not only question just what it means to be human, but also if there is ever a "right" side. It's perfect for fans of Halo, Rick Partlow (Drop Trooper), Jeffery H. Haskell (Grimm's War), and Joshua Dalzelle (Black Fleet Saga).**

Get Vision Rising Now!

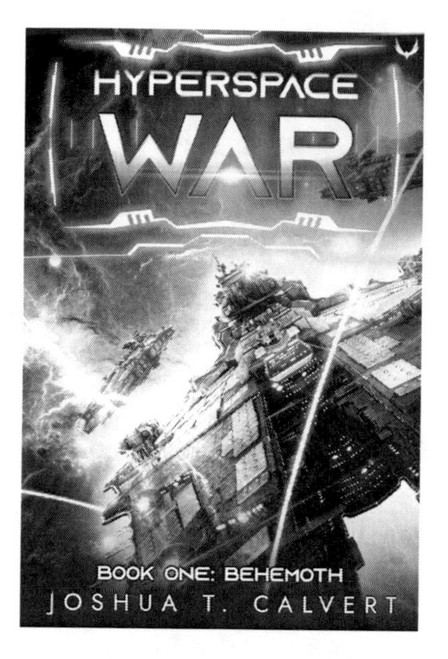

A colony cut-off. A mysterious alien wormhole. A Captain with nothing to lose... Contact with Earth has been lost for generations and mysterious waves of disappearing colonists have been shaking the five moons of the Archimedes System for decades. When suddenly a wormhole appears in the middle of the system, the Union Navy faces an ancient danger from the darkness of deep space. A merciless war erupts, and Jeremy Brandt, Captain of the UNS Concordia, is sent through the wormhole to confront the mysterious enemy. **Pick up your copy of this new Military Science Fiction adventure from bestseller Joshua T. Calvert. Aliens, War, and a Captain who will stop at nothing to defend his people, this is Sci-Fi the way it's meant to be!**

Get Behemoth Now!

For all our Sci-Fi books, visit our website.